ABANDONED BY GOD

ELIZABETH GUY

FirstRider Publishing

To
Roger:
I loved you
the first moment I met you.

Elizabeth Guy is a full-time writer. She was awarded a Ph.D. from the University of Sydney (*The Poetics of the Nation-State*) and for the past 30 years has taught Literature in Australia (Sydney and Kalgoorlie) as well as Scotland, Fiji, and Chile. Before working and trekking in South America, Elizabeth travelled extensively throughout the USA and Canada, writing, reading, and learning Spanish. *Abandoned by God* is her third book. Her first was a non-fiction, *The Alchemy of Poetry: A Reader's Guide to Poetry* and is now in its second edition. Her second book, *Take Ink & Weep*, is a fictional account of the poetic lives of the great Silver Age poets during Russia's engagement in World War 1. Outside of writing, Elizabeth is an accomplished long-distance walker. She has passionate interests in the Arts and ongoing travels in Russia. For part of the week, she lives in Sydney's inner-city with Mithridates, a little grey tabby found under a house in Dubbo, and her good-looking husband. For the rest of the time, she writes in a family home in the Blue Mountains where her daughter and son-in-law often stay.

I

The Abdication

Tsarskoye Selo, 30 km south of Petrograd. April 1917.

He stands on the steps in the icy gloaming. With his back to the doors, the man looks over the garden, its covered statues and boxed-up fountains seem strange sentries. Far away in the distance, the silhouette of trees dips and nods solemnly. He thinks to himself that it hardly feels like spring, despite being early April.

The man knows he should move indoors but remains facing his garden as it disappears into the rush of evening. He watches as the sky spirals inwards in a thick contorted roll of darkened grey and brittle white, indicating the day's end.

The man's long woollen greatcoat, undecorated and utilitarian, is a protection of sorts against the hard cold that he has known all his life. He realises, without emotion, that in one month he will be 49 but, now that he is a man without purpose or destiny, a birthday seems pointless.

All of a sudden, the honk of geese sweeps up and wheels above the man, who is still standing on the steps with his back to his home. They rise effortlessly to become a swirling mess of early evening and then soar eastward in a cacophony of homecoming. The man cranes his head back and hears the creak and flap and gaggle leave him far, far behind.

He knows the longing he feels is ridiculous — to be free, to escape. Lines from Pushkin fly through his mind, like the last goose of the skein:

I let a captive bird go winging,

To greet the radiant spring's rebirth

I was free to set aflutter

One poor captive from his cage!

The man is unaware of irony, whether it is here in the recitation of the Golden Age poet or in the everyday tasks assigned him before he was made redundant.

Well, that's not it exactly, he thinks to himself as he shuffles about to face the double doors to his home. Before he was made to resign.

He mounts the last two steps and registers the grunt of pain in his knee. The man pauses and wonders why he struggles. He loves his family and yearns for their chatter and touch but at the same time, he wants to be rid of it all. This story that is his, and by default theirs, this shame, this inexplicable loss of faith.

And there before the double doors, with one gloved hand on the doorknob, he utters a truth that lurks like a heretic in the crypt of his soul, 'God has abandoned me ...'

He senses something is amiss when he enters the home and stands momentarily in the hallway, listening. The dim pools of light before him offer no clues. He glances up to his right and there stands his wife.

A heaviness descends on the man as he moves slowly up the winding staircase. He is still not used to the cavernous space of his home that is filled with the spectres of a life now finished.

The man reaches the top of the staircase and says by way of a beginning, 'My knee is still giving me a little trouble.'

She stands quite still. If she could swim, people might have said she had the shoulders and deportment of a swimmer. Her remarkable shoulders still reveal their architecture of clavicle, scapular, and even the beautifully moulded humerus. She walks tall, straight-backed, and fluid but on this occasion, she stands motionless, in a wine-red Japanese kimono, beneath which is a flurry of floor-length silk petticoat. She is waiting for her husband to reach, not only the top of the staircase but some awareness of their situation.

'Yes, my love.' The man says quietly, with no expectation. 'What is it?'

Her grey-green eyes search her husband's tired face.

'It's Derevenko,' she whispers which is what she has been doing lately. 'He has left us.'

The man looks past his wife to the small room directly behind her and, probably because it contains bookcases, he finds himself wondering what will become of the collection of verse that he inherited long ago and loves so dearly.

'Derevenko,' she repeats insistently but he just cannot place a face to the name. They look at each other, he blankly and she expectantly.

'Of course!' the man blurts. 'Derevenko!' And he looks about as if to confront his son's bodyguard, there and then, on top of the staircase, 'Where is he? I'll have a word. I'll ...' But they both realise he cannot fix this. He cannot stop what is happening to them — to his wife and family and himself.

She rests her hand on his arm momentarily. These days her voice sounds more and more like her mother once did, 'Derevenko,' she repeats and looks away from her husband. His sad blue eyes and greying whiskers make it nearly impossible for her to continue. 'Derevenko was heard taunting ... and jeering our son ...' And her face screws up like a tight handkerchief and she begins to sob.

The man lays his head into the cave of her shoulder and neck, feeling the shudder and gulp of her grief.

They stand like this for some time.

It seems cooler here than when he stood outside and watched the geese fly east into the eternal night sky. He wonders whether the internal oil heaters have been lit or whether it is something more uncertain than a simple task not completed.

She mumbles into his coat collar and he pulls away with, 'What was that?'

His wife says, 'Everyone is leaving us …' He pats her strong back as she continues, 'It is hardly three months … since we buried …'

He wonders if she will say the name and after a moment he offers, 'Father Grigori Rasputin.'

There is a fresh flood of tears but she is nodding into the comfort of her husband's coat. And the man thinks about the priest who, for years, managed to give his family all that he could not. He wonders how they will finish up. When will the ignobility stop? And he even finds himself contemplating the blasphemy — that in his beginning must have been, and most probably is his end.

The man is brought back to the present by something she is saying to him, '… But without Derevenko …' And the woman's palms open upward in a gesture of desperation.

Before he can stop himself, he sighs and almost imperceptibly he senses his wife stiffen. How could she understand? He thinks to himself. How could she possibly understand? He has fallen so far from God's grace that he knows, buried in the dry soil of his dead hope, that there will be no redemption.

But instead, he says, 'Derevenko can go. It is my job now to care for my son … and to care for you … and all my family.' He brushes wisps of thin dark hair away from her face and adds quietly, 'All will be well.'

The man smiles carefully at his wife and she, quite unexpectedly, kisses him on the side of his face, where his beard ends and his pale skin appears.

Together they turn to walk through the small room behind, from there they will make their way, slowly, to the hall beyond and then eventually to their son's room, where a 12 year old boy, one leg contorted in a strange angle perpendicular to the rest of him, lies on his cot next to his mother's day bed. His wasted body is taut with pain, his handsome face searching the icon-strewn wall — in an attempt to manage the bloody mess of his holy disease, not to mention the bewildering loss of his beloved bodyguard.

2

For the past two hours, Captain **Pavel Mikhailovich Konoplev** has been leaning against the low wall that separates the man's home from his garden. Pavel should have made himself known and hurried the man back inside when the sun went down but something is intoxicating about the shift of power, that has, somehow, strangely, come into his own hands.

Pavel hunches over the butt end of his cigarette, the one he has been keeping, and relights it. His greatcoat is unbuttoned revealing the olive-green khaki of his single-breasted woollen tunic, and dark green breeches that tuck comfortably into black knee-length boots. Pinned to his coat are his detachable shoulder boards, faced with bright metallic lace. Once they were a potent symbol of privilege and status but recently they have become a little more worrisome.

He looks up because he hears the approach of a vehicle and so he slowly picks up his Mosin-Nagant rifle and sucks up the last hit of his cigarette then stubs it out before the vehicle sweeps around the long driveway.

Pavel has been assigned to the Sharpshooter Guards, 4th Regiment, and is more or less glad to be guarding the family under house arrest. Glad because he occasionally takes leave to visit his father, an ex-colonel, out on his forested estate halfway between Gatchina and Luga. Pavel thinks to himself that he has nothing to complain about. He has an older sister living in Petrograd. She's a teacher and very active in politics, who is always looking out for him — despite him surviving the Battle of Tannenberg.

The shrapnel wound in his left thigh resulted in a noticeable limp. Consequently, Pavel remains a great shot who prefers not to run after his target. Not that there seems any likelihood that the prisoners he is guarding could attempt an escape.

The roar of the motor cuts through the night and the gravel driveway spits and splutters beneath its heft. Some of the soldiers are mooching out of the guardhouse and sentry boxes adjoining the large entrance gate. Pavel moves into position, directly beneath the steps of the man's home, and squints across at the sound of car doors slamming, voices barking and footsteps crunching in approach.

He scoops his rifle under his arm.

'At ease, Captain,' he hears an unfamiliar voice and then a government minister stands before him. It is still early days so Pavel fumbles with his salute that more or less becomes a tug of his cap.

'Any trouble?'

Pavel thinks the government minister looks familiar and wonders what sort of trouble a middle-aged man with a wife, a sick son, and too many daughters, could actually pose and then he remembers, 'Just to report, sir ... comrade, that the sailor who acts as a bodyguard for the boy has gone.'

The government minister seems uninterested but Pavel wants to register his distaste for the greasy lard-arse who has avoided fighting at the Front by spending his days carrying about an invalid kid. Besides, one moment the sailor-bodyguard is thick with the prisoners, and the next minute he's strolling out the gates.

'Thank you, Captain. I will take that under advisement. Nothing else to report?'

Pavel scratches about inside his memory but can come up with nothing. These days it is better to watch and keep quiet unless of course, you have a weasel in your sights that needs routing before he turns on you.

'No, comrade.'

The government minister hesitates for a moment and then says, 'I need a good man like yourself, here, to keep an eye on things for me.' The minister is clean-shaven and although it is obvious he has never been a soldier he seems genuinely concerned that Pavel re-alises his importance in the scheme of things, whatever that is.

Pavel nods.

'Thank you, Captain,' adds the minister and then shoves a half packet of cigarettes into Pavel's hand before striding up to the dou-ble doors.

Pavel watches him disappear. He has been guarding the family for about a month now and it is definitely preferable to the ongoing mayhem, street speeches, and rabble-rousing of Petrograd.

At first, like every other poor hungry sod who had limped back from the Front, he was euphoric when the garrison rebelled along-side the Putilov workers back in February. They had joined the women's protest, which of course became a tidal wave of workers and soldiers marching down the Nevsky Prospect and into the Palace Square. His sister, Lidia, was there with him and had even called it a revolution! And there he was shoulder to shoulder with her and all of Russia, or so it seemed, in the very thick of it. Not that he got anywhere near the square — he had never seen so many people. He, like every other Russian, knew theirs was the biggest na-tion in the world but he sure had no idea how so many of them had squeezed into the city. But there he was — a true part of something remarkable, something joyful and unstoppable. It was as if the madness of the past had ended that day they took to the streets.

Pavel takes a bent cigarette from the packet the minister gave him, straightens it, lights it, and inhales deeply.

He had tried explaining what it had been like to his father. But it was no good. His father had grunted something about the country's determination to kill each other and that the younger generation should be more cautious. But Pavel had been there and his lungs had burst in song.

Stand, rise up, working people!
Arise against the enemies, hungry brother!
Let be heard the people's cry for vengeance
Forward! Forward! Forward! Forward! Forward!

It was impossible to describe the power he felt as he marched headlong into a new Russia chanting *End the War!* His sister Lidia shouting *The Tsar must Go!* His countrywomen demanding *Food for the People!* His countrymen roaring *Power to the Soviets!*

All bridges behind them were burned, so to speak, because there was no going back.

Workers and soldiers and peasants and businessmen and students and teachers and mothers and grandmothers and children and priests and poets and railwaymen. The unimaginable was happening. Russian people everywhere, saw, for the first time, that what they had dreamed of before the war — before 1917 — was now a reality.

Pavel looks up into the windows and watches a figure move unhurriedly along the long corridor. He inhales deeply and can't help but feel, probably for the first time in his life, utterly significant. Pavel exhales in the knowledge that, now, Russia will be righted.

3

Inside the house, the broad-chested Head Footman leans over

the balustrade at the top of the staircase and looks down on the minister who has just announced himself with *Good Evening!* Sour-faced, the Footman responds with 'The family is at supper.'

Not a person to ever falter in his mission, the minister bounds up the impressive staircase in his grey suit, coat over one arm, and, a little surprisingly, a Homburg hat in the other saying to the 60 year old servant, 'Then I shall be their guest.'

The footman recognises the face of the minister and without further ado leads the way to where the family is enjoying hot blinis with jam and the never-ending strong sweet tea, topped up from the large samovar.

As they move toward the east wing, a door at the end of a long corridor suddenly opens.

The Footman comes to an abrupt halt, as does the minister treading close behind, but unlike the minister, the aged footman bows deeply.

Before him is the man dressed simply, as an officer might, with his dark-green trousers tucked into long black boots and a loose woollen khaki tunic.

'Your Imperial Majesty. The Minister for ...' The footman's pause is, almost, indiscernible, 'Justice.'

The minister moves past the servant and walks toward the man, who had once been Tsar of all the Russias but now seems unsure of what to say or do next.

The silence between them grows, uncomfortably.

Then the minister shoots out his hand and says, 'Alexander Fyodorovich Kerensky.'

'Yes. Kerensky,' repeats the man and they shake hands, both somewhat relieved.

'That will be all, Trupp.' The sexagenarian, with his wide Finnish forehead and thinning pale hair, retreats quietly.

'Comrade Romanov,' begins Kerensky who can see it will have

to be him who takes control of the situation. 'I am here to give you an update on your house arrest and what the plans are for you and your family, as agreed by the Russian Provisional Government and in consultation with the Petrograd Soviet.'

Once again, the door at the end of the corridor flies open, and stepping toward Kerensky comes the man's wife and a shaggy black and white spaniel that skids along the polished timber floors just ahead of the kick and sweep of her long silken ensemble.

It is getting late, thinks Kerensky to himself and exhales audibly through his large daunting nose. Kerensky has promised Milyukov, the Foreign Affairs Minister, that he will swing by after he meets with Romanov. There is so much to do and he doesn't want to be caught up in the German woman's polemic.

The wife stands quietly by her husband's side.

Again, the minister takes the lead and introduces himself, 'Kerensky, Minister for Justice.'

She says nothing but watches him with those grey-green eyes.

'Are you married, Minister Kerensky?'

He is startled by the man's question but quickly regains his composure, 'Yes. Two sons. Ten and nine.'

The man seems genuinely pleased and is about to ask something more, when his wife speaks, 'Are you here to bring us some good news? Our children are distressed by this situation —which must be brought to a close, one way or another.' Her last phrase hangs in the air between them and Kerensky wonders if they have any idea of what has been openly discussed by ministers like himself.

'Minister Milyukov has been reaching out to Prime Minister Lloyd George,' says Kerensky and he thinks about the Welshman and his churlish response to Milyukov, which is quite unfathomable considering Romanov's cousin is the throne of England. 'And to President Poincaré.' Kerensky decides not to mention that while France is under siege it has no interest in offering the Romanov's refuge. 'So there are a few lines of enquiry that are very positive ...'

Kerensky watches as Romanov turns slowly to his wife and it occurs to him that maybe the man has no faith.

'The Provisional Government and the Petrograd Soviet for Workers and Soldiers are not interested in revenge or taking any punitive action against —'

'Revenge? Punitive Action!' Her Teutonic vowels sit heavily about them like immovable furniture.

'Indeed,' Kerensky looks at the man who seems to be unable to follow the conversation thus far. 'As discussed previously, we must move the Romanovs ... the family to a place where you can ... live your lives ...'

Husband and wife look at him. Bewildered, confused, and disorientated.

'Minister Kerensky.' The man speaks with infinite patience as if he is talking to a child who has somehow got caught up in the wrong crowd, 'Russians have always shown restraint ... they have shown ... devotion, deference, and duty.' The man seems delighted with his rhetorical tricolon, although Kerensky is unconvinced the man knows where he is headed, but the man heads off there nonetheless, 'Russians need God's appointee to rule, do you see? To lead this magnificent country, that has nurtured and loved us since time immemorial, into our destiny.'

Kerensky hopes that is the end of it but he can see the man thinks his audience wants more and then notices the wife is completely transfixed by her husband, a divine vision, a saintly protector.

'Comrade Romanov —'

'Our job,' the man continues because interruption is not something to which he is familiar. 'Is to continue the Divine Right and infallible rule of the Imperial Romanovs to bring peace and prosperity to Russia.'

The spaniel leaves the three people and trots back down the corridor and begins scratching the door. The aroma of blinis is far more tempting than waiting for someone to take him out into the dark scent of rabbit.

Kerensky realises the man has stopped speaking and that his wife has her eyes closed, as if in supplication and, not for the first time, Kerensky feels a great weariness come upon him.

Last November the Duma had warned the man of the impending disaster if he continued to spurn the people's demand for civil liberties and democratic representation. The man had no idea. When confronted with the people's loss of confidence in him, his only retort was that the people should simply value *his* confidence in himself.

What did that even mean, thinks Kerensky. Regardless, it is all too late.

The only reason he is still talking to this man is that the success of the revolution, internationally, is contingent on how the world sees them manage the exit of an ex-Imperial Emperor.

What the world really should be looking at, thinks Kerensky, and not for the first time, is that the Russian Provisional Government has hoisted its petard on the freedom of speech, press, assembly, and religion as well as universal suffrage and equal rights for women!

Indeed, beyond these walls of the Alexander Palace, everyone knows that it was he, Kerensky, who lobbied hard and long for this great turn in Russian history. So, what this man has to say about the needs of the Russian people is completely and utterly inchoate.

'I am hoping, when I return this time next week, I might be able to offer definitive plans for your future. The Russian Provisional Government and the Petrograd Soviet —'

'May I make myself perfectly clear,' interrupts the man. 'As I have said the day I was forced to abdicate ...' His wife's shoulders straighten and she looks unflinchingly at Kerensky as her husband continues, 'Peace and prosperity is my only goal for Russia and I will not accept any plan unless it includes my wife and children. We will not be separated under any condition.'

And that is all you have, thinks Kerensky, but he says to the man, 'As the great-grandson of a serf and a member of the Socialist Revolutionary Party, I give you my word — that peace and prosperity will come to Russia.'

The man simply looks at the minister.

Kerensky realises that forming a Constituent Assembly with a representative government, negotiating a peaceful settlement with Germany, fulfilling the desperate needs of the people, and hauling Russia into the modern world — is nothing in comparison to re-educating the man who stands before him.

A man without skills, knowledge, or any awareness, whatsoever, of the country to which he claims an unbreakable devotion.

He clings to an illusion, Kerensky thinks, as he takes his leave, promising to return next week with an update.

There is no fanfare of departure, no bowing or kissing of rings, or the exchange of obsequious witticisms. Just the cold hard fact of Kerensky leaving the man and his family, alone, with a few intransient servants and guarded by an ever-growing hostility.

A man entombed in his own making.

4

A few days later, out in the garden, the man leans back on the chair and reads the out-of-date newspaper. The chair originally stood in the hallway of the man's home, its gilded thin legs, and soft crème silk seat has never seen the light of day but here it now stands, under the budding wisteria, planted during the reign of Catherine the Great.

Someone, thinks the man, perhaps one of the guards, must have dragged it out to enjoy the heady scent of a spring morning with its buzz of bees. Indeed, the man found the newspaper, sprawled on the chair, as if the reader had dashed off to catch a train or attend to a minor task.

The man's wife and children are indoors at the moment because the girls have measles. *It's a sorry mess*, he had said to them this morning, as he moved swiftly to be outdoors.

The sun is gradually warming up the April day, as the man sits there cradling the newspaper and smoking his cigarette. He is wearing his usual garb: an infantry regiment uniform. With his eyes shut he pretends, for a moment, that life is as it has always been — with the scents of crocuses and lilacs in bloom, the rustle of the breeze in the birches, and the coo of shy wood pigeons.

The man opens his eyes.

It's a cruel game.

The truth is he doesn't believe his life will ever return. Of course, this is not what he says to his wife or to the children, who seem in constant need of reassurance. To them, he speaks of the comfort of their future life in England or Paris or even Japan — until the war ends and this business of socialism blows over.

He rustles the newspaper to drown out the memory of that wretched day ... the scratch of his pen inking his signature across the abdication papers, across the Romanov dynasty, across his son's future, and across his days until he dies.

The man knows his life is already over. The slow, gentle life that was once so bountiful, so laden with the promise of joy everlasting. Meanwhile, the weekly visits from Kerensky to discuss the plans for their evacuation do nothing but make the man realise that a life without *his* Russia is not a life worth living.

He reads the headline of the newspaper he holds: *The Foreign Minister's Telegram! The Tsar's war to continue!*

The man remembers the Muscovite historian who scrambled his

way, somehow, into parliament and became the Foreign Minister. Milyukov. The man remembers the relentless criticism this politician levelled at him for getting in the way of economic and social advancement in Russia. Milyukov was one of the those who bayed for the man's abdication during all that Rasputin business, back in November last year.

The man reads on.

Despite the Provisional Government conceding that the Tsarist war with Germany must come to an end and that to achieve peace Russia will no longer pursue the original plan to conquer foreign people or territories — despite this — the Provisional Government has telegrammed the Allies to indicate the Tsarist war WILL continue! A sympathetic friend, within the Foreign Minister's office, has shared this telegram with the Pravda ...

The man sighs. Unlike its nominative determinism, the *Pravda* seeks neither truth nor justice. It is a hysterical rumour mongering chronicle. A Bolshevik rag! How it got into the grounds of the man's house is easy to guess, considering it is the guards who can freely come and go, bringing with them such scuttlebutt.

He scans the Foreign Minister's telegram that has been reproduced for the *Pravda* readership.

Russia will stay in the war until its completion ... treasonable to think otherwise ... Russia will readily enforce the seizure of Constantinople and the Dardanelles ...

The man knows, with no uncertainty, that this is the right decision. He has to admit that Milyukov's telegram comes as a surprise to him, not because it was leaked — there are always spies jeopardising national security — but because the Provisional Government is standing by his commitment to the allies. The rest of the article is hardly worth reading, with its ire and exhaustive finger-pointing.

After a few more phrases the man gets the gist.

The Russian people are united in their stance against the Tsarist war ... they are also united against the Provisional Government ... most of whom slouched across from the infamous Duma ... We demand the resignation of the Prime Minister Lvov, the War Minister Guchkov, and the witless Minister Milyukov for Foreign Affairs!

The man lets the paper skid to his feet and leans back in the chair. He ignores the last phrase he glimpsed: *There are no progressive capitalists — only socialists or barbarians!*

More and more these days, the man feels he is slipping away from all that matters. He looks down the long walk of the garden and wonders who he is. Who he once was has disappeared ... somehow, somewhere. His wife and children look to him to be husband and father, but if he cannot protect his family, how is he worthy of either title?

The man can no longer see himself. The portraits of all his forebears hang heavily in his home, including Zubov's famous etching of Peter the Great, and yet the man sees himself as faceless. Indeed, he can barely look at his image in the mirror.

He closes his eyes.

Captain Pavel Konoplev is returning to retrieve his newspaper when he realises that the man slumped beneath the wisteria with his copy of the *Pravda* at his feet — is the prisoner, himself. Pavel pauses. He knows the prisoner is just a man and yet he feels unsure of how to go about this moment. Pavel coughs. The man doesn't move.

Pavel delivers his words sharply, 'Comrade Romanov.'

The man looks up startled as if he has found himself in a play without a script but then he seems to find it, 'Good morning.'

For a moment, Pavel is thrown, he has never needed to speak to the man until now, despite seeing him each day taking a short walk in the garden or appearing from time to time at the window.

Pavel clears his throat, not because it needs clearing, but because he feels he must assert some sort of authority, 'Comrade Romanov, that is my newspaper.'

Both the men look down at the tousle of printed media at the foot of the chair and that is when Pavel realises, he isn't going to bow down in front of the man to get it.

The man must have had a similar thought because he moves out of his chair and steps away from Pavel, 'Forgive me, I have taken your post.' He gestures to the chair as if it is a fortified redoubt from which the guard keeps watch.

Pavel looks closely at him and, in return, the man smiles. It is a strange smile. Or perhaps it is simply strange that the man thinks it is right to smile at Pavel who is one of many detaining the man from his liberty.

'I admit ...' The man speaks softly and with no hurry, 'I was catching up on the news from Petrograd.'

'It is world news now.' Pavel's sharp rejoinder comes out before he can stop himself but rather than feel elated, he feels uncomfortable.

'Quite right,' the man replies and then looks to the farthest endpoint of the garden. 'Quite right.'

For a moment they are set in their places and neither of them seems to know what happens next until the man turns back to the guard and says, 'I see you sustained injuries while fighting.'

Pavel replies slowly, 'Tannenberg.' And then adds with unveiled acrimony, 'August '14.' The entire Russian 2nd Army was just about decimated in this battle and he was one of the sole survivors of his company. He doesn't know why and he no longer cares.

'Well I thank you for doing your duty for —' The man stops himself speaking and looks about as if something or someone will make it clear what it is he must say. Then, 'Very good,' the man says as he shuffles awkwardly past Pavel. 'Must be getting back ...' And there is that smile, once again.

Pavel watches the man move back to the house and thinks to himself that when he writes his next letter to his sister Lidia, he'll be sure to mention this incident. It'll make her see why the Bolshevik's decisiveness is critical to resolving the problem of this prisoner.

2

Socialist Revolutionaries

Petrograd. May 1917.

Lidia Mikhailovna Konopleva is irritated by her colleagues and no matter how fast she makes her way home, plunging in and out of the traffic on the streets and footpaths of Petrograd's Vyborgskaya District, she cannot outrun their feeblemindedness.

Her day at the City Public School, teaching 11 year olds, started well enough. Penmanship, Old Slavonic texts, Arithmetic, Writing and she replaced their Bible studies with the song, *Jonah and the Whale*, thinking to herself, at least they can benefit from the cadence and pitch of singing in harmony.

It was the close of day that brought about the contretemps between colleagues, which isn't unexpected considering the Dual Powers — made up of the Provisional Government and the Petrograd Soviet of Workers' and Soldiers' Deputies — is all anyone ever talks about.

It is so frustrating because people are still thinking in the old ways, she thinks to herself as she waits for a tram to pass.

Someone had mentioned the war and the new posters flying about calling for recruits for Bochkareva's battalion. It was rubbish! Couldn't they see that Maria Bochkareva is refusing to recognise the soviet and is denying her female troops democratic discussion of all decisions before battle? This isn't liberation — this is retrograde!

Lidia runs across the busy road with the end of daily commuters.

Whatever their sources, and considering every political party prints several newspapers not to mention pamphlets and leaflets per week, each member of the teaching faculty is compelled to present their point of view, regardless of it being ill-informed and underdeveloped. Like herself, some on staff are Socialist Revolutionaries but the rest are reactionaries, without any philosophical framework.

Lidia weaves her way in and out of the evening foot traffic.

Indeed, some of her fellow teachers are even reiterating the views of *that* Bolshevik who had merely arrived at Petrograd's Finland Station just a few short weeks ago. A Johnny-come-lately.

Lidia crosses the tram line to Smolyachkova Ulitsa Tram Station. Her long calf-length dark blue skirt, thick beige shirt, and thin overcoat mark her as a semi-professional in the working-class district of Petrograd.

The early May evening is setting and the thin pale light reaches out in the last attempt to catch Lidia's white-blonde fringe protruding from her woollen scarf. She moves her bag to her other shoulder and looks toward the coming of the tram. She is a tall woman in her early 30s with a quiet face, as long as she keeps her eyes downcast. She has partial heterochromia, which means nothing in the scheme of things, but Lidia smudges a fraction of blue shadow on each eyelid every morning before she leaves her apartment. She can't remember when she started doing this but the eyeshadow seems to reduce the startling fact that her left eye is not light blue, like its mate, but rather a tarnished gold.

Lidia hears the *rickety rickety ding ding* of the approaching tram. And once again she sights evidence of deficiency in thinking as a man slouches beside a news vendor, reading the *Pravda* with the headline, *Lenin's Tasks of the Proletariat in the Present Revolution*. Only a Bolshevik with that much ego could arrive, after years of being totally out of the picture, and announce that he, and only he, had the map to an authentic socialist revolution!

It makes her want to scream.

She takes her seat on the tram and thinks how easy it might be for an unscrupulous political wrangler to take advantage of the frustrations, that are, inevitably, felt by the proletariat at this point. She, herself, has no faith in Prime Minister Lvov but it is her fellow Socialist Revolutionary, Minister Kerensky, in whom she, and most of the nation, places trust.

She had received a few days ago a scrawled note from her brother detailing, in spiky script, how he had met Kerensky in person. According to her brother, the Minister had singled him out and seen in him someone who could be trusted. Her heart flooded with love. She was proud of her brother and the way he survived the war, embraced the revolution, and was now guarding the nation's most notorious criminal.

Lidia watches people moving out into the late spring evening, from factories, shops, and schools. There is still a buzz in the air — a tremendous excitement everywhere. It is as if all of Russia believes that anything is possible and, for the first time, there is hope for the future. Her father thought it would never come in his lifetime and if it did, there would be bloodshed — but here it is right now and without violence.

The tram crawls past the Post Office Square and Lidia watches a soldier, standing on a flimsy wooden platform in a sea of furashkas on the heads of fellow soldiers and white cotton scarves on women workers, waving a paper document or newspaper — she can't quite see — and speaking with passionate belief.

The tram shoves on with its insistent *ding ding ding* signalling to pedestrians they should scuttle away or face the consequences.

Lidia knows that how they manage the next few months is crucial. The meeting she attended last night, at the local branch of the Socialist Revolutionaries, discussed the return of political prisoners as mandated by the Dual Powers of the Provisional Government and the Petrograd Soviet. As this means the return of many Socialist Revolutionary dissidents it was met with rousing applause but the Chair made it very clear to all attendees that the new Russia, the 20th century Russia, is still in its infancy. *We must be vigilant that nothing is lost — as we, the Socialist Revolutionaries, the true revolutionaries, consolidate power and make it our own!*

This was followed by some members of the local Socialist Revolutionary Party calling for a terrorist cell. Not just men, but women, some even younger than herself, arguing that assassination and murder were utterly necessary to secure the goals of the revolution.

Lidia thinks of the long, long road to arrive at this point in history.

'There can be no turning back,' she says quietly to herself as she sits up straight and tall on the wooden tram bench that hauls her homeward.

Already, there have been so many changes. The City Public School, where she has worked since she graduated, now extends its intake to girls because the Dual Powers has mandated that all Russians aged from 8 to 11 will receive compulsory education.

What an extraordinary time, she thinks to herself, a new Russia is rising and nothing can stop it!

The tram shunts to her stop and she alights, traipsing through a rabbit warren of side streets until she turns into Lanskoe Ulitsa. She moves aside as an old woman with a large barrow lumbers past. She almost doesn't hear the babushka mumble *cabbage*, or at least that's what she thinks she has said.

'You have something to sell?' Lidia asks, hardly daring to hope.

In reply, the old woman pulls back three wooden planks that she has managed to purloin, and there in the dirty bottom of the barrow lies a few cabbage leaves. Lidia leans in and touches their thick waxy skin and espies scraps of mushrooms and some spongy onions.

'Yes. How much?'

The old woman looks up, sees Lidia's mismatched eyes, and with the cracked spring sky fading behind, furtively makes the sign of the cross over her bowed head and chest.

By the time Lidia climbs the last stairs to the top floor of her apartment block and sees the sprawling angularity of Grishka up against her front door, labouring through something he is reading, she knows her day is going to get better.

She leans down and says, 'Hello, my love.'

His kiss is long and full. The taste of tobacco and fanaticism is on his lips as he pulls her down on top of him, right there, in the hallway.

Laughingly, Lidia disentangles herself and says, 'I am cooking my father's soup tonight.' She then reveals her earlier purchases. As he scrambles up to his full height, his army uniform dishevelled, he shows her his contributions to their evening. Vodka and cigarettes.

One of the perquisites of being elected by his regiment to the Army Committee of the Petrograd Soviet is that Grishka is always finding someone willing to part with a few items for a favour or a task that needs doing. Everyone loves **Grigory Ivanovich Semyonov**, known as Grishka to all. Although he never talks to Lidia about the last few years, he survived his time with the Russian 12th Army at the Northwest Front, and now works tirelessly, except when he is with Lidia, for Petrograd Soviet. This large city council is made up of Socialist-Revolutionaries and Mensheviks with over 3,000 members.

Once inside, Lidia scoops water from a covered bucket in the corner of the kitchenette and begins chopping cabbage leaves then mushrooms, and finally onions. She takes the half loaf of dried black bread from the cupboard and breaks it into clumps. Grishka moves beside her lighting the small gas ring, opening the bottle of vodka, and collecting two glass teacups and wide-open bowls all of which he places on the table along with a thick old church candle he requisitioned from she doesn't know where and doesn't ask.

Theirs is a tight and determined love affair. He loves her more than she loves him but that is how she has always survived. It was the mess of dark thick hair, and the way he seemed so at ease within his own body, that drew her to him one night at the local party meeting. He said he had come to the meeting out of curiosity rather than roaring self-assured zeal. That's how he discovered the Socialist Revolutionaries, which sort of amused her.

Lidia dismissed his lazy disregard for those who were taking responsibility for the future and determining the path of the Provisional Government. She dismissed it because, for all his charm and magnetism, she could see he hungered to have the faith, to have the determination to believe in something, anything, other than waking up for the sole purpose of surviving.

'It's good,' Grishka says as he slurps the next spoonful in appreciation. 'Your father's soup, huh?' And then that broad square smile that makes Lidia blush. 'When am I going to meet your father? And your brother, huh?'

He has heard fragments from Lidia about her father, who is ambivalent about the Tsar, and her brother, who is fully committed to keeping that blood-sucking leech under house arrest.

'Ex-colonels aren't so bad, are they?' He continues with the soup, 'He would love me ... all the fathers love me.'

She swats his hand away from her glass of vodka which she has hardly started and thinks he is incorrigible and needs no encouragement. He looks across at her pale skin and paler hair and thinks, he has come home — away from the mud and horror and scream of war, away from the endless talk and debate and recant of the Petrograd Soviet. Living used to make Grishka tired but here, in this old apartment, he feels more alive than ever.

After their warm repast, Lidia unties her leather boots and tucks her legs up under her skirt. She nestles in alongside Grishka on their sofa bed, which she insists on packing away each morning before she leaves for school. He suspects it is her way of curbing his desire, which is becoming tantamount to an obsession. He groans inwardly at the thought of those long pale thighs.

'I missed you last night,' she says and he reaches for her but she bends past him and places her glass on the small stack of books in front. 'The meeting was interesting ...'

He waits.

He missed her too but not because he couldn't attend one of those political meetings she is constantly running off to. Besides, he had papers to distribute to other members of the soviet from his committee.

'There's too much focus on *that* Bolshevik,' Lidia says. This is the term she uses nowadays for **Vladimir Ilyich Ulyanov**, known by all as Lenin. 'He's a trouble-maker. Besides — all of Russia is behind the Provisional Government.'

Grishka has been with Lidia now for a few months and knows better than to correct her perceptions of reality.

'Besides ...' Her forehead tightens. 'Comrade Kerensky is the best man for the job.'

And there it is. Most evenings her adoration for Kerensky surfaces, without fail. Grishka doesn't mind too much. He is still incredulous that someone as smart as Lidia, with her clean beauty and unshakeable belief in a better world, even looks at someone like him. He hasn't got around to telling her that his education was a little more ... informal. A bit of writing and reading at the local church school for a year or so, after which, he pretty much worked on the land where generations of his family had offered their labour to the landowner while trying not to starve to death.

It was the army that made him the man he had become. Indeed, not many could say this but it was his direct commanding officer who had ensured his platoon's survival back in '16. Lieutenant Viktor Leizorovich Pereltsveig, was respected for his shrewd ingenuity and steely acumen. Grishka continued to meet up with Viktor, who had also found himself on the soviet, and they often quietly discussed, just the two of them, their growing concerns about how the soviet should secure the power gained by the February Revolution.

'Don't worry about *that* Bolshevik ... Lenin.' There he had said it, 'No one is listening —'

'But he is tossing about those maxims in such a way that even my work colleagues are spouting them at each other and myself — as if *he* is the only pathway that *true* revolutionaries should follow for the future of Russia.'

Grishka pulls himself a little from her and pours more into his glass. He knows the maxims she is talking about ... *All Power to the Soviets!* To which, of course, Grishka is in full agreement ... *Bread!* God knows he has heard no plan from the Provisional Government about how food shortages are to be addressed. What would those aristocratic ministers know about hunger and food lines on the streets?... *Peace!* Well, there's a word that rings like God's truth in Grishka's heart. Up until now, only the soviet is discussing the collapse of morale in the army and that a peaceful settlement has to be made with Germany ... *Land!* He knew first-hand about the back-breaking soul-destroying filthy life of a peasant. Beasts of burden. Voiceless and invisible.

'He's banding about his thesis on what the proletariat must do to secure the revolution!' she says and there is a blush of fury rising up her lovely neck. 'In fact, the Bolshevik newspaper has nothing better to print — but it is just a bid for control and power! Why can't people see that?'

Grishka scoops up her pale fringe and kisses her forehead. She is warm beneath his touch. From the back of her neck, he pulls out her loosely gathered silk of hair. She looks sideways at him and the golden shard in her left eye pulls him closer.

'Now ...' He murmurs into the side of her face, 'What's up with that eye ...'

She smiles.

'Could God not decide —'

'There is no god,' she offers, but her voice is soft.

'So, whoever made you couldn't decide which colour ... Blue or gold? Hmmm ...' He begins kissing her, 'Blue or gold ...'

To her, the sex is still astonishing. Grishka is a great lover. He is, quite literally, a far cry from anyone else. Rather than attend cautiously to her as if she is a thing of beauty. Grishka rollicks in on her body with such intensity and certainty that she finds sex thunderously exciting. And the first time he went down on her, she nearly died from shame and desire. Even when she came, he wouldn't stop. At other times he would throw out instructions to her in the wrestle of the sheets as if she was a trapeze artist and he, her coach. *Roll over. Lift your arse. Higher. Push down. Further. Grab me. Tighter. Yes!*

Later, that night, after the soup and sex, Grishka leans over her and pulls his trousers across the floor to the unmade sofa bed upon which they sprawl. She watches him dislodge a cigarette, light it and inhale. After a minute he holds it to her lips and she takes a drag. And so, back and forth it goes, the way he had done the very first time they had gone to bed together. Strangely it is always this moment that Lidia feels most loved, most held in the moment of their lives together.

'Do you remember ...' He begins and she knows what he is about to say, 'Those marches through the streets ...?'

It's not a question. She will always remember the unadulterated February glory that led to the abdication of the Tsar and the end to centuries of autocratic rule. She was there and so was her kid brother. She, and so many Socialist Revolutionaries, had taken to the streets and joined the women's march that morphed into a city strike where every factory worker, peasant, soldier, teacher, student, and administration worker had demanded a better Russia — one where they could be heard.

'Yes, my love.' She smiles into the darkling and speaks quietly, 'I remember.'

'Do you recall that moment ...' He says with wonder and she does. 'When all of us soldiers put down our rifles and joined you.'

'I remember you guys were armed to the teeth!' She hears him chuckle.

Their skin is still wet with perspiration and sex but she feels her feet and hands growing cold.

'Petrograd was ours! Do you remember?'

'Yes.'

She squashes her hands between his back and the sofa bed upon which they lay for warmth.

'And it is still ours,' she says.

They stay like that for some time.

He thinks about the unimaginable happening. The holy Tsar abdicating in favour of his brother, his brother abdicating a day later in favour of the people. In his lifetime this great wonder has come to pass.

She thinks about all that could go wrong. The Dual Powers of the Provisional Government and the Soviet of Workers and Soldiers are still nascent and fragile. In her lifetime this great achievement could all come undone.

Lidka says, 'The Petrograd Soviet has the military support but the Socialist Revolutionaries have the backing of the peasants.'

He is not sure where she is headed with this so he says, 'But the Bolsheviks have the factory workers.'

Lidia clambers up on her elbow and looks toward him. Her outline is just visible.

'That's why it is crucial that the Party ...' He knows she is referring to *her* Party, the Socialist Revolutionaries. 'Secure power. You know ... there is talk of civil war —'

'There will be no civil war.'

'There *will* be civil war!' Her voice is rising, 'And if you have read *that* Bolshevik's *April Thesis* and believe it is not divisive, beckoning us into civil war, then you are a fool!'

Lidia unpeels herself from the crush of the sofa bed, and his body, and begins pulling on her underwear. A button-up camisole, dark woollen tights to the knee, and loose cotton drawers split in the crotch and tied at the waist. Grishka wants to reach out and stroke her long thigh and round arse, as she bends over in the shove of redressing. But he has made that mistake before and didn't go well.

'There won't be a civil war,' he says again as he sits up. 'Because the men are sick of fighting. All of Russia is sick of fighting.' She says nothing, so he continues, 'The men in the trenches have had enough. Their battle with Germany is no longer important. Their battle is now with the Russian High Command at Military Headquarters.'

Lidia watches him light another cigarette and as he continues she hears the bitterness in his voice, 'Russian soldiers witnessed, every ... single ... day, out there on the stinking Front, that those in command did not give a fuck whether they lived or died. *For the glory of Russia!* they would scream and hold a gun to the backs of those poor bastards — they were shoved out onto the battlefield — no boots, no coats, no guns ...'

She sits down beside him and after a moment moves his fingers holding the cigarette toward her lips, and in that touch, he is soothed.

He leans in and his kiss is hungry.

Eventually, Lidia says, 'All I am saying is that we have to secure what we have fought for so that people like *that* Bolshevik won't sneak in and take what is *our* future ...'

She gets up slowly and pulls the blinds and turns on a lamp. She knows they will tidy up, drink some more and read or talk or both. If he stays, they will most probably have sex again and in the morning make plans for that evening or the next. As she collects their tea glasses, she looks back at him in the poorly lit room and realises there is something more.

She pauses and he looks up. Grishka is still completely undressed. She wants to return to the sofa bed and sit with him but she also wants him to realise that vigilance and action are critical if they are to secure a socialist Russia. Grishka looks at her for a long time. He drops his gaze and reaches out for his trousers but she is not convinced.

'What is it?' The apartment seems very quiet and because he doesn't respond she adds, 'What's wrong?'

He begins, 'I wasn't going to say anything but — well — just so that you know ... I understand how we are in a critical time ... I ...'

She steps toward him, tea glasses still in hand, 'What have you done?'

Then he just says it, right there, a violation of confidentiality, 'I have volunteered for the Central Battle Unit.'

She doesn't know what this is and because she doesn't, she suspects immediately it is part of the terrorist cell in the Petrograd Soviet. The Socialist Revolutionaries had guessed they had one but up until now, had no evidence it existed. The glasses chink back down on the stack of books and she sloshes each one with a generous serve of vodka.

When she, like every Socialist Revolutionary cheered at the announcement last night that political dissidents were being released from Siberia's labour camps — a small part of her wondered how these disturbed individuals, many of whom had been incarcerated for assassinations and acts of terror back in '06, would impact on an already destabilised Russia.

Lidia sits alongside Grishka and drinks. And she thinks to herself that things are only going to get worse before they get better — especially now that her boyfriend has been recruited as a terrorist ... as an assassin.

Yekaterinburg, Urals. May 1917.

Feiga Khaimovna Kaplan cannot remember when they boarded the train in Siberia for Petrograd. It could have been last Wednesday or maybe it was Monday, she has lost track of time. She closes her eyes to the interminable *chuppchuppchuppchuppchuppchupp* of the train hauling them out of slavery and captivity. At least that's what Maria says. For days, the other women, in their dung-coloured woollen pinafores and loose-fitting shirts, sit close to Maria, listening to her talk about Russia's future. There is something fine-skinned and frail about her, despite the robust legend of surviving a Cossack gang rape, with only a smashed cheekbone and some nasty scars.

Feiga sighs.

Rape is a Russian woman's destiny, she thinks, and with her eyes soldered shut she raises her finger to push at the space just above her right eyebrow where a fierce pain pierces her head.

It is more or less always there, now that her monthly bleed has commenced. Some of the other women in the carriage have also got their period, for the first time in years. Siberia had at least offered them that relief, she thinks wryly. Feiga knows that soon she will have to move to the next carriage where there is a grim lavatory so that she can scrub the rags she wears inside her woollen drawers. Maria had helped her rip apart an old grey undershirt for this very purpose.

It must be raining now because the endless sound of the train is cut through with the *shoo shoo shoo* of the May showers in the Urals.

Feiga presses her forehead against the train window and the cool summer shower beyond. Her short brown nest of hair, pointy chin, and overlarge eyes, need only the addition of a set of whiskers attached to her nose, to complete her look of a field mouse.

She opens her eyes.

The entire carriage is filled with women who had once been prisoners at Akatoi. Some of them had been members of old terrorist societies while others were simply banished by administrative decrees without trial, without known offence, and without mercy. Many were in a ghastly state, unwashed, emaciated, and crippled. Feiga had been assigned to the bookbinding factory and not the mines, so in some ways, despite her deteriorated eyesight, she is slightly better off than others.

She knows them all, more or less, having arrived 11 years ago when she was just 16. But rather than feel part of their sisterhood, especially those closest to Maria, Feiga feels she is living out someone else's life. It has always felt this way. So, when the other women were brutally punished, she watched on indifferently. And when it was her turn to be stripped naked and left in a roofless cell, a blank Siberian winter sky overhead, or to be stripped naked and caned, by guards with lifeless eyes — Feiga let her true self, her real self, wander the forest-steppe of her homeland.

Chuppchuppchupp shoo shoo shoo ... Maria has said that the violators will win if the victims fail to testify to the injustices they suffered. Feiga watches the blur of green beyond her window and knows she will fail ... *Chuppchuppchuppchuppchuppchuppchuppchuppchupp* ...

WHOO — WHOO!

The whistle startles Feiga out of her slump and she pulls herself back from the window pane and looks about at the faces of the other women. Sure enough, she can feel the slowing of the locomotive, and then she hears someone murmur, *Yekaterinburg*. The locomotive screeches slowly alongside the platform and the women shunt forward on their seats, then pull back.

Momentarily, grey steam fills the space between her window and a crowd on the platform and then it dissipates so that Feiga can make out the faces of women, older than their years, swathed in shawls and scarves, babies strapped to their backs, and large-eyed infants clutching their aprons and skirts. There is also a smattering of soldiers, in various efforts of khaki, standing back from the womenfolk but there nonetheless. And pushing to the edge of the platform are men and women bearing the thwack of red flags or painted signs, *Power to the Soviets!* and *Long Live the Revolution!*

Feiga squints, her eyesight is appalling, and she sees some of the women hold photographs of a loved one and one woman, a small statue of the Blessed Virgin, and there further back, a few icons of the crucified Christ. Jostling, and with growing confidence, they push as close as possible to the windows of the train, knowing that this is a moment only the new Russia could deliver.

Inside their carriage, Maria stands unsteadily and looks upon the upturned faces of her fellow passengers and says, 'Comrades, this journey to freedom is not just our journey ...' Feiga has heard this before, at Omsk and before that at Novosibirsk. 'It is the journey of all Russians! We are travelling from slavery and unspeakable atrocities ...' Feiga watches as the other women raise their heads higher. 'To freedom and an unstoppable victory!'

The women cheer and Feiga hears her faint attempt but it doesn't matter because no one is looking at her. Everyone is looking at Maria Alexandrovna Spiridonova. A small-boned woman with soft brown hair and wire spectacles, who speaks with one hand on her hip and the other across the base of her throat.

Feiga tries to rouse herself to join the entourage milling behind

Maria as she steps down from the carriage and into a storm of applause and calls for *Holy Maria* to bless them. An irony not yet made clear to some of the locals by the Yekaterinburg Soviet of Workers and Soldiers.

Along the exhaustive route to Petrograd, they have been met by similar fanfare as if the trainload of newly released political prisoners is every peasant's freedom ride into a wondrous future. And despite the hollow-cheeked poverty that Feiga has seen from the window of her train journey through Siberia, she is astounded by just how much her countrymen and women want to offer. Indeed, when the locomotive needs to replenish with coal, pulling up at this or that train station, word gets out and before long, members of the soviets or the Socialist Revolutionary Party or the Mensheviks or the Popular Socialists have crammed baskets of food and other supplies into their carriages.

And so, every newspaper across the land rattles their story on and on and on and on and on!

Feiga sits in the near-empty carriage and enjoys the stillness. She can hear Maria's voice rising above the crowd outside ... *Friends the day has come ... Comrades, we are taking back our freedom ... Friends the future is ours and we must ... Comrades it is imperative that we ...*

Despite the gentle friendship that Maria has extended to her, Feiga can never shrug off the feeling that she is unworthy of this woman's attachment. Can the revolution, with all its promises, truly bridge the great divide between herself — a Jew — and an ethnic Russian?

Feiga closes her eyes and thinks about her childhood in the outskirts of Kiev and wonders if any of her siblings are still alive. She remembers the weatherboard school they all attended because of her father's passion for education, it was, according to him, their passport to life. One of her brothers was articled to a lawyer, another to the bank where her father worked, one sister returned to teach, another left to study music but only Feiga walked the path to revolutionary assassin.

It is all such a long time ago and she has had more than a decade to think about the life she once lived, God knows there was little else to do in the women's prison at Akatoi.

She remembers that fateful day when she joined the terrorist cell of the Socialist Revolutionaries but she doesn't remember why her heart quickened and her blood thrummed as if she was a bride on her wedding night. Nor does she recall the hours of preparation in binding the phalluses of dynamite into a lover's knot. She was young and virginal. What did she know back then? She was nothing but a child. The night before the assassination, she had laid awake without appetite or sleep, imagining the fanatical consummation of this love for one's country that would take place the next day.

And 11 years later she still tries not to think about the handsome young Tsar official, her target, nor the explosives detonating before she made it to his rooms.

She wants to go back home to Kiev and her childhood and innocence but knows, this will never happen.

... Comrades steal your hearts against rumours that will take us back to ... Friends we must join together and work for ... Comrades the Old Tsarist Rule made us no better than dogs ... Friends farewell until we ...

The women spill back into the carriage as the locomotive begins to cough and splutter into life. Feiga can hear the peasants calling out to Maria to kiss their babies or themselves or bless them or take them with her or return to them forever.

Perhaps they have forgotten the four bullets Maria shot into the face of the Tambov security chief, as he waited for a train at Borisoglebsk Station, unaware that the pretty young woman dressed as a schoolgirl, was his angel of death. Two and half days to die but not before he had heard the Cossack guards had taken it in turns to violate her, hence his final words: *God is just.* The newspapers had a different opinion and continued to report for weeks and months that Maria had been virginal and beautiful before the Cossacks brutalized her. Consequently, her death penalty was overturned for life imprisonment.

This all happened just after the 1905 Revolution. For the next several years Russian peasantry, with deep devotion and determination, prayed for Maria's release and the restoration of her hymen.

The bodies on the train momentarily propel forward as the brakes are released and the slow blast of *WHOOO! — WHOOO!* resounds across the township.

The crowd press up against the windows for a glimpse of the beloved Maria and call their love and respect to her, the one woman whose story they will always remember. For the other 200 ex-prisoners, theirs is a story that is too old and tired to ignite the imagination of the masses.

Feiga knows she can't wait any longer and must make her way down to the next carriage and the lavatory. The train is picking up speed and all about her Maria and her disciples chat about the revolution and the future and the love of all things Russian. Feiga feels the sticky warm blood ebb beyond the rags, now sodden and nonabsorbent. She must get up and change before it seeps into the back of her skirt. Her headache throbs with the *chuppchuppchupp chuppchupp* of the train. And her eyes close against the *shoo shoo shoo* of the rain.

She finds that she cannot move. She is just a body inside a train that will not stop because it cannot until it reaches its destination.

Podgaitsy, Ukrainian Russia. May 1917.

Sergeant Leonid Joakimovich Kannegisser has just received a telegram from Petrograd stating the first trainload of political prisoners has arrived, and he wants to be the one to tell Minister Kerensky. His boss needs good news. This morning's plan is for Kerensky to speak to the 21st Muromsky Regiment, here in Podgaitsy, just 150 kilometres east of Lviv. It is part of the morale-boosting tour that he has lowered himself to conduct, or at least that's how Leonid sees things. Although he admits all of Russia is relieved Kerensky has replaced the former Minister of War, the ineffective Guchkov. Leonid has a reputation for fastidious attention to detail as an aide-de-camp, which ensures Kerensky's brilliance to shine. Having said this, the 21 year old Kadet comes from a long line of proud and re-sourceful Jews, who grovel to no one.

'Sir,' says Leonid.

The minister looks up from his papers.

'News from Petrograd. The women prisoners have arrived safely.'

'Ahh. Akatoi, Maltsev, Kartoga ...'

Leonid shifts uncomfortably because he believes the less said about the litany of labour camps in Siberia, the better. Of course, he knows the Minister once worked as a lawyer for the Socialist Rev-olutionary terrorists, and in particular for the infamous Shesterka women who are led by Maria Spiridonova.

Unquiet souls, Leonid thinks po-faced. Assassins are mad dogs and the female assassins are demented bitches but the Kadet's stellar career is a result of his capacity to keep his own counsel.

Kerensky stands up abruptly and in his usual brusque way says, 'In many ways, the Dual Powers could never have come about with-out the bravery and selflessness of many of these early revolution-aries.' He grabs his gloves and as an afterthought, more for Leonid's benefit than anything else, 'Narodnik-inspired.'

Oh yes, the aide-de-camp contemplates drily, the Narodnik rev-olutionaries of the 1870s — nothing but upper-middle-class intellec-tuals saving the peasants from Tsarist oppression. Ignoring the fact that the peasants were devotees of the Tsar.

'Right. Time to leave, Sergeant.'

Leonid has already called round for the car, sent on their bags and so, after gathering the final letters off the desk, follows Kerensky out of the temporary Headquarters. He would be happy to never stay in this ram-shackled place again, with its surly-faced servants and flea-ridden beds. Its former name, The Grand Metropole Hotel, is a complete joke.

It takes only 15 minutes to be driven to the barracks by the Cossack. There are phalanxes of tents with soldiers milling about in the liquid sunshine of mid-May. The regiment of 1,500 men, with their washing and numerous campfires, seems disorderly and lackadaisical. Leonid gets straight to business, calling for an officer to notify the Colonel of their arrival.

The objective of the tour into Galicia and the southwest Front for the newly appointed Minister for War is to stop Russian troops fraternising with the enemy and to get them back to the bloody business of bringing this war to an end. There have been astounding stories of Frontoviks returning from the Austrian's trenches with sweetened coffee, rum, biscuits, and even boots and puttees. Some of these men are sending messages to each other, indicating when the bombardment is to commence, so that their sworn enemy can take cover!

Meanwhile, everyone knows the Germans are funding the Bolsheviks to spread mutinous discontent in the trenches and undermine Russia's national interests. The *Russian Gazette*, the Kadet newspaper, summed up this catastrophe perfectly in its editorial two days ago: *The principles of Socialism and universal peace are all well and good, but they cannot stand up against German cannons.*

Surprisingly to some, Kerensky's tour of the Russian troops has been largely successful. It has to be said that Leonid is proud to work alongside Kerensky, who has refused to accept Germany's offer of an unlimited armistice. Here is a man who will not rest until Russia is a nation of justice, a country of freedom and a land of bounty, for all.

Despite all this, occasionally, in the arms of his lover back home in Petrograd, Leonid feels doubt rise like an ominous zeppelin in his peripheral vision.

Officers of various ranks are moving the regiment toward the assembly area and the Colonel talks, head down and in muted tones, to Kerensky, who all the while watches the Muromsky Infantry Regiment, which is attached to the Russian 12th Army, amble toward him.

Slowly.

Suspiciously.

Indifferently.

It is the same everywhere they go.

Leonid notices that some of the soldiers openly continue to talk to one another, others smoke nonchalantly, still, others stand about in various displays of military undress. The Kadet watches all this, his uniform immaculate with his Cross of St George and Cross of St Vladimir winking in the sun.

Kerensky stands motionless.

Some of the men momentarily overlook the Minister because of his short, unassuming stature.

Kerensky waits.

The men shuffle and scratch and prattle.

Kerensky steps up on a crate and looks out over the men.

Insubordinate insolence continues to dart from one soldier to the next, in the spitting and laughter and yawning and talking and smoking.

'RUSSIA'S FINEST!' roars Kerensky and the startling salutation whips about their heads.

'COMRADE SOLDIERS! WE, THE RUSSIAN REVOLUTIONARY VICTORS, ARE AT A DECISIVE MOMENT IN THE GREAT WAR.'

Kerensky gazes across the hostile, the exhausted, the lost.

'THE ENEMY IS AT RUSSIA'S BORDERS! THAT IS THE TRUTH AND IT IS OUR TRUTH. THE HOUR IS NOW — I CANNOT LIE TO YOU, BROTHERS.'

This is not what they expect. The men shift uncomfortably and focus on Minister Kerensky whom they have heard of but never met.

'WITH ONE HAND WE WILL BUILD A GOVERNMENT FOR THE PEOPLE AND WITH THE OTHER WE MUST FIGHT AGAINST THE GERMAN HORDES!'

The minister speaks slowly, deliberately, and very very clearly.

'NOTHING WORTH HAVING CAN BE ACHIEVED WITHOUT SUFFERING.'

The soldiers begin to nod because this truth is theirs and it is the truth of every Russian since the beginning of time.

'MAN, HIMSELF WAS BORN INTO THIS WORLD IN SUFFERING.'

Kerensky peers across the vast horde of men and waits.

They wait with him. Some think about their mothers, some, their fallen comrades, some, their wives and small children.

The Minister continues, his voice is deep and resonant, 'THE GREATEST OF ALL REVOLUTIONS BEGAN ON THE CROSS AT CALVARY. AND IT IS HE, THE LORD JESUS CHRIST, WHO SAID ...' Kerensky pauses in the silence of more than 1,500 men, 'WHO SAID, *GREATER LOVE HATH NO MAN THAN TO LAY DOWN HIS LIFE FOR HIS FRIENDS ...*'

Some of the infantrymen make the sign of the cross while others bow their heads and still others kneel.

The words of the suffering Christ ring forth, '*YE ARE MY FRIENDS IF YE DO WHATSOEVER I COMMAND YOU. HENCE- FORTH I CALL YOU NOT SERVANTS ...*' Kerensky's voice rises above the heads of every man standing before him, '*I CALL YOU NOT SER- VANTS BUT FRIENDS!* COMRADES!'

There's a smattering of applause from the crowd but Kerensky speaks on, his beardless face making him look younger than his 36 years, but his love of his fellow Russians is palpable. And it is now that his voice seems to fill the very meadow upon which the regiment is encamped. His eyes are ablaze and every soldier has him in his scope.

'WILL YOU, COMRADE SOLDIER, SON OF RUSSIA, FRIEND TO THE DUAL POWERS OF THE PROVISIONAL GOVERNMENT AND THE SOVIET OF SOLDIERS —' The rest of his words are swallowed up in the frenzy of cheering but Kerensky will not be silenced and yells louder, 'WILL YOU — THE COURAGE OF RUSSIA — FIGHT TO PROTECT THE MOTHERLAND FROM THE BARBARIC ENEMY WHO is NOW AT OUR BORDERS!?'

The mob roars itself hoarse because, at that moment, they know themselves to be the Redeemers of Russia!

'IN THE NAME OF SALVATION AND A FREE RUSSIA, YOU WILL GO WHERE YOUR COMMANDERS AND YOUR GOVERNMENT SEND YOU. ON YOUR BAYONET POINTS YOU WILL BE BEARING PEACE, TRUTH, AND JUSTICE!'

The sky bristles with the men thrusting their weapons and fists above them, bellowing their vow: *PEACE! TRUTH! JUSTICE!*

Kerensky rises above them and with arms outstretched points to each and every one of them. 'YOU WILL GO FORTH IN SERRIED RANKS, KEPT FIRM BY THE DISCIPLINE OF YOUR DUTY, KEPT STRONG BY YOUR SUPREME LOVE OF COUNTRY, AND KEPT TRUE FOR THE REVOLUTION YOU HAVE ALREADY WON!'

The Muromsky 21st Infantry Regiment knows they have been chosen by God and Mother Russia and by this small inconspicuous man who they would follow into the cavernous mouth of hell.

Earlier they may well have been eating their dry black bread and washing it down with bracken tea while listening to the Bolsheviks among them say ... *Go home, the land will be yours, the factories will be yours ... A new life is beginning ...* But by the time the rising sun is directly overhead they are utterly committed to the war to end all wars.

And every single man knows it is down to him.

3

The July Days

Petrograd. July 1917.

Lidia is awake before Grishka and lays for a few minutes on their narrow sofa bed. It is already July and the apartment is sticky with heat that has been trapped by decades of cooktops frying onions and corner stoves warming the inhabitants. She watches the light pad across the room, slowly, still drowsy and heavy with sleep.

Grishka is tucked into the sheet but, somehow, Lidia can slide one foot, then another, onto the floorboards without disturbing him. She pulls out the small squat bucket from under the sink, the one they must use during the night, covers it with an old towel and, in her nightdress and thin coat, shoves her feet into a pair of old worn shoes and carries their night waste out their apartment, down the flights of stairs and into the back courtyard.

At this time of the morning, the privy is usually free.

The big steel tub beneath the old wooden seat in the privy is taken and emptied once a week, although most of the people in Lidia's apartment block have complained to the superintendent, and each other, that more often than not the sanitary workers have not done their job.

The door of the privy yawns open and a black batch of flies is already busy. Lidia leans over the hole and empties the contents of her bucket. Job done, she closes the door behind her, secures the latch, pulls up her nightdress, and sits down.

Outside, she can hear the long squeal of someone opening a window in the apartment block that surrounds the courtyard in which squats the privy.

She urinates and waits.

Last night was punctuated by the sporadic crack of gunfire and drunken slogan yelling. She knows it is just the usual Bolshevik malcontents attempting to undermine the Provisional Government. It's so infuriating that she mumbles, *Goddamnit*, to the spidery web of light making its way through the slats of the privy door.

Yesterday, in her district of Vyborgskaya, the workers from the shipyards and the paper factories moved from one cluster of agitation to another. A veritable tinder, sparking this speaker and that, to call for rebellion against the Provisional Government's ongoing war efforts.

Meanwhile, the newspapers shout *Great Kerensky on the Frontline! Kerensky Lifting Morale! Russia to Fight on Against the Teutonic Hordes!* At the same time, the Bolshevik leadership foments outright rebellion in Petrograd.

She agrees with Grishka, it is a bad move billeting the 1st Machine Gun Regiment near the radicalised factories of their district. Vyborgskaya Storona has always been a hotbed of worker discontent. And if rumours are true, *that* Bolshevik is in some rat hole in this very district, just streets away from her apartment, stirring up pro-German treachery. God how she hates Lenin!

Her sphincter opens and she defecates quietly.

Despite the earliness of the morning, outside the streets are strangely calm without the shrill whistle of the factories or the *ding ding* of passing trams. The last few days have been dangerously devoid of the usual comings and goings of people making a living.

Indeed, only yesterday, the Kronstadt sailors had abandoned their naval base and made their presence felt as they marched down the Liteyny Prospect, crossing the bridge into the Vyborgskaya Storona, swinging their wild red flags and shouting *The Government must Go!* and *End the War!*

These fanatics, thinks Lidia, believe they are the heart of the revolution. She shifts a little on the seat and can smell someone smoking from one of the lower-floor apartments.

The rebellion of the Kronstadt sailors seems to have put a spring in the step of every other Russian who is sick to death of taking orders from above and fighting the war. Yesterday, wherever Lidia went, people were demanding Russia negotiate peace with Germany.

She tears a few strips from the newspapers and leaflets scattered about the privy floor and, with the finger of clear morning light falling between the privy door and its frame, Lidia reads ... *Everything that is reported about money and other connections between Comrade Lenin and the ruling circles of Germany is a lie and ...*

Bullshit, she thinks, as she cleans herself. She hears someone cough beyond the privy door and knows she has a minute, at best, before one of the residents starts to hassle her.

She waits a moment. Then urinates a little more, tears another strip from a floor-lying leaflet, and reads ... *Enough demonstrations! Enough wild unrest! Enough senseless parading on the streets! The revolution needs ...*

Lidia drops her paper waste in behind, stands up, shakes out her nightdress, re-belts her thin coat, picks up her bucket, and unlatches the door. And there stands Grishka, bristling with news.

'*Izvestia* is just out. Four hundred civilians have been killed! One hundred and eighty Bolsheviks!' Lidia looks down at the newspaper in his hand. 'There's more to come,' he adds bitterly.

She has never heard him speak like this before and her own heart begins to race.

'I'm going to collect Viktor and head out to the Tauride Palace. Bloodbath there last night. Cossacks were mowed down while defending the Provisional Government's artillery.'

Lidia finds her voice, 'I don't understand. Why are you going there? There's nothing ... You can't be ...' Her mind is running around frantically. What can Grishka possibly do now that the Tauride Palace is surrounded?! Even with the wily Viktor, the two of them are no match against a mad mob.

'You need to go upstairs,' Grishka adds urgently. 'I will come up in a minute but keep away from the windows. There will be more crossfire and machine-gun fire, be sure —'

Right on cue, they both look up at the not so distant *tat tat tat tat tat* of return fire.

'Fuck! I need you to go upstairs, Lidia!'

Grishka has his hands on her arms but she is having none of it so she cries, 'I'm going with you!' She hasn't realised this is her decision until she says it. 'If things are as bad as you say they are, I need to take up my position with the other Socialist-Revolutionaries and defend the Provisional Government.'

The anguish in Grishka's face nearly undoes her resolve.

He thinks I cannot lose her, she is all I have!

She thinks I cannot stand by, Russia is all I have!

To stop him speaking she says, 'I have one of my father's revolvers in the apartment.'

Grishka is startled and opens his mouth but she adds, 'I will take it with me.' In her mind, she is already pulling the loading gate down and inserting the projectiles into the cylinder of her Nagant revolver. Locking in the seven bullets with air-tight satisfaction.

Grishka knows of her youth in Kiev hunting alongside her father but it doesn't quell the raging horror of his beloved out on the festering streets of Petrograd and in particular, Vyborgskaya Storona. He wants to hold her in his arms and force her inside, away from the unpredictability of this day, but she is already pushing past him and flying up to the apartment.

At that very moment, an elderly babushka is carefully carrying a small covered bucket on her way down to the privy, she sees the fanatical determination on Lidia's face and cautiously turns around and retraces her steps. The old neighbour has lived through these times before and knows it is better to be out of sight and mind, especially when you are unsure of your enemy.

By the time they collect Viktor and cross the Liteyny Bridge, it is nearly noon. The sun is a roiling mess behind thick clouds and there is a stillness in the air that threatens those inside and out. The three of them scurry the back streets making their way to the Tauride Palace. Whenever they hear a motorcar, they quickly take cover. But for the most part, the streets are bare except for a platoon from the city's Bicycle Regiment, rifles strapped across their backs peddling in small whizzing packs — the sole responders, it would seem, to the loss of central control in Petrograd.

Viktor's long aquiline nose, black moustache, and dark liquid eyes belie his capacity for blasphemy and profanity. But today it's different. In taking the lead he hardly speaks but rather beckons Grishka and Lidia to follow, or to stay back, or to take cover. Somehow, the two men have managed a small arsenal between them. Rifles, revolvers, hand grenades, and a couple of nasty knives. Lidia grips the textured teak handle of her revolver and knows target accuracy is a matter of life and death.

As they make their way across Shpalernaya Ulitsa they see the Palace a couple of hundred metres through parkland but the *bsst bsst bsst bsst chk chk chk* of rifle fire cracks overhead.

They throw themselves face down.

It's the Bolshevik Anarchists shooting Provisional Government supporters. Grishka grabs Lidia's forearm and together they scramble to the wall where Viktor is offering them precious seconds to scramble in beside him.

It's then that the three of them notice they are not alone.

A few metres along, tucked behind the wall, are several women completely unarmed. Lidia recognises one of them immediately, and so must the men, because, despite the heart-thumping predicament, Grishka clambers across to the fine-featured woman with wire-framed spectacles, shakes her hand, gives her his revolver, and crawls back to join Viktor.

Lidia watches Maria Spiridonova's handshake as she checks the cylinder of the revolver Grishka has just given her. The other women say nothing, their eyes are on Grishka and Viktor. Lidia pulls back the catch of her revolver and it's then she notices the young girl closest to her, humming, almost inaudibly, to herself.

'Cover me,' hisses Maria.

The command is so ridiculous it is stunning.

Lidia opens her mouth to speak but the legendary assassin is muttering grim-faced, 'Those bastards have been taking pot-shots at us for the last hour. Hooligans!' Maria then readies herself against the wall and adds, 'I didn't come this far for a coward to take me out!' And it occurs to Lidia that this is being said for the other women.

'Wait!' Viktor's arm reaches out across to where Grishka, Lidia, and the women huddle and then they all hear the *tickticktickticktick-tickticking* of bicycles freewheeling down Shpalernaya Ulitsa toward them. They catch the shout of staccato commands followed by rifle fire.

Crouched behind the wall the noise is riven with ghastly anticipation. On and on the exchange between the Bicycle Platoon and the Bolshevik Anarchists ricochets about their heads. At one point

Grishka and Viktor scramble around the wall to support the Platoon. Meanwhile, Lidia is unsure whether to follow or stay with Maria in case they need to shoot their way out.

Then there is a deafening explosion followed by another and another and another.

The bitter pungent smell of smoke fills the air.

Lidia is breathing heavily through her mouth and gestures to the women to stay low and wait. Not that any of them seem to have any intention of moving.

Then she hears a voice from someone in the Bicycle Platoon call, 'Clear!' and she hears Viktor respond with 'All clear!'

A stumble of footsteps crunch toward them and when she looks up she sees the smudged face of Grishka looking down at her.

'All good?'

'All good,' she replies and, along with the other women, begins to pull herself up.

She hears Maria speak gently to the younger one still humming and curled up in a foetal position, 'Feiga ... Feiga ... stand up now.'

'Come on!' It's Viktor. 'We have to move. These dead mongrels might have friends close by.' He looks about him and adds, 'Fucking Bolsheviks!'

They all scramble in the direction of the Tauride Palace but something makes Lidia look back. She notices the girl called Feiga is lagging behind so she drops back until they are abreast and puts an arm around her narrow waist to haul her along.

Most of them ahead are jogging it out and Lidia says, 'Nearly there,' to her thin and pale compatriot.

'I can't go on. I don't want —'

'Yes, you do,' interrupts Lidia and hauls her onward. 'You and me, together. Nearly there, little sister.'

Their feet pound the ground beneath them, the distance seems interminable and Lidia realises Feiga is probably in shock.

'I really can't ... I'll catch up ...'

'MOVE IT!' yells Grishka from the bottom of the Palace's driveway and there is panic in his face.

Lidia and Feiga's breathing is ragged and sparse.

'Together,' Lidia says as the Palace looms up ahead. 'You and me.' She is pushing Feiga forward. 'Little sister, nearly there.' She has no more oxygen but she doesn't need it because she knows they are going to make it.

Hours pass as Lidia and the others in the octagonal domed hall of the Tauride Palace wait for an emergency meeting of the Provisional Government ministers and the members of the Petrograd Soviet. Lidia watches as concerned Russians, like herself, move through the vestibule, then the hall, then the transverse gallery, and from there on to a conservatory, all to find out what the hell is happening! Around her are journalists, army personnel, and party members sitting on straight-backed chairs or scurrying between anxious discussions. The monochrome chequered marble floor, stucco pantheon, and open colonnades with Ionic columns preceding down the east and west halls suggest the calm beauty of Neo Classicism's perfect symmetry. Nothing could be further from the truth.

The only suggestion within the Taurid Palace that things have gone awry is that the high front windows have been boarded up. Probably as protection against sniper attack, Lidia thinks, but even then, the Palace transforms this anomaly into long cool shadows that soothe and calm.

Lidia muses to herself that one might be forgiven for thinking there is no looming crisis of civil war just outside the Palladian double doors. Regardless, Kerensky is rumoured to be returning this afternoon.

More and more Socialist-Revolutionaries are pouring into the Palace where the west wing houses the Provisional Government and the east wing, the Petrograd Soviet. Whoever bursts through the doors tells a similar tale to theirs. Running the gauntlet set up by thugs and anarchists, puppets of the Bolsheviks, to get here.

After a while, Lidia finds a comfortable davenport at the entrance of the east wing, and there she sits with Feiga. Maria and the other women are deeply embroiled in conversations with various Socialist Revolutionaries members, while Grishka and Viktor are off somewhere with the members of the Petrograd Soviet. She knows it is a waiting game and stretches out her long legs, brushing off the dust from her grey skirt and short white blouse. Feiga begins to do the same. She seems to swim inside her dark pinafore and Lidia wonders whether this was her prison attire because earlier Maria had said that the women were all from a labour camp in Siberia.

Feiga turns to Lidia and with considerable effort says, 'I want to say ... I'm sorry ... I'm not myself ...'

Lidia smiles and replies, 'None of us are ourselves at the moment. Nothing to be sorry about.' She realises Feiga is not as young as she first thought.

'The thing is ... I don't want to be here. I never wanted to be here. I wanted to ...' Feiga's large lash-fringed eyes look up to Lidia and then after a few baffling seconds, look away.

Lidia asks quietly, 'Where ... where did you want to go, after you left Siberia?'

Feiga's tawny elfin head turns once more to Lidia, 'Why ... your eyes are ... one is blue ... but ...'

Lidia smiles slowly, 'Yes. Yes, I know.' And then she thinks to add, 'It has always been like that, it's a —'

'Blessing,' says Feiga suddenly. 'You are blessed!'

The adoration from this small broken woman is disturbing.

'Hmmm ... some would say cursed, perhaps in the end, it is all the same,' says Lidia and instinctively she turns her face away from the direct stare of the younger woman.

It is not that she is ashamed, she learned to deal with difference a long time ago, it is because she has seen this before, in students, men, and certain women. A fascination in her, a clinging, a wanting. She cannot put her finger on why, but for as long as she can remember, she does not want people in the same way that they seem to want her.

'Kiev,' said Feiga.

'What ...?'

'I wanted to go to Kiev. I once lived there, a long time ago, before the arrest. With my family. A long way from the township itself, actually.' It is the longest speech Lidia has heard Feiga give and she cannot help but respond with, 'I lived there once myself, you know. My father was a career officer. We were posted about a bit. Kiev was one such place.'

And unbeknownst to each other, both women imagine themself there in the forest steppes with the endless wide-open grasslands whispering throughout their summers.

'That is where my father taught me to shoot, in the steppes,' says Lidia but she doesn't know why she is sharing so much with this woman, who she will probably never see again. Perhaps that is why it feels so easy or maybe it is because of what they have just been through, out there on Shpalernaya Ulitsa.

'That is where I would sometimes recite my Ashrei,' Feiga doesn't know why she has told Lidia something so private and secret, but she knows she wants to stay right here with Lidia, and never leave. And like a character trapped in a spell, Feiga sings faintly in the most exquisite monotone:

'I will extol thee, my God, Oh King.
I will bless thy name forever and ever.
Every day will I bless thee.
I will praise thy name forever and ever.
Great is the Lord, and ...'

Completely unaware, Grishka strides up to them and interrupts with, 'We're going in.'

The intimacy of what has just happened, Feiga's head bent close to hers, incanting this ancient keepsake to a god that does not exist, has made Lidia's hair stand on end.

But she rouses herself and asks Grishka, 'Is something happening?'

'The Provisional Government and the Petrograd Soviet are reconvening. Kerensky has just arrived. We need a plan and —'

'Sorry to interrupt but we are going in,' Viktor is speaking to Grishka but his right hand is nonchalantly hooked over the shoulder of a young Kadet who is wearing an immaculate uniform with the Cross of St George and Cross of St Vladimir pinned across his chest. His perfectly symmetrical features, fairish hair, and light blue eyes, in some strange inverted way, mirror Viktor's dark good looks, and Lidia thinks, what a handsome couple.

'Grishka, Lidia ...' Viktor has a ghost of a smile, 'This is Leonid Joakimovich Kannegisser.'

No one looks to Feiga who is singing Psalm 147 softly to herself as Viktor explains Leonid is Kerensky's aid-de-camp.

'Lidia,' says Maria warmly as she pushes past. 'Come and join us, we are all attending the meeting —'

'But how can I ... I'm not a member of the soviet ...' Even as she is speaking Lidia realises everyone is crowding into the enormous state hall located deep in the central axis.

'Come with me,' and Maria holds her hand out to Lidia. 'I know Yekaterina Konstantinovna Breshko-Breshkovskaya. She will vouch for all of us.'

The other women who shadow Maria's every move, her so-called Shesterka, are already pushing their way forward.

Lidia is caught in the river of Socialist Revolutionaries, Mensheviks, Kadets, Popular Socialists, Soviet deputies, and even Bolsheviks. The talk within the great hall is momentarily deafening. Maria's grip is tight about her wrist and Lidia wonders at the remarkable turn of events in this day, so far. She would never have thought she would meet the renowned Maria Spiridonova as well as Yekaterina Breshko-Breshkovskaya, the grandmother of the revolution. Both women, legendary Socialist Revolutionaries, have given their lives to a free Russia.

And all the while, Feiga is clinging to Lidia's other hand.

Grishka, Viktor and Viktor's boyfriend, because that is what everyone assumes, are close behind. Maria, without hesitation and despite the crowds and the obvious lack of available seating, leads them all the way down to the front of the auditorium and that's when Lidia sees Yekaterina Breshko-Breshkovskaya, white-haired and plain-faced, sitting at the head delegates' table, quietly writing.

'Babushka,' Maria's voice is soft but Yekaterina looks up and her face transforms into a smile.

'Doch-ka,' she calls back and then she gestures to some of the young Kadets close by and they move quickly in response, pulling chairs out of nowhere and hauling them across to Maria and her entourage.

As they settle in their seats Lidia sees the lovely looking Leonid leap up to the head delegates' table and swiftly meet, none other than, Kerensky himself.

Most of the great hall is on their feet cheering as Kerensky, Minister of War comes into view still nodding and listening to whatever it is the young Leonid has to say. Lidia has been at several meetings where Kerensky has addressed the crowd but this afternoon it is different. Just in his mid-thirties, medium height with a slight stoop, this man who was once a human rights lawyer, is now the great hope of Russia. Lidia knows she is not the only one who yearns for his success. His movements are quick and alert, his high forehead and brown hair brushed upwards seem to indicate that he is fast off his feet, moving from one major decisive moment to the next.

Lidia applauds thunderously alongside the other party members because, while the Socialist Revolutionaries suffer from factionalism and intransigence, as journalists never tire to point out, they are absolutely united in their support of Kerensky.

'COMRADES! OUR BRAVE SONS AT THE FRONT HAVE BEGUN THE SUMMER OFFENSIVE!'

The roar of approval drowns the heckling and booing from the back rows.

Kerensky raises his hand and the audience quietens, 'THEY KNOW, MORE THAN ANY OF US, HOW CRITICAL IT IS TO DEFEND MOTHER RUSSIA FROM THE ENEMY. THEIR BRAVERY IS THE VERY BLOOD THAT PULSES IN THE VEINS OF A FREE AND DEMOCRATIC RUSSIA!'

This time the Minister of War allows the great hall to applaud and yell their approval until there is a natural hiatus.

'BUT THE ENEMY WITHIN OUR NATION, IS HERE AMONGST US!'

Lidia feels herself tighten with this dangerous statement of truth.

'LET ME SPEAK BLUNTLY! OUR COURAGEOUS SOL-DIERS — THE FIRST SOCIALIST FIGHTING FORCE IN THE WORLD — WILL HAVE LAID DOWN THEIR LIVES FOR NOTHING ... IF, BEHIND THEIR BACKS, HOODLUMS AND GERMAN HIRELINGS SMASH AND DESTROY ALL THAT HAS BEEN GAINED IN THESE FEW SHORT MONTHS BY THE REVOLUTION! I DEMAND —'

'WHAT HAS BEEN GAINED!?'

As Lidia twists around with every other person in the great hall, she espies *that* Bolshevik, and she joins in the hissing, immediately.

'I REPEAT — WHAT HAS BEEN GAINED?' cries out Vladimir Ilyich Ulyanov, aka Lenin.

'ORDER! ORDER!'

Everyone ignores the chairman as the two men go head to head.

'TELL US WHAT HAS BEEN GAINED!' Lenin declares. 'THE DUAL POWERS OF THE PROVISIONAL GOVERNMENT AND THE SOVIET FOR WORKERS AND SOLDIERS PROMISED THE END TO THE WAR!'

Fellow Bolsheviks cry out their support for Lenin and the chairman is on his feet yelling *ORDER! ORDER! ORDER!*

'YOU PROMISED ...' Lenin continues, 'FOOD FOR THE PEOPLE — BUT WHERE IS IT?! YOU PROMISED —'

'When Vladimir Ilyich Ulyanov ...' Kerensky interrupts in a voice that is calm and measured, 'Was wearing short pants and a student of my father's, back in Simbirsk ...' Kerensky the master of public speaking pauses and notes the chuckling from the crowd as Lenin is reduced to a schoolboy. 'He was taught — POLICY MUST BE FOLLOWED BY PROCESS. WE ARE IN THE PROCESS!'

The crowd roars their approval but unperturbed *that* Bolshevik springs out of his seat with, 'WE INSIST LAND IS PLACED IN THE HANDS OF THE PEASANTRY AND WE INSIST THAT THIS IS DONE —'

'GET OUT OF HERE!' Yekaterina Breshko-Breshkovskaya bellows. 'GO ON! GET OUT OF HERE AND TAKE YOUR FILTHY CRONIES WITH YOU!'

The crowd goes wild for the grandmother of the revolution. It is as if the white-haired matronly figure is the only one who can stop this rude intruder.

She speaks on. 'While comrade Kerensky has been at the front, while he has been running this country, while he is both a member of the government *and* the soviet, while he has orchestrated the abdication of the Tsar, while he has ensured support from the entente powers, while he has released Russia's unlawfully held political prisoners — a blight on the very body of this nation ...' The entire hall is mesmerised by this 74 year old woman, pointing her arthritic finger at Lenin and holding him with her glittering eye. 'WHILE *HE* HAS DONE ALL THIS ...' She too is the master of the dramatic pause, Lidia thinks gleefully. 'WHERE ... WERE ... *YOU*!?'

The cheers and applause crash about the auditorium.

Kerensky, with a nod of respect to Yekaterina Breshko-Breshkovskaya, takes over the baton and enters the space she has created, racing on with his agenda.

'TO SUPPORT OUR TROOPS AND WIN THIS WAR ONCE AND FOR ALL I STAND BEFORE YOU AND DEMAND THAT THE PROVISIONAL GOVERNMENT HAVE COMPLETE EXECUTIVE CONTROL OVER THE ARMY WITHOUT ANY INTERFERENCE FROM THE ARMY COMMITTEES ...'

The Bolsheviks are not the only ones to holler their disapproval and it is at this point and Lidia wilts because she knows Grishka will feel betrayed.

'I ALSO DEMAND AN END TO ALL BOLSHEVIK AGITATION!'

The applause is thunderous and nearly drowns out the protest from the back row.

'AND *THAT* MAN, THE ONE WHO GOES BY THE ALIAS, LENIN, AS WELL AS HIS ASSOCIATES, SHOULD BE ARRESTED FOR TREASONOUS SUPPORT OF GERMAN —'

Nothing can be heard. The great hall is in chaos. Men and women are lost in the cacophony. Despite red flags windmilling in protest, Lidia thinks, Bolshevism has died! Her elation is euphoric. She looks around and that's when she sees a lone, mud-encrusted, blood-splattered soldier making his way slowly down the centre aisle of the great hall. She looks up at the delegates' table and notices that Yekaterina Breshko-Breshkovskaya also sees him.

His face is white with the dust of the summer streets but he moves on and on toward the delegates' table until he is standing directly below Kerensky. The lone soldier, who wears the uniform whose lapel markings are those of the Petrograd Bicyclist Regiment, salutes the Minister for War and then faces the entire hall.

The incongruity of the scene stops the noise.

The soldier clears his throat: 'WHILE THE RUSSIAN ARMY HAS BEEN GATHERING ALL ITS FORCES TO DEFEND RUSSIA FROM THE ENEMY — YOU WHO HAVE NEVER FACED WAR ...' He takes his time to look out over the sea of faces to the far bleachers of the hall where the Bolsheviks congregate, 'YOU IDLERS AND TRAITORS WHO SPEND TIME IN VICIOUS BABBLINGS ...' His gaze is fierce, 'INSTEAD OF FIGHTING LIKE MEN AGAINST AN INVADING ENEMY!' He points his finger at the red flags, 'YOU HAVE BEEN MURDERING PEACEFUL CITIZENS!' He is utterly unstoppable, 'ORGANISING RIOTS AND CONFRONTING US, THE SOLDIERS OF THE GREAT RUSSIAN ARMY, WITH MACHINE GUNS AND CANNON!'

The soldier stands grim-faced and appalled at the spectacle he sees before him.

Lidia, along with more than a thousand others, is spellbound.

'WHAT INFAMY!' The soldier's voice is icy and a sardonic grin stretches across his face, 'BUT ALL YOUR TREACHERY IS IN VAIN!' His voice rises with heat, 'I AM THE COMMANDER OF THE PETROGRAD BICYCLISTS' REGIMENT AND MY TROOPS HAVE DISPERSED THE RIOTERS.'

Confusion and uncertainty run through the crowd: *How is this possible? Could this be true? Are we saved?*

'HEAR ME WHEN I SAY — YOUR MACHINE GUNS ARE IN MY HANDS. YOUR FIGHTERS, SO BRAVE IN THE FACE OF UNARMED CITIZENS, HAVE FLED!'

The silence is palpable.

'AND I TELL YOU — THOSE OF YOU WHO ATTEMPT TO

CONTINUE THIS REBELLION — YOU WILL BE SHOT DOWN LIKE DOGS!'

And above the irrepressible racket of the inflamed crowd, Lidia hears Kerensky shout for the arrest of Lenin and the other leaders of this treacherous Bolshevik Party — Trotsky, Lunacharsky, Gimmer, Kats, Zinoviev, Kamenev, **Volodarsky, and** Uritsky.

<h1 style="text-align:center">4</h1>

The Departure

Tsarskoye Selo, 30 km south of Petrograd. August 1917.

The man is thinking about chopping wood. Although he has lived half a century the skill is newly acquired. It doesn't occur to him that most Russian folk would have been chopping wood for all their lives. What he is thinking is that it is practical and useful expertise that may well come in handy down the line. Yes, if he could have his life again, he would have wanted to be a woodsman. He smiles quietly at his own fancy. The man gazes out over the parkland where the entourage of Cossacks and Sharpshooter Guards flank the oncoming procession, and considers his realm, now somewhat reduced, with its abundance of birch, oak, rowan, fir, and maple trees offering some shade in the summer heat. He wonders if a man, truly, could want for more. To be surrounded by woodland and the love of chopping wood.

It's the truth of the timber.

It's the heft of the axe.

It's the heavy neutrality of the blade.

Now, he can see the clergy moving slowly and deliberately through the military guard toward his home. It is his role to meet the religious procession at the entrance of his home and lead them inside, along the west wing until they arrive at the chapel.

The man stares straight ahead, chin up and eyes aloft, thinking of his son's longing for the rough and tumble of the great outdoors. It is a perfect August afternoon, the sky an eggshell blue, the sun a holy wafer of light, from which the warmth of an old summer shines.

It is as it should be, on this, his son's birthday.

If he had been a woodsman ...

He sees the icon winking in the sunshine and is momentarily startled by its enormity, he has only ever seen it in the dark shadowy recesses of the local church. His first instinct is to sigh, thinking, what a folly.

His wife's idea, of course.

Four men labour awkwardly with the giant icon in the procession. The silver jewel-encrusted devotional painting flickers and slashes the sunlight, blinding the guards, then the Cossacks, then the man.

The procession still has a few 100 metres before it reaches the steps upon which the man stands. He has no stomach for this, anymore. He and his family will leave their home tonight and may never return. They will leave behind the Alexander Palace, in Tsarskoye Selo, an oasis in the town of Pushkin on the outskirts of Petrograd.

Quite frankly he will be glad of another life.

One less complicated, less connected to all he had failed to be.

From the back of the procession, he hears the angelic strands of *Te Deum*. The beauty of this Ambrosian hymn wraps around him and up into the birthday afternoon where larks sing and cavort in the cloudless sky.

He cannot help but recall the euphoria he felt when Kerensky told him the Russian 11th, 8th, and 7th Armies had been victorious in Galicia, routing the Austrian forces.

To thee, all Angels cry aloud.

The Heavens, and all the Powers therein.
To thee, Cherubim and Seraphim continually do cry,
Holy, Holy, Holy ...
The thurible swings on its chain and sends up wafts of sandal-wood to the swaying entourage of holy men and the holiest of all icons which all proceed to where the man stands.

The glorious company of the Apostles: praise thee.
The goodly fellowship of the Prophets: praise thee.
The noble army of Martyrs ...
Then hardly a week passed before Kerensky returned with the appalling news ... the Germans had responded and those brave Russian boys who had taken Galicia were massacred. Hundreds of thousands, hundreds, and hundreds of thousands. For what? All that had been gained in the last year, and more, was lost in a few days. A tragic waste.

And the man wonders, but not for the first time, what is to become of them all?

O Lord, save thy people: and bless thine heritage.
Govern them: and lift them up forever.
Day by day: we magnify thee ...
The man looks upon the Znamenskaya, the icon of Our Lady of the Sign. The Virgin's arms are outstretched in supplication while her son is cradled in the womb and surrounded by a halo. The bearers hold it aloft, beads of sweat visible, as they move to the bottom of the stairs upon which he waits. The Znamenskaya is the holiest of all icons, according to his wife. The one she insisted be delivered from the local church in a special celebration of their son's 13th birthday. That his son has lived so long could surely be seen as a miracle.

If you were a believer.

Some of the guards genuflect and many of the Cossacks cross themselves because out of its usual shadowy situ of the local church, the icon shocks and bedazzles.

The man looks on impassively.

O Lord, have mercy on us: have mercy on us.

O Lord, let thy mercy lighten upon us: as our trust in thee.

O Lord, in thee I have trusted: let me not be confounded ...

The priests carrying the two-metre high icon stagger slightly and the man realises it is his cue to lead the way into his home where his family awaits.

He thinks about the emperor of yore who solemnly paraded this icon as a paladin on the city walls and then carried it out on the battlefield to meet his foes. He knows when he looks upon the icon he is looking upon a biblical truth: *Be it done to me according to your word.* And he wonders whether the Virgin Mary doubted, whether she faltered or whether she flat out did not believe there was a God — just a hurried fumble, pregnancy already showing and a vague promise to marry someone who had already abandoned her.

The man turns and leads the way into his home, through the passageways and crosswalks to the main hall which leads into their own Alexandra Chapel, all the while thinking about the satisfying *thunk* and *thwack* of axe blade hitting the grain of wood, slicing it clean, nicking its knots and chopping and chopping until all that is left are splinters and chips that eventually, over time, will become part of the undergrowth.

2

It is Captain Pavel Konoplev's job to oversee the move from Tsarskoye Selo to west Siberia for the man and his family — and it is making his head swim. It's enough having to put up with their perverse attachment to the old ways. This afternoon's ridiculous charade, bearing the icon from the local church through Tsarskoye Selo and into the chapel, is a case in point. Pavel had distinctly told his men to remain in formation and show no subservience to the man or his troubling practices, but a few allowed the past to get the better of them ... genuflecting or crossing themselves as if they were old peasant women on the feast of the Assumption.

Pavel stands at the entrance of the man's home and is glad it is nightfall. Soon they will be on their way. Colonel Kobylinsky will return presently but until he does Pavel must ensure the luggage is hauled down to the siding station.

As far as he is concerned, the sooner they move the man and his family out of sight, the better. There is already too much talk in the ranks about the filthy Citizen Romanov and what should be his fate.

Siberia, of all places, he thinks to himself as he reassembles some of the luggage awaiting pick up at the entrance of the man's home. But it can't be helped. Orders are orders. Although some of the men are having trouble with this concept.

The late summer air crackles and pops with tension. The family's endless crates of clothing, household items, and foodstuffs, as well as the furniture that they insist on taking, never seem to end.

Pavel looks askance at the growing hill of excess and bounty that the man and his family have no hesitation in flaunting. Piles and piles of wanton waste and indulgence block the entrance.

They have no shame, he thinks and walks back into the hall where the candles are aflutter with all the bodies toing and froing. The Head Footman rushes past Pavel, full of outdated loyalty to a master who has failed more than 100,000,000 people.

Then the boy comes bounding toward Pavel with a black and white spaniel underfoot, 'Captain!'

Pavel doesn't seek familiarity with the boy, who is naïve and trusting.

'Captain — did you hear? We are leaving tonight!'

Pavel gazes down on the perfect skin and upturned face of delight and replies dourly, 'That's correct, comrade.'

The boy loves this appellation which, to him, is so full of new and easy friendships. 'My sisters are hoping for the Black Sea but I have heard some of the soldiers talking ... about Siberia!' The boy lowers his voice to add confidentially, 'You see, one day I want to be a Cossack or a sailor. Did you know that the Siberian Cossacks are very fierce?'

Pavel begins to pull away as guards sullenly shoulder more luggage past. He doesn't like to be seen with the boy or any member of the family.

Sensing the window of chat is closing, the young boy's voice rises, 'Siberian Cossacks wear red cap bands and epaulettes. Green breeches!'

The 13 year old then runs after the spaniel who is darting for the open door and the possible snack of kit fox, while their mothers are out hunting frogs and rabbits.

'Your men are asking to be paid!' cries the red-faced Head Footman to Pavel. 'They are meant to be guarding and protecting ...'

Pavel looks past the elderly servant who is at boiling point and sees three guards walking nonchalantly toward him.

One of them squares up to Pavel and says, 'Cap'n, this job is more than we bargained for.' Pavel watches the hairy brute, carefully. 'So, as a member of the soviet, we are asking for six roubles. Each.'

His comrades stand shoulder to shoulder with their spokesperson.

After a second or two, Pavel's laconic response is quiet, 'Fair enough.' He knows which battles to fight. He has heard of fellow officers shot by the rank and file for less than this. Besides, the unnecessary trunks and suitcases are pissing him off.

Pavel turns to the Head Footman and says, 'Three roubles per soldier.'

There is something in the Captain's eyes that makes the elderly servant mumble, 'This is a matter for Count Benckendorff, the Grand Marshal.'

Pavel asserts, 'There are 25 of my men lifting furniture and luggage for the family.' The three guards before him are cracking grins so wide they look disturbing as they stand about listening to the Captain berate the prisoner's servant. 'So that is 75 roubles which you will give to this man.' Pavel nods at the hairy beast, 'Whose job it is to distribute the money, fairly.'

The beast pushes back his shoulders and surveys his minions.

'And if it is not distributed fairly ...' The Captain's menace is unmistakable, 'Then these two fellow guards and I will report him to the soviet ... and he will be dealt with severely.'

The Head Footman storms off with the three guards in tow, most probably to find the Grand Marshal if he knows what's good for him. Pavel sighs. This is what it has come down to ... there was a time when soldiers deployed to safeguard the Emperor would dutifully give their life if the Crown was threatened. And although thankfully, those times are gone, Pavel wonders where will it all end.

It takes a few more hours into the night to complete the enormous task of transferring the goods of the man and his family down to the siding station. Now, all they can do is wait. Not just for the Colonel and Kerensky, who are due tonight, but for the railwaymen to complete their discussions and vote in favour of moving the locomotives into the siding to transport the prisoner. The debate is fierce.

It has been a long day. Pavel heads to one of the temporary redoubts, set up outside the man's house, to take the weight off his left leg. He need not report the incident of the soldiers demanding extra pay to the Colonel. What would be the point? Colonel Kobylinsky is navigating his way in the dark, like the rest of them.

Pavel pushes open the door of the small shed, nods to two guards who are just leaving, and makes his way to the samovar to pour a glass of tea. He reflects dryly on how things have changed. There are some moments when he misses the old ways ... Where a batman would organise one's meals and refreshments ... Or where soldiers just did as they were told by their officers.

He sits back and enjoys the quiet. He probably has ten minutes before he needs to be back out there. The guards are being fed in, what used to be, the man's grand dining hall. And the family is back in the chapel. Praying.

There was enough praying this afternoon by the man and his family, not to mention the syphilis-infected clergy, to last Pavel a lifetime. It was unsettling to hear the priests ask God for a prosperous journey for *their Majesties* and their children. And this, of course, started the man crying.

Pavel spits into the corner of the redoubt.

The man is always crying. Or trying to talk to Pavel and his men. Or trying to chop wood, as if it is some sort of hobby. And every so often, Pavel catches the man smiling kindly at him and he has to turn away.

If I failed in my job as catastrophically as he has, I would have the balls to do myself in, thinks Pavel as he finishes the dregs of his glass.

When he steps out of the shed, he is caught up in the sweep of headlights that crunch up the driveway. He tucks his rifle under his arm and moves toward the vehicle. As it pulls up he can see it is Kerensky and his aid-de-camp.

'The Prime Minister to see Comrade Romanov,' says the aid-de-camp smartly.

Kerensky moves swiftly around the vehicle but his voice is tired when he says, 'Good evening, Captain.'

Pavel shakes the Prime Minister's hand which has become their ritual, having stumbled awkwardly around salutes and the word *comrade*, when they first met. Pavel has admitted to his sister that Kerensky trusts him. Their connection has developed with the weekly visits to the prisoner but Pavel has noted a growing sense of defeat in Kerensky as he has morphed from Minister for Justice to Minister for War to Prime Minister. Regardless, this great leader of the revolutionised Russia has reminded Pavel often that he is his eyes and ears on the ground.

'The carriages on both trains are packed and ready. Just waiting for the locomotives,' reports Pavel but he knows the Prime Minister is not interested in the details.

'Well done, Captain. And no problems with the religious service this afternoon?'

'The Znamenskaya has been returned to the local church.' Pavel notices the aid-de-camp is finding something amusing and he bristles, thinking he has been taken for a religious fool.

'Excellent job, Captain. Now I will just have a quick word with Comrade Romanov.' Kerensky turns to his aid, 'Sergeant Kannegisser, check the automobiles are brought up from the bottom of the drive.'

Ahh, thinks Pavel as he watches Kerensky move swiftly up the front stairs to the man's house, his assistant is nothing but a Jew.

Inside the man's house, Kerensky hurries through the various passageways and halls until he finds the family, cluttered about one another in the woman's lilac sitting room. Its quaint out of date French silk wallpaper and yellow wood furnishings make Kerensky feel claustrophobic. The man is reading aloud to his needleworking wife and daughters, his son is playing draughts with Dr. Botkin.

It's a tableau vivant, thinks Kerensky as he hears the man read Tolstoy's *How much does a man need?* and wonders if any of them have a sense of irony.

'Ahh, Prime Minister,' it is the little doctor with his tonsure of hair and sweet-natured smile who speaks.

The others look across at Kerensky, a little startled, still unused to the comings and goings of mortals in their inner sanctuary.

'Kerensky, thank you for seeing us off tonight,' says the man, as if this was a mere courtesy and not the most highly anticipated secret that Kerensky has personally orchestrated.

'If I could have a word in private, Citizen Romanov?'

And the man follows the Prime Minister from the family's anxious faces to the Palisander Room, just beyond. The man waits for Kerensky to speak because he has learned that people prefer it this way, now that his duty to God has been rescinded.

Kerensky has no time to waste. Petrograd has gone mad. First the massacre of Russian troops at the southwest Front, then the stupid missteps of Kornilov to ignite a coup, and now the Bolshevik-stacked soviets stymie every move he makes.

'Look, as I mentioned last week, things are heating up in the city. We've arrested Kollontai and Trotsky ... there are others. Lenin is on the run.'

The man says warmly, 'Yes I did catch that in the newspapers you have kindly sent my way.'

Both of them ignore the fact that when the news does arrive it is days old and the *London Times*, with its Russian royalists' letters to the editor, has been completely omitted from the stack of newspapers delivered to the man.

'Yes, well, as a result of these arrests the rioting in the city has settled and Lenin has scurried down some rat hole — but all the same, I need to have you away from the city, should the situation flare up again.'

The man nods sagely, completely unaware that his life is in peril.

And people wonder why I am tired, thinks Kerensky. It is getting harder and harder to protect the prisoner because he doesn't believe he is in danger. He realises the man is incapable of understanding the representative governance that he, the Prime Minister, is attempting to put in place. He must just get him out of the way.

Kerensky clears his throat, 'So, I am here tonight to respond to your suggestion to be sent to Livadia on the Black Sea —'

'Where the Dowager Empress resides and other members of my family —'

'Yes, yes. Where the ... where your mother resides.' Kerensky is exhausted by this man who should be grateful that they had wrangled any place at all for him other than the grave. 'Well, it is just not going to happen.' There, he has said it, and decides it is best to plough on, 'Too far, you see, too many ... The train would need to pass through many hostile villages, so it won't do ...'

The man blinks. Hostility is a new concept to him and Kerensky realises he is trying to process what has just been said.

'It won't do. So — Tobolsk. Siberia. Best choice. There's a Governor's residence at your disposal. Good climate. Small garrison. Look, it's a bit of a backwater —'

'My dear fellow,' the man interrupts, again. 'It sounds just right. Perhaps this is closer to Murmansk anyway, should we ... need to ...'

'Yes. Yes. Exactly.' Kerensky wonders if the revolution's feu de l'esprit has reached Japan, because any effort to get the family to England or France via Murmansk and the Barents Sea, had been refused point-blank — Japan is now their only hope.

'Look,' Kerensky begins quietly. 'Tobolsk is isolated. Still a lot of the Old Believers ... I am hoping that will work in your favour. And the thing is —'

'I trust you,' the man interrupts. Then he adds as if to reassure both of them, 'I am not afraid —'

'Be that as it may, the Bolsheviks are coming after me, and make no mistake, they will be coming after you.'

The two men look at each other for some time. The younger one knows his power is slipping and it will only be a matter of time before he is unable to stand between the man and retribution. He has tried. God knows ...

'If you say we must leave and Siberia it must be, then I accept. My family is all I have now.' Kerensky is used to seeing the man's eyes fill with tears and thinks back to the last meeting of the Dual Powers, where deputies diced for the lives of the man and his family as if they were pieces of silver.

'Right,' Kerensky's voice is decisive and signals the end of their conversation. 'Colonel Kobylinsky is in charge of the transfer.'

He turns to leave because there is nothing else he can do for the man, at this stage. His hope of course is to move him out of Russia but things being as they are, who knows when this might happen.

Over his shoulder he throws, 'Another good man with you is Captain Pavel Konoplev.'

Surprisingly the man catches the lifebuoy and says, 'Yes, he is our friend!'

Kerensky walks briskly from the drowning man thinking, *No, he is not.*

Meanwhile, out in the waning summer evening, with still no resolution from the railwaymen, Pavel is a little surprised by the question from the young Jewish aid-de-camp, who has probably never known a day's combat in his perfectly worn uniform, resplendent with medals.

'Well ... I am not a member of any party, as of yet. Yourself?' responds Pavel who feels surrounded by guards who are simply focused on the Army Committees to the soviet but as for wider party politics that is not part of their day-to-day conversation. End the war, nationalise land, and bring food into the cities, especially Petrograd where many of their families reside, are the topics that loop over and over and over amongst the guards Pavel works alongside.

'Kadets,' is Leonid's answer, as he leans against one of the vehicles he was sent to organise and is now parked, waiting, in the man's driveway. Pavel is also waiting, nonchalantly, for Kerensky to dash out of the man's house and give him instructions, as is his custom. They stand together, the two of them, awkwardly. Pavel smoking a cigarette from a pack he doesn't bother to offer Leonid.

'Ahh,' says Pavel. 'That makes sense ... the Kadets are stacked with non-ethnic Russians promoting non-Russian national cultures.' He does not need to be careful with this Jewish aid-de-camp, he is nothing but a servant to the Prime Minister and largely replaceable, besides, it is a relief to let caution drift when speaking to a lower-ranked officer. Pavel is warming to the conversation, 'I think Lenin regards you lot as counter-revolutionaries.'

'I don't give a fuck what that imposter thinks,' spits Leonid which makes the Captain smirk. Not because he necessarily agrees but because he sees a chink in the aide-de-camp's perfectly manicured armour. Pavel thinks of his sister, a strident Lenin-hater, and wonders what it is about this leader of the Bolsheviks that gets under their skin. He's just as fanatical as the others. At least the Bolsheviks want the soviets to run the country and, personally, that's what Pavel believes the country needs.

So, he says to the young Jew, 'People are rioting because 400,000 Russian bastards died in that bullshit Galicia offensive, last month!' Pavel wonders when the Kadets and the Socialist-Revolutionaries and the Mensheviks and the Popular Socialists and all the so-called progressive reformers are going to get it through their heads that no one wants the war — especially those rotten sods who are sent out to fight it.

'They're not rioting anymore,' Leonid corrects Pavel. 'Now that the Bolshevik ring leaders have been arrested and Lenin remains nothing but a filthy fugitive.'

'Listen to me, Lenin's not the problem. This war has to end and he is the only one saying that it will end as soon as he comes to power —'

'Let the *people* say whether the war has to end!' The interjection makes Pavel inhale deeply as Leonid rolls on, 'We want a Constituent Assembly so that the peoples' voice can be heard — on the matter of the war as well as land nationalisation and other issues, for example, whether there should be a Ukrainian Rada, you know, their parliament.'

This young overconfident aid-de-camp is irritating, thinks Pavel. 'So, you think we should carve up Russia, now, do you? What about a Siberian Rada or —'

'I'm sure many of those in Siberia would welcome the opportunity to have independence.'

God help me, thinks Pavel, the guy is like lice, just makes you want to scratch and scratch and scratch.

Pavel points his cigarette at him to emphasise his point, 'Lenin, thinks the Constituent Assembly is loaded with right-wing Socialist Revolutionaries, who are mere supporters of the bourgeoise.' The look of repugnance on the handsome fair-haired young Kadet encourages Pavel to add, 'There is no representation from the Left, no supporters of socialism!' There, thinks Pavel, got you in the bag.

'Captain Pavel Konoplev!' calls Kerensky.

Both of them abruptly turn as the Prime Minister jogs down the steps toward them.

Kerensky asks, 'Any word from the railwaymen? We need to get the family on board that train and gone before daybreak!' Kerensky's looks harried as he scans the late summer evening.

Pavel responds, 'I will call them again but —'

'No. I will call,' says Kerensky and with that, he returns just as abruptly back to the man's home.

Pavel is relieved because the railwaymen are far more likely to jump if Kerensky makes that call. After all, Kerensky is the leader now of revolutionary Russia. It is then that he notices the aid-de-camp looking at him, quietly.

He turns away to avoid the scrutiny and hears Leonid comment, 'I may have met your sister. A couple of times. She mentioned she had a brother guarding the Tsar. I just didn't realise it might have been you.'

In the time Pavel had spent with Lidia in February he had met a number of her friends, including the very likeable Grishka, but Pavel is sure this guy had not been one of them.

The aid-de-camp continues, 'Lidia Konopleva. Hmmm ... Grigory Semyonov — Grishka — her boyfriend.'

And without hesitation, Pavel puts out his hand which is quickly picked up by Leonid and they shake.

Leonid says, by way of apology, 'I didn't hear your name — when we arrived but she told me about you ... and ...'

Pavel takes the squashed cigarette packet from his trousers and offers one to Leonid, who doesn't smoke but accepts it all the same.

'My sister, you'll find, is very Left. A real socialist actually,' Pavel's irritation has dissipated and in its place is his usual sangfroid.

'Sure. The first time I met her she was surrounded by the Shesterka.' Leonid adds, 'Maria Spiridonova and the assassins of 1906.'

Pavel nods because it doesn't surprise him that Lidia is making connections with those sorts of women. Indeed, according to her last letter, the Socialist Revolutionaries need a more radical approach to eradicate counter-revolutionaries.

Then Kerensky is flying down the steps, once again, announcing, 'Done. Now, Captain if you will get your men to assist the family to board these vehicles and meet us down at the station.'

The exhaustion of the past few months has evaporated and Kerensky turns briskly to Leonid, 'Sergeant, the drivers are not to draw any attention to the entourage. Hurry. We need to get ourselves down to the station.' He adds grimly, 'The sooner we get this show on the road the better!'

The Prime Minister then turns back to Pavel, 'Captain, God speed,' and shakes his hand vigorously.

As Leonid is reiterating a terse instruction from one vehicle to the next, Pavel takes the opportunity to call out, 'Sergeant!'

Leonid looks back.

'Give my regards to my sister, when you see her next,' says Pavel.

Leonid nods.

'And tell her to be careful with the company she keeps!'

The aid-de-camp grins broadly.

Pavel turns about and returns to the man's home thinking that it may be a long time before he sees her again.

3

The man's wife moves slowly. Her children, even her son, are bundled up in travel rugs and excitement. Her husband follows the self-assured Captain Pavel Konoplev as if he is a shining agent from heaven. She tries to smile at her second eldest daughter who watches her every move. The smile doesn't take, so she turns aside and pretends to check on the others. The first vehicle, her son and husband. The second, her two youngest girls chatting happily with her lady in waiting. The third, her eldest daughters, Olga and Tatiana. And the fourth, Dr. Botkin, the Head Footman, and Cook Kharitonov with his kitchen boy.

The woman has prayed.

Indeed, she has stormed the communion of saints, wept supplications on the breast of the Virgin, and fasted until she fainted with weakness and was carried back to her sofa. The woman knows that the Infant Christ will never be abandoned by his mother, he is held tightly against her beating heart. It is an unfeigned knowledge that runs in her veins. And it is because of this that she knows the Mother of God will never forsake them.

The Captain looks directly across at her as she stands in the driveway in the breezeless summer darkness.

She knows it won't be long before light creeps back into the night sky and they must be away. She moves to the third vehicle that contains her daughters but there is a restless voice agitating for her to look back and gaze upon her home. She knows she should not. She wants her children to think and her husband to believe that she, too, is excited about their new adventure.

A train trip to God knows where.

She pushes the thought away and grasps the golden crucifix around her neck. She knows it is too late to look back but the desire to do so is physical. A yearning in her belly that no food could fill, a tugging at her heart that no caress could replace.

She pauses. Her back to her home.

'Get in the vehicle.' The Captain's voice is cold and probably because she has never been addressed by any of the guards, it shoots through her like mercury.

All she wants is to look one more time at the Neo-Classical façade that has become her most precious home. She gave up her Lutheran faith, her country, and her language to marry her husband, and not for one minute of one day has she regretted it. Until this moment.

The grief that swells in her throat, as she stands in the softening darkness of an August pre-dawn, is nearly too much to bear.

In her peripheral vision, she sees her husband speak from his open window to the Captain. He is a man reduced to begging. She loves him for this and, at the same time, is filled with fury as he chats on earnestly.

She feels the symmetrical beauty and calm of her home press its warmth against her and she longs to look back at what has become her own true country. This one home. This native place has been hers. She thinks about the chapel at evensong and the way light showers through the stained-glass windows, she remembers the singalongs with friends in the Maple Room, and her fingertips quiver at the memory of the silken embroidery on the quilts left behind.

'Hurry. Get in.'

She doesn't look at the Captain when he says this but sees before her the anxious faces of her eldest daughters and knows she has little time. She crosses her arms to steel herself from looking back. She needs to forget the marriage bed that was blessed by her daughters and her beloved son. The marriage bed where she was his Sunny and he was Russia's Saviour.

The woman glances over her shoulder and looks back.

A cramp of pain catches her breath and she presses her hand into her abdomen. She makes no sound. Still twisted away from those waiting, her eyes stitch together and she grinds her teeth. The roar inside her goes on and on and on.

Who will care, she asks herself? Who will even know we are gone? And what will become of this home, this eyrie, this bema?

The woman's body feels flaky and to her horror, she can taste salt from her tears. She needs to turn back and clamber into the vehicle and motor toward the station and board the waiting carriage before the pearlescent dawn points them out to the ever watchful.

She needs to go now but her swift legs are rooted to the ground.

As Captain Pavel Konoplev moves toward the woman to man-handle her into the waiting vehicle, he thinks, Mother Russia is a madwoman.

5

The October Revolution

Petrograd. October 1917.

Slowly, and without Lidia noticing, the sky's brittle darkness softens. It is far too cold for the third week of October and it is far too early to be awake. She knows she has been up since 5 am but without looking at the old clock in the living room she would estimate the time to be about 6 or 6.30 am.

Feiga is still asleep on the sofa bed and every so often Lidia hears her snore.

The men are due home soon. She tries not to think about all that could go wrong, but they are armed and sure-footed in the Vyborgskaya district. For the past week or so they have been attending meetings and discussing options, often at night, to gauge the situation. She's disinclined to go with them because what would be the point? Everyone knows it has been eight months now and still no land has been given to the peasants, no factories have been given to the workers, and ... Lidia looks out the kitchen window and sees the opalescent smudge of dawn ... no peace.

The Bolsheviks have hijacked the soviets throughout Russia if the newspapers are to be believed. And she does believe them because it is true.

She looks back down at the letter she is writing to her brother, Captain Pavel Konoplev, and knows he is safer there than she is here.

She continues writing.

And it concerns me Brother that you are so critical of the two commissars who are now in command of your post. They are harmless. Don't engage. You say they are ...

She breaks off from writing, pencil hovering above the paper, and reads over the earlier part of the letter to him.

You write about 'Old Socialist Revolutionaries — turgid doctrinaires' who have taken it upon themselves to politically educate you and your men. Regardless of how uninspiring they may well be I cannot fathom your talk of Bolshevism. It seems you have become infatuated with these apes and I shouldn't think that the PM, who singled you out to 'be his eyes and ears', would be pleased with such a treasonous thought.

Lidia toys with an unlit cigarette as she considers the Post and Telegraph Censors, but there is mayhem everywhere and by the time this letter finds its way to Siberia, who knows what might be considered censorable in the interests of national security. She glances across at Feiga and decides not to reach for a match.

I urge you to make your decisions cautiously, Brother. For the last few days, it has been so volatile in the streets that my friend Feiga and I have stayed indoors. Grishka and Viktor, bring back supplies and the latest wild news.

She thinks about Viktor turning up unexpectedly a month or so ago with his quiet lover. At that stage, Feiga had not moved in and it was just Grishka and herself. She watched as the wiry and dark Viktor was unable to keep his eyes off the young Kadet, Leonid Kannegisser. The fair-haired Leonid had wanted to meet her to tell her that he had caught up with Pavel, her brother.

Being Kerensky's man, Leonid had ensured the transfer of the Tsar and his family to Siberia. As well as, the fair handsome officer added drily, their skeleton staff — two valets, six chambermaids, ten footmen, three cooks, six kitchen hands, a butler, a wine steward, a nurse, a clerk, a barber, and two pet spaniels. Accompanying them was a Colonel, 300 guards, and half a dozen officers of which, and most importantly, was Pavel.

She drifts back to the letter she is writing him.

So much is happening here in Petrograd since you have gone. No doubt you have heard — THAT Bolshevik has come out of hiding to lead his party while the hideous Trotsky is heading up the Petrograd Soviet. The last four or five weeks have been uncertain. Nothing to buy. School cancelled and then reopened and then cancelled again. People striking, bullied back to work, and then walking out to join another protest or demonstration.

She doesn't want to think about the five or six officers who were rounded up and thrown off the Liteyny Bridge into the grey river below. And the pot-shots that followed as a crazed mob of Anarchists, Bolsheviks, and newly released criminals, finished the officers off.

Lidia can't help but think that Russia is collapsing and she wonders if the madness has always lurked in the dark recesses of its imagined self.

You must take care of yourself, Pavel. Write to me and tell me if you need anything because, as you know, Grishka is very resourceful and wouldn't hesitate to help you. Leonid Kannegisser, who is a frequent visitor now, assures me that my mail to you can be sent via his office — a far more secure post. In a week, I intend to get out to see Papa — as I promised him I would visit by the end of the month. Just as soon as all this business calms down in the city.

Without even realising, Lidia strikes a match and lights her cigarette. She inhales deeply and sees the light stirring outside her kitchen window. The corner wall stove has been on most of the night but she clutches at the neck of Grishka's woollen pullover, the one she wears so often that he has more or less forgotten is his. Her long grey pinafore has snaked about her thick tights as she sits with her long legs folded up beneath her on the kitchen seat.

Feiga stirs and sits up. Tousled nest of short brown hair, she blinks slowly several times at the wall across from her.

Signing off for now, darling Pavel.

Your affectionate sister

L xx

PLEASE Keep Warm!

She folds the letter and thinks how grateful she is that Leonid brings over whatever news he hears about the internment of the Tsar and, of course, his guards and in particular, Pavel. He reported that the four-day train journey to Tyumen went without incident. Leonid suggested that the trains transporting the Tsar, his entourage, and the Regiment of Sharpshooters, were disguised as part of the Japanese Red Cross Mission.

Lidia smiles as she remembers the way Viktor playfully wrestled Leonid on the sofa when he told them this, saying over and over, *The wonder boy! My very own wonder boy!*

'Why are you smiling?' Feiga asks with a yawn as she wanders over to the kitchen table.

'I was just thinking about Leonid. Viktor's Leonid.'

Feiga screws up her nose and sits down on the other kitchen chair and looks across at Lidia then at the letter.

She is just a scrap of a girl in her mid-twenties. Feiga had come back to Lidia's apartment, that evening after they had all met at the Tauride Palace. Lidia couldn't put her finger on it but as the months went by and Feiga returned again and again to visit her, she realised they had fallen into some sort of sisterly friendship. Feiga seems to love her devotedly. Lidia soon found out that Feiga was living a hand-to-mouth existence with nowhere to count as home and before Lidia had thought it through, she had offered her apartment to her, as a temporary place to stay.

'You have written a letter.'

Lidia smiles and thinks she might refresh the samovar, 'Yes. To my brother. And meanwhile, you have been sleeping —'

'I know. Forgive me. It's just that ...'

'You don't have to explain.' Lidia doesn't feel the burden that Grishka says Feiga has become.

'It's just that — you know — my eyes. I need to shut them and ... it helps the headaches as well. I'm not sure why ...'

Lidia leans across and holds the warm hand of her friend for a moment and then uncurls herself from the seat and starts bustling about the kitchen.

The samovar is from Tula and was once her mother's. It is always on a small bench just below the kitchen window. She dips the jug into the water bucket and then carefully fills up the samovar. She will need to open the kitchen window to let out the smoke from the small attachable chimney but she will do that last because it has begun to rain. Lidia takes the thin splintered wood, that Grishka stores beneath the sink, and pushes it into the vertical tube running up the middle of the urn. She lights some newspaper and with the last thin stick shoves it down to the base of the vertical tube then replaces the cap of the samovar and adjusts the knob on the side so as not to suffocate the fire.

Behind her, Feiga is moving between cupboards and table. Plate of small apples, dry brown bread, and sushki biscuits. Feiga takes the pot of kulesh, that they made last night, and pops it on the stovetop. By and by the samovar begins to smoke and Lidia removes the cap and inserts the chimney-piece which reaches the kitchen window, perfectly. With a grunt, Feiga opens it. The rain outside is cold and needle-sharp.

Lidia places the teapot at the centre of the table and adds tea leaves and a blob of precious jam, 'There!' She knows the men will be here any minute and although she loves them, she cannot help but enjoy Feiga's quiet, easy company.

Grishka is not a person who is often put out, so his privately hissed comments to Lidia had come as a surprise: *Why did Feiga have to find her way to your doorstep? She's like a lame dog who's followed you home.*

For the past few weeks, Lidia has soothed his frustrations, telling him it is only temporary until Feiga is strong enough to find her family. The younger woman has sent letters to her family in Kiev but there has been no reply. Perhaps they were dispersed back in '06 after Feiga committed her crime against the state.

'That's what she is telling you,' says Grishka to Lidia when they are alone. 'But I'm not buying it.'

He wants to be the one who beds down with Lidia on the sofa, not this myopic, wide-eyed blinking mouse girl.

'They're back,' Feiga's voice is faint.

'What ...' Lidia waits and is just about to tell Feiga she is mistaken when she hears the familiar stomp of boots up the stairwell.

Feiga lights the single stovetop ring and stirs the lard and vegetables about in the kulesh.

2

'But the difference is the Bolsheviks are better organised than we are, they're more active than we are — they have a definite political program. Whereas —'

'Oh Grishka, we have a vision that has been tried and tested for decades and decades, we have a philosophy that —'

'No one's arguing philosophy. They have that too, Lidia!'

'Oh, is that what they're calling it now?'

Lidia glowers back at Grishka in their ever-shrinking sitting room. Viktor is leaning back on the sofa next to her, smoking and taking a break from the arguments that have been ping-ponging across the little flat between Lidia and Grishka and himself, during and after breakfast. He is here most days up to a certain hour but after that ... he often meets up with Leonid. Viktor smiles his secret smile between lusty inhalations of his cigarette and thinks, I must give these up, it is the one thing Leonid abhors.

'What I am saying, my love is *their* power is centralised,' Grishka pauses and looks across at Lidia's magnificent mismatched eyes. 'Trotsky utterly supports Lenin.' Grishka needs her to understand the state of play in which the city finds itself, 'The Military Revolutionary Committee's sole purpose is to build a militia from factory workers, sailors and soldiers, all of them are disenfranchised —'

'But the Military Revolutionary Committee's mandate is to protect Petrograd ...'

'I know, my love. This is what I am telling you. It's lies, all lies!'

The room is warm, now that the meal has been cooked and eaten and dishes washed and put away. Cigarette smoke wafts upward. Lamps have been extinguished even though it is grey with rain outside. Grishka adds a tad more fuel to the corner tiled stove and plonks himself back down into the overstuffed armchair opposite Lidia and Viktor.

Feiga is resting, once again, her head snug in her crossed arms on the tabletop.

Lidia has an inkling that all this talk about what the Bolsheviks have and what every other party, including the Socialist Revolutionaries, doesn't have is not really what Grishka wants to say.

She looks across at Feiga and sees that her eyes are closed.

'You're talking as if you admire those Bolsheviks!'

She knows what she says to Grishka is rubbish but she is at a loss to know what to do with the criticism she is constantly trying to sidestep about her party. She knows it is not personal, because Grishka loves her, fiercely — so why does it feel so personal?

'He doesn't admire them, Cat-eyes,' Viktor rearranges his long limbs until he is sitting forward on the sofa. 'He's facing facts. We all need to face facts.' His dark handsome face clouds momentarily and then he adds, 'This militia — the Red Guard or the Red Army whatever you want to call it — is seizing power quickly and we need a plan ...'

Lidia waits because she knows that the two men are part of the Central Battle Unit, a terrorist cell. Privately, Grishka admitted to her that he believed he was recruited because of his ingenuity in gleaning resources and finding information, but she knows that all recruits are ultimately recruited to assassinate a key target.

And in the darkest room of her mind, locked and bolted from others and even from herself, is the belief that assassinations of key Bolshevik leaders would secure the aims of the revolution.

It occurred to her last night and the nights before, that Grishka and Viktor are probably mobilising a counter-strike if the Bolsheviks seize power.

Perhaps there is no *if*, she thinks to herself lugubriously.

Lidia feels as if her mind and body have been filled with the tension and mayhem of the last few days and nights. The random rifle fire and explosions and shouts and running feet and the bells of Saint Sampson's Cathedral clanging with alarm! Her nerves are shot from days of waiting indoors, along with so many others, for yet another cleansing of her nation. And she thinks to herself, Russia is forever in a state of purgatory.

THUMP! THUMP! THUMP!

The men are on their feet and Lidia's heart is racing at the pounding at the door — how did no one hear footsteps coming up the stairs!

Feiga begins to whimper.

Viktor holds his Iver Johnson revolver aloft and nods to Grishka who approaches the door slowly and growls, 'Who the hell is it?!'

And then they hear a familiar voice, 'Leonid! Open the door!'

When Grishka pulls open the door the young fair-haired Kadet seems to tumble into Viktor, saying, 'I figured you'd be here.'

The urgency is palpable in his pale blue eyes and Viktor's hand goes tenderly to his lover's shoulder.

'What's going on, brother?' asks Grishka.

'What's happening —' Lidia stops when she sees Viktor's hand come away from Leonid, smeared in blood.

She hears a quick intake of breath behind her and then Feiga is scooping water from the kitchen bucket and moving about collecting towels. Meanwhile, the men are lowering Leonid onto the sofa bed and Lidia kneels next to Viktor who is tenderly unbuttoning his lover's wet coat, and jacket, and shirt to reveal a pale muscular shoulder.

'What's happened to you,' Viktor croons. 'Looks like a flesh wound. Wonder boy ...' he moves Leonid's upper arm to the left and looks closely at the snarl of flesh and blood that keeps oozing.

'Here,' says Feiga as she carefully hands Lidia a bowl with water and a small clean towel but it is Viktor who takes it and like a mother with her newborn baby, he presses the damp towel gently to Leonid's wound.

'We have brandy,' announces Grishka and moves off into the kitchen, banging through the cupboards while Lidia thinks, no we don't. But sure enough, he is grunting about with a corkscrew until there is a vague *pop* and then he is handing a small bottle of French brandy to Viktor.

Leonid's eyes are closed but he rouses at the smell of the alcohol when Viktor presses it to his lips. The Kadet drinks.

'Why are you in the Vyborgskaya?' asks Viktor who is not the only one baffled. All of them know that a great unruly mob scouting the streets for victims would target someone like Leonid. He is frequently seen alongside Prime Minister Kerensky and there is just something about him that makes him more vulnerable than the rest of them.

'I had to see you,' came Leonid's answer as he tries to sit up on the sofa but Viktor pushes him back down and holds him firmly.

Grishka has passed their rudimentary first aid kit to Viktor, who quickly and methodically unravels a bandage, soaks it momentarily in a little brandy, re-checks the wound, then swiftly secures it over and around Leonid's shoulder, as if he has played the role of medic many times before.

'I'm fine — let me up,' says Leonid.

'In a minute.' Viktor strokes Leonid's face and adds, 'Little Feiga's here, behind you.'

'Hello, Leonid.' Feiga's voice seems to come from far away.

'And Cat-eyes has made us eat the most awful breakfast ...'

But Leonid is shuffling about trying, once again, to sit up and this time his boyfriend lets him. Propped up in the sitting position Leonid begins to speak, 'It's tonight. That's why I had to come and find you, Viktor.'

The small crowd waits.

'The Red Army and the Kronstadt sailors are already pouring into the city. They've taken the army garrisons, the Central Post Office on Pochtamtskaya Ulitsa, and ... the lower bridges across the Neva.'

Lidia stands up and reaches for Grishka. This is it then, she thinks and presses herself into his strong tall body.

'Yesterday, Kerensky ordered the arrest of the Bolshevik leaders.' Leonid looks about urgently, 'That's what started the ball rolling!'

This is because the November elections have been announced and the Bolsheviks don't have a chance in hell, thinks Grishka furiously.

This is because the PM handed 40,000 rifles to the workers of

Petrograd back in August, thus enabling an uprising, thinks Viktor disgustedly.

This is because last night Kerensky closed down *Pravda*, that Bolshevik's mouthpiece, thinks Lidia bitterly.

Feiga doesn't think this is because of anything other than the Lord's will and she says quietly, '*I will show portents in the heavens and on the earth, blood and fire and columns of smoke. The sun shall be turned to darkness, and the moon to blood, before the great and terrible day the Lord comes.*'

No one responds to Feiga because Leonid is saying to Viktor, 'I've come to warn you. There'll be blood on the streets!'

'We suspected as much — we must all stay together,' replies Viktor as if this alone will right the terrible wrong.

The younger man ignores him because what he has to say next is the beginning of the end, 'Lenin has called the Central Committee to arrest Kerensky's government — tonight!'

No one speaks.

The rain roars outside.

Each one of them, in their way, has anticipated this moment, and yet, now that it has arrived, no one can seem to move.

'The government is tottering.' This is the ghastliest statement Leonid has ever uttered and as he says it, he realises, he is crying, 'Lenin has commanded the government be dealt a deathblow ...' He thinks of the months and months and months of travel and organisation and administration and preparation and packing and unpacking and negotiating and overseeing for the one man, the greatest man this nation has ever known, working tirelessly to save Russia. And then, imperceptibly at first but then more and more noticeably as the nation became quicksand, he knew Kerensky was never going to be permitted to save Russia from itself.

'I haven't got long ... I have to get back to Kerensky —'

'You're not going anywhere!'

'I have to get back to Kerensky,' Leonid continues, completely ignoring Viktor. 'I need to get him out. But I couldn't leave without ... I had to warn you and ...'

'Well, I'm going back with you, *Moi dragoi*.'

Lidia feels tears prick her eyes because she has only ever heard Viktor use the satirical appellation *Wonder boy!* and never *Moi dragoi* — My dearest one.

'We must all stick together,' says Viktor evenly. 'The Vyborgskaya district here is nothing but a hotbed for Bolshevik agitation — all of us need to get out of here for at least 24 hours — or until we see the lay of the land.'

'Let's head out to Maria Spiridonova's on the other side of the city,' suggests Grishka.

'Yes, let's go there —'

'Look,' Leonid interrupts Viktor. 'You can take me back to the Winter Palace but then you must leave me.' Leonid's calm demeanour doesn't fool anyone, least of all Viktor.

'Right. Help me up.'

Regardless of their protestations, everyone can see that Leonid will not be stopped, besides Viktor is already re-buttoning his lover's shirt and jacket and damp coat.

By the time the five of them leave the apartment, the icy rain has turned to sleet. Leonid, assisted by Viktor, moves quickly through the maze of streets heading towards the Liteyny Bridge. Grishka and the women follow close behind. Each one of them knows that moving about outdoors is a bad idea and yet staying indoors at this apex of the crisis, when God knows what could be happening, is worse. Besides, other Socialist Revolutionaries could be calling for armed support against the Bolsheviks, and Lidia for one has no intention of waiting for those murderers and thieves to come knocking at her door.

The sleet stops and starts.

In the distance, they hear the town clock chime eight. Lights behind curtained windows reflect off silver puddles on the narrow roads, forming a strange chiaroscuro quiet, through which the five of them scurry. Normally on an autumnal morning like this, hundreds of people would be darting to the brick kilns or sugar refinery or breweries or spinning yards, but because all factories and schools and administration centres and trams and buses transporting the workers have closed down over the past few days, there is an eerie emptiness lurking in every wet side street and bordered up shop front.

'Red Guards up on the bridge,' hisses Viktor over his shoulder and Lidia presses herself and Feiga into the food storehouse frontage that overlooks the Neva.

The men confer in whispers and then Grishka says quickly to Lidia, 'We think they've seen us, so let's push on and if asked, give them the answers they want to hear.' He moves two or three paces then turns back to her, 'Get ready.'

Lidia nods because her revolver is loaded and held tightly inside her coat pocket.

'Comrades!' roars Viktor as he moves confidentially across the bridge.

Grishka has his arm about Leonid as if guiding a fellow drunk, and the women are close behind.

'Declare yourself!' shouts the posse of Red Guards with their rifles bristling with purpose.

'Comrade Viktor Pereltsveig and friends. Heading back to the Smolny!'

Very clever, thinks Lidia, but there is a crackle of tension between the five of them as they wait for the Red Guards to allow them passage.

A burly young man, reeking of alcohol, moves towards them, two of his fellow fanatics are close behind. 'Never heard of you — where have you come from?'

There is static popping and hissing along the tram wires.

'Listen up,' says Viktor as he leans towards the Red Guards with insouciant menace. 'I'll tell you where I'm going ... lad.' There's no mistaking the edge in his voice, 'To Lenin's Headquarters.' The brutish young guard doesn't blink. 'You might be forgiven for thinking Smolny is still the Palladian Institute for Noble Maidens,' Viktor takes out a cigarette, strikes a match on the bridge railing, and inhales. 'You might be forgiven for not realising this is the nerve centre of the revolution,' he exhales. 'But lad — you will *not* be forgiven for getting in the way of Lenin's orders that all members of the Bolshevik Central Committee report immediately to Smolny.'

The rifles of the posse sag.

Some of the Red Guards have moved back to their small makeshift fire that is threatening to extinguish with the slush of rain and sleet. The young lad looks behind and sees not one of his comrades is looking his way. So, he nods to Viktor, as if to say, this is not worth my time.

The five of them hurry on avoiding Liteyny Prospect and then make their way through the Field of Mars.

As they move stealthily, Lidia hears the smashing of glass followed by people yelling then shots firing. 'Looters!' warns Grishka. 'Keep your wits about you!'

Right on cue, footsteps are charging across the field toward them and as one they flatten against the shrubbery. An aristocratic woman in a nightdress, one hand presses a sable fur against her front and the other hand clutches strings of pearls and gold, whizzes by with nothing on her feet, her husband in breeches wielding a sabre follows, then more slowly and less committed, come a bunch of frightened maids and finally a struggling butler.

After two or three seconds a volley of gunshot fire overhead.

Lidia ducks as do the runners and someone screams until they don't and there's a sickening thump.

'Come on!' yells Viktor and they peel out of the bushes and head away from the rioters and down the northwest pathways toward the Winter Palace. Lidia grips her revolver, as her father taught her, and runs with her other hand locked into Feiga's.

People are darting in and out of alleyways, footpaths, and entrances shouting out *Don't shoot!* or *Out of my way!* or *Comrade, turn back!*

'In here,' calls Grishka as he finds an alleyway with a wheelless carriage looming thick in the shadows. They race in behind him and crouch down behind the carriage. Lidia struggles to catch her breath and she hears Feiga panting on one side and Grishka on the other side, inhaling deeply to slow his breathing.

Leonid breaks off from his tête-à-tête with Viktor and turns to the others.

'Right. I will go on ahead to the Winter Palace. I have to secure Kerensky's safety. Viktor will take the rest of you to Spiridonova's, behind the Mariinsky Theatre.' Leonid's face looks ghostly in the wet disfiguring morning light.

'I'm coming with you.' Lidia realises she has spoken out loud because Feiga and Grishka together say *NO!*. She can't look at Grishka's hurt expression and says to Leonid, 'I don't know what your plan is for getting the Prime Minister out of the palace, but I know where he can find safety —'

'Look, I think we all need to get to Maria Spiridonova's!' Grishka interrupts, trying to calm himself. 'She is the leader of the party's Left.' He tries to pull Lidia to him but she is already squirming across to Leonid. 'Lidia,' cries Grishka urgently. 'We need to show our support to either the Left Socialist Revolutionaries or the Bolsheviks! Now is the time we must choose if we are to survive!'

And Feiga adds, 'You can trust Maria, Lidia ...'

Then Viktor says quietly, 'So where is this place of safety, Cat-eyes?'

Grishka needs Viktor to be on his side but maybe his question, so neutrally asked, is a forerunner to his reasonable explanation of why there is no way Lidia can risk her life and go anywhere near the Winter Palace.

Lidia wishes more than anything that she had kept her own counsel and simply followed Leonid without fear or explanation but instead, she answers calmly, 'My father's estate.'

Grishka has to admit it isn't bad. She has told him that her father's estate is a rambling place surrounded by woodland and the ex-colonel has his veritable armoury.

'Please, Lidia,' pleads Feiga who sounds like she is on the verge of tears. 'Come with us. Maria will — she will ...' The younger woman doesn't know what the legendary assassin will do, but what she does know is that without Lidia she is utterly alone.

'Maria Spiridonova will vouch for all of us,' adds Viktor meaningfully. 'Look — here's the thing. The tide is turning and we, my friends, are without a raft.'

No one speaks because each one of them knows what he says is true.

Grishka makes another attempt, 'If we are to survive today — we have to throw our cards in with Spiridonova. Or the Bolsheviks —'

'Never!' spits Lidia.

But it is Viktor who changes the moment as he turns from Lidia to Leonid and in the putrid inky alleyway declares, 'I cannot let you go, my love ... I cannot ...' And then in the muffle of two bodies embracing Lidia hears Leonid reply, 'I will be alright. I promise you. I told you I would never leave this city without telling you — and I kept my promise.'

Lidia knows she should reach out and embrace Grishka but if

she touches him her resolve will dissipate. Besides he would feel her trembling and insist he goes as well.

'Your father's estate ... Are you sure?' Leonid asks Lidia

What she is sure about is that without Kerensky, Russia will have no future.

Lidia scrambles to her feet and says, 'Of course.' She needs to be gone before her fear weakens her resolve. Leonid is already pushing past her and she can hear Feiga whimper and just as they stop at the entrance to the alleyway, Leonid scanning the way forward, she feels Grishka's strong arms around her. Lidia turns immediately into his long tender kiss and when she breaks off to follow the sound of Leonid's boots crossing the cobbled road she hears Grishka call, 'I will be waiting for you ...'

3

For the next ten minutes, Lidia is either running at breakneck speed behind Leonid or squashed up beside him as they hide from the oncoming motor cars or foot traffic. He seems to have momentarily diverted them from the Winter Palace and it is on the tip of her tongue to ask him if he knows where he is headed when he points to the 12 column portico of the Rumyantsev Mansion, home to the embassy of the United States of America, just 50 metres along the embankment on the Angliyskaya Naberezhnaya. They reach the small maze of parked Model T Fords, that constitute the embassy car park.

'Stay low. I won't be long,' says Leonid and ducks off into a side road.

Lidia crouches between two of the vehicles and waits. She knows that if she has to, she can talk her way out of this situation if confronted by authorities as to why she is hiding in amongst the embassy's cars, but if she is confronted by brutes and troublemakers she knows she will have to shoot her way out.

She looks up at the pediment of the mansion's ornate frontage, dull and bleak in the autumn rain, its alto-relief of Apollo and the nine muses seem utterly irrelevant to this moment in time.

Lidia is conflicted. Despite her fierce loyalty to the Prime Minister and the Socialist Revolutionaries, she understands why so many of her fellow Russians, with their empty stomachs and no true political representation, are participating in this uprising.

She hears footsteps pounding down the embankment. She presses herself even lower between the vehicles. Then someone is running down the side street toward the parked cars in which she crouches and she pulls out her revolver.

'Just me!' cries Leonid as he scoots in next to her. 'We have five minutes!'

She has no idea what he means but she is up running behind him down another alleyway until they come to an abandoned barricade and she picks up her long grey skirt and slides herself over it. Lidia realises they are out on the Neva once again and to her horror espies a couple of naval ships quietly pointing their guns at the back of the Winter Palace.

Leonid grabs her elbow and pulls her with him into a doorway saying, 'They're doing repairs on those naval cruisers. Don't be alarmed.' Days ago, maybe, she would have accepted this explanation at face value but Leonid is fooling himself if he thinks they are not a threat.

She hurries behind him into a cool and darkened passageway where soldiers from the Women's Battalion, heads shaved and faces grim, salute Leonid.

'Right. Wait here,' he says and leaves her.

Lidia stands about the shadowy recesses of what could only be the back of the Palace. In front of her is the closed doorway through which Leonid has disappeared and behind her stands an armed and uncertain soldier, ready to defend the Palace — with her life. Lidia leans against the cool stone wall and watches a thin ray of sunlight struggle through the window to pinpoint the nondescript corridor in which she has found herself.

The girl, because on close inspection that is what she surely is, whose duty it is to guard the egress of the Palace doorway through which Leonid has disappeared, looks at Lidia with open curiosity. Her round face softens her features. She must be from the countryside, thinks Lidia, and tries to offer a smile but the girl spots Lidia's mismatched eyes and instantly recoils, tightening her grip on her rifle.

When they were first recruited by Maria Bochkareva, even Lidia had to admit it sounded like the answer. These women were to imbue Russia with inspiration and strengthen the morale on the Front. But as time went on more and more reports indicated that Bochkareva had no intention of allowing her troops access to the Army Committee. So, unlike the rest of Russia's Army, her battalion would not be offered the democratic rights that Kerensky had insisted all soldiers were entitled.

Lidia looks across once again at the soldier, who peers back with undisguised anxiety. The door cracks open and the Prime Minister stands in front of Lidia.

'This is the woman I spoke of, Lidia Konopleva,' says Leonid quietly.

'Captain Konoplev's sister, no less,' responds Kerensky and shakes Lidia's hand vigorously.

She is startled for a second but then realises this is how Leonid would have vouched for her and she says quickly, 'Yes, Prime Minister. Pavel Konoplev is my brother.'

She realises he is looking intently at her eyes, shifting his gaze from her left to her right eye and back again, a familiar gesture.

'My aid-de-camp here says you have a plan?'

She is taller than Kerensky and although this is a common occurrence for her with many men it surprises her because she is standing up close to the man who will save Russia.

'Yes. My father has a place south of here. Between Gatchina and Luga. Inside the forest.'

She realises Kerensky is looking at her as if to say, *That's it? That's your plan?*

'My father is, or rather was, a Colonel for the 8th Moscow Grenadier Regiment.'

She hears Kerensky grunt, whether it is one of approval or resignation she cannot discern but then he is all action striding ahead and off past the soldier as she stands to attention and salutes. Leonid is right behind him saying something about the US embassy and then Lidia is running behind them not wanting to be left behind in this cavernous underbelly of the palace where women younger than herself are waiting for the naval guns to begin blasting the Palace into ruinous tombstones.

When they push out into the daylight, the icy rain of earlier has returned. There, a metre or so from their exit are two cars with their motors running. Leonid leans in and speaks above the chatter of the T Model Ford to the driver who is nodding carefully.

Kerensky is not looking at the exchange or Lidia and she turns to follow his gaze at the flat grey Neva, upon which sits the *Aurora* battleship.

'I'm afraid I must go first to Gatchina HQ ... and mobilise the troops and come back and restore law and order,' Kerensky says as he drags his eyes off the *Aurora's* forecastle gun.

He looks at Lidia and says, 'But I thank you for your loyalty and your family's offer to give me sanctuary should I need it ... but today is not that day —'

'Sir,' it's Leonid. 'We must be on our way!'

She doesn't know why but she finds herself being bundled into the back of the second vehicle, a Pierce-Arrow touring car. Beside her sits Kerensky, Homburg hat pulled low over his forehead and the collar of his grey overcoat turned high. Leonid climbs into the T Model Ford waiting up front in the passenger seat and the driver slips off the brake.

As the vehicles chortle out beside the Neva, heading south with the US flags fluttering gaily from the bonnets of both vehicles, Lidia's heart fills up with Grishka, Feiga, and Viktor and she wonders if they have made it safely to Spiridonova's place.

She can hardly think back on the madness of this October day — that had begun innocently enough with a letter to her brother, of all things!

4

Feiga is dreaming.

At first, the long cylindrical body moves imperceptibly and beautifully above her. She wonders whether she is underwater, looking up at a huge bellied whale. Then she realises that the whole city is underwater and she is looking up at the zeppelin as it passes slowly overhead, above the treetops, above the apartments, and above the dome of the cathedral.

There is no one else about ... such a shame ...

Out of the drifts of mist, the long talked of spectacle emerges but she can't quite put her finger on exactly what has been said nor why everyone waits with bated breath. She hears the purr of its motor as the cylindrical body moves across the sky above her, with its nose pointing ever forward and its tail heavenward. The mammoth bulk is held afloat, impossibly, by four dwarfed rotary propellers. It moves ever onward, a somnambulant slipping and sliding across the skies.

She mouths the words, *hydrogen gas*, schooling herself in something she cannot quite remember.

She drifts upwards and sees the canvas stretched tight across its straining body. The ropes, still attached to its dirigible expanse flutter downwards and she dreams she sees, in the glass cabin attached to its underbelly, the face of a uniformed captain staring out.

White, expressionless, certain.

Slushing past the monolithic zeppelin are clouds, presentiments of more rain and sleet and snow. She begins to feel cold as she cranes her head ever upwards to the changeable sky, watching the great moving beast overhead. On and on and on ... glissading past factories and schools and shops.

Unable to stop ... unstoppable ...

She dreams she hears sirens and knows the rest of the city will come running with their buckets of sand and shovels ready to save a city on the brink of incineration. There are shouts and cries as people push past her — yelling, directing, instructing — and it is then that she realises the vast cylindrical airship hovering above her is the reason for the alarm.

Her heart rate whirrs and whirrs and whirrs until she knows the air raid siren is coming from her chest.

Frenetic bodies push past, racing for shelter but she cannot move. Her feet and legs are locked to the ground. The rest of the city, a million dwellers, scurry this way and that to find loved ones, to find safety, to find redemption. Silence hauls on and on and on overhead and she can do nothing but watch in icy terror.

The zeppelin looms over her, its taut skin straining to burst.

And that's when she hears the ticking time bomb deep inside its ballooned belly because it is about to give birth to an incendiary device. People around her, mouths agape with inaudible screams point at the airship.

The behemoth creaks and grinds. Its gargantuan body lolls from side to side until it comes to a shuddering halt. She knows — if she doesn't run now, nothing will save her. She cries out again and again and again but even as she does, she knows, she makes no sound.

When Feiga wakes, she knows that Maria Spiridonova's crowded apartment is just about empty. She can hear some murmurings from the kitchen and then the clock chimes and she realises it is later than she thinks. Feiga moves quietly through the bedroom, where she shared some blankets with a few other women, and into the cramped kitchen filled with too many chairs, unwashed dishes, scattered newspapers, and two oversized men.

There sits Viktor and Grishka. Maria and her Shesterka are gone.

'Any news?' she asks and Viktor turns around to face her, pulling out the chair next to his.

'Yes. Leonid sent a message this morning. They are outside the city. That's all we know.'

Leonid had telegraphed from Gatchina that they had arrived safely and, despite the upheavals and counter-revolutionary fracas, they would be moving Kerensky very soon out to the estate of Lidia's father.

Feiga watches Viktor speak and she wishes she could press a hand to his lined face and unshaven stubble. He is always kind to her which is more than she can say about Grishka who sits across from Viktor and herself, smoking, not quite looking at her but not quite looking away.

'You should eat something, Feiga,' Viktor half stands and fusses about the samovar and teapot then pushes across some black bread that lays torn and belly-up on a plate.

'And Lidia?' asks Feiga.

'Well, Lidia is with Leonid.' Grishka's voice sounds strained as if he is trying to keep his temper in check. 'So we can only assume she is safe.'

After a beat, Viktor adds, 'Of course our Lidia is safe.'

Viktor places a glass of tea in front of Feiga and with her hands still inside the long sleeves of someone else's knitted cardigan, she cradles the steaming beverage.

'I dreamt of a zeppelin,' she says as she looks from Grishka to Viktor and then back to her tea.

'Hmmm,' Viktor moves a small plate of cheese and pickled herring toward her. 'So a rough night?'

Russians are either eating or trying to get hold of food to eat, thinks Feiga. Lidia has said to her on more than one occasion that she needs to use the opportunities to eat as a way of refuelling because no one knows if there will even be a next meal. But she sees how sparingly Lidia eats and knows that she, too, struggles.

Feiga pushes the plate away.

'No need to worry about zeppelins.' Grishka stubs out his cigarette. 'Lenin has delivered a proclamation to the citizens of Russia.'

With that, he pushes across a copy of *Pravda*.

'There is no German enemy, anymore.' Grishka leans back in his chair and adds, 'Allegedly.'

How can so much happen in such a short space of time? Feiga wonders to herself, as she blinks at the front page of the newspaper.

The Provisional Government has been overthrown. The state power is now completely in the hands of the Soviet of Workers' and Soldiers' Military Revolutionary Committee.

The men watch her small nest of hair pull close to the text as she reads on.

The achievement of democratic peace, the termination of landlord-held property, the control of all means of production by the workers, and the creation of a soviet government — is now guaranteed!

Feiga doesn't know how this has happened. Kerensky is no longer the Prime Minister, but rather a wanted man.

LONG LIVE THE REVOLUTION OF WORKERS, SOLDIERS, AND PEASANTS!

Feiga stares blankly at Lenin's proclamation and tries to remind herself that this is what they had all been fighting for since as far back as she can remember. It certainly was all they ever talked about when they were imprisoned in Siberia for the best part of their youth. Yet now she feels no dedication or zeal in creating a better Russia, especially under the aegis of the Bolsheviks.

Grishka says, 'I think we need to get going. We need to see for ourselves what exactly is happening —'

'I think we need to attend the emergency meeting at Smolny,' says Viktor purposefully. Grishka looks surprised at this suggestion to go to the Bolshevik Headquarters. Viktor continues, 'We need to be in at the ground floor. We need to have our eyes and ears about us.' He gives up on the clichés because Grishka is nodding assent.

Both of them know that their training in the Central Battle Unit requires they are ready for any eventuality and should an individual in power derail the revolution they need to respond, immediately and with deadly force.

It makes complete sense that the two of them should be present at the meeting Trotsky has called for today, as well as the one Lenin is to chair. As members of the Central Battle Unit, they need to know the goals of this, the second, revolution. They need to be ever vigilant that those now leading the country don't dilute the true purpose of the February revolution.

Concerningly, Lenin has indicated in today's newspaper that terrorist cells will no longer be tolerated. Viktor and Grishka are freedom fighters, not terrorists, and they had been trained to safeguard the aims of the revolution. If egotistical dictators rise and block the most fundamental aim of the revolution — the will of the people determining the future — then they have no other choice but to implement the most effective use of terror: assassination.

'I will come with you ...' she says but Grishka scowls and Feiga knows it is hopeless.

'No, Mouse.' Viktor pats her hand explaining, as one might to a child, 'It will be dangerous outside.'

Feiga looks back down at the front-page article.

The men busy themselves about in the cramped space. Pulling old newspapers that they'd stuffed into their damp boots last night, shoving them on, and lacing them up. Now, snug and dry. They bundle themselves into their coats and pull their caps down low.

Feiga peers at the grainy photo of Lenin at the centre of the page.

Grishka and Viktor check their revolvers.

There is something about the face of the Bolshevik leader, here on the front page, that makes her shudder and frown.

The men shove their revolvers into their coat pockets and Viktor says, 'Right. See you tonight, Mouse.'

Feiga glances up distractedly. Her over-large eyes stare but she doesn't see either one of them. Grishka wonders if this is one of Feiga's moments of episodic blindness that Lidia warned him about. Still, he can't help but feel irritated by this diminutive girl who looms so large in his girlfriend's concerns.

'This is the Captain,' Feiga's voice is faint and although she is not looking at the front page of the newspaper her finger is pointing at Lenin.

'What's up?' Viktor is impatient to be gone, now that the morning streets have quietened.

Feiga looks down at the newspaper and says, 'I saw him. Last night. In the zeppelin.'

5

The streets are disturbingly calm. Grishka follows Viktor in and out of the narrow roads and alleyways to avoid rioters and the Red Guards. Yesterday, there had been hand-to-hand combat, sniper fire, running soldiers, screams of victims, and shouts of the victorious leading up to the storming of the Winter Palace. Today, no one seems to know if there is a curfew so the city stumbles on, uncertain, head down, hesitant. A part of Grishka wants to deviate from their route to see with his own eyes, whether the *Aurora* fired a single shot at the Winter Palace or if it showered the site of Kerensky's government with live fire. The rumours are rife. The Russian cruiser had been in the Neva since February, hence the *Aurora* had come to represent the revolutionary aspirations of the people. But, instead, Grishka follows Viktor. Destination Smolny.

Petrograd is filled with mist and rain, giving an ashen hue to the bordered-up shop fronts, shuttered apartment windows closed cinemas, and sleepy tram stops. The two men are on high alert as they make their way up and across town. They speak quietly and move cautiously. Viktor is not thinking about the *Aurora* nor is he thinking about the storming of the Winter Palace or the battle that raged there between the Red Guards and the Women's Battalion who had been protecting Kerensky's government. Viktor is thinking about Leonid and hoping his young lover will not risk everything for the Prime Minister, who is now on the run.

They navigate through the old markets, which are grimy and bereft of customers, and move swiftly across the small canal footbridge at Lomonosov, ever vigilant of passing vehicles or fellow pedestrians.

Many a late-night, in bed he and Leonid had smoked and talked about the state of the nation, after and before their unruly sex. The problem, they agreed, was that Prime Minister Kerensky had isolated himself and had failed to end the war. Moreover, the fundamental management of the troops had been savagely mishandled or simply forgotten in the excitement of the Tsar's abdication and the revolutionary gains of February.

But that was just the thing, Viktor thinks to himself, espying the old Greek Church on Ligovsky, Russia spends most of the time talking and then at the eleventh-hour dashes about with a makeshift plan.

They move on steadily to the park of the Tauride Palace, not too much further, Grishka thinks to himself, and we shall be at the Smolny. The anger in his chest comes in fits and bursts and then he realises that all he wants to do is to wrap Lidia in his arms and protect her. Why is she risking so much for Kerensky? And yet he knows that she would shoot to kill more readily than he would if truth be told.

He crouches behind Viktor as they let two armoured vehicles slouch past.

For the last few weeks amongst factory workers, returned soldiers, and desperate peasants searching for work in the city, Grishka has only met discontent. The people cannot eat process, they cannot eat philosophy, they cannot eat promises.

The two men move on when the street is empty.

Grishka sees Viktor pause at the corner and knows the Smolny is up ahead. It has been a strange journey here. Instead of seething with the chaos and mayhem of the last few days, the city has turned its back on itself and gone inside. The Neo-Classical Smolny, squatting across from the leaden Neva, is now Headquarters to the Bolsheviks and its Palladian countenance seems to frown as they enter.

By the time Viktor and Grishka reach the assembly hall the Chairman of the Petrograd Soviet, Comrade Trotsky, is already convening the emergency meeting that is pre-empting today's Congress of Soviets. Over 600 bodies are packed together, their metacommentary is overridden, for the most part, by the Chairman and his flamboyant rhetoric.

'... Kerensky had surrounded himself with young officers and a battalion of women soldiers!'

There's an outbreak of laughter, then a flurry of defensive shouts, countermanded by booing. Viktor and Grishka find themselves on the outer rim of the 600 delegates as the Chairman of the Petrograd Soviet pushes on.

'But where is the former Prime Minister? He has run away ...' He ignores the cries of protest from the Left Socialist Revolutionary Party members. 'He called his ministers to hold the Winter Palace while he summarily ...' Trotsky's eyes glitter and his voluminous dark head of hair is thrown back, dramatically flicking his fingers in a gesture of dispersal, 'Vanished!'

The Chairman hauls onwards in his address to the delegate of soldiers and workers of Petrograd.

'The military blockades we set up and the agitators we sent out, like our great Comrade Volodarsky ...' The crowd roars and Viktor strains to see the editor of the *Red Gazette* at the front of the hall. A stocky man with an aquiline profile and lively eyes that seem to watch the proceedings with great intensity. Volodarsky is rumoured to have brilliant organisational abilities and an erudite clarity to complex theories.

'It was comrades like Volodarsky who ensured our bloodless up-rising. This was not a conspiracy. It was a rising up of the popular masses — which, Comrades, requires no justification —'

'Will Comrade Trotsky assure the Russian people that the Con-stituent Assembly and its elections will still be held next month?' Her voice is not loud but it is electric and even Trotsky lowers his enormous Cubist head and looks around the crowd until he finds her.

'Comrade Maria Spiridonova, knows more than most of us the price that has been paid for Russia to throw off the shackles of its past ...' The rest of Trotsky's rhetoric is drowned by the wave after wave after wave of applause and hoorahs for Maria Spiridonova, leader of the Left Socialist Revolutionary Party.

As usual, her Shesterka women flank her frail body.

'Will Comrade Trotsky assure the Russian people —'

'Of course, the Constituent Assembly and the elections will proceed as planned,' Chairman Trotsky bellows over Spiridonova. 'The millions of workers and peasants who are represented at this Congress have put their faith in us and we will deliver PEACE, LAND, AND BREAD!'

While the delegates shout and yell and cry and bellow and cheer and boo and heckle and applaud and insist on being heard the Chairman — Comrade Trotsky, the man who was once Lev Bronstein — ruminates on this morning's conversation with Lenin who said, laughing in disbelief, *We went from persecution and being forced underground ... Straight to power... Es schwindelt,* and his hand circled about his head.

The Chairman abandons the reverie and cries over the hullaballoo.

'I SAY TO YOU, MY COMRADES, THE PROVISIONAL GOVERNMENT IS NO MORE! I KNOW OF NO OTHER EXAMPLE IN HISTORY OF A REVOLUTIONARY MOVEMENT INVOLVING SUCH A VAST MASS OF PEOPLE WHICH PASSED SO BLOODLESSLY!'

The afternoon goes on and on in the way only Russian political meetings can. At one point Grishka and Viktor make their way to Maria Spiridonova and her Shesterka, who are surrounded by other Left-wing Socialist Revolutionary Party members. Something is reassuring about the calm-faced leader of the Left as she talks to this one and that, regardless of the speakers who have taken the podium after Trotsky.

While the mood is ebullient, Grishka feels the tension rise because there are delegates who are uneasy with the speed and ferocity with which the Bolsheviks have mobilised an army to bring down the Provisional Government and chase Kerensky out of town. On the other hand, there is a sense of relief that the negotiations for a peaceful settlement with Germany begin tomorrow.

Volodarsky takes the floor at one point and his metallic gun-fire approach is mesmerising. He is the newly appointed Commissar for Propaganda and as such controls all information — real or imagined. Grishka darkens when Volodarsky asserts that counter-revolutionary efforts cannot go unchecked. When these words are spoken Grishka catches Viktor's eye. They have been utterly committed to the Central Battle Unit where they have trained to ignite terror by assassinating key targets who continue to block the will of the people. Viktor and Grishka know they are doing this because someone has to safeguard a truly revolutionised Russia.

Rumours abound as they wait for the leader of the Bolshevik Party to arrive. Some say that the ministers of the Provisional Government have been imprisoned in the Peter and Paul Fortress, some say that Maria Bochkareva's women's shock troops have been raped in the Winter Palace, and some say that the aristocracy has been chased out of their houses, hunted down and shot.

Just before Lenin appears, Grishka and Viktor regroup.

'Word is Lenin is to replace Kerensky,' says Grishka. 'And Trotsky will be his new Tereshchenko!'

'With the negotiations that are needed to resolve the conflict with Germany, Lenin will need a miracle worker, not a Foreign Minister!'

Grishka looks at his friend and says, 'You think there'll be trouble with the Kaiser? I would think he would want to end the bullshit going on at the Front ...'

Viktor looks at the men and women jostling about him, calling out to each other that Lenin is about to take the floor. 'That well might be the case,' Viktor keeps his voice low. 'But the Bolsheviks will need to take the Tsar and his family out of the picture — otherwise, the Kaiser might put his cousin back on the throne and the revolution would have all been in vain ...'

The rest of Viktor's musings are lost in the tidal wave of cheering accompanied by red flags hauling back and forth over the heads of the delegates. Grishka and Viktor, along with the other Left Socialist Revolutionary Party members, are in the minority, and as for Mensheviks, they seem to have disappeared.

'COMRADES!'

The assembly settles immediately as all eyes are fixed on the leader of the Bolsheviks, Comrade Lenin.

'The Military Revolutionary Committee has, with superhuman organisational effort, worked day and night, night and day for the past month to bring about the bloodless revolution that we achieved in the last 48 hours.'

'And during those long days and nights, the chair of that committee, Comrade Moisei Uritsky, never slept. He and his committee members, a handful of men of great stamina and strength, did not allow exhaustion to sabotage their work. Uritsky calmly drew in all the threads and issued directives, knowing that our time for this mighty revolution would come!'

So rumours that the Bolsheviks were plotting a second revolution all along are true, thinks Viktor, in the din of the cheering for the pugnacious Uritsky who waves from the front of the crowd, tobacco pipe in one hand. Viktor watches as Uritsky makes his way to Lenin for a handshake then back to his position amongst the chosen ones.

'Tomorrow, Comrade Trotsky will commence negotiations to settle peace with Germany, and Comrade Uritsky will work closely alongside him. I am told that Comrade Volodarsky spoke to you earlier today. He will work with me to let the Russian people know the truth.'

Lenin is in full swing now, leaning away from the podium and pumping his right arm up and down in rhythm with his call and response rhetoric: arm outstretched and low, 'And what does our new soviet government propose with immediate effect?' Arm raised high, 'DEMOCRATIC PEACE TO ALL NATIONS AND ARMISTICE ON ALL FRONTS!' Arm low, 'And what shall be transferred to the peasant committees?' Arm raised high, 'ALL LAND BELONGING TO THE LANDOWNERS, THE CROWN AND THE MONASTERIES — WITHOUT COMPENSATION!' Arm low, 'And how will the soldiers be protected?' Arm raised high, 'THE ENTIRE RUSSIAN ARMY WITH BE DEMOCRATISED!' Arm low, 'And what of the workers?' Arm raised high, 'ALL INDUSTRY WILL NOW BE IN THE HANDS OF THE WORKERS!'

Lenin pauses as the crowd throws their caps in the air and cheer. Both Grishka and Viktor offer a good imitation of the same, as do a number of the Left Socialist Revolutionary Party members. Most of them have heard the panacea of promises before. Indeed, after the revolution in February, versions of these same goals were offered to people by Kerensky and indeed, the legislative wheels of change had begun to turn but now, it would seem, they must start all over again.

Grishka argued many a time with Lidia that the endless debating and argument within the Socialist Revolutionary Party stymied action, turning the newly revolutionised Russia into a dangerously impatient beast.

'Comrades, I tell you, the Constituent Assembly and elections *will* take place next month on the appointed day! But more importantly — more importantly comrades — the soviet government will supply the cities with bread and the villages with fundamental necessities because ...'

The assembly has erupted into euphoria and no one is thinking of Kerensky's watershed cry for freedom of speech, press, assembly, and religion — not to mention universal suffrage and rights for women.

'BECAUSE! BECAUSE COMRADES ...' Lenin regains the crowd, 'The soviet government will secure for all nationalities within Russia the right to self-determination! Therefore, all power will now be transferred to the Soviets of Deputies for the Workers, Soldiers, and Peasants, which is charged with the task of revolutionary order!'

The leader of the Bolsheviks raises both arms above his head.

'TO THE WORKERS, SOLDIERS, AND PEASANTS — I SAY, COMRADES ... RUSSIA IS YOURS!'

6

West Siberia

Tobolsk, West Siberia. November 1917.

Captain Pavel Konoplev is homesick.

Four days on a train and then another two days travelling up the Tura and Tobol rivers on a steamer. For what? To arrive at Tobolsk, a godforsaken village in west Siberia where they have been living for the last several weeks.

Pavel looks out of the sentry box and watches the snowfall. He thinks about his father, snug in his estate south of Gatchina and his sister, in her Petrograd apartment. He knows she will realise it is his birthday today but has doubts his father will remember. He gazes over the snow-covered fence that, a few weeks ago, framed a garden for the man and his family. Pavel knows he has nothing to complain about. Meals, accommodation, and regular pay. It sure beats the Front ... digging trenches, digging graves.

Instinctively, Pavel looks back at the month-old newspaper he has just finished reading.

The Russian 4th Army has joined forces with Romania in defending this last vestige of Europe from the Teutonic hordes. A battle near Mărășești. It has tied down over a million German troops and is regarded, according to the newspaper, as the only point of light in the East. The fact that it was the Romanian army, not the Russian, that dealt the strongest blow to the Central Powers in the last 18 months is evidence enough that the Russian soldiers on the Front are exhausted, ill-equipped, hungry, and sick of it. What are they fighting for?

Pavel lights his cigarette.

The snow is never good. Of course, it means the end of the rain — more or less — but they will soon have to contend with frozen water pipes, damp wood for the fires, and slow supplies, all of which will only increase the tensions that have already begun to build amongst the soldiers who are guarding the man and his family.

He leans against the doorjamb and watches the palisade cap in icy snow.

Pankratov and Nikolsky, the old doctrinaire Social Revolutionaries who have come to be the commissars here at Tobolsk, have done nothing but stir up resentment in their bid to re-educate Pavel and his men.

Pavel spits the loose tobacco from his mouth.

It is as if these two old men — one a retired teacher and the other a former office worker for the West Siberian Steamship Company — believe it is their role to give evening lectures on the Socialist Revolutionaries' political philosophy. Pavel wrote to Lidia about it, admittedly to stir her up a little, but also because he is sure the Socialist Revolutionaries have got it wrong and the Bolsheviks have got it right. Russia must suspend its war effort and feed its starving people and the only way to do that, thinks Pavel, is to nationalise the farmlands and end the war.

Pavel inhales and gazes at the back of the Governor's house, a dilapidated white two-storey affair that houses the man and his family.

When they had first disembarked the steamer in Tobolsk, Pavel had looked across at the crumbling fortress, lavish church cupolas, and mud as thick as molasses, and wondered where on God's earth he had arrived. It was so far from his childhood in Kiev and his military training in Moscow, let alone the outer regions of Petrograd where he had been assigned to the Sharpshooter Guards.

Why would anyone live here? Was the first thought that came to mind, the second was one of concern as he watched illiterate peasants kneel and bless themselves as the man and his family made their way to their appointed residence.

Pavel had gotten to know some of the family, such as the boy who was always asking a million questions about the various battles he had been in as well as the weaponry he had used. Pavel had also become acquainted with the eldest girl, Olga Nikolaevna Romanova — he never thought about her former title, the Grand Duchess. It was the second night on the steamer when, rugged up and high spirited, she had made her way to starboard where he had been smoking in the night sky. He would never forget the way she stood there … quite still, head high and gaze direct. He'd kept smoking, too nervous to do anything else. She had asked him something about the time or the weather or the route they were taking and he had waited a few moments before replying. Out of the long lonely river seemed to have flown a night-bird and he had no intention of spooking it away. They had talked quietly — him carefully, her playfully — and the sound of the steamer went on and on. Two young people with only the thick autumnal nightfall above them and the invisible passing of land somewhere beyond them. Before she had turned to go she had laughed about something he had said and his blood pumped warm long after her lavender-scented body had left. Not too long after arriving at the Governor's house, she — he liked to think of her as *his Olenka* — would seek him out when others were busy creating a life for themselves.

The back door to the Governor's house opens and Pavel watches her walk quickly toward the sentry box. A wide knitted scarf covers her shoulders and neck and most of her face. Her skirt kicks up in front as she makes her way toward him and despite finding himself in exile, Pavel forgets his homesickness.

His smile is slow, 'I was wondering if you were going to brave the elements this morning.'

Olga looks boldly at the Captain and says, 'Well unlike some I'm not cowering inside the guard's shelter. I've been permitted to go outside and even, possibly, ski later this afternoon — if the snow keeps up.'

'Is that so?'

He moves aside for her to enter and she steps lithely into the guardhouse, surveys the game of draughts on the bench, the unwashed coffee cups, and the folded newspaper, and then turns her blue-eyed gaze on him and asks, 'Is this newspaper newly delivered? Has Papa read this copy?'

He has to admit, her direct approach is both disturbing and exciting. He does not allow himself to think too much about his interaction with the man's eldest daughter. She, on the other hand, thinks differently. He knows this because she has told him — in the way she has sought him out at least once a day if not more, in the way she offers him her secret smile revealing that small gap in the middle of her front teeth, and in the way she has asked him, innocently enough, if he would ever marry someone who just wants to live in the country with spaniels and never have to deal with court officials.

Pavel watches as she bends over the second-hand newspaper, her wide Slavic cheekbones carve beauteous plains across her flawless skin.

'Romania,' she murmurs and reads on.

He knows she is smart. She has told him the books she has read, many of which Pavel has never heard, and she has explained the reasons why she has learned English and French, and even German.

Pavel looks across at her thick woollen cardigan that is tied with a belt and her blue serge skirt that stops mid-way at her calves. He feels a gush of tenderness when he sees clumps of snow precariously balanced on the toes of her black boots.

'Hey, you're making my place slushy,' he teases.

She looks down and then stomps her feet. 'Well then, it's about time you cleaned up,' she says with a grin and then returns to the newspaper as she unwinds her long knitted scarf.

He wants to reach over and pull her to him but instead, he forces himself to look back out the sentry doorway.

There's a slight pause and then he hears her voice, 'Are you going to offer me coffee, Pavel?'

'Of course!' Pavel bustles about with the coffee beans, filling the pot with water from a tub beneath the bench, gathering dry kindling. He steps outside and uncovers the small fire pit used for cooking. He lights the fire. Then carefully places a grill over its growing roar and balances the coffee pot gently on its surface. He knows she is not the only one who has come to love this ritual between them. It is as if they are husband and wife and she has simply asked him to make the coffee so they can enjoy the peace of the morning in the countryside (would spaniels be lazing about their warm feet?) he wonders indulgently.

He knows she will be reading the newspaper from beginning to end. In many ways, this has been the reason why he has developed such a voracious appetite to read whatever is sent through. But he can hardly keep up with her. Unlike the rest of her family, she seems to be following what is going on in Russia and, more curiously, doesn't falter in offering her opinions on politics, economics, philosophy, theology, literature, or nursing. He has never met a woman like her and knows he most likely never will.

'Coffee's ready,' he says as he stomps inside the sentry box. 'Do you have the cups?'

She turns her face toward him but doesn't speak because she is still inside a battle near Mărășești. This happens, occasionally, and he has learned to just give her a moment and sure enough she will return.

He pours the steaming coffee into two of the cleaner cups. For the first time in years, he drinks real coffee and eats good food. This bothers him and he wonders what the Bolsheviks, who have filled the ranks of his company, would make of it, considering they too enjoy the benefits of guarding the most despised prisoner of Russia.

'You know, I went to Romania, once ...' she says and he realises she is back and passes her the coffee. He takes a seat but she remains standing. 'Maybe three years ago now ... yes it was just before the war. I remember Tatya and I refused to wear our hats because we wanted to have sunburned noses so he — so they — would think we were too ugly!' She laughs a little and looks at him, 'They were terribly serious, out there, you know.'

He sips his scalding coffee and thinks about the way she lifts her chin when she talks to him. 'Were you visiting one of your suitors?' Pavel asks.

She blinks then answers, 'Well I suppose I was there to consider him as a match. Prince Carol.' She bends over the coffee but keeps her eye on Pavel, 'But I didn't fall in love with him. I didn't feel anything. It was — you know — there was ...' She sips the hot coffee and pushes herself away from the cup, 'There was no rapport.' She thinks: Rapport. A French word, from the verb *rapporter*. Harmony, agreement, intercourse. She pushes her fingers against her lips. Roots in Latin. To bring back.

'Prince Carol was very charming — and brave!' she adds and points at the newspaper, languidly.

'But no rapport.' Pavel's statement is final.

She waits and then a wide mischievous grin appears, 'You know what? I just can't remember ...'

He rolls his eyes and crosses his legs, relieving the pain in his left thigh.

'Anyway, I was also meant to marry the English Prince of Wales. But I could never leave my beloved Russia. I would rather not marry!' she says warmly and just beneath her pale skin he sees the blush of passion creep up her throat and cheek.

Pavel has finished his coffee but she has yet to drink all of hers. Before he can stop himself, he says, 'Drink up, Olenka. My love.'

This is not the first time he has used a term of affection. When he first did, he convinced

himself it allowed him to get close to her so he could be the eyes and ears for the Prime Minister. When she first used an endearment, she convinced herself that maybe there was a chance that she could remain here in the countryside, in another life, with him. She puts her cup back on the bench and leaves her fingers around its porcelain warmth. He leans across and, with the lightest touch, traces the outline of her fingers. An electric current shoots through her body. She does not remove her fingers but stares ahead because she thinks she can see the impossible ... a young married couple enjoying a break from their daily cares.

And perhaps because it is too hard to end the fantasy, the chestnut blonde asks the Captain, 'Are you happy here?'

And they both stay with the question for a moment, pretending they are already in their future.

Eventually, he answers, 'Here? No. I am homesick.'

She pulls her fingers away from the now cold cup. He watches her face cloud and he realises his mistake.

'What I mean is ...' He is leaning forward as he speaks. 'I don't like this remote Siberian town. I want to be near my home. I miss my life there.' He doesn't really know what he is talking about. His former life with the 8th Moscow Grenadier Regiment is over. His childhood home in Kiev is gone. All that is left is an uneasy relationship with his father, back on the forested estate between Gatchina and Luga, and a sister in Petrograd.

'I understand. I do.' She puts her fingers back on the cup and he carefully places his hand on hers. She adds wistfully, 'I miss Tsarskoye Selo ... I miss — well — some of my former life.' She laughs quietly and all of a sudden he feels ashamed of his glib comment while she has no idea where she and her family might be taken.

'I don't miss home ...' He struggles to express what it is that he feels but there is something in the intensity of her blue, blue eyes that makes him push on. 'I think I have been homesick all my life.'

He pauses.

She waits.

'I think ... I think it must be that I am homesick for Russia. I — I — can't explain it ...'

What an idiot, he thinks to himself, and looks down at her boots that have puddles beneath their toes.

'You're homesick for the promise of your country.'

He looks up at her. That is it exactly, but he has no idea how she knows that, she who was once the Imperial Grand Duchess of all the Russias. What would she know about the burden of growing up in a nation that endlessly discusses a better and more inclusive place of belonging? But know it she, somehow, does.

'Yes,' he smiles and lets her place her soft hand in his.

Over the past weeks, they had come to know a great deal about each other, in the undetected encounters they have managed to steal beneath the very noses of the other guards, not to mention her ever-present family. He knows that she is close to her father but her relationship with her mother is tricky. Pavel does not find her father to be clever nor is he convinced the man is much of a believer, despite the great show of faith and prayers and church-going. There is something about him that strikes Pavel as someone who is acting out a role for the benefit of others. And as for that German woman, well, Pavel has nothing good to say of her considering she has prolonged this war by letting the Kaiser know Russian military secrets and plans! And even if this is only rumour, he knows that there is no way this sweetheart before him could care for either of them.

Olga flips a draught over and then another and slowly a third. She looks up at him and her smile is a gift. In him, she finds a kindred spirit. Someone who knows the darkness. He told her he was at his most depressed when he was ordered to send his men back to the slaughterhouse of the battlefield, again and again, and again. That was their reward for serving Russia, he had said darkly. Back then he had drunk. In her case, they had given her arsenic injections to cure the darkness. The thick dark clouds of sadness rolled over her until she thought she would never see daylight again. Nothing had helped either of them — not the alcohol or the injections — and the unsaid between them is *until they had found each other*.

She pushes her hair behind her ears and he can almost feel its silky promise.

He knows that she had nursed during the early part of the war. When he was fighting in Tannenberg. He told her that no nurse as pretty as she had attended to his injuries. She had giggled and said that she would have had to roll up her sleeves and cut his trousers so that the surgeons could get at the shrapnel in his thigh and he had grown stiff and useless at the thought of her cool fingers touching his calf, then knee, then thigh. He momentarily forced himself to think of nothing.

'It's strange,' she muses. 'You and I were in Kiev at the same time ... all those years ago.'

He doesn't interrupt but watches her in their protectorate with the snow falling gently outside.

'Back in '11 when Tatya and I went to the opera ... with Papa.' They are both thinking of the Rimsky-Korsakov production made infamous by the Prime Minister. 'Poor Stolypin,' she murmurs and pulls a moue at the memory of him being shot in the face.

Pavel had been living with his family just outside the city of Kiev and remembered the newspapers reporting that the two Imperial Princesses, who had witnessed the assassination, had not even fainted.

'To think ...' she looks across at him blithely, 'We could have encountered each other back then, in Kiev.' She thinks: Encounter. From Old French, *encontre*. Opportunity. Or the Latin, *incontra*. To be in front of. She lets herself imagine standing in front of him. Close. Naked.

'I will be 22 soon,' she blurts and worries that he might wonder at her train of thought.

'Really? Well, that's interesting ... because it is my birthday today —'

'I don't believe you!'

'When have I ever lied to you?' and his voice is warm and his deep brown eyes are clear.

She laughs and looks away but she can feel the heat rise from her breasts to her throat and up her cheek. He thinks if the snow would just keep falling then no one will come and nothing will change and we can go on like this forever — drinking coffee, chatting, holding hands. She thinks if only I could marry and go far away from where I won't be recognised, where there are long summery days that lift the hem of my skirt and long wintery nights that is filled with him.

He asks, 'So, tell me how old do you think I am — and don't be cruel!'

They laugh easily together and she looks across at Pavel, one hand on her hip the other on her chin affecting the look of a doctor examining her patient.

'Hmmm ...' her face is stern. 'Now that you ask me, I have to say ...' Sharp intake of breath, '40?'

He grabs the newspaper and swipes her with it. She giggles and he wants to grab her right there and pull her to him. But instead, he says, 'I am 26, today, and —'

She swoops in and kisses his cheek, her lips are butterfly wings.

He is stunned. He is startled. He is — he cannot know. He tries to speak. And then tries again.

'Happy Birthday, Pavel,' she says as she takes a seat demurely.

And he wonders to himself whether she did kiss him.

Then she cocks her head to the side and adds, 'Wait — what, how old are you?'

He thinks it's part of the luxurious libidinal game and leans in this time, in readiness, and repeats, '26.'

She sits perfectly still and her beautiful eyes widen as she says, 'I will be 22 soon — the age mother was when she married. And you are 26 ...' He waits and then she offers quietly, 'The age Papa was when he married her ...'

They sit together. The noonday sun peeps behind the thick tumble of snow clouds and for a moment the snow pauses, somewhere, high in the skies.

He has no interest in her parents' story. He has come to think of her as his. The Tsar and his wife, who ruled this nation ruthlessly, mercilessly, and shamelessly have nothing to do with the wondrous curves of her body nor the light-catching planes on her face nor the way she tilts her perfectly upturned nose to the heavens when she laughs.

She wonders how she could convince her parents that this is all she ever wants. He is a captain after all, and educated, and from a military family. She knows he would protect her and love her forever. Yes, she admits that she had been in love with Pavel Voronov, but she was a child then and he, an officer ... Besides it was another time, another world back then. And of course, there was Dmitri Chakh-Bagov, he was one of the wounded soldiers she nursed during the war, but he had not lived. No. Mother and Papa would eventually come to agree that this is the best decision.

'Pavel?'

'Yes, Olenka,' he looks past her and notices that the snow has started once again and realises she is probably going to ask him to ski with her this afternoon. The thought of the two of them, alone, away from the guards and the commissars and the family and the village folk, who often thrust gifts at her for the Imperial Family, fills him with longing. The revolution, in so many ways, is yet to reach them out here in west Siberia.

'Why has the country turned against my father?'

He is unready for this question. Her mind is mercurial, its quicksilver unsettles him.

'I mean — I have read and read and read newspapers from all around the world offering their opinion.' She is staring past him, deep in her world of concentration, 'But at the end of the day, just like England, Germany, and the Hapsburgs, Russia is a monarchy. Always has been. Always will be.'

Pavel stands and stamps his left foot to recirculate the blood flow. He thinks about the revolution's promise of a democracy, where every man stands equal and worthy of the right to food and education and land and justice. To live with his shoulders back, proudly independent and gloriously free.

'Besides, like George 5th, Wilhelm 2nd, and Charles 1st, the Tsar is chosen by God,' she adds.

Please stop speaking, thinks Pavel, as he gathers up the coffee cups and the newspaper and the draughts that are scattered across the bench.

'It is Papa's destiny, his fate, his sole purpose for living.'

He looks down at this young woman and realises he has nothing but pity for her ... that she should be manacled to this appalling human being, this man, who just about destroyed Mother Russia. And somewhere in the muffled secret of the snow, he thinks he hears the back door of the Governor's house open.

He gathers himself together and looks away from her and says to the bench, 'The reasons the country has turned against your father go right back to your grandfather.' He hears the crunch of footsteps approaching and adds, 'Your grandfather revoked all the progressive and lawful plans for the people that had been set down by *his* father.'

Without missing a beat, she replies, 'Ahh yes. But then my great grandfather was killed by the very people to whom he was offering freedom. By an assassin ...' She thinks: Assassin. From the Medieval French, *assissini*. And before that, from Arabic *hashīshīn*. People who are faithful to the very foundations of their beliefs.

Commissar Pankratov's small beadle body stands in the doorway. For a moment he can't seem to make sense of the scene before him and then he realises it is not one of the local women chatting amicably with the Captain but rather, the Imperial Highness herself.

Pavel is the first to break the tableau, 'Good day, Commissar.' Under the Provisional Government, the term *Commissar* is now used for the officer responsible for the organisation and political education of strategic units. Olga notices that Pavel puts people at ease with his quiet ways but at the same time she wonders if they are aware of his eternal vigilance.

'Yes. Yes. Umm ...' The Commissar turns to Olga saying, 'Good morning, Your Royal — Your ...' He gives up, 'Right. Konoplev there are nuns with sugar and cakes at the entrance — send one of your men, will you, to relieve them of these gifts.' Pankratov is blinking excessively behind his thick spectacles, 'And ahh ...' He turns aside as if to speak to Pavel alone and in sotto voce adds, 'Please tell the nuns not to bring any more ...'

Olga looks between the men and affects a pout.

This immediately has the desired impact on Pavel who chortles and says to the bewildered Commissar, 'I will send one of the men directly and instruct that the goods be distributed amongst the guards and ensure —'

'Well hold on a minute! Hold on a minute, Captain ...' Pankratov's mass of grey hair swirls about his head as he turns back and forth between the eldest girl and the quietly spoken Captain, 'Wait a minute ... wait a minute ... We don't want this to cause trouble amongst the men and — well — it wouldn't hurt for the Imperial — the Royal — the family to have one or two extra supplies. Especially the little chap ...' Pankratov looks at Olga and beams. He has become quite fond of the youngest member of the family and has, once or twice, told him stories about Siberia, a topic of which he never flags, just to keep the little fellow's mind off the pain.

'Oh, Commissar Pankratov,' says Olga sweetly. 'Colonel Kobylinsky has permitted my sisters and me to take a walk beyond the confines of the fence this afternoon.'

Pankratov glances nervously between the girl and the Captain. He hasn't been told of this by Kobylinsky. It should be him who makes these sorts of decisions, not Kobylinsky!

'Well, I would have to consider —'

'With your permission, Commissar,' interrupts Pavel smoothly. 'I can accompany them this afternoon. If that is your wish. To ensure there is no unwelcome attention from the villagers.'

Both Olga and Pavel keep their eyes on the small commissar who was once a school teacher and spoke to his students about socialization of land and government but then was branded as a dangerous enemy of the Tsar and sent to prison at the tail end of Siberia.

Despite his limp, the Captain is never lazy like the other guards, so Pankratov replies with, 'Yes. Quite right. I give my permission.'

Pankratov wonders whether this might be a good opportunity to speak to both the Captain and the man's eldest daughter about the Narodnik, the forerunners of the Socialist Revolutionaries. Part of Pankratov's job, in overseeing the internment of Comrade Romanov and his family, is to take whatever opportunity presents itself and re-educate not only the prisoners but also the guards. The Commissar's parents were part of the Narodnik movement and worked tirelessly amongst the peasants to raise their awareness of communal ownership and shared production. They were also committed to creating a Russian Marxism, one that believed in skipping the transitional phase of the dictatorship of the proletariat and going straight to modern socialism. It is this element that Pankratov feels moved to share with Captain Pavel Konoplev and the girl, both of whom have had little to do with the peasantry of Russia.

Sensing a recrudescence of a political lecture, Pavel asks, 'Is there any news from Petrograd?'

The Commissar frowns, 'Actually, Captain, that is why I came looking for you.' He glances at Olga who shows no sign of leaving or lacking curiosity. 'Organise your men to gather in the upstairs hall of Headquarters, today, in the next hour ...' Pankratov likes to refer to the Governor's house, where the man and his family are incarcerated, as HQ. 'There have been some critical developments in Petrograd. I wish to inform everyone at the same time.'

Pavel feels his chest tighten with apprehension. Already this year has run away from him. Last Christmas he had gone to his father's estate along with Lidia and discussed, at length, the military failures of '16, all of which could be laid squarely at the feet of the Tsar. Russia's most hated incompetent. The only event worth celebrating at the family gathering was the slaying of Rasputin. Who would have known that one of the aristocracy would have the balls to bring about justice?

Olga is hit by a wave of hope and thinks to herself that there must be news of their imminent departure and if this is granted then it will only be a matter of time before she might be able to persuade her parents to let her live a quieter life ... after all, they have been through... here, perhaps, or somewhere close by where she and Pavel could live simply and happily.

'I have informed Comrade Romanov to attend the meeting as well. So, if you will deal with the nuns at the gate Captain and ...' The Commissar's tone becomes vague, 'And um ... gather your men ...'

'As you wish,' responds Pavel but instead of striding past Pankratov and pushing out into the snowy noonday world he stands and laconically rearranges the draughts as if he might commence a game at any minute.

After a moment of hesitation, the Commissar says, 'Right. Right you are. I will leave it in your hands, Captain.' Then he nods to no one and leaves the entrance of the sentry box free, retracing his steps to the Governor's house where he shares an office with his truculent Deputy.

'Maybe Prime Minister Kerensky has managed to secure our transport overseas,' Olga cannot help herself and reaches for Pavel's hand.

'Maybe,' his reply surprises her because instead of reflecting the hope in her own heart his voice seems wary and subdued. More likely, he thinks to himself as he smells her lavender scent, there has been more havoc and now the government is requiring all soldiers, despite injuries, to return to the Front.

'This is the only way,' she insists. 'Otherwise, we cannot be together ... I must leave Russia until this all blows over and then I know I can convince Mother and Papa to allow me ...' Although many would say she is too young to know love, she knows she is running out of time being nearly 22! This is the love story she has been waiting for, and she will stop at nothing until she is free of the past so that they can create their future. She looks at Pavel but he will not return her steadfast gaze.

'Pavel,' she pulls at his hand with seems lifeless in her own. 'Pavel, please ... Don't you want to be together? Don't you want to —'

He moves suddenly and scoops her up in his arms. Her tall wiry body is warm and it opens up into his long kiss that is hard and urgent. When he eventually releases her they are both catching their breathing. He looks down at the chestnut blonde of her hair, her clear blue eyes, and those wide cheekbones and knows he can never leave her.

'Of course, I want to be together ...' and with that, he kisses her quickly on her retroussé nose.

2

The man's wife has an earache. She has had it since yesterday afternoon. She knows it started when Schneider washed her hair in the fuss of their first bath time since their arrival, two months ago, here, in this godforsaken outpost of Tobolsk.

The to-do of bath days!

The huge cast iron bath on stubby legs has to be manoeuvred upstairs by five of their footmen. Trupp, the Head Footman, orders the staggering men this way and that, with spaniels barking at their heels and the three youngest Romanovs chasing each other about with towels and cakes of soap. The bath then has to be scrubbed and rinsed by some of the chambermaids.

Water is drawn from the tank supply by the other chambermaids who, complaining quietly to each other, carry the buckets into the kitchen, heat pans and kettles and pots of water, then haul them up the slippery staircase and down the hallway to the back bedroom, where the man's wife insists is the best place for their bathing.

After innumerable trips, the bath is filled. Then the kindling is brought in, much of which the man has chopped himself, a pastime from which he never tires, and lit in the small fire next to the bath.

The water is then stirred with lavender and salts until it is piping hot. Well, at least that's what Baby calls it.

First, her husband bathes, with the assistance of his senior valet and when he is done, Baby climbs in allowing only his Papa to help him wash his back and hair. After much cavorting and sloshing about, with water all over the floor, Baby finally accedes to his mother's pleas made outside the door, to get out and dry off.

Hours pass as the chambermaids empty the bath, one bucket at a time: along the hallway, down the slippery staircase, and out the backdoor of the house, where they toss the dirty water onto the frozen yard. The bath then gets refilled from the freshwater drawn and heated.

And on it goes. Up and down and up and down and up and down.

Olga, then Tatiana followed by Maria share the next bath. After this, the water again needs replacing before Anastasia then finally the woman herself, bathe.

The chambermaids' long skirts and aprons are soaking in soapy bath water as they lean over the females and scrub soap into their scalp, then rinse, using a small porcelain bowl; then rub vinegar into the roots, rinse; then pour cold black tea through their hair, rinse; and finally brush one egg yolk into the ends, and rinse.

The woman knows this is what caused the earache.

Schneider is always careful, but the two other maids attempting to cover her ears with towels were not so concerned.

Meanwhile, the house steams up with the freshness of towelled skin and damp hair and hot tea with pancakes and jam that has been brought into the upstairs drawing room, all to clean and rehydrate the pink-skinned fresh-faced family.

Today, the woman sits in the quiet of her husband's study on a damask settee he has thoughtfully had brought in for her so that she can take time for herself, or chat with him, or look through the window onto the fenced-off yard or into the town beyond, with its comings and goings. Schneider has brought her a hot towel and she leans her right ear down into its comfort.

On the stout Gueridon table next to her are a stack of novels that her husband devours. She turns her head and reads their spines: *The Scarlet Pimpernel, The Ninth Wave, On the Mountain, The Robbery, A Tale of Two Cities, The Marriage, Dracula.* She closes her eyes and listens to the scratch of her husband's pen on the letter he is writing to his mother, safe and sound, in Crimea.

She feels her eyes well up with yearning, not just for the endless summer water of the Black Sea but for the calm of Livadia Palace ... where the plock of tennis playing or the splash of bodies diving or the laughter of her children are the only sounds that can be heard. Looking back, she doesn't know why she didn't take the children from Tsarskoye Selo and flee to Livadia when those radicals took hold of Petrograd. If she had done this her husband might have turned around and followed them. His mother, the Empress Dowager, had gone on ahead to the Crimea as had several relatives and if that wasn't motivation enough, the revolutionary chaos should have spurned him to follow his family and flee.

She opens her eyes and watches her husband read through the letter he has completed. She readjusts her position and places the warm towel on a cushion which she holds against her tender ear.

'Any better?' he asks but his eyes don't leave the page he is reading and she thinks about the way his mother has tried, for nearly two decades, to erase her.

Alone together in a room the Empress Dowager never speaks or looks toward her daughter-in-law because she is a foreigner and incapable of drawing affection from the Russian people.

Unlike the Empress Dowager, thinks the woman bitterly, who still believes she is loved by the entire nation — despite being a Dane!

'Yes. I will be fine. Thank you.'

The man grunts at her reply and then folds his letter, pleased with its contents, and rings the bell on his desk.

'I have to join Commissar Pankratov in the hall,' he says as he checks the carriage clock on his desk. 'Now is there something I can call for you? Would you like —'

There is a faint knock at the door, followed by a junior footman.

'Yes,' says the man and picks up the letter he has just written and hands it to the approaching servant. 'See that this gets delivered.'

After the door closes softly behind, the man's wife removes the cushion from her ear, stands, and walks gingerly across to the window. She gazes out at this story that has become theirs.

'It's still snowing,' she says to neither herself nor him and looks at the relentlessness of the world outside — the newly constructed head-high wooden fence surrounding the house and the sentry boxes where guards, who once ensured intruders were kept out, now make sure they are kept in.

She longs for her mother or the idea of her mother. Of course, her mother saved her when she was only six years old living in her beloved childhood home of Neue Palais, Hesse-Darmstadt. Her sweet mother nursed her through the painful sore throat, the chills and fevers that she and her father, brother, and three sisters suffered. She doesn't remember the actual death of her favourite sister, even though they shared a room, but she will never forget the way her mother roared like a wounded beast when it happened. Two days later, their mother was cast down by diphtheria and they were told later that it was this that lead to her heart giving out. But she knew it wasn't the epidemic that killed her. Maternal love is life-giving and life-taking, the woman thinks, as she gazes on and on and on at the snow that will not stop.

'Wait,' she peers closer to the glass pane. 'Why that's ... is that —'

Her husband moves swiftly beside her and follows her gaze to the sentry box out in the fenced-off yard and then says unsteadily, 'Well it's Olga ... she must have dropped off a message to Captain Pavel Konoplev ...'

And just as he says this they see their daughter step out of the sentry box, turn back, pull at the waist of her cardigan, and say something. Now the Captain appears and leans up against the doorjamb, he lights a cigarette, and then he returns a comment.

The two standing sentry upstairs, watch this mime show intently, uneasily.

Suddenly, Olga laughs and moves back toward the Captain. She raises both her hands and pushes him playfully in the chest. Pavel pantomimes a stagger and moves back out of sight into the dark bolt hole of his post and then Olga leans in after him so that only her outstretched skirted leg and boot can be seen.

There is something about the stillness of that small part of Olga's seen body that causes the imagination to run. The woman inhales sharply. The man fumbles with the catch on the window and then remembers it has been nailed shut. The woman has spent the last few months fearing this. It is high time her eldest two are married and settled but this cannot happen until the war is over and they are safely restored to their lives as the royal family of Russia. Indeed, she and her husband have privately estimated that by the time Christmas rolls around and the madness of this year is behind them, everything will have calmed down. The other Entente Powers will restore peace and the family will be back in the Alexander Palace, Tsarskoye Selo. And this year will be remembered not at all or, if so, as a distant memory of something best forgotten.

She wills her daughter to pull back out of the darkness and into the light. Her mind flies to her most treasured icon of the Mother of God, a replica of the Znamenskaya. She closes her eyes momentarily and prays for Olga's swift rescue and as she does the Virgin's words come to her disturbingly unbidden, *Be it done to me according to your word.*

'There!' her husband says as he spots Olga walking out of the sentry box oblivious to the momentary earthquake she has just caused her parents.

Meanwhile, like a bear inside his wintery den, Pavel, stays out of sight.

The woman and her husband watch as their eldest child crunches her way back to the door of the house, every footstep toward them releases the tension that moments ago stopped their hearts.

Olga is just herself. Sure-footed, shoulders back, and chin up.

All is well, thinks the man and turns away from the window, his wife needs to relax and trust that the girls will not form inappropriate dalliances with the officers. Besides, the last few months have been filled with peace and tranquillity. Far away from the boiling fracas of Petrograd, they have been able to read and walk along the river, when permission is granted, and spend time as a family. Sometimes, he can even imagine another life for himself, one blind to the memories of his past and deaf to the call of his conscience.

All is not well, thinks the woman as she presses her forehead against the cold pane of glass, eyes downcast upon her daughter who has paused at the steps leading to the door of the house in which they now reside. She watches Olga press two fingers against her lips then with the tip of her finger she touches the very tip of her nose.

The woman's earache is a sly hot knitting needle that slides slowly through her right ear and into the back of her head.

3

Pankratov takes off his spectacles, rubs them vigorously with the bottom of his gymnastyorka, all the while squinting at the guards settling in the hall. The guards have moved in alongside their Captain and standing uncomfortably near the doorway, is the man. When Pankratov informed him that there would be a meeting and that he should attend, the prisoner had smiled courteously and replied that he would check his schedule. If only he knew what I know, thought the Commissar. Personally, Pankratov had no vendetta against the man, despite never having been given a trial, not to mention justice, and being incarcerated in a Siberian state prison for more than a decade. What Pankratov wants is a new, educated, and fair Russia.

Colonel Kobylinsky is not present Pankratov notes with a tut and pushes his thick spectacles back up the ridge of his nose. He will have to seek him out and explain, once again, that all meetings must be attended if they are called by the Chairman of the Soviet of Soldiers in Tobolsk, in other words, himself, Commissar Pankratov. These old school war veterans like the Colonel are a nuisance, he thinks, as he raises both hands to indicate he is about to commence.

'Men, I now open the 23rd Meeting of the Soviet of Soldiers in Tobolsk. As your Chairman I will commence by informing you of the events that have taken place in Petrograd —'

'Speak up, Pankratov,' yells his gnarly Deputy standing right behind him. 'The men at the back need to hear! On you go!'

The Deputy is a thorn in Pankratov's side but he takes a deep breath and pushes on, 'The battleship *Aurora*, which has been anchored in the Neva across from the Winter Palace, where, as you know the government is now located ... opened fire on the Palace ... at point-blank range ...'

There is a moment when no one speaks then everyone is shouting and gesturing and calling for more information. Pankratov is pleased he kept this information to himself after the telephone call because it is one more lesson to the men and the prisoner, not to mention his Deputy, that he is the Commissar in charge as well as the Chairman of the Soviet of Soldiers in Tobolsk.

'Quiet down! Quiet!' Pankratov calls and the men immediately do so and he sees the prisoner looking back at him, wide-eyed and pale-faced. 'As you know, next door to the Winter Palace is the Hermitage and Russia's foremost treasures ...' The teacher in him wants to pause and bring their attention to the collection accrued by Catherine the Great but he stops himself and continues, 'So, men, as you can see, this is a turn of events and one we are all trying to make sense of —'

'It'll be *that* Bolshevik behind this!' interrupts the Deputy. 'Mark my words, Lenin and his Jew-comrade, Trotsky!'

This snowballs into a cacophony of bellowing and accusations and reprimands from the men until Pankratov again raises his hands. The men sullenly shut up only because they want more news and to ascertain what this next dramatic shift means for them. Already the grain of fear that many may be sent back to the Front is growing.

'As a committed Socialist Revolutionary, like our noble Prime Minister, I must admit that our Party's decision a few months back to quit the Congress has left it packed with Bolsheviks.' The men growl their irritation because they want direct news about what is going on in Petrograd and what this means for them and theirs — not a retrospective of inter-party fighting. Pankratov pushes on, 'The Bolshevik's feeble little newspaper, *Novaya Zhizn*, has misinformed the people and, as a consequence, there is some support for the uprising that has followed in the streets of Petrograd —'

'What uprising!? Speak to us, man!' roars his Deputy.

Pankratov raises his voice and shouts, 'THAT'S WHAT I'M TELLING YOU! THAT'S WHAT I AM TELLING ALL OF YOU! ON LENIN'S COMMAND, THE NAVY IS FIRING AGAINST THE GOVERNMENT AND THE BOLSHEVIKS ARE ATTEMPTING TO TAKE POWER!'

No one speaks and Pankratov himself feels out of breath, faint.

Then from far down the back of the hall, at the doorway, the man says over the heads of the few hundred gathered there, 'So are you telling us, Commissar, that Russia is undergoing a second revolution?'

No one turns around and looks at the speaker because everyone knows what he looks like and has known what he looks like since as far back as they can remember. His image was the one image that hung in their homes, in their schools — if they were lucky enough to attend, and in their churches. Before this year, these very men would have dropped on one knee to have seen the man or heard him speak.

Then, the Deputy's bilious retort, 'So from the most idiotic war that an imbecile forced us to fight we find ourselves now in yet another radical social upheaval!'

Pankratov needs to take back his meeting and says with authoritative certainty, 'It has been referred to as a second revolution by those in Smolny. Which is in complete violation of the promises made to the people of this nation, who are patiently awaiting a Constituent Assembly to vote —'

'IT HAS TAKEN THE GOVERNMENT TOO LONG!' cries out someone in the crowd.

'WE HAVE WAITED TOO LONG!' yells another.

'BREAD, PEACE, AND LAND — NOW!' roars a third.

Pankratov knows he must seize the moment now or forever be lost so he shouts, 'THE BOLSHEVIKS HAVE TAKEN THE PETROGRAD TELEGRAPH AGENCY!' A few of the men boo and hiss but it seems to Pankratov that there is an unhealthy amount of cheering coming from some others.

And so he continues with, 'THERE'S SHOOTING ON NEVSKY!' A salient reminder, surely, that only a democratic vote system can save Russia.

Hecklers audaciously call *SHOOT THE POLICE!* and *DEATH TO ARISTOCRACY!*

The crowd is a powder keg and Pankratov must keep it dry so he reaches out his hands imploring them to hear the truth of what is going on, 'KERENSKY'S GOVERNMENT SENT ARMED SOLDIERS INTO THE FRAY TO RE-ESTABLISH CONTROL BUT THESE SCOUNDRELS WENT OVER TO THE BOLSHEVIKS!'

Instead of seeing the Commissar's point of view and soberly understanding the implications of a government forced into defeat by Bolshevik bullies, the men, are now a mob euphoric with the thought of Lenin's promises of peace and bread and justice coming to fruition.

They are like children, the Commissar thinks to himself — when they don't get what they want in the shortest time possible, they riot. And as Pankratov looks over this imbroglio, all he can feel is tired. He still needs to tell them that the government ministers and supporters of Prime Minister Kerensky have been imprisoned in the Peter and Paul Fortress. He still needs to tell them Kerensky has gone missing. And, most importantly, he still needs to tell them that the Socialist Revolutionary democracy has been snatched out from underneath them.

The men jostle about the hall calling to anyone who will listen that the *TIDE IS TURNING!* and *WAR WILL END!* If there is one thing everyone knows it is Lenin and the Bolsheviks won't stand for war! At last, the nationalisation of land and factories will now take place! Men yell across to each other that Russia will truly be theirs and now at last there will be bread in the shops!

The crowd fills up on the jubilation of the hall and begins to think that maybe, just maybe, this time it will be better ... Bread for their families. Land for them to farm. Peace for all of Russia and young bodied men will never again walk into the fray, without boots, without rifles, without cause, and with only their flesh and bone and blood to defend Russia. The mash, the darkness.

Meanwhile, Captain Pavel Konoplev fills up on the euphoric

hope around him and finds himself cresting its wave. Now, for the first time, he can truly allow himself to think that this could be their moment, their opportunity, their chance for freedom! Hers and mine!

4

The man returns to his study. He closes the door and notes with relief that his wife must have retired to her bedroom chamber. Perhaps Schneider is making up one of her balms. Ginger and garlic in warm oil, he thinks distractedly. A dutiful attempt to alleviate the pain of his wife's relentless earaches.

The man goes over and over in his mind what he just heard the Commissar say. He is trying to figure out what it all means. He doesn't ask himself, how is this possible, because after February anything is possible in this meaningless, purposeless, ridiculous reality. He looks for some time at the dwindling fire and notes, without the usual satisfaction, that there is chopped wood waiting to build it back up. He remains standing.

What will become of them, now? He wonders, then realises that his initial thoughts are solely for himself and his own family. He thinks he should be driven by a profound concern for his nation, after a lifetime of putting its sovereignty before all else. But he doesn't feel anything. He knows their future, once uncertain, has now become terminal. The hope he had recently allowed himself to entertain, that they would be moving up to Murmansk then on to Japan or England or even France, once the Entente Powers had defeated the belligerents, has now vanished.

He is completely alone.

The man knows he should be thinking about Russia. He knows he should be thinking about the Bolsheviks, who threaten the freedom of every man, woman, and child born into this great nation,

Mother Russia. The greatest of all nations. The only nation. He knows that the Bolsheviks will condemn the Constituent Assembly and, in so doing, move the people into a dictatorship and abandon this short-lived democracy. The man knows he should feel outraged.

What is the point of his abdication, if it means the country will be dictated by coarse and indifferent men, who theorise and postulate but have no tradition and no understanding of what Russians truly want and no authority, whatsoever, to lead the country to victory?

The man should feel horrified, but he doesn't.

He sits down heavily on the damask settee and looks about, as if for the first time. The noise of the men beyond the room in the hall and spilling out of the house and into the yard below is full of elation. It is as if they have heard a different announcement from the Commissar.

The man watches the room fill with light as clouds beyond the window shift and move. He imagines he sees a zeppelin lolling like a somnambulant toward him. The clouds shift again and he shakes off his madness.

The man turns away from the window and looks at the pile of books. He picks up one, cracks open the cover, and reads.

It was the best of times, it was the worst of times, it was the age of wisdom, it was the age of foolishness, it was the epoch of belief, it was the epoch of incredulity ...

The man looks at the dying fire in the hearth and wonders whether history is repeating itself or fiction is foreshadowing truth. The man pushes on alone, numb.

It was the season of Light, it was the season of Darkness, it was the spring of hope, it was the winter of despair...

The man thinks about his wife, stoic and uncomplaining in the destiny that has become hers, he thinks about his oldest daughter, bright-eyed and sure-footed, and he thinks about his other children but particularly his son, who seems to have embraced their new lives with complete confidence. And yet the man knows himself to be deserted, forsaken, and cast aside. God has left us, he thinks, and with the snow falling outside and the light making havoc on the walls inside, the man reads on.

We had everything before us, we had nothing before us, we were all going to Heaven, we were all going the other way …

5

Several weeks later, it is minus 30 outside and the west Siberian snow is unrelenting. Bone-breaking cold. Even with the fires roaring, the Governor's house is an icebox.

'Hurry up! Everyone, *please* take your seats!'

Captain Konoplev and Colonel Kobylinsky are the special guests tonight and scramble into the family's drawing room that has been converted into a makeshift theatre.

'Quiet, everyone!' Anastasia has taken it upon herself to act as Master of Ceremonies.

Earlier this evening her mother had said that this is the end of the worst year of their lives, so everyone is to put their best foot forward. Anastasia stands alongside her brother, her closest ally. There is giggling from Baby, in a false beard and a borrowed footman's uniform. He is already positioned downstage, as the thespians would have their guests believe. The bearded footman looks at his 16 year old sister and winks, which sets her off in a peel of titters. From the audience, Dr. Botkin places a silent finger on his lips and nods at her. He is seated in one of the straight-backed chairs alongside the children's mother.

'Tonight's performance, Ladies and Gentlemen, is the one-act farce by Chekhov,' says Anastasia, her little round body and short legs a surprising comparison to the tall willowy figures of her other sisters. They have assured her, time and time again, that they too went through *the chubby stage*.

'Our dear tutor, Mr. Gilliard ...' She pauses so that the audience can offer him polite applause. 'Has been teaching us the great masterpieces of Russian Literature!'

Her mother knows that her youngest daughter can go on all night and so she taps her second eldest, Tatianna, on the shoulder, the one most like herself, and Tatianna responds with, 'What is the *name* of the play, Ana?'

'Oh yes, *The Bear!*'

Applause and laughter follow as Pavel, his usual shyness replaced with a bold familiarity, stands, and bows, pretending that the play is a nod to him. Not to be outshone, the incorrigible Anastasia curtseys and runs off stage and throws herself next to Marie, the sister only two years older than herself, so that all three sisters are now sitting on the damask settee facing the stage.

As Pavel takes his seat the Colonel says sotto voce, 'Our Captain is as strong as a bear!' Right on cue Anastasia squeals but then everyone hears their father's voice from the wings urging them to *Get the show on the road!*

Coughing.

The crackle of fire.

Action.

Luka, the trusted old servant (Baby): *It isn't right, madam .... You're just destroying yourself. The maid and the cook have gone off fruit picking and every living being is rejoicing, even the cat understands how to enjoy herself ...* Baby speaks directly to the audience, and his rendition of Luka, the old trusty servant of Lady Popova, is done in a raspy voice.

Lady Eleni Popova, beautiful widow (Olga): *I shall never go out ...* The audience watches as the beautiful Olga strides across the stage supposedly carrying a framed picture of her husband, who died seven months ago. Her 22 year old skin shines under the hanging candelabra and her blue eyes are startling.

Lady Eleni Popova, beautiful widow (Olga): *My life is already at an end. He is in his grave, and I have buried myself between these four walls ... We are both dead.* Onto the Gueridon table, she places the framed picture but not before the audience sees that it is a photograph of the Empress Dowager. There is laughter. This is cut short by someone knocking off stage and the Colonel Kobylinsky responds by calling out *Who's there?* The audience erupts into more chuckles and even the woman, who still regards herself as the Mother of all of the Russias, smiles, but her thoughts have iced. The most recent letter from Empress Dowager said that the rampaging villains, who had stormed the Winter Palace during the October Revolution, slashed the Serov portrait of the Tsar.

Luka trusted old servant (Baby): *Somebody wants to see you, Madam. He pushes himself right in!*

Lady Eleni Popova, beautiful widow (Olga): *Very well ...*

The woman watches her daughter on stage but her mind stays inside her mother-in-law's letter. The villainous revolutionaries had gone into her bed chamber and destroyed the very bed where she and her husband ... No! She will not think about it.

Lady Eleni Popova, beautiful widow (Olga): *How these people annoy me! What does he want of me? Why should he disturb my peace? No, I see that I shall have to go into a convent after all.* Laughter from the men in the audience, boldly led by Colonel Kobylinsky.

Lady Eleni Popova, beautiful widow (Olga): *Yes, into a convent.*

Then a roar of appreciation from the audience as the man, who was once Tsar of all the Russias, stands on stage. He blinks into the crowd and then, standing in a tailored tweed suit, obviously made by someone in Saville Row, delivers his line to the widow Popova.

Smirnov, the wealthy landowner (the man): *Your late husband died while owing me 1200 roubles. As I've got to pay the interest on a mortgage tomorrow, I've come to ask you, madam, to pay me the money today.*

Anastasia and Marie are giggling and pointing at Baby who is hamming it up on stage, rubbing his beard and quizzically looking on at the acting between his father and sister, or more accurately between Smirnov, the wealthy landowner, and Eleni, the widow Popova. Pavel takes this opportunity to move back to the fire and throw a few logs into its slumbering grate. He finds it hard to cover up his contempt for the man who is doing nothing to save himself or his family. Pavel's clandestine love affair with Olga has burned. Meanwhile, the Bolshevik uprising in Petrograd has sparked versions of revolution in Moscow, Kazan, Novosibirsk, Yekaterinburg, Nizhny Novgorod, Samara, Omsk, Chelyabinsk, and Rostov-on-Don. Pavel shunts the iron poker into the burning kindling and returns to his seat. He had let Olga hope but deep in his gut Pavel knows their chances to be together are slight.

Smirnov, the wealthy landowner (the man): *I don't want the money the day after tomorrow, I want it today.*

The man's wheedling voice and accompanying hand on hip, makes the audience hoot. Pavel can feel rage, bilious and bitter, at the back of his throat, and then he looks at Olga, her wide Slavic cheekbones and upturned nose. He thinks of her long white thighs and perfectly shaped buttock ... he closes his eyes and the smell of her warm neck nuzzles its memory to his lips. *Olenka, my own,* he murmurs audaciously under the clamour of the performance.

Lady Eleni Popova, beautiful widow (Olga): *You must excuse me, I can't pay you.*

Smirnov, the wealthy landowner (the man): *And I can't wait.*

Olga strides back and forth across the small stage. A chinoiserie privacy screen brought from the Alexander Palace in Tsarskoye Selo, cordons off the backstage.

Lady Eleni Popova, beautiful widow (Olga): *Well, what can I do if I haven't the money now!*

Smirnov, the wealthy landowner (the man): *You mean to say, you can't pay me?*

Pavel feels himself bristle at the man who is, whether on or off stage, always a fool.

Lady Eleni Popova, beautiful widow (Olga): *I can't.*

Smirnov, the wealthy landowner (the man): *Hmmm! Is that the last word you've got to say?*

Lady Eleni Popova, beautiful widow (Olga): *Yes, the last word.*

Smirnov, the wealthy landowner (the man): *The last word? Absolutely your last?*

Lady Eleni Popova, beautiful widow (Olga): *Absolutely.*

And Pavel stands, ostensibly to stretch his dodgy leg, and turns his back on the performance.

Smirnov, the wealthy landowner (the man): *Thank you so much. I'll make a note of it.*

Colonel Kobylinsky prides himself on his ability to handle the most precarious situations. He is a survivor. And he intends to remain a survivor until he can retire to his daughter's home in Odessa. He has had enough of the war and now this bloody mess of revolution. Scoundrels and criminals of the worst kind.

Smirnov, the wealthy landowner (the man): *I'm going to stay and sit here till you give me the money. You can be ill for a week if you like, and I'll stay here for a week ... If you're ill for a year — I'll stay for a year. I'm going to get my money back! You don't fool me with your widow's weeds and your dimpled cheeks! I know those dimples!*

Chekov's tale of the alazon, a character who thinks he is more than what he actually is, has somehow been lost on all of them, thinks Pavel. Oh dear, thinks the Colonel as he hears the Captain poke the fire savagely behind him as if it was Comrade Romanov himself. He has heard the rumours about his quiet handsome Captain and the headstrong filly up there on stage. You don't get to be in your late fifties and see what he has seen to not know a thing or two.

Smirnov, the wealthy landowner (the man): *Or do you think I'm doing this for a joke?*

Lady Eleni Popova, beautiful widow (Olga): *Please don't shout! This isn't a stable!*

The doctor next to the Colonel finds this the wittiest line so far and claps loudly. Tatiana, the second oldest daughter turns around and frowns. Ahh so much like her mother, thinks the Colonel, as the Captain sits down heavily beside him.

Lady Eleni Popova, beautiful widow (Olga): *You don't know how to behave in front of women!*

Pavel imperceptibly tenses. Olga is looking straight at him as she delivers her lines.

Lady Eleni Popova, beautiful widow (Olga): *You're a rude, ill-bred man! Decent people don't talk to a woman like that!*

Pavel smiles back, openly and proprietorially, at the glorious chestnut blonde and the fourth wall broken. Meanwhile, the man looks from his daughter to Captain Pavel Konoplev then back to his daughter. The play's suspension of disbelief stumbles and the mother, three seats away, leans forward quietly and looks across the Colonel to the Captain.

Then Anastasia hisses from the front of the audience, *Get on with it!*

Smirnov, the wealthy landowner (the man): *Madam ...* The man struggles to regain his composure after what he saw or thought he saw between his eldest daughter and the Captain.

Smirnov, the wealthy landowner (the man): *Madam ...* The man looks back into the audience. His wife sits straight-backed and imperious. Perhaps she is right. Perhaps Olga and Tatiana should be married by now. He will write to his mother to arrange a suitable match. And fast. Then the man thinks, *My lines?!*

Smirnov, the wealthy landowner (the man): *Madam, three times I've fought duels on account of women. I've refused 12 women, and nine have refused me! Yes! There was a time when I played the fool, scented myself, used honeyed words, wore jewelry...*

The man lacks self-knowledge and perhaps the daughter is the same, thinks the Colonel. He knows that a lack of self-knowledge is dangerous. He watches her. She is the young damsel, endowed with confidence and intelligence, not to mention beauty, who has thrown herself in the path of ... the Colonel glances at the Captain next to him ... a wounded warrior. What does the ingénue think? That it can go on like this until their dying days?

Lady Eleni Popova, beautiful widow (Olga): *I'll tell you that of all the men I know, the best was my late husband ... I loved him passionately with all my being ... But after his death I found in his desk a whole drawerful of love letters, from when he was alive — it's an awful thing to face!*

Baby knows the spotlight has moved away from him and seems to shine on his sister and, strangely, Captain Pavel Konoplev. He thinks fast and reaches out for the framed photograph and turns it face down shaking his head solemnly. The audience loves it and claps and laughs — even his oldest sister, the rather astonishing Lady Popova, smiles indulgently.

Smirnov, the wealthy landowner (the man): *Give me my money ...*

He is persistent, thinks the Captain as he listens to her father gabble on as Smirnov. Persistently stupid.

Lady Eleni Popova, beautiful widow (Olga): *You're a boor! A coarse bear! A Bourbon! A monster!* Olga stamps her foot and clenches her fist, as so many Lady Popova's before her have done.

Smirnov, the wealthy landowner (the man): *Pistols!*

The man's demand on stage is lightened by the Colonel who again interrupts in sotto voce: *Out of the question!* The girls, seated in front, giggle, knowing that it is somehow their role to unravel the dangerous intricacies that seem to bind the adults in the room. But unfortunately, the lovely Olga, their oldest sister, the one who will go head to head with anyone, even their mother, seems hell-bent on taking more and more risks. She locks eyes with Captain Konoplev.

Lady Eleni Popova, beautiful widow (Olga): *Bear! Bear! Bear!*

(Later, Pavel will remember it differently from Olga. He will say, her mother stood up, right there in the middle of the performance, and asked to be excused *after* Lady Popova agreed to use the pistols and fight a duel to the death with her father.

Smirnov, you mean, corrects Olga. To fight a duel with Smirnov.

Yes.

No, you're wrong, Olga replies. It was when I was accusing you of being nothing but a coarse bear.

You mean, Lady Popova ... corrects Pavel. Was accusing Smirnov of being a coarse bear.

Yes.)

Smirnov, the wealthy landowner (the man): *These are excellent pistols. They can't cost less than ninety roubles the pair ... You must hold the revolver like this ... Then you cock the trigger and take aim like this ... Put your head back a little! Hold your arm out properly ... Yes, a little higher ... Like that ...*

Pavel thinks about the newspapers from the cities that will not stop coming. Russians killing Russians. Gunfire on the streets. Snipers on the ready. Unquiet country. The latest reports have indicated that the peace negotiation with Germany is going well and he thinks of all those men, slaughtered for nothing.

Lady Eleni Popova, beautiful widow (Olga): *Get away from me — I hate you!*

Pavel tells himself this is Olga, his Olenka, speaking with unmitigated hatred to her father. The whole play has been a ruse for her to assert this truth, their truth. This will be the key to unhouse her from Romanov's fate, he thinks to himself. Pavel knows the Bolsheviks are the answer, with their swift reforms to private property ownership, marriage, and divorce, not to mention the establishment of the legal status of women. He tries to forget what so many are saying will happen to the family, now that Kerensky is on the run.

Lady Eleni Popova, beautiful widow (Olga): *Stand back, or I'll fire!* Yells the Lady Popova, Olga, Olenka, himself, and all of Russia.

Smirnov, the wealthy landowner (the man): *Fire, then! You can't understand what happiness it would be — to be shot by a revolver ...*

Some time afterward, when the man's final lines have been said and the applause has died down and the lady in waiting has come to retrieve the woman's precious brood back to their rooms and the doctor and the tutor and the Colonel have accepted a nightcap of French brandy in the man's study, Pavel makes his way, slowly, down the stairs and out into the frozen night sky.

He lumbers across the snow-covered road over to the barracks. Pavel knows he must turn Olga against her father and her family if they are to have any chance of escape. He will bind her to him and she will love him because only he can save her. They are destined for each other. Tonight, she showed such courage, and even though it was just a play it was still in her — the intensity of emotion, the capacity to feel the full colour of rage, and the ability to choose her path. By spring they will be gone. He and her. North. And then abroad.

He smiles to himself. Anything is possible. Everything is possible.

7

The Fugitive

Forest beyond Luga, 140 km south of Petrograd. December 1917.
Kerensky's boots crunch through the snow of the forest floor. In these last few weeks since he escaped from Gatchina and his arrival here at the estate of the ex-Colonel, he has become ever watchful. He is a trespasser, an exile, a banished interloper. He is no longer the Prime Minister. Now he is prey, game, kill. The afternoon sun behind the birch throws darkened bars across the ice crystals underfoot. He trudges on, with nowhere to go and nothing to do but wait.

Somewhere in the back of his skull, like a sniper's crosshairs, he feels the onset of madness.

The people's will is God's decree and he knows he must bow to its capricious nature. He has been blessed and cursed with salvation. For the time being. This forested estate, away from civilisation, away from purpose, away from righteousness is now his redoubt. Kerensky knows he should have shouldered a rifle. Lidia's father had tried to foist it onto him, but his nose for fatalism twitched and he refused the offer.

Not that Lenin's army should spend even a day worrying about his bird-brained, empty-stomached, frail-chested self. His value is nothing. The Bolsheviks have bigger concerns than him — simply because he had grabbed the baton of democracy and tried to run.

He staggers and holds the slim broken-skinned limb of a birch. The trunk is indistinguishable from the other thousands that shoot up from the snow. Kerensky steadies himself and feels his mind split open.

Lunacy.

Vertigo.

Hysteria.

And his heart races about the forest floor scooting this way and that until he knows he is mad and can do nothing but let himself fall at the base of the tree and slump against its back-rest.

Kerensky knows that many will believe the newspapers that he abandoned his people. That he fled well before the Winter Palace came under siege. That he left his ministers to face the bombardment of the *Aurora*. That he left women and young men to defend a failed government. The truth doesn't matter because all is lost.

His memory is bird scratch. Fleeing from Petrograd. Stopping at Gatchina. Rallying an ill-fated counterattack against the enemy. Behind his back General Krasnov, the commander of the Don Cossacks had formed an armistice with the Bolsheviks and, as a consequence, demanded Kerensky surrender to the mob.

Bolsheviks.

Barbarians.

Vandals.

He escaped Gatchina disguised as a sailor. To find himself ... to lose himself ... In this bleak mid-winter hold out. This cold unfeeling redoubt. This estate — somewhere in the forest en route from Gatchina to Luga.

What is the point? he asks himself. Is this what the people want? A country that will get what it deserves.

Kerensky knows he must stand up and keep walking if he is to make it back to the house before dark. He watches the shadows reach out, long and menacing. He yearns for his sons, for their adoration. He tries not to think about his wife who cannot forgive him for the affairs. He knows his family will be hunted down because of their association with him. He has already sent word to his wife to flee with the boys until order is restored.

I am womanless, he laments, as he stands and forces himself to push onwards. God has exiled him. Once the most powerful man in Russia, he is now someone lost and hidden in the winter birch. How is it possible that he once strutted forth with the command of his nation to bless troops and shape destinies — but now he moves from rocky clefts to crystalized ivy bushes and narrow estuaries. There is nobody here to call him Prime Minister ... there is nobody here ... there is nobody here ... His mind is flotsam and jetsam ... and there is nobody here ... His thoughts wash up and spew back ... nobody here ...

He stops.

Light is fading. He feels striped like a winter tree, empty, nude, devoid of protection. The canopy of thin branches reaching above him forms a heaven that doesn't exist or a chapel for the missing. A part of him wants to kneel in the frost encrusted snow and pray for forgiveness. But another part of him whispers that there is no God, only a manhunt to expiate his sins.

Hunger begins to gnaw at his innards and he looks about knowing that the fading colours of the day could simply be leading him to his circular madness. A wolf pack on his heels. Lamentations and regrets snap and snarl around his person.

Perhaps it has been the shock of the battle ... the one he has fought over the past few months ... past few years. All his life, if truth be told. He has only ever wanted to fight for what is just and right. Is that so wrong?

He looks down.

Footprints. Large. Certain.

His heart races.

Then he realises they are his footprints and he has, at last, come upon the path he trod earlier.

The afternoon sky is an indigo bruise. He thinks he is a ghost. A madman diarising his decent. A character from Gogol. I have left behind a dead kingdom, he thinks as he follows his footprints that have become softer and weaker in the greying twilight. His home-land, his beloved, his Russia offers him nothing now but heartbreak. And doubt ... which nibbles away at his mind until he knows that there is nothing much left but spasm and outrage —

Branch snap!

He doesn't move.

Holds his breath.

Heart punching chest.

Then, slowly, the thud of snow from tree to the ground, and time thaws, and he carefully puts one foot in front of the other, and moves quietly on.

Savage henchmen lurk in every shadow of his mind. Crouched in the mask of their own deceit. He wonders if an assassin has been sent to finish him off. He tries to tell himself if this is the case, then this is what he wants. To be shot. To be bone and offal seeping through the clean glistening snow. Then nothing. He sighs.

Fate is a long drawn-out affair.

He pushes on knowing he has more or less 15 minutes left of day-light. He is sure this is the path back to the estate. Perhaps I could learn to live happily here, he thinks. Amongst the birch and the ivy and the pine and the oak and the rowan trees. Where there is no hurry to live, only the slow beginnings of the morning then the long onset of the evening and a deep expanse of time in between. Where, like Lidia's father, he would hunt. Nothing more.

A life contingent on survival, not ideology.

Quietly, the bone-white skeletal trunks begin to thin out. Up ahead, Kerensky sees the long vaporous tongue of the homestead's chimney smoke calling him home. The wolves may well be loping away from their chance to kill, but it is just a matter of time. His mind addles out into images of Bolsheviks howling at the moon for his blood. His mind scuttles over escape possibilities, the balm of the fugitive, the mocked, the abandoned. Himself.

Kerensky sees how the forest has morphed into parkland which opens to the estate. Up ahead in the homestead the windows are alight in readiness for the thick night ahead. Chinks of hope. The best he can expect is a pilgrimage to a foreign land. One day he might meet his sons again. He presses his gloved fist into his mouth, stopping the yaw of grief. After a moment he pushes on to the homestead.

Where did his nation's affection go? They were lovers once — unable to sleep unless he dreamed of her and she of him. Russia was the bride he had longed for and all the nation saw that they were entwined, enamoured, committed to each other. He was nothing without her and she made him believe it was the same for her. And yet here he is, tramping through the cold. A bag of skin and bone, heart-culled, blood-thinned, mind nothing but a wasteland. And there she is, in the arms of another lover.

Russia is his unrequited love, his lost whore, his Russia no more.

Kerensky sees his host moving about inside the homestead and wonders if the ex-Colonel has sold him out to his enemies. It is only a matter of time. He imagines the Bolsheviks following the forested road between Gatchina and Luga, circling the property ... rifles ready. *The righteous one will rejoice when he sees vengeance, and he will wash his hands in the blood of the wicked.* But who is the righteous one? he asks himself as the Old Testament's bloodlust surfaces. *Vengeance belongs to the Lord,* comes back the answer.

But in his mind, he offers the heretic's addendum: *Vengeance belongs to whoever is lord, make no mistake.*

By the time he reaches the back door, the evening has already fallen from the sky and blanketed the snow in darkness. He can smell the bubble and boil of supper inside. He has lived a lifetime in a country that knows only one certainty: hunger. A people who have always been starving or on the brink of starvation. A desperate appetite to survive forces them to live off the meagre scraps of an unjust and disreputable system. Kerensky knows himself to be Russian because he has been ravenous for love, justice and for a life worth living. He stamps the snow off his boots at the back door. His thighs are ice and his mind unhinged with the thought that the Red Army waits within — ready to eviscerate him.

Once he was Cicero, now he is a bare-faced raving madman, who can do nothing but raid the naked woods of his imagination to conjure up an end.

He opens the door and his host nods him in. There's a warm glass of homebrew already waiting next to the open hearth in which a stout bellied pot contains some sort of stew. Above the stone fireplace is an old crucifix.

Almighty God, the godless Kerensky prays, perhaps I deserve this ... gutted and miserable as I am. I chose beloved Russia, the idea of her, the seduction of the imagined other, rather than her people.

Could that have been it?

He tries to quieten his mind. He keeps his eyes on the burning flames and not the recrudescence of memory. He sits like a man acting like a man. Attempting to ignore the panic rising from his entrails. He is a dereliction of his former self. He is a scuttler, a thread-bare, terror-afflicted idealist gone rogue. Even within the safety of the estate, he sees heads pursuing him. The bonnet rouge and emblazoned eyes, singing *La Marseillaise*. Lenin's beloved hunting him down. He was once their King of Kings, their Lord of All.

Now, on this night, holed up in some stranger's home, he sips the warmed intoxicating cider.

The ex-Colonel's daughter is a true believer of the Socialist Revolutionary Party, the Provisional Government and its Prime Minister. His son is the Captain of the Guards watching over the Tsar and his family. The ex-colonel is a tall man of few words and no hair, whose sole passion seems to be hunting and hunters. What one stalks and traps is neither here nor there.

The two men sit in the den of warmth and flickering light, listening to the screech of a wind that begins its performance in the wintery dark.

Kerensky knows that out there wolves run in packs. He picks up his spoon and bowl of stew. And he thinks he should be driven out, he is a madman that should be chased off the body of the beloved as she squirms to be rid of him from their sweat-stained sheets. Perhaps he should not eat the stew of steaming root vegetables and salted venison.

The host bows his head and gives thanks for this food, God's bounty.

And at the back of his skull, Kerensky is certain that he is been offered Christ's body. Despite his lack of faith, he finds himself pushing a cautious spoon through the stew and repenting solemnly.

Let me atone, Lord, for the error of my ways,
Let me do penance so that I am no longer persecuted,
Let me not be cursed, forgotten and forsaken, Lord.

...

Lord?

Outside, it is snow-black.

8

A Bleak Mid-Winter

Petrograd. January 1918.

The day is filled with so much possibility, thinks Lidia, as she lowers herself down onto the Neva.

January's uncompromising winter has calmed the turbulent river into metallic ice. There is no one else around. Lidia has left her father's estate and come back to the city. Her tall thin frame is thickened by two woollen skirts under which she wears a pair of men's trousers. Her long-sleeved knitted jumper is stuffed beneath an old military greatcoat. Lidia's chequered scarf is wound several times about her pale hair, nose, mouth, and neck, so that the only exposed part of her body, her eyes, smart with the hard white cold of noon.

She gingerly takes a few steps beneath the first riveted span of the Troitskiy Bridge. Lidia thinks about the elections last month that resulted in a Bolshevik minority — an outcome that was immediately overturned by Lenin.

Bastard, she murmurs to the godforsaken cold.

She knows the ice is harder on the Neva than any road surface in the city but despite this, her mind's eye sees the ice crack and the roiling black river below swallowing her whole. She shivers. Lidia has travelled night and day to get here. The broadsheets posted on street bollards and across shopfronts in Petrograd are heady with a mixture of wild rumours, piecemeal reporting, and scathing criticism.

Lidia crouches over her small knapsack and pulls out her brother's adjustable skates. In the last few weeks, she has made good use of them across the forested lakes that hide Kerensky at her father's estate, hidden in the birch forest between Gatchina and Luga. All of Russia is intent on finding Kerensky and there he has remained at her father's for the best part of two months. But she cannot stay away, any longer, from her Petrograd, the hotbed of politics. Besides, the Socialist Revolutionaries must take back their power and authority, otherwise, Lenin will drive them all into a destiny that was never meant to be Russia's.

She tugs the steel skates over the soles of her boots and binds them with a thick cord. Her leather gloves lay on the snow alongside her. She works quickly but already her fingers are growing numb. Lidia stands up and stamps her feet a few times, more to show her inner terror that the ice will hold. Indeed, she assures herself, it will sally me forth into the arms of Grishka! This will be the first time she has seen him since that night when she and Leonid whisked Kerensky off to safety. Since then she has moved back and forth between the Gatchina Palace and her father's estate. And although Leonid had once delivered a badly scrawled note from Grishka, she had been more than two months without his hard hungry body and she was starving.

It's hard to believe so much has happened in just a few short months. Even her father, who is never ruffled by anything, having survived the war with Japan in '05, fears she might be shot by a Bolshevik. *They're bastards and hoodlums,* he would say again and again. But she knows he takes comfort in Lidia's marksmanship. A gift he gave both his children.

Lidia looks ahead and a kilometre or two away is the Liteyny

Bridge — she plans to pass under the Liteyny and then scramble up the Vyborgskaya side of the Neva. The bridges are controlled by Red Guards and they are renowned for detaining pedestrians, demanding their identification, and generally making life difficult. More concerningly, no one is doing anything about the hordes of unruly soldiers returning from the Front and menacing the unwary.

Lidia pushes off and skates slow and relaxed, beneath the Troitskiy Bridge. Up ahead are some old men bent over in coats and blankets, fishing beneath the bridge. She leans into the *shuu kk shuu kk* of her rhythm.

A few minutes later she taps her right foot a few times as she meanders about the first old man, who doesn't even look up, and the second, who grunts with her sudden appearance. She wonders if they are catching perch or roach. *Shuu kk shuu kk* ... Lidia drags her left skate behind her right, creating friction, until she glides slowly to a stop, at the third fisherman. He doesn't look up straightaway but tugs and toys with his fishing line that drops down into the thick hole he has screwed into the ice.

'Any luck, grandfather?' she asks.

He nods quietly as he sits like an enormous bear on his three-legged stool.

'Perch?'

'Perch,' he agrees and she realises there is a tobacco pipe tucked inside the dirty scarf wrapped about his face.

She wants to get on but there is something in his stillness and in this ordinary task out on the iced river that makes her long for the past, the time when she was a girl and there was nothing to fight for, except the reeling in of a good catch on a winter's day.

'You headed to Vasilyevsky?'

She is surprised by his question because the Vasilyevsky Island is in the opposite direction to her home in the Vyborgskaya but then again the Troitskiy Bridge, beneath which she skates, is halfway between the two.

'No. I'm heading home.'

'Good.'

It is then that he looks up and sees the only uncovered part of her. Her eyes. One blue, one gold. And then, taking all the time in the world, he moves his gnarled hand, the one not holding the taut fishing line, and makes the sign of the cross. Lidia looks past him to the red rostral column that is visible from Vasilyevsky Island and even from this distance, she can see a large group of people gathering. She wonders what the old man has heard but he is already anticipating her question.

'A rally in support of the new Constituent Assembly ... I read the poster.'

His pride in the fact that he can read trumps any threat she might pose as someone with heterochromia. She thinks about one of the first implementations of the Provisional Government early last year: *Education for all*. Not only did schools become coeducational but people beyond school age were being taught the basics of literacy in soviet meetings. Indeed, for these last 12 months, all of Russia seems to have been reading. And it is impossible not to want to learn to read when every single organisation is producing pamphlets interpreting the political and economic seismic shifts of their nation. It is no wonder that in cities, towns, and villages there is a frenzied effort to make sense of the future.

Lidia digs her skate into the ice and pushes herself off and as she glides away she hears the old man call behind her, 'Take care, granddaughter.' And even though she knows her revolver is in her coat pocket and not in her knapsack, she reaches in and feels its hard reassurance. *Shuu kk ... shuu kk ... shuu kk ... shuu kk ... shuu kk ... shuu kk ... shuu kk ... shuu kk ...* There is less snow beneath the bridge and although it is rough going Lidia begins to warm up and enjoy the freedom of the day. One in which she can nearly, but not quite, forget the endless worries about the future of her beloved homeland.

As she leaves the underbridge behind and moves out across the river toward the Liteyny Bridge, it begins to snow. The lonely quiet flutters around her and Lidia thinks about her imminent arrival home. She has missed her small functional apartment. Grishka will be there and he will be relieved. She wants his hard lean body. *Shuu kk ... shuu kk ... shuu kk ... shuu kk ... shuu kk ... shuu kk ... shuu kk ... shuu kk ...* Lidia skates across the moment where the Bolshaya Nevka River turns in from the north of the city to join the mighty Neva, this signals the end of the Petrogradsky district and the start of the Vyborgskaya. Her home.

It is unusually quiet and she wonders if it is the rally over on the Vasilyevsky Island, or, maybe people are already making their way to the Tauride Palace for this afternoon's first Constituent Assembly.

She hopes Grishka has not yet left the apartment. Her heart fills up and she leans into the kiss of snow and skates toward her boyfriend. And swirling about in her mind is Tolstoy's skating scene in *Anna Karenina* ... The ice rink at the zoological garden ... Kitty's arm linked through Levin's ... Gliding on and on into the blush of tender longing ... The bright hoar frost ... The promise of more ... *Shuu kk ... shuu kk ... shuu kk ... shuu kk ... shuu kk ... shuu kk ... shuu kk ...*

Lidia slows her rhythm as she espies Red Guards up ahead on the Liteyny Bridge. She had planned to scramble up the right embankment and make her way through the labyrinth of streets to reach her apartment but there is something about the quietness of the guards, a watchfulness, that makes her slow down. She drags her left skate behind her right until she comes to a shaky stop. And she stands there, quite still, until she hears the mighty frozen Neva thrum, crack, and pop as if there are a thousand heartbeats caught somewhere far below or a strange battlefield trapped in a distant underworld.

With her skates still attached, she uses the stone pylons to pull herself up the side of the Liteyny Bridge. She feels the Red Guards watching her.

'Where are you headed?'

She looks up and sees a round mashed face with dark squinty eyes. The other Red Guard joins his mate and peers over the railing of the bridge, he scratches his thin beard then starts working on his nose. They both wear cone-shaped bashlyk caps and khaki brown overcoats.

They watch her untie her skates. Lidia takes her time and then packs them into her knapsack. She pulls her scarf low over her forehead before she answers them.

'I'm headed home. I teach here in the City Public School.' She hopes this will indicate she is known in the district.

The one who spoke first sucks on a dirty cigarette and says, 'Come here.'

Straight away, as if on cue, the thin one slurs, 'Pedestrians, as well as vehicles, are to be checked.'

She tells herself this is to be expected. Her city, her country, is in the grip of revolutionary change, not to mention the shadow of civil war, and so it goes without saying that these imbeciles relish their new found power. Lidia makes her way toward them on the bridge. She tells herself she has done nothing wrong — except help Kerensky, the most wanted man in Russia, escape. She puts this fact out of her mind and composes herself.

Her destiny, like every woman before her, is problematic. On the one hand, she knows she must not pose a threat but on the other hand, she cannot be seen as a target. She stands tall and straight before them, eyes downcast. Then she realises with dismay that she can hear a cart rumbling away off into the distance, as it exits the far side of the bridge. Apart from that, there is nothing but an eerie stillness.

Mash Face looks her up and down, 'So you're a school teacher? Daddy must be rich ...' He opens up his pudgy eyes as best he can, shifts his weight, and adds contemptuously, 'So you went to school, huh?'

This isn't going well, she thinks.

The thin one has stopped digging around his nose and asks, 'What's in the b-b-bag?' He takes a swig from his canteen and she knows it's not water.

She wonders if the next passer-by on the bridge will stop. She does a quick calculation and figures it to be past noon, maybe one o'clock. Surely someone will be coming soon but somewhere in a dark corner of her mind she knows that all over Russia, people are putting their heads down and moving quickly by. The only way to survive, many think, is to see and do nothing. Lidia opens the knapsack and places it carefully between herself and the men. Keeping her head low she glances to the farthest end of the bridge. Not a soul.

Mash Face watches on, smoking his cigarette, as his colleague goes through the contents. Skates, no food, only some of her brother's woollens.

'What is your name and who do you live with?'

'My name is Lidia Mikhailovna Konopleva and I live with my husband,' Lidia keeps her eyes lowered but knows the bigger one is moving imperceptibly closer to her.

'Take off the s-s-scarf,' says the thin guy, quietly.

The instruction is delivered so unexpectantly that she thinks at first she has misheard and she glances up at the thin guy. He is smiling and she can see an assortment of condemned teeth in his mouth. Lidia waits. She cannot believe that they have asked this of her. She squints across at the bigger guy who is finishing off his cigarette.

'Right,' Mash Face says and flicks his cigarette butt over the bridge. 'Stasevich, place her under arrest and I'll take her to the ... err ... our quarters.'

This is not happening, she thinks to herself, there is a mistake and she opens her mouth to explain, demand, question, plead — but Mash Face hits her hard in the stomach and she crumples to the ground, desperately trying to breathe. Then one of them has a vice grip around her arm and the other is tugging off her scarf. She feels a thick paw in her hair and she wants to stand up and shoot the bastard — but she has no breath to do so.

'You shouldn't have resisted arrest,' Mash Face says, laconically.

Her chin is jerked up by the thin guy and she looks into his rheumy eyes and the grinning black hole of his mouth. He steps back suddenly and lifts a holy medal from around his neck, kisses it, and sloshing his words about in his filthy mouth says, 'Look, b-b-boss. Com-Comrade. She's ... her ...'

Mash Face grabs the back of her hair and hauls her up on her feet and the roar of pain to the back of her head is savage and brutal.

'Open your eyes, bitch.' He has his huge hand clamped about her face. She opens them and looks into his eyes and sees nothing. Meanwhile, he is scrutinising her gift, her curse, and his dark piggy eyes dart between her gold and blue eyes.

And then she does see something in his eyes. Loathing.

'Stasevich,' Mash Face calls back as he begins moving her off the bridge toward the warehouses. 'Keep a lookout. I will interrogate her first. Then it will be your turn.'

She hears the thin one spew forth a giggle as she is shunted ahead of her captor into a side street that runs parallel to the river. He has locked one of her arms behind and grips her hair mercilessly.

Lidia frantically searches the windowless buildings for someone, anyone, but Mash Face adroitly shoves her through a warehouse doorway and, she knows, there is no one to save her. He still holds her arm behind her but has let go of her hair. She cannot feel her skull. She cannot feel her arm and wrist.

They stand together. Woman in front, man behind. Close. Intimate.

Then she sees a table where there are some papers and the remains of an earlier meal as well as two chairs and she tells herself this is where he will interrogate me and test my commitment to the Bolsheviks.

She steadies her breathing. She tries to calm her panicked mind and remember some of the truism brandished about by the Bolsheviks but she cannot seem to remember a single thing and that's when she hears him behind her — tugging at the belt across his greatcoat.

'Please — I can give you food — in my apartment — close to here ...'

She hears the belt drop and he pushes her toward the table.

'I have some jewellery — my mother's — gold — please ... I —'

With his free hand, he swipes the table's paraphernalia onto the floor and then slams her face down so that she is bent over the table, her feet scrambling on the floor, both wrists now clamped behind her in his cracking grip.

'My name is Lidia — I am — my husband ... my husband ... Grishka —' And to her shame she begins to sob as the animal behind reaches up under her rucked skirts.

Although well-seasoned in the art of violence, having been a Frontovik and now an ardent believer in a Russia that promises to put him first, Mash Face realises, with a grunt of irritation, she is wearing trousers held up with a cord. He balls up his free fist, thumps her hard in the side of her head. Her sobbing is exchanged for a whimper. He then yanks sharply at the cord holding up her trousers. Once, twice until it gives away.

She no longer struggles.

His cock is rock hard and without difficulty, he slams it into her. He. Will. Teach. Her. A. Fuck — ing. Less — on.

She watches the upturned chair on the floor.

His blood is up and he is the king of the goddamn world. His brain roars. He goes at her hammer and tong. Thrusting and thrusting and thrusting. This middle-class bitch won't forget this ride!

She stares at dust particles caught in a sliver of fading light.

He is nearly there but he wants to slap this tart across her soft white skin before he climaxes — the exciting urge to do so makes him shove harder and harder into her — *uh uh uh uh uh uh uh* — he wants to hit her so hard but he can see the muck of blood and snot on the upturned side of her face.

She gazes at the grooves in the wooden table, beneath her.

He explodes. And then he slumps across her and breathes heavily. His stinking breath reeks across the side of her face and just for the hell of it, and because he can, he wrenches her long fair hair back so that her face lifts off the table, and as his soft wet cock slips out, he bangs her face back down on the table. Satisfied, he pushes himself back away from her, readjusts his trousers, and stoops over to retrieve his belt.

'Get up, whore.'

She hears him light a cigarette, inhale and blow out the smoke deeply.

'Stasevich will be in next, so wipe your fucking face ...'

She moves slowly because she is not there. She pushes herself up and leans against the table because her legs are shaking and the rest of her body is not hers. She turns around, bends slowly, and then drags her trousers up to her waist, pulls and tugs down her skirts, and closes her coat. She watches him. As if from a great distance.

He buttons his fly and clips together the rectangular brass buckle of his belt. The buckle is stamped with the double-headed eagle. The all-seeing magisterial power of Russia. He fusses with the brown leather ammunition pouch attached to the side of his belt.

And that is when she makes her decision.

He never looks up at her because she is nothing. She is not a threat and she no longer offers value. He buttons the chest flap of his brown khaki greatcoat. He has forgotten her. He turns aside and picks up his bashlyk cap and momentarily looks down at his most prized possession, his sapogi, high-top black leather boots.

It is only a pause — but this is all she needs. She pushes her hand deep into her coat pocket, grips the teak handle of her Nagant revolver, and drags it out.

He is using his cap to hit away at the warehouse grime that has somehow found itself on his boots. He has forgotten the bitch. His shift will finish soon but anyway he and Stasevich will leave early like they do most days. It's as cold as his wife's face out there on the bridge and he is tired. He doesn't hear the click of the revolver's hammer as she pulls it back. And he doesn't see her cup her left hand about her right, as she grips the revolver and aims at his ear.

She knows the cylinder is loaded with seven shots.

He knows it's time to go and let Stase have a go, that is if he can get it up, being, as he always is, three sheets to the wind.

The table creaks against the lean of her thigh and he glances back at the sound. At first, he can't make sense of what he is seeing. The warehouse is filled with shadows and the slut is a mess of clothing — but then he sees her tangled snarl of white-blonde hair and remembers something about her eyes, but he can't quite recall what ... her face is bloodied and ballooning ... and then he sees it.

'You fucking —'

BANG! BANG! BANG!

She knows it is a waste. The first bullet takes out the left eye and the rest of the side of his head and he flounces like a rag doll. The second sends bone and blood splintering from his clavicle. And the third explodes the chest of his greatcoat.

One, two, three. Three seconds, if that. There is no need for the second or the third bullet. He is dead with the first. But strangely his body stands until the final death blow is delivered and then, in its quiet surprise, collapses upon itself.

The warehouse fills with the smell of sulphur, dust, and dampness.

Her arm and wrist and fingers hum. She breathes deeply and her body is calm. This body that now feels like hers. She still grips the revolver, its strength, and its power. Every hunting trip with her father, every target practice with her brother, every incidental conversation about firearms has brought her to this moment.

Her mind is alert to the empty street beyond the warehouse door. She doesn't care if the other one has been alerted to the gunshots because she will kill him, too. She knows she only has minutes. She picks up the bashlyk cap near the dead Red Guard, shoves it on her head to cover her hair, and moves swiftly to the doorway of the warehouse.

Outside it is snowing and growing dark and there is no one around, not even the thin Red Guard. She picks up a clump of snow and holds it to her face, in her other hand the Nagant revolver is ready. Lidia looks back down toward the bridge but there is no movement or sound. It is as if what happened, never happened. She turns the other way and with her back to the warehouse and moves quickly into the maze of streets.

2

'... This is our right as people of the revolution — to have our *first* Constituent Assembly!' And the crowd's response from the Vasilyevsky Island can be heard far away by some lone fishermen who sit on the icy Neva River under the Troitskiy Bridge, the very ones who less than an hour ago were interrupted by a young woman skating home. Now they are po-faced and committed to taking home fish to eat so that they and theirs will not starve.

The speaker behind the bullhorn continues, 'Our *first* Constituent Assembly is what the whole country has been waiting for! This is a new dawn, a new day. Comrades! We are united in the common pursuit to build a better future for ourselves and our children and our grandchildren! And we will not be intimidated or threatened or dispersed as we march with pride to the Tauride Palace today!'

The sea of people roars their courage and Feiga looks up at Viktor and Grishka wedged on either side of her and is filled with such exultation that she feels tears prick her eyes. Indeed, Viktor's beautiful angular face turns down to her and beneath his dark moustache appears a smile.

'Today my friends, we *are* Russia! We seek to change the bourgeoise world order to a working-class world order which will pave the way for a classless society. Together we will forge a philosophy and the Constituent Assembly will ensure that the *whole* of Russia decides on a clear-sighted political agenda with a political program that *will* transform Russia!'

The crowd sways with the nearness of the promised land. They are crossing the sea that the revolution helped part.

'We will march to the Tauride Palace today, where the first Constituent Assembly will take place, and we do this to safeguard justice and democracy!'

Feiga wonders whether it is true that the working class can unite a nation of over 178 million. A nation that covers millions of square kilometres from the Baltic Sea to the Pacific Ocean, from the Black Sea to the Arctic Ocean.

'LONG LIVE THE REVOLUTION!' Cries the speaker and punches the snow-flaked sky.

'LONG LIVE THE REVOLUTION! LONG LIVE THE REVOLUTION! LONG LIVE THE REVOLUTION!' Shout the crowd over and over again and their bodies move forward and back and from side to side, like hundreds of corks tossed about on a shipwrecked sea.

Viktor yells at Feiga, 'You alright, Mouse?' His dark eyes, a mix of amusement and brotherly concern.

She nods. She does feel faint and a little breathless but earlier this morning Grishka had suggested he and Viktor go alone to the rally at Vasilyevsky Island. The crowds would be too big, he had said, in answer to her request to join them. Red Guards were stirring up trouble everywhere and accusing innocents of counter-revolutionary activity, he had added. She knew there would be troublemakers every step of the way across the Dvortsovy Bridge, recently renamed the Republican Bridge, and probably all the way down the Nevsky Prospect and up Liteyny — but she wanted to be with the crowd when it reached the Tauride Palace.

And truthfully, a part of her was a little nervous because they were expecting Lidia any day now. Feiga had tried to make herself useful after returning to Lidia's apartment — cleaning and making meals with whatever Grishka and Viktor had liberated on their endless trips about the city. She had tried to make herself scarce when some of their comrades had turned up, gathering in clandestine clusters to discuss politics and strategies. She knew they spoke of striking terror in the hearts of the Bolsheviks ... and of targeted assassinations. They called themselves freedom fighters — with the holy mandate to secure the revolution for the people (and not for the Bolsheviks!).

Viktor mushes the top of her headscarf with the ball of his fist, an affectionate gesture as another speaker takes the bullhorn and shouts truths to the crowd.

Feiga thinks to herself, at least I can show Lidia when she comes home, today or tomorrow, that I am back in the land of the living and participating in the revolutionary wave of change! Today will be proof of Feiga's commitment to the revolution. It will mean she is of value and believes in what her friends believe and that this might persuade the beautiful Lidia to let her stay on ... for a time ... because, quite frankly, where else can she go?

'We are driven by the principle — that all nations have the right to self-determination! Without this the Socialist Revolution in Russia is impossible!' Feiga joins the crowd and claps rigorously but thinks about her lost youth holed up in a Siberian prison camp and wonders if political action is worth that much.

'Our efforts today are to protect and advance the revolution! Over the past nine weeks, there have been 25 major decrees —'

'The Bolsheviks have no right to take control!' a man behind Feiga heckles.

'Decrees that cover issues such as ...' The speaker ignores the man, 'Peace, land, civic rights, abolition of estates and titles, the judicial system, security, economic planning, workers' control of industry, nationalisation of the bank, civil marriage, the press ...' The crowd boo and hiss at this point signalling their objection to the shutting down of the Socialist Revolutionary newspaper, *Delo Neroda!* by the Red Guards because it refused to submit to the censorious controls of Lenin's government.

The speaker takes up the disquiet and shouts to his crowd, 'That is why my friends — that is why comrades, we must march to the *first* Constituent Assembly being held this afternoon to show our complete and utter support for a fully representative and responsible government — one that is democratically elected and answers to the will of the people!' Feiga's ears hurt with the fiery response from the crowd and, even though she joins in, there is a dark quiet place inside her that ... doesn't believe. Now that the Bolsheviks have the power, why would they ever give it up?

'Make no mistake, we are still in the midst of the greatest proletarian revolution which is about to transform the machinery and practice of the state into a vehicle of working-class rule!' The crowd goes mad for this newfound language because, for the very first time in Russian history, they are placed at the centre of the nation's narrative.

Feiga forgets to join in and closes her eyes, which are so tender in the daylight. She feels the softest snowflakes touch her eyelids. She thinks about the working class and rather than be filled with hope, she feels dismayed — how can the hope of a nation be in its most uneducated, its most unenlightened, its most uninspired, she wonders.

All of a sudden there is a shift in the crowd.

Feiga opens her eyes and looks about. Heads are craning, people are shoving and then voices start chanting: *KERENSKY! KERENSKY!* Feiga can see nothing except the backs and shoulders and heads of those around her.

Viktor shouts across her to Grishka, 'I told you!' And both men are grinning like they've won the lottery.

The speaker up ahead who has control of the bullhorn is trying to regain the crowd. 'Comrades let us make this a monumental day —'

'KERENSKY! KERENSKY! WE WANT KERENSKY!'

'People! People! Please, we need to move in an orderly fashion across the Republican Bridge and then up the Nevsky —'

'KERENSKY! KERENSKY!' There's a heady mix of laughter, nerves, and excitement. The entire crowd is convinced that the rumours of Kerensky attending this rally are true.

Feiga's heart begins to race.

People all around her in the crowd are confirming to one another that at this very moment that the Prime Minister is returning! Any moment now!

The organiser on the bullhorn tries a different tack: 'Let us remember that the idea of the Constituent Assembly has been in the hearts and minds of the greatest Russians for the past hundred years and so today holds enormous significance —'

'KERENSKY! KERENSKY! WE WANT KERENSKY!' The crowd is steadfast in its knowledge that here and now Kerensky will appear. If the revolution has taught them anything it has taught them they have the power. They can make imperial autocracy tumble. They can bring oppression to its knees. And they can turn the tide of history — because there is nothing more powerful than the will of the people. This is their truth!

'We, conscientious workers and honest soldiers are gathered here in the name of Russia and we demand those in charge, the Sovnarkom —' Booing and hissing follow because the Sovnarkom is the Council of People's Commissars, Lenin's government, and the rally has been organised by the Socialist Revolutionaries.

'We demand that our current leaders are held accountable! And we will demand that this, our *first* Constituent Assembly, is the beginning of a new Russia! LONG LIVE THE REVOLUTION!' Cheering and euphoria as the great ocean of people commence their exodus from the Vasilyevsky Island and head over the bridge to reach the Tauride Palace.

The crowd chants, 'LONG LIVE THE REVOLUTION!' as well as, 'KERENSKY NOW!'

News has spread that Kerensky is out of hiding and is joining the rally today. Many of the protestors believe he'll be re-elected by the Constituent Assembly as the rightful leader of the Revolution and, therefore, the government.

Feiga looks back but all she can see is a human wave pouring ever onwards and then she thinks she hears something else, something wrong.

Grishka and Viktor have both stopped and one of them reaches out for her as they move to the side of the bridge. All three are looking back and then other members of the crowd are doing the same until it cannot be denied that there are catcalls and jeering and taunts of derision being spat at the marchers: 'BOURGEOISE! ... INTELLIGENTSIA!'

Viktor growls, 'Red Guards!'

'Come on!' Grishka grabs Feiga's arm, 'Let's get ahead of these brutes and move to the front of the crowd.'

Viktor moves in swiftly behind herself and Grishka, and together the three of them push and shove their way through the supporters who, up until this point, have been filled with hope, goodwill, and cheer. Their pace quickens.

Feiga finds herself quickly out of breath but there is no getting away from Grishka's fierce grip and just as they make it across the bridge, the pushing and shoving become more deliberate, more aggressive. The infiltrators are now openly causing havoc. She sees Grishka glance across at Viktor and something passes between them — a knowing, a strategy already devised, a decision made in the lead up to this day. And Feiga thinks about how the Bolsheviks, like those in power before them, will stop at nothing to curb and condemn individuals who refuse to bow down to their authority. If there is one thing she has learned it is that freedom never, ever belongs to everyone. No matter what they say.

Then bottles are flying through the air and smashing on railings, cobblestones, and the crowd.

Whistles blow in a frenzy of disruption and the Red Guard infiltrators are roaring *DOWN WITH COUNTER-REVOLUTIONS!* over and over again.

'Hurry!' Grishka has his arm around Feiga's head and shoulders. 'Let's move out of the Palace Square. Come on!'

Some of the crowd has turned to face the Red Guards to argue they have the right to march in support of the Constituent Assembly. Viktor, Grishka, and Feiga want to get out of the Palace Square but the Nevsky Prospect is tight and narrow with buildings that tower on either side of them. It doesn't take them long before they are crossing the Moyka River but the Red Guards are pouring into their procession from the side streets. Feiga grips onto Grishka's coat and she can hear Viktor cussing.

The rally has no intention of dispersing: 'LONG LIVE THE REVOLUTION! LONG LIVE THE REVOLUTION! ... KERENSKY NOW! KERENSKY NOW! ... DEMOCRACY AND LIBERTY! DEMOCRACY AND LIBERTY!' The call and response rebound off the buildings and it would seem that all of Russia is in accord. Then a barrage of stones is airborne and one narrowly misses Grishka's unruly mess of hair.

'Keep together!' calls Grishka to Viktor and Feiga because now bodies are heaving past them.

'Over to the cathedral!' yells Viktor and the three of them barge through the crowd until they reach Our Lady of Kazan's small semi-circular colonnaded walkway. The columns will surely offer them protection, thinks Feiga, but that's when she hears the first gunshot.

There is a moment when the crowd on the Nevsky seems to freeze. No one moves, speaks, breathes. Then the moment vanishes and people are running faster than they have ever run in their lives. The pell-mell of young people, old people, women, children, factory workers, and soldiers cannot drown out the noise of gunfire and Grishka is pushing Feiga down behind one of the colonnades. He is crouching alongside her with Viktor on the other side. She stops hearing the relentless staccato crack of gunshots. She stops hearing the pounding of boots running hard. She stops hearing the screaming and yelling. She stops hearing Grishka shouting. She stops hearing Viktor swearing. All she can hear, with her eyes, screwed shut and her mouth open in an anguished maw is the wounded sending up their harrowing grief to a God who has forsaken them.

'We need to get her to safety,' Grishka says as he picks up Feiga, who seems almost weightless. 'We need to take her over to Maria Spiridonova's apartment.'

Viktor is already in the lead pounding along the Catherine Canal that will eventually take them to the Mariinsky Theatre near where the well-loved leader of the Left Socialist Revolutionaries lives. The mayhem caused by the Red Guards still reverberates behind them as they run for their lives. Has Feiga fainted? Grishka can't tell, he sees her eyelids flutter against his chest as he charges behind Viktor.

'Look out!' Viktor shouts and Grishka jumps back from the curb just as a vehicle careens around the corner. The driver squeals to a halt. A head pops out of the driver's window and both Grishka and Viktor can't believe it.

'Leonid! What the hell?'

Kerensky's aid-de-camp leaps out of the braked vehicle and hugs his beloved and then looks down at Grishka's bundle exclaiming, 'Good God, tell me she hasn't been shot?'

'No, no.' Grishka speaks quietly as if she is sleeping, 'Shock. We think it's shock.'

'You know those bastards up there have just opened fire on innocent people!' spits Viktor.

Leonid puts a warm hand on Viktor's neck and says, 'Yes, we heard as much. That's why we have changed our plans.' He nods towards the vehicle, 'I'm headed to Finlyandsky Station. To make sure he gets out — we never even made it to Vasilyevsky Island.' Everyone knows it is Kerensky but no one will say his name, not now, not after the blood has been shed for even suggesting it could be the will of the people to have him reinstated. 'Look, I don't have much time but I can take you guys to a hospital or ...'

'No we are headed to Spiridonova's,' Grishka says quickly. 'Can you take us there and then I think Feiga should be ...'

'Of course —'

'Actually,' interrupts Viktor. 'I'll go with you to the station. Grishka, will you be alright with Feiga? I can then go on foot along to Lidia's apartment and see if she is there and let her know where you are ...'

Viktor is looking at Leonid with such longing that Grishka needs to look away. He tells himself that it makes sense. After Leonid sees Kerensky off at Finlyandsky, they would want to be together, their time is always short-lived.

'We've got to go!' calls Leonid as he whips into the driver's seat.

'You don't mind, do you?' Viktor is never this solicitous and Grishka immediately feels guilty because, of course, he does mind — he wants to be the one who bursts open Lidia's door and enfolds her in his arms, without another person present.

'We'll be fine,' Grishka assures his friend as they clamber into the vehicle, its engine already thrumming. 'Just make sure you tell Lidia what a goddamn hero I've been to Feiga.'

In the corner of the back seat sits a railway worker with a ragged beard, a cap jammed low on his forehead, and hands ingrained with grease. It's Kerensky.

3

For almost a hundred years the finest Russians have lived by the idea of a Constituent Assembly ... In the struggle for this idea, thousands of the intelligentsia and tens of thousands of workers and peasants have perished in prisons, in exile, in hard labour, on the gallows, and by the brutal bullets as ordered by the Tsar.

Viktor shakes *The Grey Overcoat*, the Socialist Revolutionary newspaper, and reads on.

Rivers of blood have been spilled on the sacrificial altar of this sacred idea because the People's Commissars, Lenin's Government, gave orders to shoot down the people demonstrating in honour of the first Constituent Assembly.

And Viktor thinks, Maxim Gorky's critique of the infamous events of yesterday is nothing less than a coruscation of truth.

The Bolshevik propaganda mouthpiece, Pravda, lies when it writes that the demonstration yesterday was organised by the bourgeoise and the bankers. Pravda lies because it knows that the bourgeoise has no reason to rejoice in the opening of the Constituent Assembly.

Viktor looks up because he thinks Lidia has stirred but he is mistaken.

Pravda also knows that the workers of the Obukhov and the Patronny factories took part in yesterday's rally. And it was precisely these workers, among many others, who were shot by order of the Cheka, Lenin's secret police, and however much Pravda lies, it cannot hide this shameful fact!

Viktor sips his lukewarm tea and thinks about his unmitigated hatred of the Cheka and its growing reputation as a brutal shock troop rather than a militia upholding order. This organisation of secret police is running amuck in its attempt to ensure the will of the ruling class. He sighs and looks out the dirty kitchen window of Lidia's apartment. It's nearly midday but the day has no intention of waking up. It slumbers on in the hard riot of steel-blue clouds above.

Again Viktor glances back at Lidia, still as death on her sofa bed in the living room that is just an extension of the kitchen. He lights a cigarette and picks up the other paper he managed to get hold of this morning. But instead of opening the *Pravda*, he watches the top of Lidia's blonde head and the way her body disappears into a bundle of rugs and coats. He inhales then reaches out and ashes his cigarette over his tea glass.

Yesterday, Leonid had disclosed that Kerensky left the estate of Lidia's father sometime in early December. Leonid had helped Kerensky move to Novgorod, then back to a hunting lodge at Bologoye, a railway junction halfway between Moscow and Petrograd. A week ago Leonid had taken Kerensky to Belenky at some timber merchant's property but a few days later Kerensky insisted he come back to Petrograd, where he was to make a surprise appearance at yesterday's rally.

Once they got to Finlyandsky Railway Station Leonid dashed off with Kerensky but after several minutes, with the whistle of the steam train screeching in the background, had run back to say there had been a change of plans. Kerensky was insisting Leonid go with him to Finland. *For the time being*, added Leonid as he stole a furtive kiss from Viktor in a hug goodbye, and flew back. So, Viktor made his way to Lidia's, alone. He was more than a little dispirited.

When Viktor had arrived at her apartment yesterday, he was horrified. There's no other way to put it. He had knocked on the door and while there was no immediate response, something made him wait.

He knocked again.

The old lady next door opened her door a crack, and it was the way she looked at him that made him unable to walk on down the stairwell.

He knocked a third time and then he heard it, the rustling of a wounded animal.

'Lidia,' he had called gently. 'It's me. Viktor.' Pause. 'Open the door, Cat-eyes.'

Then he heard a few unsteady footsteps, the door unbolting from inside, and there she was. As soon as he saw her, he knew. He moved into the apartment cautiously, not wanting to scare her, and bolted the door behind. She returned to the kitchen chair where she had been bathing her face and hands and God knows what else. He saw how the left side of her face was so swollen her eye was shut and there were cuts and abrasions on the right side. Her bottom lip jutted out unnaturally and there were bruises around her wrists and up her arm. She didn't speak.

After a while, he went to the sink and said, 'I'm just going to make us some tea, Lidia.'

Eventually, the tale came out in fits and bursts. Her voice had been monotone and never once did she look at him. By the time she got to the part where she was raped in an empty warehouse, she had stopped bathing her wounds.

Viktor had picked up her glass of tea and gently held it to her lips until she opened her poor mouth and sipped painfully. He heard himself say *Good girl* and *There you go* and *One more sip* and *Well done*. His voice was serene. His heart, a broiling rage of hate.

Later, as time disappeared into the cracks of the room, he helped her undress in the moonlit darkling. He had heated some water and slowly assisted her to step into the large wide bucket that she kept to sluice her body.

Last night her pale limbs looked like broken saplings, white and luminous.

He took the washer and moved warm water across her back and around to her neck and arms, he even reached down and wiped those long legs of hers. Perhaps he was repeating endearments to her, he cannot remember, but she was his daughter, his mother, his sister ... she was every Russian woman — and a certain Russian man — who had been forced against their will.

Wonton destruction. A spoiling that would be carried deep beneath the skin.

At some point, Lidia took the washer from him, and while he went back to the kitchen stove to make up more hot water he had heard her whimper as she attempted to clean the most soiled part of her body.

When it was done, he had made up the sofa bed, tucked her in but despite the sub-zero temperatures outside, she had begun to burn and tremble. Her body was flushed. He ignored her requests to open the window. He had seen this before after the battle had been fought, where the so-called survivors had rattled and sweated their way back to the present tense.

But before she had fallen asleep, she had forced him to promise he would say nothing to Grishka. He regretted it even before he gave her his word that he would never mention anything. She had clawed at his arm with such ferocity that there was no other choice. Besides, it was her truth to tell, not his and yet … She slept, or so he thought. He had given her some brandy — he knew where Grishka kept his supply — and as he tucked himself into a mess of thick blankets on the floor, he drank the rest of it. Time passed and in the dark, with the moon outside watching with complete indifference, he found himself crying.

Viktor rustles the Bolshevik rag, *Pravda*, open and begins to read.

Yesterday the first Constituent Assembly took place in the Tauride Palace. A right-wing demonstration had been held earlier, marching in from the Vasilyevsky Island through the city. This was mostly attended by the petty bourgeoise: bankers, clerks, and intellectuals. They were easily dispersed.

Viktor gives a derisive snort. Guns do make dispersing unarmed peaceful marchers easy.

This botched insurrection added to the tension of recent days where the plans of a right-wing Socialist Revolutionary terrorist cell to abduct and assassinate Comrade Lenin and Comrade Trotsky had been leaked.

There are no plans, you fuckers, Viktor says to himself. The Bolshevik's inner circle is being infiltrated by the Battle Unit but the specific details of targeted assassinations are strictly prohibited between members. Everyone in the Battle Unit operates as a singular cell and the less said about how one plans to strike terror in the souls of the all-powerful Bolshevik party, the better.

Despite this insurrection, the Constituent Assembly took place. However, as very little was achieved because so much had already been realised in the decrees issued by Comrade Lenin, the Constituent Assembly is now obsolete.

Viktor blinks at the last word he has read. Surely, this is not happening.

The Constituent Assembly, a bourgeoise obsession, was bound to become an obstacle in the path of the Revolution and soviet power. Accordingly, the Central Executive Committee resolves that the Constituent Assembly is hereby dissolved.

What utter bullshit, Viktor thinks. They will never get away with it! He tosses the newspaper aside. Yesterday was the turning point. Today and for every day to come, he will work tirelessly, with like-minded others, to take back the reins of the revolution for the Socialist Revolutionaries! Their way is democratic and intolerant of the radical manipulation of truth and justice. The power of the Revolution must be returned to the people!

Viktor stands up. He needs to piss and he also needs to dash back over the bridge to his apartment to bring back some supplies. He'll be back before Lidia is awake. Viktor glances once again at her and unbolts the door, then heads on out.

When the door closes behind him Lidia opens her eyes but she has been awake for a long time. She lets herself think about the moment when Viktor turned up but she will not think of what happened earlier. She turns her head and looks out the window. The day is a turbulence of clouds and she watches them nudge and push each other across the cold cold sky. She doesn't touch her face, she doesn't need to. She can feel the swelling has subsided but she is stiff and sore even when she shifts, momentarily.

Lidia closes her eyes and thinks of the forest around her father's estate and how she spent most of the past two months there. She tries to hear the sound of snow falling from the branches and twigs. She tries to remember the crunch underfoot and the way the snow crystalizes and shards. She tries to feel the touch of the weak mid-winter sun on her upturned face.

Lidia stands in the forest and reaches her right hand high above her head until it touches a low-hanging branch. The snow is clean and pure. She scoops some up in her fingers and brings this down to her lips where it runs cool and bright into her mouth and its healing powers illuminate her body until she stands tall and strong a powerfully lit beacon.

She is unspoiled.

She is whole.

She is found.

After a while, her mind comes back to her apartment, the sofa, and the damaged broken parts of her body, which, once again, don't feel as if they are hers. She opens her eyes and the tears that slide down the side of her face and into her hair cannot be stopped.

9

Love and Daring

Tobolsk, West Siberia. January 1918.

'In French! In French!' Pierre Gilliard says, good-humouredly, as he gazes out the study window to the snow-filled yard below. He hears Alexei flop back on his wooden chair and exhale noisily.

This is then followed by the young 13 year old Tsarevitch saying laboriously, in French, 'The usurper wants the new calendar to force the peasants to work on feast days.'

Tutor Gilliard turns back to his pupil and a quick smile appears beneath his moustache and above his goatee, 'Hmmm, that could be one's opinion, or, one might consider the history of Russia and acknowledge this has been a decision the whole of Russia has been moving toward for quite some time. One might say...' The tutor unravels the rubber bands from the slingshot that is being constructed by Alexei about his pencil, 'One might say that embracing the Gregorian calendar is in keeping with the zeitgeist.'

The Swiss scholar waits behind the pupil's chair and as if coming out of a deep slumber Alexei bobs his head up and says, 'Zeitgeist — I know this one — hang on — we did it yesterday or the day before ...'

Gilliard loves his charges but they would test the patience of Job.

'Yes! German. Or Swiss —'

'German,' intones the tutor.

'Yes, well same thing — only kidding.' The boy stifles a giggle and tries to catch the thread of memory before it returns to the canvas of boredom, 'Yes! German. *Zeit* means time and *geist* means ghost — no — spirit. So the spirit of one's time!' Alexei triumphantly swings back on the hind legs of his wooden chair and in his usual measured way, Gilliard gently pushes it back so that the young pupil is safely sitting on all four legs of the chair.

'Go on.' Gilliard walks on by and warns, 'In French.'

'Let's go out to Papa, please Tutor Gilliard! I can hear him chopping wood and he promised I could help him this morning!'

Gilliard doesn't even look at the fine-featured little fellow with his earnest grey-blue eyes.

Alexei whines, 'Or what about tobogganing?!'

There's no way the Tsarevitch, also known ridiculously as *Baby* as well as the less obnoxious but still infantile *Alyosha*, is ever going to let up, thinks Gilliard.

He sighs, 'It is far too cold outside for you to go tobogganing, and that rough and tumble stuff is ...' He is going to say *dangerous for you, with your condition* but knows better than any of them this is too cruel. So, he ends his sentence with, 'Too undignified for the future Emperor of Russia who must be linguistically capable in the many languages of Europe.'

The young boy groans and continues in monotone with his French Conversation class, 'Today is February 14 according to the new Gregorian calendar, but according to the old, the Julian, it is February 1. The usurper —'

'Comrade Lenin,' corrects Gilliard because if there is one thing he insists upon it is that language should be used to ensure your survival — never mind the survival of the language.

'Comrade Lenin,' Alexei thumps a fist lightly on the table as if to register his protest at being banned from using a pejorative moniker. 'Has — Gilliard how do you say commanded but, you know, like to —'

'Decreed.'

'Yes, that's it. I knew it was decreed ... Lenin has decreed that the new Western European calendar will keep Russia in harmony with other civilised countries — Tutor Gilliard?'

'Yes, Tsarevitch Alexei?'

'How are we going to keep in harmony with England and France now that the Bolsheviks have prohibited the Russian soldiers to fight alongside our allies?'

From the moment he arrived in Russia, some 14 years ago, the Swiss tutor noted how Russians did not shield their children from knowledge. He looks out the window and watches the man lining up a felled tree across a forester's log bench.

'A good question, but one that will be considered in our lesson *after* supper when the newspapers have been read.'

In some ways, he hopes this topic might be forgotten by the impressionable young lad because Gilliard knows he needs to carefully navigate the topic of Trotsky's peace discussions with the Germans. As a born and raised Swiss he is, of course, disinterested in war and believes the best plan is to educate the nation's population into a civilised people so that, as a consequence, war will become an obsolete tool for nation-building. His theory is troubled by Germany's compulsory education program and yet it remains a belligerent nation like no other.

'Please continue your precis on the events of today with the introduction of the Western European calendar.'

Alexei already knows there is no getting out of it and wonders to himself, what difference does it make? Sure, when he woke up this morning and remembered the day's significance, he ran into Mother's room and told her that she looked nearly two weeks older than when she had kissed him last night! She had tried to grab him and give him one of her long cuddles but he managed to skip past her ever-reaching arms and hurry along to his dyad'ka, Nagorny, to be dressed and readied for the day ahead ... which he knew would be exactly like the day before and the day before that.

'There are some who are concerned with the introduction of the new calendar but their concerns have been ignored ...' Gilliard over-looks the insertion of opinion rather than fact and Alexei moves on swiftly, adding, 'The holy Russian Orthodox Church notes that the introduction of the new calendar means that many sacred holy days will now be lost ...'

The boy pauses not because he minds Gilliard, in fact, he rather likes him, despite his strict manner, but because it is boring to speak French and boring to talk about the calendar which is not going to make a single iota of difference to him because nothing is ever going to ever happen to him again! Indeed, he longs for the days when he was at Army Headquarters with Papa and soldiering about with the men.

The boy notices that his tutor has lost interest in the topic be-cause the voice of the fresh-faced dimpled-smiling Shura can be heard just outside the door of the study. The maid is giving some last-minute instructions to Anastasia. Alexei latches on to the dis-traction, particularly in the light of the fact that his tutor seems to have turned to wax with a silly faraway look on his face.

'I think Anastasia's maid has a crush on someone in the house-hold,' Alexei has abandoned French in preference of Russian.

After a few moments, the tutor breaks out of his private reverie and is now sternly re-tightening his tie which really couldn't be any tighter, saying 'Get on with —'

'But it is true! My sister told me that Shura has a sweetheart,' he asserts in Russian even though he hasn't been told anything of the sort. Alexei is ever observant and knows that the young maid to his sister is pretty enough, with her sweep of auburn hair and small hands. She could be anyone's sweetheart and, as far as Alexei is concerned, Gilliard needs something to distract him from these tedious French Conversation topics.

'She told me ...' Alexei is enjoying himself now that he has left the odious French behind and can allow his imagination to run amuck in Russian, 'That she likes someone ... She said he is the smartest and kindest ...' Alexei doesn't know what else to say, already it sounds too soppy for words, 'Oh and handsome.'

Then to his surprise, his tutor asks, 'Did she say who?'

The question hangs between them for one then two then three seconds until the young boy adds thoughtfully, 'Actually, Shura didn't say his name but I can tell you who it is *not!*'

'Oh yes?' responds Gilliard vaguely.

'It is not Pavel — Pavel Konoplev. The Captain of the Guards.'

Gilliard thinks to himself that this is a strange comment, not only because he never really thinks of the guards as part of the household but because some memory niggles at the edge of his brain ... something that happened several weeks back at the children's presentation of the Chekov play ... something that he is just not quite able to put his finger on.

Then Gilliard hears his young pupil say in a stage whisper, 'Captain Konoplev is in love with Olga and she is in love with him!'

Alexei has forgotten all about Shura and is now keenly watching Gilliard's face which changes like clouds in a windy sky — first confusion, then realisation followed finally by adult censorship — an expression to which Alexei is more than familiar.

'One should never speak about personal matters, especially those of the fairer sex, and especially never about one's own family —'

'But it's true! I saw them together tobogganing —'

'No. No. It will not be spoken about again. This is not right and I am sure your father would be disappointed if he knew that your

French Conversation lesson today has been wasted. We will return to our topic of the adoption of the Western European calendar by Russia. Please continue.' Gilliard turns his back to his pupil and he hears the boy stumble about in French, listing some facts concerning the new calendar and adding a few embellishments or opinions.

The women's voices outside the study door move on and the tutor, despite his best efforts, has gone with them. Shura ... Everywhere he looks he sees her. Somehow she is there at the top of the staircase as he runs up to commence the lessons with the Romanov children. And as he dashes from the house across the road where he resides, along with the Doctor and several other household members, Shura is there laughing with one of the other maids or house girls. She is ever-present. And although she never really looks directly at him, he feels more conspicuous and self-conscious than in anybody else's presence.

'... And the farmers and peasants are also inclined to ignore the new calendar and get on with their working day lives in the same old way as they always have according to nature ...'

The breath-taking beauty of nature, Gilliard thinks as he looks out the window at the endless snow that wraps the hills beyond, cowls the town's collection of small buildings, covers the road that divides the residences of the staff from that of the family and fills the yard below him. There he watches the man sawing off the branches of a tree after which he commences cutting the trunk into logs. How strange the world has become, Gillard thinks, and yet it all feels so normal. Somehow all this — this sense of entrapment, where the great imperial ruler is now the forester, where the princess yearns for a lame Bolshevik and the scholar of several languages — it nearly makes him wince — is in love with an illiterate housemaid. There I have said it, he tells himself.

'... And so the great Emperor of Russia, Tsar Nicholas 1, believed that taking on the Gregorian calendar would offer no advantages to Russia, whatsoever, and it would only lead to inconveniences and difficulties ... That was my great grandfather — No, wait ... My great-great grandfather ...'

Should I ever be, one day, someone's grandfather, the tutor muses as he watches Alexei's oldest sister step out through a side door of the Governor's house and wrap a long knitted scarf about her face. Gilliard doesn't think about the unfortunate fact that he is 39 and still a virgin. Surely in this strange new world in which they find themselves, everything and anything is possible? Would the young 20 year old Shura give him children if they ever did marry? But what is he thinking! This is nonsense.

He watches the Grand Duchess call out something to her father and head toward the gate that is guarded by soldiers who still treat the family deferentially. Gilliard ponders Olga and Pavel's alleged affaire de coeur and wonders whether it all just makes complete sense. After all, every one of them has been thrown into this brand new world where the old ways are no longer viable and, if anything, the new calendar surely reinforces to every Russian that these are our times, our destiny, our new world!

'... Up until the end of the 15th Century, the new year in Russia began on March 1. Then Peter the Great — my great great ... never mind — decreed that the new year would be January 1 which comes before the birth of our Lord, which is January 7 ... Oh — and I forgot, but the real reason is that the Julian calendar has too many leap years ...'

Perhaps, one must take a leap of faith, Gilliard tells himself as he watches the Grand Duchess leave the gated house and walk alongside a limping captain who carries a wooden toboggan under his right arm and ... surely not ... holds the gloved hand of Olga in his left?! A leap of faith, the tutor thinks aghast. And just like that, Shura's voice is heard once again outside the study door and his heart leaps!

Gilliard turns about and sees that his pupil has left the desk and is now hidden behind the large settee at the back of the study. He can't see the child but he knows he is there. His books are scattered about and his chewed pencil rolls quietly to the edge of the desk and plops off onto the rugged floor.

Gilliard knows he needs to get back to the job at hand and to set the next day's topical discussion for the French Conversation hour. Indeed, getting off task never would have happened in the palace or wherever they travelled before the family's house arrest. Of course, he had been given the option to leave and abandon the family but he had realised they were all he had. These rather ordinary people with their simple delights and secret fears. Besides, as the children's tutor, he has meaning, he has a purpose and it is greater than just the teaching of languages. Being the tutor has, he realises, become the very reason he exists because, without him, these children would have no one. And so he chooses to continue with them — out here in this godforsaken wilderness of Siberia and yet it is here that he has found the greatest surprise ... that there is someone for him, someone who might, one day, love him.

Gilliard forces himself to come back to this present moment in the study. He coughs affectedly and says, 'Lost your pencil, Tsarevitch Alexei?' He hears a stifled snort from the boy. He should let Alexei have an early mark, he ponders to himself. Maybe he should be allowed to go tobogganing ... Gilliard looks back out the window and thinks, maybe I should give myself an early mark. Because what he wants more than anything is to be out in the soft undulating snow with Shura and that dimpled laugh of hers.

2

The eldest Romanov girl and Captain Pavel Konoplev, who carries her wooden toboggan under his arm, walk slowly toward the

Kremlin walls of Tobolsk. Olga doesn't think about their destination — the steep slopes on the other side of the Kremlin that plunge to the sweep of the river plain — where her sisters and some of the household staff are tobogganing. Nor does she think about the stuffy house where winter and politics imprison her and frustrate her longing. What she does think about, is Pavel. Their walk slackens and he stops, leans down, balls up snow in his gloved fists, stands, and pulls back his arm as if to lob high and away but she has seen this ruse before and jumps behind him.

'Ahh — you have no faith, Olenka.' And his snowball flies high and splats against a tree.

'I can't trust you.' Olga is thumping together a small tight snowball, 'I have learned the hard way — that you are untrustworthy —'

'You be careful with that weapon — remember — you are only a girl —'

'I'll show you what a girl can do!'

And Pavel watches on amused as she runs back behind him to use him as a target.

'Don't you get any ideas, girl!'

Her snowball hits him square in the right shoulder and he half collapses like a man wounded by shrapnel on the battlefield. He's groaning and staggering and she is nothing but a peel of laughter and for a split second, they are ordinary sweethearts playing about in the snow, cavorting with the familiarity of newlyweds whose successful nuptials draw them deliciously close to one another, again and again.

And just as quickly as it starts, it stops.

The couple stroll closer to the Kremlin walls and espy the onion domes of the Cathedral of St Sophia: midnight blue and God's gold. They both know that these moments alone are getting harder and harder to snatch.

'Will winter ever end?' asks Olga as she leans her back against one of the trees that line the path. She looks beyond Pavel but she wants him to press his strong body against her and say *I love you*. She knows he does love her but she needs to hear the declaration, once again.

Pavel picks up a thin branch and begins switching it back and forth against another tree.

'What's wrong?' she asks. Their time alone is precious and normally he takes advantage, as does she, of any excuse to kiss and hold each other close.

At first, Pavel doesn't respond but then he drops the branch and comes across and slouches alongside her, 'Everything is happening in Petrograd and yet here we are ... This huge moment in history is taking place but ... God ... Siberia of all places! We might as well be in ...' and he fails to name the farthest place from Russia, so finishes his despair with 'Some strange foreign country!'

She pushes her shoulder and arm against his because this is all she wants — to be here with him, just him and her, just them — here or there, it doesn't matter where, as long as they can be together. Forever. She tells herself to take it slowly and speak to him calmly but she also feels the tug of tears in her eyes.

'Pavel, I don't understand ... at least we are together, and ...' She tries to keep her breathing steady but she realises he is the one reason why she hasn't lost hope. In him, she has a future. In him, she has a belief that there is a purpose for her being on this earth. Without him, she would have lived 22 years for no reason, whatsoever.

'Olenka ...'

She turns her face close to him but instead of kissing her, he looks into her eyes and then pushes some stray hair back up into her knitted woollen scarf that is wrapped about her head and face, and neck.

'But I thought you said it was possible ...' She can hear the panic rising in her voice as she continues, 'You said it was possible — we could escape and get away together and ... in the spring — you said in the spring ...' And she grips his hand like a woman drowning.

He looks away and says, 'But so much is happening. Not just our future — but everyone's future is uncertain ... At least if we were in Petrograd we could be better informed and know exactly what is happening — I mean we are still receiving newspapers a week late, who knows what's happening right now — '

'We could be happening right now.'

Pavel lets her pull him a little toward her and then he is unable to stop because she is the most wonderful girl he has ever met and her retroussé nose is adorable and her cheekbones are exquisite and her tall slim body is strong and her lips are soft and generous. They kiss and kiss and then he buries his hands up inside her thick coat until he can feel the slight rise of her breasts and he pushes against them hard and her mouth opens in response and he thinks he hears her groan and he knows they should stop but he presses himself up against her and she groans again and this time it is unmistakable and he knows that she wants him.

At the same time — slowly — reluctantly — he begins to pull away and says, 'We have to stop ...' He is unconvinced by his own words.

She continues kissing and he hears her mumble, 'Why? Why Pavel?'

'I have to stop — because — because — I love you and ...'

They peel apart and he knows, without looking at her, she is smiling but his heart is crowded with a litany of anguish and heartache. He tells himself to toughen up. They watch the clouds scoop and flounder above them. They cannot hear her sisters' having fun on the other side of the Kremlin nor can they see the dark Tobol River far below — it is just the two of them here, right now. Olga rests her head on his shoulder and he has her hand and arm entwined in his and they lean up against the tree as if they have all the time in the world, despite both knowing this is not true.

'The thing is ...' Pavel hears his voice before he realises he is going to speak, 'The thing is ... There's a new constitution now, in Russia, and ... Well now that Russia is a Soviet Republic ...' He is surprised she hasn't begun arguing which is her want whenever they talk about the current state of politics, 'And any previous ruling classes are barred from holding power, so that means, well what it means —'

'That we can be together and live ordinary lives,' she interrupts and her voice is without hesitation or angst. 'In other words, no one will expect me to live out a life that is filled with imperial obligations — I will be — I will be just an *ordinary* ... person ...' And her voice trails off in wonder. She thinks: Ordinary. From the Old French, *ordinaire*, and before that Latin, *ordinarius*. Suggesting order is restored by the commonplace, the normal. This is better than anything she had dared hope. Now Papa and Mother must approve of her marrying Pavel because all her sisters will have to marry ordinary men and so — let me be the first, she thinks.

'Well ... it's a little more complicated than that, my love.' His voice is soft, 'You see all power is given to the workers and the soldiers —'

'But Pavel, *you* are a soldier and I — well I can be ...' She hesitates then adds quietly, 'I can be your wife, a soldier's wife ...' She wonders why he cannot see how wonderous this brave new world is — where a love that once would have been unimaginable is now real. Besides, anything is better than being stuck in the Governor's mansion as a prisoner!

'All power will be with Comrade Lenin.' He knows the bluntness of this truth is brutal but she needs to hear it from someone and preferably someone she can trust because God knows that ridiculous father of hers needs to understand that the time has come for him to separate himself from his family — if the rest of them are to survive. 'Olga.' The abandonment of his affectionate use of *Olenka* makes him sound strangely formal and she looks across at his dark features as he continues, 'There is a massive mobilisation going on now, as we speak, by the Red Army against counter-revolutionary forces. And as I am a committed Bolshevik I believe ...'

She pulls away from him and pushes herself off the tree trunk. 'Why do you always have to bring our discussions around to those — to those — bloody Bolsheviks? How can you be a Bolshevik when you fought for your Tsar just a year ago against the Germans?'

'Yes that's right, and men — my comrades — were dying like flies because their lives meant nothing to him — their lives were just wasted on a useless cause! Can you understand me when I tell you no one cared for us — out there at the Front — no one! Not the colonels, not the generals, and not the goddamn Tsar!'

She has turned her back on him and he thinks he won't be able to bear it, to be outside of her orbit of love. He knows he has gone too far. He knows he should make his plan and go through with it but he knows he cannot live without her. Pavel also knows that his beloved must distance herself from her father and family if she is to make it with him, she cannot come encumbered by them. Besides, the whole of Tobolsk is rapidly becoming Bolshevik and he needs to get her away from here as quickly as possible, and up north ... somewhere. He knows he needs to do better than this vague plan but so far this is all he has — *go north* — and then, in time, return to the anonymity of the city of Petrograd, or better still Moscow.

'Come here.' She doesn't respond to his request and so he says, again, 'Come here, my Olenka.'

She turns and her face is pale as she says, 'Did you know that the Polish Legion has declared war on the Bolsheviks? And other loyalists will follow! The Poles don't want to end the war —'

'The Poles don't want to end the war *yet* because they don't want to be subsumed into the Russian or German empires. They want to fight their way into an independent Poland —'

'How stupid —'

'Be that as it may ...' Pavel pulls her close to him and wraps his arms about her tightly, 'Comrade Trotsky is already negotiating a peace settlement with Germany. The fighting has been going on for over three years and Russia is worse off than when we started.' No soldier who has seen the Front desires the war to continue. It has all been a sickening waste of time — one that he can barely bring himself to think about. No matter what, the war must end.

'But *that* Jewish weasel is going to concede so much of Russia's land and resources to those filthy Huns!'

He hears the pain in her voice and he admits this is something he finds very hard to stomach but if the alternative is the return of even one Russian soldier to the Front then he wants Trotsky to negotiate peace. But he decides on a different tack.

'Spring will be here soon, Olenka.'

She knows what this means and she straightens up in his arms and looks him in the eye because she wants to be very sure that he is as committed as she.

'And when it comes, my love, you must be ready to leave ... You and me. I know it will be hard. But you are a grown woman now ... And if you love me ... If you love me ...'

She presses her lips to his and they are soldered there for an eternity and she has forgotten the tobogganing, a ploy to get away and be alone. In the arms of her lover, she thinks of the shock and mayhem of the word *love*. Love. From Old English, *lufu*, meaning romantic sexual attraction. Before that from the Old High Germanic, *liubi*, meaning joy, with its roots in *leubh*, to care.

He pulls back and says determinedly because they have so little time left, 'I will make all the arrangements. You will bring nothing but yourself and the clothes you are wearing on the day. Do you understand? And we will go. North, first. And then ... You will take my name. When it is safe we will go to one of the big cities. I will always look after you. You know that, don't you Olenka? You will need no one but me. You and me. Just us.'

3

The young 13 year old sits at the top of the stairs on the enormous silver tray, engraved with the United Kingdom's coat of arms. A treasured wedding gift from his mother's English grandmother, Queen Victoria. He has always liked the lion but is particularly fond of the unicorn. He drags himself so that he is perilously balanced on the top step, its carpeted descent an exciting downhill slope, which he has every intention of tobogganing.

Ten minutes ago, when Gilliard gave him an early mark, he was surprised. But he was even more astonished when he saw his tutor make a hasty retreat from the study, down the staircase and out the front door. Alexei pressed himself against the window to watch the Swiss scholar dash across the yard and then down the road as if he, too, was on his way to the slopes where his sisters and the pretty housemaid, Shura, would be.

The boy had knocked loudly on the window to attract his father's attention who had finished cutting the wood and was chatting to one of the guards in the sentry box. The man never looked up at his son in the window.

The boy guesses his mother is napping just down the hall.

Sitting on the silver salver he balances precariously on the very top step of the staircase. The boy now holds the banister with his right hand — he is cross-legged so that all of him is on the tray, left arm aloft. He tilts forward a fraction and then backward. The sensation in his stomach swooshes with delight and fear and the boy laughs quietly.

Yes, it will work! They can all go tobogganing without him but he will show them — he is going to be the champion — he will practice and practice until he knows how to pull this off with great speed and skill!

He leans back and the tray slips a fraction, he grips the banister and manages to get the leverage he wants.

And for a fraction of a second, he balances, perfectly, between the motion and the act, between the static and the descent, between the idea of himself and the reality of all he can be.

He lets go of the banister —

He is flying!

Silver salver, magic carpet!

Arabian nights, shooting star!

Soaring lion!

Winged unicorn!

And for a breathless moment, he is the greatest mountaineer, the fearless adventurer, and the fastest living hero who dares to make the audacious flight down Russia's Mt Elbrus.

Then the edge of the tray catches a balustrade.

The boy cartwheels.

Legs.

Arms.

Over, over, over.

Thud.

Smack.

Clunk.

The body of the boy lies still and strangely contorted on the tiled floor.

10

The Cheka

Petrograd. February 1918.

Viktor sees the three men as soon as he steps up to cross the Liteyny Bridge. There is something about their studied nonchalance that makes his nerves twitch. He knows he can turn and dart back down the side of the bridge and hot-tail it back past the closed factories in the Vyborgskaya until he reaches Lidia's apartment but if they are waiting for him here, on the bridge, then they know both where he lives and where he often stays. Viktor slows his walk and looks straight ahead as he nears the men who have begun to peel themselves off the bridge's railing.

The one in a leather coat that is too big for him asks softly, 'Identification?'

Viktor waits and looks past the men blocking his path.

The man adds, 'Show us your ration card, comrade.'

Viktor has no intention of taking out his ration card for these three thugs but then again he also knows this is only the beginning. Everyone in Petrograd is paranoid, now that the Cheka is growing and flourishing, not just here in their city but in Moscow, Novosibirsk, Yekaterinburg, Nizhny Novgorod, Samara, Omsk, and Kazan. The secret police are ever-present.

'Ration card,' commands a large pock-marked brute with a spray of sour breath.

Viktor reaches into his inside pocket and pulls out his ration card and hands it to the smaller leather-coated thug, who is obviously in charge. The third nondescript Chekist has stepped behind Viktor, with the ease of someone who has done this time and time before. Viktor is effectively trapped with the bridge's railing on one side, Pock-face on the other, Leather-coat in front, and the other guy, behind. An inordinate time is given to the examination of the document and to Viktor's surprise, it is eventually handed back to him.

'Where are you headed?'

'Vyborgskaya. Friend's place.' Viktor wonders whether his willingness to pre-empt the next question, *Why?* might result in his quick release. He keeps his face expressionless. But inside, Viktor seethes. When did his revolutionized Russia sign up for this? Haven't we endured enough with the Tsar and his cronies denying us our civil rights? But the Sovnarkom, Lenin's government, claims counter-revolutionary activity must be dug out and exterminated. The Cheka is Lenin's dog.

'That would be the apartment of Lidia Konopleva.'

The assertion by Leather-coat rattles Viktor but he responds coolly with, 'Do you mind telling me what this is about?'

'Let's turn around, shall we?' responds the Chekist who is sweating heavily in his leather coat in the nascent spring heat. 'And we will take this up at Cheka Headquarters.' With that Viktor is swung around by Pock-face who fumbles about checking him for weapons and then frogmarches him back over the bridge.

Viktor hisses, 'I'm a lieutenant in the 12th Army! Unhand me.'

He is wedged between the three men who appear, to those witnesses skulking quickly aside, to be escorting him to some place of detention. Minutes later he is bundled into the back of a Black Maria. The engine roars and they take off quickly.

It was just yesterday, thinks Viktor bitterly as he watches the shopfronts and side streets flick by, that he and Grishka agreed that all opposition to the government is being marginalised. Petrograd is hot with disturbing rumours that arrests are happening everywhere. Grishka is right, Viktor thinks as they turn down the Gorokhovaya Ulitsa that leads to the Cheka Headquarters, Russia will soon become a one-party state if this continues. Viktor knows that he, for one, will not go so easily into that dark night.

'I have a right to know why I am being arrested,' Viktor's voice is flinty.

'Take it easy, Viktor.' Leather-coat's mocking tone draws a chortle from one of the others.

Viktor responds, 'Before you and your party were rounding up Russians what exactly did you do? Fight in the war? I think not —'

'Comrade, you're not the one asking questions, so shut the fuck up.'

The automobile brakes and as Viktor unfolds himself out of the back seat he looks up, and behind the Cheka Headquarters, sees the majestic dome of St Isaac's. He is taken swiftly inside a nondescript building that was once part of the Admiralty situated just a stone's throw across the park and is escorted up to the fourth floor.

Hours later, when he is still detained in a large unfurnished room filled with at least 20 other men, Viktor wonders to himself whether he should have run when he was back there on the bridge. Neither he nor Grishka had worked out a plan, should something like this come to pass, but this is something they need to do. The small of his back is aching. There is nowhere to sit except on the hard polished floorboards. Every so often a Chekist comes to the door and calls a name. The one who responds is both relieved and full of dread. Viktor knows why most of his fellow cellmates are keeping to themselves. Association with someone unknown can have a very sticky outcome. It is better to keep one's head down and convince whoever will be asking the questions that there has been a mistake.

Blaming it on one of those ignorant bastards who detained me will be easy, thinks Viktor.

He and Grishka have worked hard to ensure there is no trace linking them to the Battle Unit and, in fact, attending the 4th Congress of Soviets in Moscow, just the other week, was done so that no one could accuse them of being anything other than Bolsheviks. Despite all of this Viktor is fractious and wary.

He needs to calm down and so Viktor thinks of Leonid and their clandestine love. Who would have thought, a well-educated Ukrainian Jew, with a heart of a poet and an eye for detail, would fall in love with him. *Someone older* Leonid would tease. *Someone wiser*, Viktor would qualify. He smiles quietly to himself.

The door scrapes open and Viktor thinks, at least Leonid is safe.

The short leather coated guy who apprehended him hours earlier looks inside the fetid room.

'Viktor Pereltsveig.' There's no question in his voice but rather a statement of fact. Viktor ambles across to the open door. 'This way,' says the goon, almost courteously, and Viktor follows him into the halls of his destiny. What he is expecting is for Leather-coat to begin a series of tedious official questions in an attempt to ascertain Viktor's allegiance to the governing power.

What he is not expecting is Moisei Uritsky.

Viktor takes the seat that is indicated to him, opposite the iconic and ever-present revolutionary leader and now Chief of the Cheka here in Petrograd. Comrade Moisei Uritsky. In another moment in history, thinks Viktor to himself, this fellow would appear almost homely. His crumpled suit and half pulled tie surprises Viktor. Western dress is not the usual outfit of choice for the Bolsheviks. He looks past the Uritsky's rounded face to his ever-alert eyes and rather than feel intimidated, as perhaps he should, Viktor senses an equal.

'Go.'

The instruction to the small leather coated thug is more than dismissive and Viktor begins to think that maybe, just maybe, something else might be happening here. Leather-coat slouches out and pulls the door quietly behind him but still, Uritsky is yet to directly address Viktor. Perhaps this is a sort of recruitment, thinks Viktor, and he begins considering how he might avail himself of such an offer while pursuing his true goals in the Battle Unit.

'Viktor Pereltsveig,' Uritsky says in an almost friendly manner and then returns to the papers before him. 'Lieutenant in the 12th Army. Served in Lodz, Galicia ...' He squints closer to one of the papers he holds loosely in his hand, 'Ahh, and the siege of Przemysl ...' He lifts his face and stares at Viktor through his small round spectacles.

'That's correct, sir. And then Warsaw.' Viktor doesn't know why he adds further bio-data, it is obvious that Uritsky knows Viktor's history but there is something in the Chekist's easy-going manner that makes him think he is being recruited.

'And your view of this war would be ...?'

'A debacle from start to finish, sir,' There is no hesitancy in Viktor because it is a view he has always held while serving at the Front. The decisions made by those in command of the Imperial Russian Army were catastrophic.

'Ahh, and yet you held rank?'

'That came about solely because of attrition, sir.'

Uritsky accepts this as making a great deal of sense because his head continues to nod as he reads through his notes.

'And Viktor, what is your view of Comrade Romanov and his family?'

For a moment Viktor is not sure who he talking about, not because he is a Royalist by any stretch of the imagination, but because now that the revolution has succeeded, the Tsar no longer matters. Russia has washed her hands of the Tsar, and Viktor along with the entire nation rejoices.

'Look, sir, I think he and his family are parasites. I fought for this revolution and I am proud to be a Russian witnessing the start of our new, fledgling democracy ...' *Careful,* a quiet voice inside his head warns.

The word democracy triggers Uritsky to jot something in the margins of one of the papers before him.

Viktor then asks, 'Would you mind telling me what this is about?'

Uritsky, with a pleasant half-smile on his lips, continues to read the papers in front of him. After a moment or two, he looks back up.

'And what is your view, as I believe you attended the 4th Congress of Soviets in Moscow, of Comrade Trotsky's achievement?'

Viktor doesn't pause but smoothly responds, 'Well, like every other Russian, I am relieved that at last, the war is at an end. The Treaty of Brest-Litovsk had to happen.' Viktor, like many who fought in the war, despises the agreement Trotsky and Lenin have drawn up to appease the Germans. Surrendering one-third of Russia! Lithuania, Latvia, Estonia, Finland, Ukraine, Poland, and Belarus are now so-called independents and no longer Russian.

'Hmm. Not every Russian would agree ...' mumbles Uritsky.

Viktor watches the shrewd eyes behind the spectacles and responds, 'If you are referring to the walkout at the Congress of the Socialist Revolutionary Left, sir, I consider that a weak and ineffectual protest against the Sovnarkom.'

'You mean the Russian Communist Party?'

'Yes. A weak protest against the Russian Communist Party.'

He and Grishka had decided when the walkout occurred to distance themselves from the Socialist Revolutionaries. It was a strategy to aid their infiltration into the Bolshevik Party. From that moment onwards, the Russian government was entirely Bolshevik — there were no dissenting voices left, so it was paramount they remain.

The quiet between Viktor and Uritsky grows but so far it is more amiable than tense.

After a while Uritsky says, 'As you know, being a well-informed individual ...' The pause is there but Viktor is not sure what to make of it, 'Chairman Lenin has given his undivided support to me to round-up the enemies of the people.'

Viktor is convinced he is speaking about others because he would give his life for Russia, especially Russia with the revolutionary ideal of democratic rights for all.

'I run a tight ship, here, Viktor, and we can get through a great deal of business every day.'

Viktor has indeed been informed by the press of Uritsky's extraordinary capacity for work.

'The Russian Communist Party knows that these are fragile times and we must work tirelessly to eradicate the dissenters to stabilise the goals of the revolution. Do you agree with this objective of the Party, Viktor?'

Viktor knows himself to be a cunning survivor and someone capable of great courage and ingenuity under fire, 'Of course, sir.' He knows himself to be smart. Street smart and wily. And he knows he will not be out-witted by this fox. It is then that Viktor decides to throw a curveball to see what Uritsky might do. 'As you know, I am a member of the Party.' Viktor crosses his legs and continues speaking evenly, 'I, like many of my fellow Russians, am wondering who decides what debate is useful and what is considered dissenting?' Viktor leans into the table indicating a desire to be informed by Uritsky.

The Chief of the Cheka responds immediately, 'That's interesting you ask, Viktor because many of *my* fellow Russians are wondering who decides what members of Party leadership are to be targeted by assassins.'

Viktor doesn't flinch.

'You'll need to explain, sir.'

'I'm hoping you might, Viktor ...'

Viktor waits.

Uritsky waits.

Then Uritsky returns to the papers and moves them about even though Viktor suspects the papers are nothing more than a prop. After a few minutes, Uritsky selects one sheet and reads it closely, then lowers it and begins to pack up the file.

'What happens here, is done for the good of the people. I hope you understand that, Viktor.'

Viktor doesn't understand. He doesn't know whether this meeting is coming to an end. The Cheka only has powers to conduct preliminary investigations and yet people are reporting that those arrested and detained by the secret police have gone missing or been found dead. The Cheka is failing to hand over suspects to the revolutionary tribunals. Obviously, the Cheka is now judge, jury, and executioner.

'We are the sword and the shield of the revolution, Viktor. Without us, the revolution will not survive.'

For an absurd moment, Viktor wonders whether Uritsky is speaking about the both of them and then realises this is the motto used by the newly appointed secret police.

'My team is made up of ideological and ... let us say ... energetic men, and they are commissioned to fight against banditry, sabotage, speculation, and counter-revolution.'

In the last fortnight the capital has moved to Moscow and the incorruptible Head of the Cheka, the emaciated aesthete, Comrade

Dzerzhinsky, has left in his place the erudite but dangerous, Uritsky. Reflecting on this Viktor is under no illusion that Comrade Lenin needs the secret police to consolidate his power.

Uritsky says quietly, 'I know your sphere of influence is growing ...'

Viktor wonders whether Uritsky has the right person and then wonders whether he is referring to the Battle Unit to which he and Grishka belong. Quickly and effectively the newly recruited have been moved into operational cells, where targets and means of elimination are decided. Indeed, the numbers of those committed to taking back the revolution from the illegitimate hands of Lenin and his cronies, are growing. Perhaps those who attempted and failed to assassinate both Lenin and Trotsky a few months back had been caught and forced to confess their connections. And yet, Viktor had never met the two who had botched that effort and so how could his association with the terrorist cell be verified? Nothing is linking me to them, Viktor tells himself and ignores the cold sweat on his back.

'And as a consequence of this growing sphere of influence ...' Viktor frowns and looks directly at Uritsky as he continues, '... I want you to be fully informed about the powers of our reach and why we exercise this control ...'

Ahh, at last, thinks Viktor, I am here to be threatened. He watches every move Uritsky makes, which now appears nuanced and sinister.

'Sometimes, people back the wrong horse.' Uritsky speaks as though he is sharing a great intimacy with Viktor, 'They want to be winners but the race has started and their horse has no way of winning. None. Whatsoever.'

Viktor listens politely.

'What compels a person to back the wrong horse, you might ask.' Uritsky eyes Viktor almost playfully, 'Well, this person might be vulnerable or leading a life without direction or have found themselves to be left behind ...'

Viktor waits through the growing hiatus then sees Uritsky make a decision.

'I believe Viktor, that there are a few misled individuals out there who think that a planned attack on the Russian Communist Party, particularly in these early days, may result in a better outcome. But I am here to tell you that such an attack, large or small, will only result in a violent retaliation that has been hitherto unseen ...' Uritsky looks out across the desk at Viktor with largess and warmth that is unquestionable. 'Viktor, someone with your ... how should I put it? Charisma and military skills could make a great contribution to the Party. To the nation. I could make use of you here in the Cheka —'

'I could never inform on my fellow Russians.' Viktor regrets it as soon as he says it. Perhaps he is more on edge than he realises but this slip might cost him.

He waits.

'That's a great pity,' Uritsky's tone has changed and the room seems to reduce in space. 'Obviously, you have misunderstood this meeting. The Cheka, as I have taken pains to explain, works *against* saboteurs, bandits, and would-be assassins ...' The word hangs quietly in the room and just as he is reminding himself, once again, that nothing is connecting himself or Grishka to the failed attempt to kill Lenin and Trotsky, shrapnel explodes at his feet.

'You are a homosexual, isn't that right, Viktor?'

He is always vigilant and yet today, here at 2 Gorokhovaya Ulitsa, Viktor feels himself cartwheel backward. He frowns again, leans back, and uncrosses his legs.

'Your information is incorrect, sir. My girlfriend is Feiga Kaplan. She was one of the —'

'Yes, yes, Viktor we know who Feiga is ...'

This throws Viktor back into the crater of unpreparedness.

'No. I am referring to your illicit relationship with Kerensky's boy.'

Viktor scrambles back up to the battlefield. 'What?'

'Yes. Ahh ... Leonid ... um ...' Uritsky makes a show of reopening his file and looking through a few papers, whether or not he finds the information there is irrelevant.

Viktor already knows the enemy is about to fire again.

'Leonid Kannegisser. Kerensky's aid-de-camp. Currently, in Finland, I believe. It would be unfortunate if Kerensky were to return home ...'

Viktor says nothing. He crosses his legs and waits. He doesn't care. They cannot hurt Leonid and that is the only way they would ever hurt him. The Cheka is fucked. He knows it. They know it. They can hail explosives down on him of every kind but they will never destroy him while Leonid is safe.

And these two men sit opposite each other. One, a studied enactment of nonchalance, and the other, an expressionless recipient of threats. But what these threats are, in the long run, Viktor still cannot completely understand. On the one hand, Uritsky is warning him that the Cheka is now in place to eliminate the Battle Unit, which exists only as an unfixed and fluid group of individuals, disconnected to each other except in their commitment to wreak havoc and terrorism on those individuals who have unlawfully seized control of the revolution. On the other hand, the Chief of the Secret Police seems to be telling him, indirectly, that he and Leonid will be targeted if they assist in the return of Kerensky.

At least that is what he thinks is being said.

'We will be in touch.' And with that Uritsky flicks a dismissive finger at Viktor as if he is nothing more than an annoying insect.

Despite his confusion, Viktor stands and without a word leaves the room. Unstopped by any leather coated imbecile, he continues down the stairwell until he reaches the doorway of the building, through which he exits.

Petrograd. March 1918.

Feiga's eyelids flutter. It is as if she wants to open them, but cannot. Her head groans from side to side and the sheet is wet beneath her. Lidia has all the blankets she owns on top of Feiga but still her tiny body shivers and shakes. Lidia thinks her friend looks like a child possessed — thin limbs jangle, tiny chest rattles and waxy doll hands panic the covers. Feiga has been like this for days and if the news on the street is right, it is the *Blue Death*, cholera has descended on Petrograd.

Lidia stands up and stretches her tired legs. She has been crouching alongside the sofa bed on and off all morning. She moves across to the kitchen and pushes the window open as far as it will go. It is early spring but in her heart, it still feels like death. Lidia hears Feiga moan and so she dips some boiled water, now cooled, from the kitchen bucket into a bowl with a facecloth and returns. The cool water is sponged across Feiga's perspiring face and neck and collarbone. Again Lidia sees her friend attempt to open her eyes but she is far too weak. She reaches in under the blankets and places her hand on Feiga's heartbeat. Weak. Fluttery. Fast. She scoops up more water in the face cloth and squeezes drops into Feiga's dry mouth.

Lidia tries not to think about the newspapers that speculate cholera has come about because of contaminated water which will undoubtedly lead many to an early grave. Petrograd has been dogged by cholera for decades. Some say it is the canals used for both the disposal of sewerage and the collection of household water, others say it is the cesspools dug close to the wells. Whatever the cause, amulets, crucifixes, and medals of the Archangel Rafael, patron saint of healing, are now for sale everywhere.

Lidia dampens the crown of Feiga's head with cool drops of water and her friend seems to calm. Grishka and Viktor will be back soon and Lidia promised them she would rest while they were out. But how can she? *Wash your hands, Cat-eyes, as much as you can remember to do so.* Viktor's advice had been said gently to her but in the black dust of her heart, she wonders why it wasn't her who had caught the sickness. She would not have struggled — not the way she watches Feiga struggle. Lidia knows she would have surrendered and gone to the cold dirt grave, without a fight.

'Arghh ...' Feiga slowly brings her legs up to her stomach and groans again, 'Ughh ...'

Lidia leans in and says, 'I'm here, dearest. You'll soon be well ...'

Feiga's face is grey and her eyelids open partially but all Lidia sees are the whites of her eyes and then she smells defecation. Lidia gets up, once again, and grabs some newspaper off the kitchen table, and scoops up another bowl of water. When she comes back she gently pulls back the covers and the smell is nearly unbearable. She breathes through her mouth.

'Poor thing. Let's just clean you up and you will be fine.'

Feiga trembles. Lidia rucks up her friend's damp nightdress, scrunches the newspaper into the water until it is soggy, and then begins wiping down Feiga's legs and buttocks. The pale watery stool slips off Feiga's skin and Lidia rolls her gently to the other side so that she can clean her lower back. The diarrhoea will be the death of her, Lidia thinks, but there is something about the small-boned girl with her dinky chin, overlarge eyes, and cropped feathery brown hair that seems determined to live. Lidia pats dry Feiga's feverish back and buttock and thighs, and then covers her up, once again.

Viktor has been insistent that she wrap any soiled waste from Feiga's endless shitty discharge and take it down to the incinerator. He and Grishka have seen cholera when they were at the Front and warned her that the patient is highly contagious.

Lidia is tired but stands up again and bundles the dirty newspapers up into her old string bag. She stands at the kitchen sink and scrubs her hands with soap that Grishka got just as soon as he realised Feiga's headaches and nausea were getting worse. Lidia leans against the sink.

She will not let herself think about what happened a few weeks back in that warehouse. Days later, when Grishka had turned up at her apartment filled with excitement at her arrival followed by confusion at her withdrawn manner, he had gently tried to ask if something had happened ... Perhaps when she and Leonid had secured Kerensky's escape from the city ... Or maybe when she was at her father's estate ... Because, he said, she seemed *wounded* ... There was no other way to describe it. Yes, there is, she had thought bitterly at the time. She told Grishka that she was just fatigued with the journey home and then as the days and weeks passed she explained to him that she was having severe and ongoing period pain. Being the man he was, he bustled about and made tea then made himself scarce. Feiga on the other hand never asked her what had happened, even though everyone seemed to treat Lidia differently. More gently, less robustly.

Lidia looks out across the apartment courtyard below and into the pale blue sky that has the promise of summer at its edges. She wishes ... she wishes ... She shakes her head and collects the bag filled with fetid newspaper and moves quietly across to the door and closes it behind her as she leaves the apartment.

Feiga hears the *whoosh shoo whoosh shoo* of her grandmother's long skirt. She doesn't turn around because she knows she is there behind the hen house. The smell of chicken shit and spring rain fills her mind. Her grandmother says something to her and, try as she might, Feiga cannot quite understand her. She watches the pale yellow hen watch her. Its eye, a bead. The other hens, brood and cluck and caw, heating up the dilapidated shelter with their single-mindedness until she feels her skin flush.

Feiga looks up and sees her father and his lolling gait. She thinks he is heading in her direction at the bottom of the yard, where she is supposed to be collecting eggs. Then she remembers there are mourners in the house who kneel at her mother's thin body laid out in a pine box. There are so many more chores for her to do now but each seems to take so long. Her heart races with the effort of the task at hand which is to snatch the smooth fresh eggs here in the hen house but she is so out of breath she can barely stand up. Her father heads toward the old gnarly lemon tree behind the hen house. Perhaps he doesn't see her. Perhaps she is in the house kneeling at her mother's coffin.

Whoosh shoo whoosh shoo. Feiga wants to see her grandmother but when she turns around she realises she is not in her childhood home but back in the prison dormitory with the other women. She is surrounded by Siberian cold and prison stone. She wants to wrap herself in fur and tilt her head upwards into radiant light — but there is no fur or light, just days and weeks and months and years of bone-hard hopelessness. Feiga tries to cry but she cannot. She tries to open her eyes but they have welded shut. She tries to call out to her grandmother but she has forgotten how to make a sound. If only she could remember the name they used for their mother — was it *Mumma?* That doesn't sound right. She has no memory of her mother's name, her face, her skin. So she presses her lips together and says nothing.

When Lidia returns from the incinerator in the courtyard, Grishka and Viktor are already seated at the small kitchen table. Lidia notices that one of them has made tea and there's a cup for her, already poured, alongside black bread and jam. She knows this is their way of trying to make things easier for her. These last few days have been distressing, nursing Feiga night and day, all the time trying to make her drink some boiled water. *Clean water*, the doctor had said severely. *Only clean water.* Hence, the samovar seems to be boiling constantly. She glances down at Feiga who is caught up in a twist of sheets on the sofa bed but for fear of waking her, Lidia moves past. Viktor continues to quietly read the newspaper aloud to Grishka and when she walks to the sink her boyfriend leans back and reaches for her. Lidia holds up her hands and grimaces and he seems to understand the dumb show — she needs to wash. After cleaning her hands, Lidia takes the seat next to Grishka and cradles the cup of tea which is still hot.

Viktor continues reading aloud from an underground newspaper, '*The Bolsheviks are already poisoned by power as they demonstrate a shameful attitude towards freedom of speech —*'

'Do you want more jam in your tea? Is it sweet enough?' asks Grishka, and Lidia glances across at his face, it is lined and thin and his eyes seem to have lost that cheeky glimmer she once loved so much.

'It's fine,' she replies in a hushed tone, as they all do. She keeps her eye on the sofa bed with its crumple of blankets.

Viktor reads on, '*The breakneck speed with which they are moving can only implode into anarchy —*'

'Have some bread, my love, when is the last time you ate —'

'For God's sake, man! You're not her goddamn nanny!' Even Lidia smiles at Viktor's faux outrage, 'Leave the woman alone!'

Grishka begins sawing away at the bread, which is dry and tough. The table watches him as he smears the bread with jam and then proceeds to slice it into bite-size pieces. Lidia looks away because Grishka's tenderness is unbearable.

'*Lenin is not an omnipotent magician,*' Viktor reads on, understanding everything that is playing out between Grishka and Lidia. '*But rather a callous juggler —* he's good, right?' says Viktor looking up at them because Maxim Gorki's polemic is, as always, brilliant. The bundle of blankets moan and quiver and the table turn their heads to see what happens next, but nothing happens, so Viktor reads aloud, '*A bullet is not a ballet and a bayonet is not an election manifesto —*'

'Just eat another piece. Take this one —'

'*What happened to freedom of speech and what happened to freedom of the press?*'

'It's Volodarsky,' says Grishka to no one in particular, his hand still poised with the piece of bread for Lidia. 'Who the hell is he? I mean — we were all here, right? Fighting at the Front.' He drops the bread he is offering back onto the plate and Lidia continues to sip her tea. 'He comes out of nowhere ...' Grishka rants on about Volodarsky, the Commissar for Propaganda, and his ilk. 'I mean who are these stooges? We were the ones fighting for our country against a foreign enemy and we came home and had to fight another battle! We were dying out there at the Front and now, *here*, in our city, we are still being shot at!' Grishka is filled with the vitriol of his own words, 'These fucking trouble makers turn up out of nowhere and start telling us what we can and cannot do — I mean, this is the latest bullshit — only the *Red Gazette* and *Pravda* can be published — everything else is to be banned! It's unbelievable! By having this newspaper, here in our own home ...' Grishka stabs his finger at the *Novaya Zhizn*, the underground Socialist Revolutionary newspaper, from which Viktor had been reading, 'We could be arrested and imprisoned!'

No one says anything because this is something they speak about often. Besides, Viktor wants Grishka to push himself to the point of no return. The Battle Unit has a mandate, to eliminate targeted individuals, which Viktor has every intention of fulfilling — ever more so after his encounter with Uritsky, the Chief of the Cheka.

'We risked our lives making sure the revolution happened!' Grishka is unstoppable, 'Making sure the Tsar and his lot were shut down! We did everything — for God's sake we fought on these very streets and then out of a hole climbs a cockroach-like Volodarsky who is immediately made one of Lenin's right-hand guys and is telling us what we can and can't do!'

'Telling us there will be no counter-revolutionary newspapers,' supplies Viktor sourly.

'Exactly! I mean what the fuck? Where did he come from? Is he even Russian —'

'Yep, but, you know, has been in the comfy lap of USA for the last ten years or so —'

'Exactly! What the hell would he know?' Then Grishka's voice lowers remembering that Feiga is sleeping, 'You see, all these outsiders have arrived after we have done the hard work for them! And now they think they have the right to tell us how to live our lives in the new Russia that we bloody well fought for and many of our comrades died for! Who the fuck are they?' Grishka's rhetorical question hangs in the air as he seethes with the injustice of it all which somehow includes the inexplicable change in his girlfriend.

'I'll tell you who they are,' Viktor answers effortlessly as he looks across at Grishka and then Lidia. 'They are Lenin and Trotsky and Volodarsky and Uritsky — I mean the list goes on and on! Leaders of the party. They are dangerous and I'll tell you something else, if we don't do something soon ... it will be too late.'

The friends sit together at the table.

Grishka worries about the state of his nation but somehow he knows it is tangled up in his rising panic about Lidia. Since her return from her father's a couple of months ago, she is different. Pale. Thin. Withdrawn. He wants her to confide in him but there is little opportunity with Feiga needing care and Viktor hiding out here after his run-in with the Cheka.

Lidia stares down at the newspaper on the kitchen table and cannot remember a time when she felt so abandoned. Nothing can save her, nothing can clean her, nothing can heal her. In the last few days she has tried to lose herself in the care of Feiga and she admits to herself she has been grateful for the excuse not to leave the apartment and if she catches cholera, so be it.

Viktor pours himself more tea and pushes away the rumour they heard on the street this morning that the Cheka is rounding up ex-army personnel and accusing them of counter-revolutionary activity. Hundreds and hundreds of army officers, if you are to believe the rumours. He knows that he and Grishka must act — now. Uritsky will try and arrest Viktor to get to Leonid and Kerensky. What might happen to Leonid while under the Cheka's arrest cannot be contemplated — it just cannot happen. Uritsky's threat is clear. Leonid and Kerensky must remain in Finland.

Viktor sighs, Feiga stirs and Lidia moves over to the sofa bed to check on her.

'Are you awake yet, Feiga?'

Viktor watches Lidia. Her upper body and limbs have become nothing but the skeletal remains of a dead tree. It is then that Viktor makes up his mind. Lidia must tell Grishka what happened to her. It will be this and only this that will tip Grishka into action. What happened to Lidia is not only an affront to her and all women and men, but it is an affront to the new Russia they are building. When Grishka hears what has happened the fight will become personal. And the targeted assassinations of certain high-ranking Bolsheviks must come to pass. The Battle Unit, he and Grishka have been recruited to, cannot fail — not now — not at this critical moment in history.

Lidia leans into Feiga and says, 'Dearest one, I'm going to make you some tea.'

Even now, as Lidia moves back across to the kitchen, Grishka is up and getting the samovar firing. Lidia is Grishka's only preoccupation and Viktor knows this must come to an end.

'Right,' Viktor says pushing back his chair and standing up.

'Here's the plan. I am going to look after Mouse and you two are going to catch a train out to the countryside for the day.'

Both Lidia and Grishka look at him blankly.

'I am serious. As you know, 200,000 factory workers have been laid off and all unemployed have been granted free travel to the countryside to find food —'

'Free travel to the unemployed *factory* workers, Viktor.' Grishka is frustrated because he would give anything for an excuse to take Lidia out of the apartment and be together, alone — even if they are surrounded by 200,000 unemployed factory workers.

'Oh ... You think railway guards are checking all 200,000 ration cards held aloft by the unemployed as they board a train? ... Come on, man!'

He's right, thinks Grishka, and what does it matter if they do or don't get on a train? They could have the rest of the day together — in fact, Viktor's apartment is vacant now that he is here looking after Feiga, and Grishka is well-liked by Viktor's old landlady ...

'Let's do it!' Grishka has grabbed Lidia's hand and the intensity of his gaze makes her look away.

'No ... I really can't. I really ... I must ...'

'Lidia,' Viktor cuts through the impasse. 'You really must take a break. Do it for all of us, please.'

She has no will to argue. She looks across at Feiga and then back to the kitchen window where, ironically, the washed-out sky with its grey clouds has cleared to reveal a sweet picture postcard of spring, and so she says, 'I'll get my coat.'

Grishka doesn't care that Lidia wants her coat, even though it has been warm for weeks now, and he doesn't care that she seems to have no interest in the excursion. All that matters, he thinks to himself as he watches her wrap an old checked scarf about her head, is that his beautiful Lidia is stepping out with him today.

She opens the cloak press and pulls out her coat, feeling for something deep within one of her pockets. Grishka turns to Viktor and says something out of earshot and, as he does so, Lidia closes her hand around the cool hard reassurance of her revolver.

When the two of them leave the apartment, Viktor returns to his newspaper.

Feiga wants to open her eyes but she is too tired. Time passes and she feels droplets of tea squeezed from a cloth into her mouth. She swallows. This is repeated and she can hear Viktor's distinct voice, warm and assuring. 'Mouse ... Mousey ... Drink a little more ... Little one ... Well done ... Soon you will be guzzling Grishka's hidden brandy ... Good girl ...' She loves Viktor. She hears him sigh. She must try harder. Viktor. So handsome. So kind.

She drifts back into the thick heat of a Kiev summer. Feiga walks back up to her house and realises there are warm eggs in the pockets of her apron. She listens intently but cannot hear the *whoosh shoo whoosh shoo* of her grandmother's long skirt. She moves slowly in case the eggs break. Then she begins to sing *El Malei Rachamim*, the song of the dead.

I, who have picked flowers up on the mountain,
And looked upon all the valleys ...

By the time she gets to the back door she is surprised because the house seems empty. The mourners must have gone.

I, who have brought dead bodies from the hills,
Can tell that the world is merciless ...

She moves into the home of her childhood memories but cannot find her siblings. Even her father is nowhere to be found.

I, who have stood undecided by my window,
Who counted strides of angels ...

She walks from room to room and notices the old clock that once belonged to her grandparents has stopped ticking. No heartbeat.

I, who must solve riddles against my will

Know that the world is merciless ...

And the interior of the house fills up with cold. Its old wooden floorboards, the heavy furniture, and the smell of damp in the walls make her shiver.

If the Lord was not merciful
Then mercy would not have been seen throughout the world ...

She doesn't want to be here, she doesn't want to be here, she doesn't want to be here.

Oh, merciful Lord ...

Viktor doesn't know what has woken him. He thinks he has been dreaming of a funeral and he touches his left breast to assure himself that he only dreamt of the act of Keriah and is satisfied when he realises his shirt remains untorn. It has been a long time since he has thought about his Yiddish background and the rituals that marked his childhood. Such trappings of the past are a hindrance. He blinks about the room a few times and longs for his bed in his apartment but he has promised to look after Feiga. Lidia and Grishka have been gone for hours. Then he hears a sort of slow murmur from the sofa bed and hauls himself off the floorboards and his own nest of coats where he has been resting.

'What about some tea? How are you feeling? Mouse?'

Although she doesn't speak her eyes open a fraction. She is bone-thin, even her skin seems dried up and tired. How can someone with so little, hold on so tenaciously? *Poor thing*, he thinks as he goes into the kitchen, fills the samovar, and splinters some wood to fire it up. It is then he realises boots are climbing the stairwell. There is something quiet and sure-footed about them.

Viktor stands perfectly still. The footsteps slow as they reach the apartment door. He looks across at Feiga and to his surprise, she is looking at him. The footsteps stop dead at the door. Viktor gestures a finger across his lips to Feiga and wishes his revolver wasn't in his coat pocket in the small cloak press on the other side of the room.

Starik ... the word is whispered on the other side of the wooden door and it startles Viktor into a grunt and then he is at the door unbolting it and pulling back the latch until Leonid, blonde-haired and pale-eyed, looking older than he should, is in his arms. They have not seen each other for months. The two men hold each other for the longest time and then Viktor is pulling him inside into the safety of the apartment. Leonid laughs and tries to take off his coat but Viktor has him again in the tightest crush saying over and over again, 'Wonder boy has come home! Wonder boy!' Then they are both laughing and Viktor is ruffling Leonid's hair and his younger lover is rubbing his knuckles over Viktor's unshaven chin, repeating *Starik* ... *Starik*. This term of affection, old man, is Leonid's way of reminding Viktor he is nine years younger — *Nine years less experienced*, Viktor would always laugh back.

'What's this?' Leonid realises the bundle of sheets and blankets is, indeed, Feiga and pulls himself, somewhat reluctantly, out of the steel embrace of Viktor. Feiga tries to smile but it doesn't happen. She knows Leonid understands because he is crouched behind her stroking her little feathered nest of hair.

'Right.' Viktor is clearing his throat of the unexpected emotion that has come with the arrival of his greatest joy. 'I was about to make tea. Feiga needs tea. So, tea.'

Leonid laughs again and it is a sound that has not filled the apartment for months. We are all home, thinks Viktor to himself and kisses Leonid on his ear and cheek as his young lover leans over Feiga and continues to stroke her. We are all home, now. After Feiga has been given droplets of cooled tea and seems to have slipped into a drowsy slumber, the two men sit back on the kitchen chairs, by themselves.

'I've missed you, moy lyubov.' When Leonid speaks these words of love, Viktor leans in and kisses him deeply on the mouth. Everything about this boy is wonderous, Viktor thinks, as he strokes Leonid's pale blonde hair.

'What's happening with Kerensky?' Viktor doesn't want to ask but he can only delay the question for so long. A part of him just wants to pretend that his lover has come back and the world is as it should be. A part of him doesn't want to face the possibility that their time together is nothing but a ticking bomb.

Leonid sighs and looks out the kitchen window and it is as if the spring sky is completely uninterested in the plight of the world. 'There's no hope, Viktor. He has come back. But only to get a visa. Kerensky is leaving Russia. He is leaving us ... We will have no one.'

The abyss yawns open in front of them. Viktor can barely believe what he is hearing. If it was anyone else who had brought this news he would have scoffed at such a ridiculous reprehensible claim. But Leonid is the only one who knows Kerensky's movements and his objectives. How can this have happened? So much has been invested into Kerensky's escape from the Bolshevik revolution in October, keeping him protected first at the secluded estate of Lidia's father and then on to other bolt holes so that no one could trace his whereabouts. And all this time Leonid has been there alongside the great leader, risking his own life and future — for what? So that Kerensky could now scurry off to where? America? Viktor tries to shake off his ire when he realises Leonid is saying something.

'How can we take back Russia, without a leader? What are we expected to do?' Neither of them speaks and then finally Leonid adds mournfully, 'What has this all been for?'

And then it hits Viktor that this might have been the reason the Cheka arrested him. They have spies everywhere and perhaps they found out Kerensky was already organising his escape.

'Wait, where is Kerensky? Does anyone know you are here? Were you seen?' Viktor asks sharply, his body now tense and alert.

Leonid frowns but knows Viktor is usually ahead of the pack when it comes to strategizing.

'I got off at Finlyandsky Station early this morning,' says Leonid carefully. 'Kerensky has continued to Moscow. He is disguised and with a handful of people we can trust.'

If only he and Grishka had already struck, thinks Viktor. Assassinating their targets would strike terror into the very heart of the Bolsheviks. He and Grishka must unleash the dogs of war against the Bolsheviks. Assassination is the only way to bring these tyrants to their knees.

'How can we be expected to go it alone?' Leonid asks vaguely and slumps a little over the kitchen table where cold glasses sit in disarray.

'Leonid, listen to me, does anyone know you are here?'

'I don't think so. No. I don't think so ...'

Viktor exhales heavily. If only he could find a cigarette in this godforsaken apartment, he thinks and then he says, 'When you were away — I was taken downtown to Uritsky.'

The name hangs between them like a portent.

'What did that Jewish bastard want?' Viktor can't help but smile at Leonid's pejorative remark because like Uritsky, Trotsky, Volodarsky, and Viktor himself, his young lover is also Jewish.

'I think he wants to get to you, through me. I think he wants Kerensky.'

'Well, he won't catch him.'

Viktor pauses and looks at Leonid for a moment and then decides it is in his best interests to know. 'Moy lyubov, listen to me.' Viktor pulls up one of Leonid's fine hands and presses it to his lips. 'They know about us. Uritsky knows about us. He knows it is you who has been moving Kerensky about and keeping him out of their reach. He knows. I think he is coming for me — for you — for Kerensky. You must return to Finland. You are not safe here ... '

Leonid is shaking his head and pulling himself away from Viktor, 'No. I'm not going to be separated from you anymore. I want to be here. This is my country. I want to be here and fight ...'

Viktor looks at his beloved who is all youth and passion and light. Leonid continues talking about the growing alarm of civil war throughout Russia and how every individual committed to the revolutionary objectives of February last year must stand and fight the pretenders — the Bolsheviks. And while he speaks, Viktor thinks about Kerensky hot-tailing it out of Russia while Leonid remains the bait.

British, French, and even American forces have landed in Murmansk and are joining General Kornilov and the White Army to fight against the Bolsheviks. Viktor hears these statements from Leonid and acknowledges them duly but feels as if they are already sitting shiva, the seven days of mourning.

'The net is closing,' Leonid says in an attempt to rally Viktor's confidence. 'Around the Romanovs.'

'Who cares about the fucking Tsar?!' Viktor says with bitterness. 'Trotsky is bringing him to the capital for a show trial. The Tsar must be prosecuted and punished for all the crimes he has committed against our nation. And I'll take a front-row seat — I want to see that bastard face his fellow man.' How can they have arrived at this point? Kerensky, their leader, running away and leaving the Bolsheviks in charge? Now, the only thing that matters is getting Leonid to safety. Viktor knows then and there how he is going to do this.

'Leonid. Something happened to Lidia — when you were away.'

Leonid waits.

Feiga doesn't open her eyes but she has heard Viktor's last statement. If anyone should know about Lidia it should be her. She waits.

'What? Tell me ...' The pause seems to stretch on and on across the kitchen and into the loungeroom where Feiga feigns sleep.

'It was that day we saw you. When we had been caught up in the protest and you pulled up and gave us a lift. Remember? You were headed to the station with —'

'Of course, I remember. What happened?'

Lidia belongs to Feiga. She loves her more than anyone could imagine. Lidia is her mother, her sister, her daughter, herself. She wants to call out but cannot.

Viktor realises he is stuck. It surprises him. Up until now, he hasn't uttered a word of what happened. He hasn't even brought it up with Lidia who is always here in the apartment. Viktor knows he just needs to say it. He has thought often about that day ... Kerensky in the back seat rigged up as a railwayman, en route to Finlyandsky Station — they would have crossed the very bridge where Lidia was raped ... Did they cross before or after this despicable assault happened? Viktor still thinks he should have warned her before she returned to Petrograd — he should have written and said that the streets were becoming ever more dangerous. Particularly to women. But he hadn't. He had been thinking about Leonid, not Lidia. Viktor knew he had failed to protect her so how the hell is he going to protect his darling, Leonid?

Feiga waits. She already knows. Someone did to Lidia what had been done to her again and again when she had first arrived at the prison in Siberia.

'A Red Guard raped her.' Viktor forces himself to speak on, 'Here, in Vyborgskaya. She was just coming home. To Grishka. To all of us.'

Feiga is no longer on the sofa bed ... She is there with Lidia ... Head smashing against the ground ... Fist slamming into her stomach ... Fingers wrenching her hair ... Knee crunching into her thigh ... Clothes ripping ... Filthy hand over her mouth ... And then the dry hard shunting in and out and in and out and in and out until she leaves the room and hides in a dark dark corner that smells of vomit and shit and blood.

'That's why I need you to leave.' Viktor's voice is strange when it is filled with tears. 'You have to take Lidia back to her father's estate. She will not recover here in the city — with every fucking Red Guard eyeing off women and raping whatever comes their way ...'

Leonid is still so shocked that the beautiful Lidia has been brutalised by these apes that he can't seem to think straight.

'I need you to take her.' Viktor steadies his voice, 'Grishka and I have to see something through — no, no — I will tell you more later ... When we join you down there. At her father's estate.'

Feiga doesn't want to be left behind. Has Viktor forgotten her? She needs to go to Lidia. Lidia! Where is Lidia? Why is no one answering her?! Feiga hears voices and vehicles in the street below. Everything is wrong. Where is Lidia? How can she be abandoned by the others? She cannot be left behind!

Then Viktor's voice, pleading, 'Will you do this for me? Leonid? Please.'

Feiga squints across the room and sees Viktor put his arm around Leonid's shoulder and she wonders whether the younger man is crying because his head is bent over and he lays it against Viktor's chest.

Eventually, she hears Leonid say, 'Yes. But you must come. I will only wait there for a few days. If you do not come, I will —'

'I know. I know, my love. I will join you there.'

There are more voices on the street below but now Feiga hears people running and vehicles braking and doors slamming. She sees Viktor cradle Leonid's pale head against his dark beauty. It makes her feel utterly alone. No one has spoken about what is to become of her. She is the one who should be with Lidia. She alone can understand what has happened. Raised voices, more vehicles screech, and then a shout followed by *RAT TA TATATATATA* of a machine gun.

Viktor reaches the window before Leonid. Feiga tries to pull herself up on her elbow. She collapses back onto the sofa bed.

'Stay back from the window!' Viktor speaks sharply to Leonid and steps back a pace of two himself and looks down at Feiga.

'Who is it?' Leonid barks. 'Red Guards?'

'Worse,' answers Viktor, after glimpsing a truckload of detainees. 'Cheka.'

With that, he spins around and looks again at Feiga, 'Right. Lay down Mouse, you're not going anywhere.'

The three of them hear the front door of their apartment block thud open and boots are crunching about followed by urgent voices.

Viktor looks at Leonid and says calmly, 'They're coming for me. You need to do as you promised and get Lidia and Feiga out of the city. We will all meet there at the end of the week —'

'NO! —'

'Yes. Uritsky won't abandon me. The Cheka want me as some sort of double agent. They want the Battle Unit. And they want Kerensky. And you, moy lyubov, can lead them to Kerensky ...'

Now the boots are ascending the stairwell. Feiga starts whimpering.

'Tell Grishka nothing changes. He will know what to do. Targets are locked. Tell him that! He is not to stand down!'

The cacophony of boots pound ever upwards. Feiga hears neighbours bolting their doors.

'I am coming with —'

'No, you are not! We can't let anymore happen to Lidia! You are staying out of sight here and I am going out to meet them. They might come in but Leonid you must hide and ...' He twists around to Feiga and says to her, 'Nothing will happen to you, Mouse. I promise. You are infectious — tell them you are infectious — warn them. Can you do that Mouse?'

She is sweating and shaking and with a superhuman effort croaks, 'Blue Death ...'

The boots halt at the floor below and there are sharp voices and the distinct *chick chick chick* of revolvers cocking.

'Yes, Mouse,' Viktor's voice is a whisper and he is already at the door. 'Blue Death will scare them ...'

He looks once at Leonid and spits, 'Get in the cloak press.'

The boots are climbing their way to the final floor and Viktor looks back and says to Leonid, 'Do it! Now!' And reluctantly Leonid steps into the narrow cloak press.

Viktor breathes in deeply and waits in front of the door for the knock that will come.

And Feiga ... Feiga runs and runs and runs and runs up from the hen house and over the uneven backyard. Her arms are pumping and her chest is about to explode but she charges on and on. The house is so far away and her legs are tired and she shuts her eyes and strains to hear the *whoosh shoo whoosh shoo* of her grandmother's skirts except there is nothing but the sound of her ragged breath.

When she opens her eyes the sky has churned into a dirty grey and she tells herself to push on, hurry, run harder because she knows now that her mother is somewhere in the house and if only she can reach her before the sky fractures, she will be safe. Her mother must be anxious for her but when she tries to shout, as she staggers closer and closer to the house, nothing comes out of her mouth but a dry wheeze. She slows down and squeezes her eyes together and attempts to shake her head but there is so much pain behind her eyes. And the pounding on the apartment door crashes about her head.

11

On the Run

Moscow. March 1918.

The Scotsman knows the soft knock at the door is Kerensky. He waits a second and thinks, for the hundredth time, this could be a cruel hoax. The call this morning at the British Consul-General office had been brief and disturbing but the person on the other end of the line, in heavily accented English, addressed him in person.

'Mr. Lockhart, I am a friend of your government. My name is Alexander Fyodorovich Kerensky,' there had been only the slightest pause. 'Russia's Prime Minister before the Bolshevik Revolution.' Lockhart had waited. 'And I need papers.'

Meeting at the Consul-General was out of the question, hence the shadowy rendezvous at the Scotsman's Moscow apartment on Tverskaya Ulitsa.

Bruce Lockhart picks up his Smith & Wesson pistol, a Doughboy's drunken effort to square off a gambling debt. He cocks it and moves to the door.

'Just a minute,' Lockhart calls.

He has no reason to make the man outside his door wait other than the fact that the whole of Moscow is filling up with spies and double agents. He has never met Kerensky before but, of course, he has seen photographs and newsreels of the charismatic leader. Indeed, as part of his brief to unsettle the Bolsheviks, it has become his business to know who's who and, if he gets lucky, have a go at knocking off Kerensky's nemesis, Comrade Lenin.

Lockhart cracks open the door and at first doesn't recognise the soldier standing before him and then realises that it is Kerensky and, as promised, he has come alone. Once inside the apartment Lockhart pockets the pistol and offers the fugitive a whisky, *Laphroaig*, one of the perquisites of the job.

Kerensky shakes his head and gets down to business, 'I need to leave Russia.'

Lockhart takes his time to empty his crystal whisky glass and then, rather deliberately, looks calmly across at the man who had tried to steer Russia in the right direction.

'That might prove a wee bit difficult.' Lockhart is 31 but assumes the manner of an older, more worldly man with his wide-open face and brilliantine dark hair. He is a man who takes sporting men seriously and beautiful women to bed. 'My boss is out of town this weekend and so I'm afraid I am unauthorised to sign off without his say so.'

Lockhart has gestured to the overstuffed armchair so that he might take its opposite, but the small compact Kerensky remains standing.

The former Prime Minister looks at the foreigner and wonders whether this Scotsman is speaking English. He can't quite figure out what he is saying but understands there is a problem. He sighs inwardly. Kerensky considers whether Lockhart, who fills out his suit with a life of good food and wine, is wanting a bribe but he looks about the apartment and sees that there is everything here a foreigner would wish.

Lockhart follows Kerensky's line of gaze and sees it alight upon his mistresses' shawl. A lavish affair of deep plum silk with embroidered peonies and tassels of liquid pink. The men's eyes meet and Lockhart shrugs.

'Countess Benckendorff' he says by way of explanation.

Kerensky knows Countess Benckendorff, she and her husband are Tsarists through and through, but what he doesn't understand is this foreigner's complete lack of discretion.

'I must have papers, under a ... a ...' Kerensky gives up and continues in Russian, 'A false name because I am a fugitive. I assume you know that Lenin holds my nation hostage at this point. He wants me dead. I aim to drum up sufficient support overseas and then return to overthrow this pretender!'

Lockhart sits in the armchair and again gestures for Kerensky to do the same. Finally, and with undisguised frustration, the Russian takes the chair.

'We must hurry,' adds Kerensky who has been in hiding for near on six months.

I can do nothing, thinks Lockhart. He has already had his knuckles rapped by the Ambassador, a typical English prig, for his affair with Maria Benckendorff. Lockhart leans forward and pours himself another whisky, his suit straining across his chest and middle. God what is a man supposed to do, he thinks, pouring himself a little bit more than he had intended. His wife, Jean, is all set up in London and refusing to come across to live amongst *those Slavs*.

'The thing is ...' Lockhart takes a generous sip of his drink and settles into the armchair, tugging at his trousers to relieve his crotch. 'The Ambassador has taken off, you see, just for a few days and although I am in charge of all domestic matters, this matter — your matter — is another thing entirely.' Lockhart gives Kerensky his signature quizzical brow to indicate that it is a tricky business and one that has him stymied.

'Mr Lockhart,' begins Kerensky. 'I am a patient man. Six months on the run has taught me that patience can be the difference between life and death.' He continues, 'I have people. These people have worked for months to line up an exit for me. But I now only have a matter of two or, at the most, three days to get to ...' He hesitates and then decides that if he cannot trust Lockhart then who can he trust, 'To get to Murmansk. You must help me.' Because there is no one else who can supply the identification papers and visa on such short notice, he thinks. Maybe he is imagining it but Kerensky suspects this foreigner has a proclivity for adventure and for making up his own rules.

'Murmansk, you say?' Lockhart drains his glass, 'That's a long journey and one that —'

'Please don't worry yourself about the details of my travels. This has all been taken care of because there are many many Russians who want the government, *my* government, who won the majority, to be returned to power. And as I said, I must rally support from our allies, overseas, as quickly as possible.'

Lockhart is not only working for the Consul-General but has been hand-selected by Lloyd George for MI6. Needless to say, he is absolutely in support of any efforts to derail the Bolsheviks and all the other Lefties in Russia. Furthermore, Lockhart is more than aware of the clash that seems to be growing day by day between the White Army, Tsarist supporters, and the Reds, Lenin's motley crew of ex-criminals and army deserters. Lockhart looks across at Kerensky and decides he likes this man. A man's man, bit like himself really, and not a namby-pamby, like the Ambassador, a Sassenach ... or, as he likes to think of the English, a milk-sop.

'You'll need more than papers. You'll need a disguise.' After Lockhart says these words he realises he's in. He will sign off on this man's escape to freedom even though he has no authority to do so. But if the Ambassador insists on his weekend retreats to the country, with his over-powdered and over-stuffed matronly wife (*No fun in that* was Lockhart's first and lasting impression of her), then these were the consequences.

'A disguise. Yes. What would you suggest, Mr. Lockhart?' And Kerensky indicates with a small nod of the head toward the *Laphroaig* whisky that he would, after all, like a nip.

The men listen to the glasses fill as the sound of a trolley bus a long way off tings its bell merrily.

'Za Vstrechu!' says Lockhart as he clinks his glass against Kerensky's, knowing he will deliver in this meeting in a way that will shape history. He is a descendant of the Bruces, the Hamiltons, the Cummings, the Wallaces, and the mighty Douglases! There is not a drop of English blood in his Scottish veins! Did he say that out loud? His head swims.

'Za nashikh milikh dam,' says Kerensky and holds his glass aloft to the delectably languid silk shawl that drapes across the settee like some post-coital odalisque. Lockhart's eyes slide back to the shawl and as he throws back his whiskey he thinks sagely that his indiscretions might be his downfall ... but what a wonderful way to go down.

Before long they hatch a plan. Kerensky will depart Moscow as a Siberian sailor en route to his naval base in Murmansk, after a short furlough in Moscow. For someone who claimed, initially, that he was unable to sign off on identification papers without the approval of the Ambassador, Lockhart certainly has all the equipment necessary to do so, right here in his attaché case. Lockhart writes out the appropriate verification of identification, followed by a visa as if he is an old hand at subterfuge. Kerensky offers a suitably sounding Siberian name and then watches Lockhart press the seal of the Consul-General into the thick melting wax at the bottom of the document. The Scotsman finishes the sting by adding his signature with flourish and pride.

Yet as Kerensky takes his leave, accepting the handshake from

Lockhart which, mid gesture, becomes a strong hug, the ex-Prime Minister feels a wave of mixed emotions ... Relief, despair, joy, frustration, and the never before experience of homesickness that flows painfully through his veins.

I am leaving Russia, he thinks. The only mistress I ever wanted.

I 2

The Journey

Tobolsk, West Siberia. April 1918.

Sometimes, when she is alone, she looks closely into the looking glass and wonders how she got to be this old. Forty-five. Forty-six in June. And the man's wife thinks, that's only two months away.

Today she looks at herself without seeing the ornate oval frame of the large mirror above her dresser. Pale skin, as pale as her daughters' but certainly not as moist as theirs. She leans in and notes the thin lines across her forehead that run to the edges of her greying hair. She turns slightly and watches the crow's feet that fan the sides of her eyes, and without looking she tugs the loose skin of her neck. Finally, her finger traces the fold lines that bracket her mouth and she thinks to herself, *thin lips*.

Once she thought there would be dignity in growing old, with her reign established and her mother in law, the Empress Dowager, long forgotten by the Russian people. But these days she knows, with absolute certainty, that there is no dignity in her destiny.

She pushes herself away from the dresser and runs her hands down her breasts, then her stomach, and around to her bottom. She is losing more and more weight. There is hardly anything left of her.

Her nerves are shards of glass that make walking not only painful but virtually impossible.

She hears the Swiss tutor reading to her son in the room next door. These days it is rare to hear her 13 year old boy chuckle or argue with Gilliard. Besides the lessons, his tutor plays cards with his young charge, trying to engage him. Since the day of her son's accident, crashing at the bottom of the household staircase, Alexei has known nothing but agony and bleeding; indeed, the haemorrhaging in the groin brought him close to death and left him yellow and slight. She blinks back tears and glances across at the icon of the *Stabat Mater* and thinks, as she does several times a day, that only the Blessed Mother of Christ knows what it is to suffer for the torture afflicted upon her son.

'Excuse me, Madam,' she turns slightly and sets her profile to Schneider, her maid, in whom she has detected the slightest change in temperature over the past few weeks. The maid no longer uses the correct address, *Empress of Russia, Your Imperial Highness,* or even *Tsarina.* Instead, Schneider's manner has been cooling. It is as if the maid is blaming her for this house arrest that has ridiculously extended to more than six months.

'You have been requested in the study.' Schneider closes the door behind her.

How she despises the maid with her pert face and equally pert breasts that cannot seem to be disguised beneath her uniform and apron. A German maid, she thinks and the corners of her mouth turn downwards. She has no memory of the elation she felt when she first learned that an intimate member of the household staff had come from her native land. Rather, she thinks about the pernicious German demands made at Brest-Litovsk.

She looks back into the mirror and pinches the tops of her cheekbones until the flush brings some level of colour into her sallow face.

One third of Russia, she had read somewhere 643,000 square kilometres, will be the cost of peace: Poland, Finland, the Baltic states, Ukraine, Crimea, and the Caucasus. It is utterly unconscionable. Nicky had wept when they were alone in their bed that night. *Sixty million Russians*, he had said over and over again, as she held him like any one of her children. Sixty million Russians were paid as ransom to the Kaiser by the Bolsheviks.

She dabs some Eau-de-cologne on her wrists and neck and cannot remember the last time she and her husband had sex. These days, if they even share a bed, it is for weeping privately and then for the comfort given, as a parent might a child.

She glances one more time into the mirror and sees her mother, long since dead, looking back at her. A face filled with the shadows of grief and a life, not hers. A narrow face. A hard face that is of no interest to anyone. Not to her son, who she knows feels smothered by her; not to her younger daughters, who want nothing but the outdoors, especially now it is mid-spring; not to Tatiana who has somehow outgrown her mother and become someone to whom her siblings turn; and certainly not to her eldest daughters Olga with her wild secrets and moodiness.

She leaves the mirror and her room and makes her way along the hallway to the study. She knows Nicky has asked for her to meet the new Commissar who has been sent to oversee their fate. Her husband and the Commissar have been locked up together for the past half hour or so. She wonders whether the Commissar has originally come from Petrograd or the new capital of Russia, Moscow. She has always felt Moscow the more stable of the cities, far less filled with bilious socialist agitation.

As she walks she feels a sharp pain dart from her left hip down her leg. Her sciatica is getting worse.

When she reaches the study, the door opens and Trupp is there with a tray in his free hand. On seeing her, the footman immediately steps back into the room and bows. It is as if the last six months never existed and they are back in her beloved Tsarskoye Selo. His livery is worn with pride. She steps through and immediately Nicky and a tall stranger, who has the black hair and the physique of a Tatar, stand up to greet her.

Her husband cocks his head to the side and mouths the word *Sunny* and she knows this is all he can do because the love he has for her is so full, so needy, that there is nothing else besides. Then he turns to the stranger and says, 'May I introduce ...' and she watches her husband stumble and she feels the blood rise to her face because she would not have faltered, as he so often does.

The tall dark stranger bows and to her surprise speaks in the most cultured manner, 'Your Imperial Highness.'

She cannot help herself, and the corners of her mouth lift and she opens wide her lovely grey eyes so that he can see she is the very title he has offered her. She joins the two men who have just been served coffee by Trupp.

'This is Vasily Vasilyevich Yakovlev,' says her husband, who seems delighted by the arrival of this strange portentous Commissar who has come to orchestrate the next chapter in their lives. Unlike her husband, she looks into her heart and does not see hope — only the endless suffering of her son, as he and his sisters lose their youth to the vagaries of an illegitimate and uneducated mob rule.

'I can only assume you are here to tell us what is to become of us.' She had not wanted to sound so crisp, especially as the Commissar had made such an impressive start, but she is overtired and tense. She had noticed the Commissar's arrival late last night with an entourage of over 100 horsemen. Already the household staff is gossiping that he had brought with him his telegraph operator because he will be communicating directly with Lenin. Rumour or truth, she did not know.

Vasily looks at this woman, whom he has heard so much about, and realises this is the strength behind the man who once ruled all of Russia. The Commissar had been seated with the man for the past half hour, unable to make sense of the man's kindliness in asking if the accommodation was suitable for him and his men. The man had then followed this up with a rambling account of an English novel he had read concerning the French Revolution. Vasily wondered to himself if the man was intimating that he understood the plight of the masses as they struggled to gain peace, bread, and land.

'I have heard from our household staff that you are replacing Commissar Kobylinsky.' To her statement, the tall dark-haired stranger nods and simply watches her for a few seconds.

Then, nonchalantly, quietly and almost casually, the Commissar says, 'He was not considered reliable.' Adding with an imperceptible shrug, 'For the job.'

'And what is the job, Commissar?'

Hmmm, Vasily thinks, she doesn't miss a beat. He looks away from her face that has no womanly softness and thinks about his wife and children in Tomsk and what will become of them if he doesn't pull off the plan handed down to him from Sverdlov.

'You see,' begins the man, who was once Tsar of all the Russias, glancing deferentially to his wife. 'We always found Commissar Kobylinsky quite reliable. And the thing is …' His wife does not watch her husband, 'The thing is, the children don't like change. It's disruptive. Do you see?'

Vasily, again, offers one of his nods and continues sipping what could only be described as the most delicious coffee he has ever tasted. He has no interest in these people. He knows what his task is and he intends to execute it successfully. The consequences of his actions will change the course of history. So, can he sit here and endure this buffoon and his sour wife? Of course, he answers himself smoothly.

'I have been sent to Tobolsk,' Vasily's voice is completely unflustered. It moves low and evenly over the agitated surface of the couple. 'From the Kremlin ...' His pause allows them to remember the formidable red citadel that was once theirs, 'With this message ...' Vasily places his coffee cup down on its saucer and turns his full attention to the man. 'I am a special representative from the Moscow Central Executive Committee. I have been sent to confirm what you probably already know.' He moves slowly and looks directly at the man's wife, 'The Germans are advancing on Petrograd.' He watches the blush move up the woman's neck and into her hollow cheeks, 'And a Bolshevik delegation is preparing to sign the German treaty at Germany's Headquarters on the Eastern Front.' The Commissar leans back and keeps his face still.

She wants to spit at this peasant. She wants to slap his face and scream that she is not German, nor has been for the last 24 years of her reign, and if the Kaiser and his men are marching on Petrograd then the Commissar and his stinking Bolsheviks only have themselves to blame! But instead, she sits there quietly.

Meanwhile, her husband's chest and face fill up with grief and shame. His Russia is lost. Under his watch, the most beloved of all nations, Mother Russia, has been handed over to foreigners. Failure. He drops his head and closes his eyes. I am a failure. I have failed, he thinks.

'It is paramount ...' Vasily's phlegmatic voice breaks into their thoughts as he directly addresses the man, 'That you allow your children and wife to go free.'

The man looks up at the Commissar. Perhaps he didn't hear correctly. The man looks across at his wife but her face is a steel trap and those grey eyes of hers remain vigilant. 'I'm sorry — I'm — I don't understand ...' The man is bewildered. Lost. Alone.

'You must surrender yourself,' Vasily speaks evenly. 'And return with me to Moscow. But more critically ...' His voice begins to rise as he sees the woman about to speak, 'You must set your wife and children free so that —'

'Out of the question! He will —'

'I refuse! I absolutely refuse —'

'We will not be separated! His Majesty will —'

'I refuse to be parted from my family. I just simply will not —'

Surprisingly, the couple stops when Vasily's hand rises in a gesture of halt.

The man reaches out and holds his wife's fingers with a tenacious grip. Everyone in the room knows the unsaid. If the man is made to co-sign the Peace Treaty, in conjunction with the Bolsheviks, then the world will know that the blood of 2,000,000 Russian soldiers is on his hands. I have nothing left, the man thinks to himself, everything has been taken from me. There is nothing left.

For a moment she catches herself thinking about her son and the possibility of taking him abroad, perhaps to England ... where he could be healed ... But then she steadies herself. She cannot allow her husband to stride, once again, into the lion's den without her. She thinks about the Imperial Manifesto of 1905. Her husband signed this and brought about an elected parliament and a fundamental blow to the ancient Russian absolute monarchy. Then, the Abdication of 1917 which he again signed and set their house arrest in motion. And now the Peace Treaty with Germany! It cannot be endured!

'Please. I urge you both to be calm.' Vasily slowly lowers his hand, 'You must be calm.'

She knows she will never allow her husband to sign the Peace Treaty. All of Russia must know it was the Bolsheviks who sold Russia out to the enemy.

The man knows there is no God. History and his beloved Russia are racing on without him, with absolutely no need of him. Once he was Tsar of all the Russias. Once he had been ordained by God to rule his people. Now he is godless.

'If you do not release your family ...' The Commissar leans into the man, 'I cannot vouch for their safety. It is you they want ...' Vasily sees the man's face pale and he doesn't care. He also knows it is a tight rope he must walk if he is to pull off the plan he has been given — not by the Bolsheviks but by the German Ambassador. Vasily's handler, Chairman Sverdlov of the Central Executive Committee, has been working with both the Bolsheviks and the Germans — the show trial in Moscow is nothing but a cover. The true plan is to dispatch the man off to the German Ambassador. Vasily inhales deeply because Sverdlov has instructed him to reveal the real plan to the man if he needs to seal his cooperation.

'As I said, I am a *special* representative ...' Vasily waits and looks at the woman, then the man, and then back to the woman, 'I have been assigned a mission of great importance ... I have my orders from my superior, Yakov Mikhailovich Sverdlov.' He looks the man in the eye, 'Russia expects you are to be tried in Moscow by Comrade Trotsky. But. In fact. You — alone — are to be taken to the German Ambassador, Wilhelm von Mirbach. Your family is to be left behind. They will be safe ...'

The study is quiet. No one stirs outside on the top floor and even below them, the household seems to be outdoors on the burgeoning spring day.

Vasily realises he must say what he knows to be true, 'The German Government has plans to protect you.'

The so-called Western Allies are not coming. They have turned their faces away from the fate of the Russian Imperial family. The man thinks about the 15,000,000 Russians he sent to fight a war for these Western Allies. Two million of them never returned. A war, that now, makes little sense.

The special Commissar speaks on in muted tones, 'The German

Government needs to quash the agitation for a Socialist Revolution in Germany ...' Again he pauses, wondering if the man is aware of Lenin's call for *World Revolution* and the impact this is having particularly on Germany. 'The Kaiser believes, now that we are at peace, that it would be best if you were ... given succour.'

Both men hear the woman whisper, *God is merciful*, as she makes the sign of the cross.

Vasily says, 'You must be ready to leave before dawn tomorrow —'

'But surely it is not safe! The river is still frozen and —'

'Our son cannot yet travel —'

The commissar's sigh is audible. He stands up and adjusts his belt across his shirt tunic. He has much to do and little patience with these people who seem unable to grasp the urgency of their situation.

'We leave before dawn. If you insist on being together then you must leave the children in the care of your household and when your son is well enough the children will join you —'

'I refuse —'

'If you refuse, my orders are to take you by force. But I advise you ...' The Commissar towers above the seated man with his wife, 'If you do not cooperate, less scrupulous men will replace me.' He lets that statement of fact descend upon them. 'It is better you accept this decision and come with me. Say nothing except that you are to be moved and the children are coming later when the boy is well.'

As Vasily walks towards the door he is surprised to hear the woman gulp back a sob. He had not believed she was capable of tears. He doesn't turn around but hears her croon something about her children, her babies, her daughters, her son and he opens the door of the study, pauses, and says quietly back over his shoulder, 'You must be calm.' Vasily steps out and closes the door softly behind him.

2

Olga's face is flushed after her breathless disclosure and Captain Pavel Konoplev thinks to himself, she is the most beautiful girl in the world! They have stolen a little time in the woodshed at the back of the Governor's house. Meanwhile, the newly arrived Commissar's horsemen have, more or less, taken over Tobolsk, galloping or trotting about proprietorially and the household is abuzz with packing, laundry, and a general feeling of festivity. Pavel knows that this is the very moment they have been hoping for and Olga seems equally exhilarated at the prospect of this upcoming logistical move.

'So, you are absolutely sure, Olenka, that it is one of the *other* sisters who is accompanying your parents tonight?'

She wants to reach up and kiss his furrowed brow but clings instead to his strong shoulders and says, 'Yes! Marie has been chosen by Mother and Papa to go with them — not tonight but before dawn tomorrow morning. Wait, I guess that is more or less tonight — anyway — yes! I am to stay back with Tatyana and Anastasia to look after Baby.'

He looks down at her silky skin still blushed with the wonder of her news. They must stick to their plan, he thinks, because there will not be another opportunity. It is now or never.

'Alright, my love, now listen ...' he says but can't resist her soft chestnut blonde head and kisses it quickly. 'When your parents depart with the new Commissar and his horsemen, we will wait till the end of April —'

'No!' groans Olga.

'Yes,' insists Pavel and pulls her lovely tall willowy body to him, 'Yes. It is only four or five days away ...' He kisses her on her upturned nose and she lifts her face to him as if he is the sunshine that will offer her everlasting life. 'Then we will leave as we planned. We will head north then eventually, west —'

'How? But how? Won't the rivers still be frozen?'

He looks down at her anxious face and knows he would do anything to save her — he would shoot to kill so that she would be free. 'Don't worry, I have it worked out.'

Pavel did not have the plan worked out but he knew they must head finally into northern Siberia first until things settle, and then west to Petrograd to reach his father's estate. Once there, she would be safe. Thousands of Russians were on the move and one more couple in amongst the throng would go unnoticed. Besides, it was spring and they would move by train, carriage, river, and foot until they were clear of this godforsaken place. They had months and months and months before the hard cold set in at the other side of autumn.

'I will miss them though ...'

He is brought back to the present by her whimsy. Their time together here in the woodshed is running out. And more than ever they must not be seen by anyone, they must not let a single person suspect something is afoot.

'I know Baby will be fine. Tatyana is the most annoying bore telling everyone what to do but in some ways, this is good because it means I can just visit you and read and think, and ...' She looks at him coquettishly and repeats, 'Visit you.'

'No, my love. Now we must be more careful than ever.'

Olga begins to protest but he presses his calloused fingers to her darling mouth and Pavel says softly, 'We can't do anything until your parents have been taken away from the approaching enemy ...' The White Army is days away from Tobolsk and the Bolsheviks need to move the Tsar to a more secure location.

'Loyalists are not *my* enemy —'

'The White Army *is* the enemy,' interrupts Pavel. 'And when we eventually get to Petrograd you will see that *my* enemy is *your* enemy.' And then he is kissing her face and slowly she feels his fingers push past her lips and touch the tip of her tongue. Olga knows she can trust him with her life and she bites down softly on his fingers and hears him groan. Then her hands are in his hair and he is kissing her with such passion that she cannot think. His body is firm and muscular and pushes her hard against the chopped timber so that her head swims with its ambrosial aroma.

Outside the woodshed, the spring afternoon recedes and the sky peels back to a palette of pearlescent grey and pink and egg-yolk yellow. The lamps are being lighted in the Governor's house and household staff and members of the family can be seen bustling hither and thither with luggage that is growing at the bottom of the stairs, at an alarming rate.

Neither Pavel nor Olga hear the approach of footsteps so when the door to the woodshed squeaks open they are whiplashed apart — he to the door itself so that Olga is secured somewhere behind him.

'Captain?' Anastasia's little face bobs around the door. 'Papa would like to speak to you and has asked if you wouldn't mind — Olga! Where have you been? Tatyana is ordering us all about and I have been doing most of the work! What are you doing here?'

Pavel thinks fast, 'She has come to ask me if some of my men might begin loading one of the tarantasses with ...'

'With Mother and Papa's luggage,' supplies Olga as she pushes past Pavel to face Anastasia who is still hanging on the doorknob. Her cool demeanour is so impressive that for a second he wonders whether, in their passionate pushing and pulling, she has indeed asked for the carts to be brought around but then he sees the corners of her wide mouth twitch with the faintest of smiles.

'Oh, for goodness sake,' exclaims Anastasia, who is far too precocious for her good. 'Mother won't want her precious things slung into the back of a peasant's cart.' Inexplicably, this sets the young 16 year old off in fits of chuckles but Pavel is grateful for the distraction.

'Please tell your father I will be with him shortly,' says Pavel easily. 'After I drop some wood off to the sentry boxes for the samovars.'

Olga hooks her arm through Anastasia, an uncommon gesture that fills the younger sister with love for the eldest, even though Olga usually has little time or interest in her, and they saunter off back toward the house. Pavel knows then that nothing will derail their plans. His beloved Olenka is courageous and resourceful and, more importantly than anything else, on his side. Outside the woodshed, the expansive Siberian spring evening, with its rush of stars and promises, forms an eternal canopy above. The Captain of the Guards, Pavel Konoplev, limps slowly across to the house.

Inside, chaos flurries about with servants packing and repacking the luggage which is stacked precariously in the entranceway. Pavel climbs up the staircase, his wounded leg causing him more trouble after the day's use. An inner voice cautions him to keep his head down and not look about in case he espies Olga.

'Papa! The Captain is here!' cries Anastasia as she disappears into the study.

Pavel hears her mother reprimand her for raising her voice indoors. He waits at the top of the stairs for the man to come to him. A minute or two passes and the man who was once Tsar moves quickly out of the study and, to Pavel's alarm, strides towards him with his arms outstretched.

'Let me embrace and thank you, Captain, for the great care you have taken of us till now!' And then to Pavel's horror, the man attempts to wrap his arms around him. 'You have shown my family great kindness and I thank you for all those hours you have spent with ...' The man pulls back and holds the Captain at arm's length, staring straight into his eyes, 'My son and letting him beat you at draughts, or so I believe!'

The man is a fool, thinks Pavel, but accepts the gratitude with a shrug of his shoulders. The sooner they leave the better.

'So, no doubt you have heard the news — we are leaving Tobolsk!'

Pavel is unconvinced by the man's performance. He looks at his gaunt face and greying beard and is sure that he must know it is the end of the line for him and his wife. This is the best decision he has made to date, cutting himself off from his innocent children. At least that will give the rest of them a chance. Why he insists on taking one of his daughters is a mystery that will, indeed, become her tragedy. But Pavel is not concerned about the man or his wife or even the other girl's fate. The only person in his sight is Olga.

'And, we are not exactly sure about where in particular we will end up, but we know it is a step in the right direction!'

The Captain looks at the man and wonders whether he was always like this or whether the war and its grinding failures made him this way. Everyone knows across the length and breadth of Russia that he has failed them and failed God. But now that there is no God, as Lenin reminds them in most of his maxims, the man has, disgracefully, failed himself. Pavel feels quite sure, no matter what, he will never fail himself.

'So, the thing is ... The thing is, Captain Konoplev ...'

Some of the children tumble out of the backrooms and scoot past them with more bundles of what appears to be furs and coats to be added to the stockpile downstairs and it strikes Pavel with surprise that they think they will make it to another winter. This is the one truth from which he has shielded Olga. All Party members know that Trotsky is planning to put the man on trial after which he will be shot by firing squad for treason. Every Bolshevik knows that the man's days are numbered.

'Papa!' It's Anastasia shouting again at the bottom of the staircase. 'The Commissar is here!'

The man ignores his daughter and the mayhem about him and takes Pavel's hand and says with complete sincerity, 'Yes, the thing is we have chosen you to come with us, to be part of the few household members we have been permitted to take ...'

Pavel is so horrified he forgets to maintain his impassive visage and roughly pulls back from the man's surprisingly tight grip.

Vasily reaches the top of the steps to find the man looking perplexedly at the Captain of the Guards. The Commissar has heard from his men that Captain Konoplev is an ardent Party member, a trustworthy comrade, and someone who understands the dynamics of the family under house arrest. But Vasily is already frustrated by what he has chanced upon downstairs. A mountain of suitcases and bedding and paintings and icons and books, as if the impending departure is now to be a travelling circus rather than a highly strategized and secretive exit.

The man looks at the Commissar who stands before him and says, 'I'm afraid that the children are very unsettled by the news that we are to be separated and they have insisted we take with us as much of their luggage as possible — I'm sure it is a way of reassuring themselves that we will be all reunited, very soon.'

Vasily does not hide his irritation from the man and addresses Pavel, 'Captain Konoplev.'

Pavel replies courteously, 'Commissar.'

How strange, the man thinks to himself, that these two, who are insignificant players in the great scheme of Russia, toy with my fate and that of my loved ones. It has all become rather confusing, really. When they were first under house arrest in Tsarskoye Selo, the man had assured his wife that the Western Allies would come to their aid and help them escape, and when the madness had blown over, they would return to Russia. As the months passed he had then said to her, after Kerensky had delivered the news that the Allies were *not* coming, that his mother, the Empress Dowager and his brother and relatives in the Crimea, would finance their escape to the Crimea. Sadly, those plans had come to nothing. But his cousin the Kaiser, once referred affectionately by him as Willy, has a plan. In some ways, it would be a relief to not have to face the Allies or his relatives and endure the shame of all he could not be. As long as he has his beloved children about him he knows he can be a man, who, perhaps, might start again, somehow, someday. Not as the Tsar of course but as an ordinary man who would eventually begin to find his place in his beloved homeland. Reading. Cutting wood. Taking long walks. That sort of thing. He has accepted that he can never go back to the role given to him by God because he knows it is completely over. That contract, that oath, that holy vow to fulfill the role which was *his* by right of birth — all of that no longer exists and in the rubble of his soul, he would have to say he is glad.

As Pavel turns to leave and to get on with the tasks requested of him by Vasily, the man breaks out of his reverie and says, 'Commissar, I have just requested Captain Konoplev accompany us tomorrow. I know most of the guards are being dismissed because you have sufficient men but the Captain has proven very reliable and, if you are in agreement, Commissar, we would like him with us tomorrow.'

Pavel stares at the man and thinks to himself, he has no bloody idea ... No idea whatsoever about Pavel's plans with Olga, about the man's impending doom, or the future of their beloved Russia.

'That is, of course, if Captain Konoplev would be so kind as to come with us. You see, it's my wife ...' The man lowers his voice as if the three of them standing at the top of the staircase are equals and are interested in the minutia of each other's private lives. 'You see, the thing is, she would be more — well, um — settled if we had a familiar face, there alongside us on our travels.'

'Your household staff is already travelling with you,' Pavel cannot help himself and knows that his tone is laced with sarcasm.

The man blinks and moves his head this way and that as if taking in this information and then adds, 'Yes, well some are coming with us tomorrow, isn't that right, Commissar? It is just that, we thought, my wife thought ... But if you cannot be spared, I quite understand.'

The man stops talking.

Pavel is sick to the back teeth of this ridiculous man and his situation. Pavel has a great deal to achieve, not only in getting the man, his wife, and young daughter on the road before dawn but, more importantly, in securing transport for himself and Olga to escape Tobolsk and head north as soon as possible. Over the past few months Olga has brought to him several items for them to pawn so that once they are on their way, they can purchase railway tickets, accommodation, and food. She insists that it is her way of preparing, as best she can, for their journey. Meanwhile, he knows he can handle anybody who might get in their way — he has seen enough in war to know how to survive.

Just as Pavel turns to descend the staircase Vasily says, 'Captain, actually that might help me.'

Pavel looks at the tall dark-haired Commissar in disbelief.

Anticipating Pavel's refusal the Commissar continues, 'Your reputation as a Party member is impressive — the men all regard you as trustworthy and fair. I have good men with me but I would not refuse your support. Your knowledge of the household and ...' All three know Vasily wants to say *the family* but instead offers, 'Those who have been involved here, over the past six months, would be quite useful.'

There is no way he can refuse. To do so would be to call upon himself retribution from the Party. Kobylinsky — white-faced with shock — had told Pavel he had been dismissed by the new Commissar. He said he was ordered to comply without delay or he would be court-martialled by a revolutionary tribunal and put to death.

Pavel turns away from Vasily and hears himself say, 'If that is your wish.'

'Thank you, Captain,' responds Vasily but Pavel can only hear a terrible roaring in his ears because his plans to escape from Tobolsk with his beloved have been destroyed with the velocity and execution of artillery fire.

3

Several hours later, but well before dawn, the man, his wife, and one of the younger daughters are unceremoniously bundled into one of the two tarantasses — carts without springs or seats. The calvary escort makes up the pre-dawn cacophony in their preparation for the long journey ahead.

Just before their departure, Pavel catches a glimpse of the second oldest girl, Tatyana, giving orders to this one and that while her mother tries to offer a teary farewell. The second oldest daughter shoos her off into one of the awaiting carts. And no matter how much he searches for her, Olga never surfaces, even though everyone else does, even the crippled boy. Pavel makes a fuss checking that the luggage left in the entranceway has, indeed, been packed, and then when he can find nothing else to delay the inevitable he too mounts his horse. Of course, he wants just a moment, a second, with Olga to reassure her that they will escape just as soon as she and the others re-join her family. And then he hears the man say to his wife that Olga is not well enough to see them off.

This is not an omen, Pavel tells himself as he kicks his horse to move up behind the cart carrying the prisoners. This is not an augury but a young girl's heart breaking. Nothing more. If only he could have told her that their plans are on hold. And soon, when they meet again, they will escape without delay. But for now ... for now, he has been ordered by Commissar Vasily Yakovlev to ride behind the prisoners. And so, Pavel rides on, frustrated and angry but not defeated. Wherever it is they are headed, and rumour has it that the next place will be the family's final bolt-hole, Pavel promises himself that he and Olga will escape.

The sun is just coming up when the escorted prisoners with the Commissar, over 100 horsemen, some of the household staff and Pavel, arrive to cross the confluence of the Irtysh and Tobol Rivers. Some of the horsemen dismount and move gingerly over the ice. The rest wait and watch. From where they stand they can hear the thick dry cracks pulling out from under the cautious footsteps of the first brave few who are testing the ice. Spring is a tricky business in Siberia. Rivers such as these ice over for most of the autumn and all of winter, then, in spring, they are predictably, unpredictable.

The signal is given for the rest of them to cross the icy river. The horses, with their riders walking beside them, whinny, flare their nostrils and toss back their heads, but the men shuffle on, cautiously watching the glassy world beneath their boots. It is an undulating steel-grey river of ice where once there was water. On and on it stretches. Here and there are wild skeletal branches of trees that protrude up out of the surface but for the most part, as far as the eye can see, there is nothing but the unrelenting stretch of hard ice.

Pavel tells the man, his wife, and their daughter to get down from the cart. Trupp, the family's footman, fusses about the luggage but Pavel is impatient to cross the river lest it splits and drags them down into its clutches. He hurries them along.

Halfway across Pavel looks over and sees one of the carts drop its wheel into the slosh of broken ice and the river gurgles menacingly around the ankles of those hauling the cart. The sound of the ice never stops. It pops and crackles and chinks and gives out low guttural groans as if it is a living breathing leviathan with its skin stretched tight over the clamour of life trapped beneath.

The man walks ahead of his wife who seems to lean on their daughter, as they cross the huge icy river. If Pavel did not know who these three were, he would have thought them ordinary Russians, part of the great diaspora moving either away from or toward, the ever-approaching Red or White Army. It is the White Army Loyalists who are closing in on Tobolsk.

Pavel is not the only one worried about the crossing. Apart from the horses protesting, no one makes much noise — there's a grunt or two from the cart haulers but apart from that there is just a hard, quiet, primal fear moving from one person to the next.

A terror.

A dread.

A horror of the swift implosion of ice — a roar of falling — burning cold — suffocation — drowning — asphyxiation — forever locked beneath its shimmering surface.

By the time they reach the other side of the frozen river, they are thigh-deep in the broken icy sludge and they scramble, on the verge of tears, to the blessed footfall of land. Pavel looks back and sees the last of the men crossing and imagines the White Army on the other side and Vasily, Moses-like, closing the river over them. As he raises the mighty Red Banner the ice screams and the White Army falls and drowns within its frozen depths. Men and horses and weapons engulfed in the horror of an eternal winter. Pavel moves on.

Days pass slowly with numerous remount stations, as the detachment moves on and on through the Siberian spring. A journey filled with the constancy of ice and cold and hoar frost. It is tired and tedious going and, for the most part, without incident until a curious moment arises, witnessed by Pavel and a handful of others.

The horses snort and clang up against other horses as they navigate themselves through a small nondescript Russian village called

Pokrovskoye. The villages are all the same ... same muddy toe-paths, same wooden churches, same dilapidated hovels, and same toothless peasants staring. Vasily's men usually take their time to egress the villages so that enterprising villagers can sell homebrew or dumplings. At this particular village, a few of the men are negotiating a ridiculously cheap price, when a woman of indeterminate age steps out beside the tarantass in which the man's wife half-sits, half-lays and tries to reach out and touch her. Pavel watches as the man's wife recoils from the soiled arthritic fingers of the peasant. And then he hears the one seeking supplication or justice, he cannot tell which, say, 'Grigori. My husband. Grigori.' Pavel watches as the woman who was once called Tsarina, now a prisoner of Russia attempts to bat away the annoying incident, but the peasant woman is having none of it and reaches both her hands up above her and cries out, 'Grigori. My husband. Grigori Rasputin.' And for a moment Pavel has to search his memory because the name is familiar and yet here, in this godforsaken lost world of peasants and poverty, where war and politics mean nothing and weather is God, it makes no sense what is being said. Then the prisoner gasps audibly, sits upright and reaches out her white hand and, above the filthy scarfed head of the peasant woman, makes the sign of the cross. Some of Vasily's men around the tableau kick their horses wanting to charge past what they are witnessing. A frisson of irritation and then anger seems to whip around them. Even Pavel finds himself grinding his teeth wondering whether it might have turned out differently if the syphilis-infected charlatan had remained at home, in this wretched village, rather than made his way to the home of the Tsar and the bed of the Tsarina.

4

The wide-open Siberian plains are easier to pass through than the villages and with each day the weather is warming, so except for the fact that his lovely girl has been left behind and their escape plans, for the time being, thwarted, Pavel can't help feel a sense of freedom after months of being confined to Tsarskoye Selo, outside of Petrograd, followed by the interminable post at the Governor's house, in Tobolsk.

As they set up camp one night, to Pavel's surprise, Vasily sends for him. The Captain of the Guards has not seen much of the Commissar throughout the journey so far. He makes his way through the men as they unsaddle their horses, light cooking fires, unpack supplies, and generally make ready for another night under the stars. Over the past few days he has heard their respect for Vasily and they, in turn, seem to treat Pavel with a certain wary deference, possibly because they know the Commissar has selected him to join them. But more probably because to cross their tall dark-haired leader, is more or less to ask for trouble.

'Captain,' Vasily says plainly as Pavel enters his tent which is equipped with a small writing desk, chair and cot. 'I'm sure you have been wondering where we are headed?' The Commissar speaks quietly and there is something about his manner that makes Pavel feel he is being taken into a confidence.

Pavel replies, 'I can only assume, Commissar, that we are either headed to Moscow ...' Something passes across Vasily's face and it makes Pavel explain, 'There has been much in the newspapers about Comrade Trotsky and the Romanov trial.'

The Commissar seems satisfied with this explanation and allows a pause to follow that indicates they have all the time in the world to haul the ex-Tsar across Russia.

'I see you are keeping your post in the rear guard, close to the prisoners.'

Again the two men wait and Pavel shifts his weight off his left leg.

Then Vasily adds slowly, 'I have received information ... There are Red Guards ... Twenty kilometres this side of Tyumen ... Waiting for us.'

Pavel is unsure where this is going but considering every Red Guard contingent he has come across answers to their own local soviet or no one at all, he can only assume Vasily, quite rightly, is apprehensive about the upcoming encounter. Everyone knows that the Red Guards will stop them and ask them their business, and most likely want to take over, especially when it is known that their cargo could be ransomed.

Vasily looks directly at Pavel and says, 'Keep close to the tarantasses tomorrow, should there be any trouble.'

Pavel nods his agreement and adds, 'I take it the Romanovs will be put on the train at Tyumen —'

'Correct. Heading west.' Vasily watches Pavel for a moment then curiously adds, 'Or southeast ... It is yet to be decided.' The Commissar looks away as if he hasn't spoken and for a moment Pavel is almost convinced he hasn't but then he realises he is been dismissed so he turns and leaves.

On his way back to his makeshift bedding under the stars, Pavel reflects on what just happened. He realises he is being warned that a melee might ensue tomorrow when crossing paths with the Reds, but he also thinks there was some kind of test of loyalty. Something about the route southeast ... as opposed to the anticipated route west. The mention of two different possible directions by Vasily is strange. It is as if Vasily is inviting Pavel to draw his conclusions or maybe even voice a protest or ask a question. Pavel moves through the exhausted bodies of Vasily's loyal horsemen, individuals who do as they are bidden, proving night and day that they will go to the end of the earth if this is what the Commissar requires.

And then it hits Pavel.

Of course, he almost says aloud in the dark. Omsk is southeast!

And in Omsk is a T-junction with the east-west train line crossing the north-south train line ... Thus the Romanovs would find their true north — all the way to the Arctic Ocean and its promise of escape! Pavel's heart is racing and he knows he will find no rest this evening. Is Vasily attempting to gauge Pavel's capacity to turn a blind eye if the prisoners were assisted to make their escape? Pavel tries to think. Suddenly it occurs to him that maybe the best way to save Olga, and her siblings for that matter, would be to enable the Tsar to escape to freedom. Without a doubt, the rest of the family back at Tobolsk would be whisked north to join him.

Pavel cannot sleep and pushes himself up against the wheel of one of the supply carts. He could leave now. Maybe this is what Vasily is suggesting — if he is unable to abide by the Commissar's decisions. But why was he selected and taken along in the first place? It makes no sense. Pavel listens to the horses and the occasional grunt or fart from the sleeping, other than that, no one stirs. His mind and heart are racing — he is convinced this is an escape plan for the man and his family. So is Olga to be taken to some foreign land? Shouldn't he be glad she would at least be safe even if it means they can no longer be together? But deep in his dark heart Pavel knows only he can save Olga and the night sky billows above him, swirling with stars that light up all of Siberia.

The next morning, a posse of 20 mounted Red Guards simply appears out of the morning mist. It happens when Pavel and the others are striking camp. The Red Guards ride in, shoulders back and rifles ready, believing whoever is in charge will surface fast. Pavel moves across to the cart in which sits the man's wife and daughter. He has little interest in the man but if anything happens he at least will try to protect Olga's sister.

Vasily walks nonchalantly across to the Red Guards and his sharp cheekbones, glistening black eyes and slanting eyebrows impress them sufficiently to halt. Many of Vasily's men move in close behind him, mounted high on their horses.

Everyone watches the scene.

Vasily takes his time to light a cigarette and then tosses the packet to one of the Red Guards closest to him. Finally, he says something, and a few of the Red Guards chuckle and visibly relax in their saddles. Pavel sees the Commissar wave a vague hand toward the supply cart and the Red Guards turn their heads and look. Vasily's body is long and lean and completely comfortable as it rests against the rump of one of the horses of the Red Guard. He smokes and talks and listens and nods occasionally and ... keeps smoking.

Pavel notices the man's wife crane her head out of the cart as she attempts to scrutinise the faces of the Red Guards. He doesn't know what she is expecting to see. After a while, she seems satisfied and he hears her reassure the teenage daughter that they, *Look to be good men.* Pavel tuts softly to himself. What he sees is a group of desperate men, possibly Army deserters, and most probably hungry and trigger happy. Pavel is a Bolshevik, as is every horseman in the contingent, including Vasily himself, but none of them will be strongarmed or harried by these thugs.

Then Vasily begins to walk away amicably, peacefully, decisively. He mounts his horse and signals for his men to follow which they do immediately, leaving in their wake a tangle of carts and horses and Red Guards jostling to move forward or around or backward or to the side. The Red Guard interlopers are put in their place, quite literally, at the tail end of the march forward.

Before long, Vasily and the men are on the road to Tyumen.

The day passes uneventfully but Pavel, like all of Vasily's men, glance occasionally at the Red Guards who now ride 100 metres or so behind. By sunset, they have made it to the train station at Tyumen. Normally the railway station is a tired little affair but tonight it is busy with train drivers and railway workers and Vasily's men and Red Guards all getting ready to move three prisoners across Russia. Everyone has been watching or participating in the endless shunting of carriages and loading of goods and beasts. There have been two trains brought forward and the Commissar has ordered that the 1st Class carriage of the second train be made ready for the prisoners. Soldiers and workers are bustling about and Pavel is in the throes of moving the man and his wife and daughter to the carriage when Vasily looms in front of them.

The Commissar addresses the man, 'I will be travelling with you and your wife and daughter when we leave tomorrow morning.'

Pavel is unsure why the prisoner needs to know this, except, perhaps, the Commissar wants to reassure them that they are in good hands and the end is in sight. Just what exactly is that end makes Pavel jumpy. Meanwhile, the man seems to be squaring up to this next chapter in his life. It couldn't have been comfortable or easy to be half-sitting, half-lying in that rickety cart for the past week, but the man nods his head with thanks to the Commissar and looks hopefully across at his wife.

'Captain Konoplev, ensure the family is inside the carriage,' Vasily gestures to the one stencilled with *1st Class* along its side. 'No lights. Curtains drawn.'

Pavel notices the man's wife open her mouth to ask a question but then decides against it.

'Wait inside with them,' is the Commissar's final instruction to Pavel.

There is so much unsaid, thinks Pavel, as he replies, 'Yes, Commissar.'

Vasily's private telegraph operator appears and says something to him.

'I will send a telegram on your behalf,' Vasily declares as he looks directly at the man. 'To let your other children know you are proceeding safely.'

Pavel has a distinct feeling that this is not the only telegram Vasily will be sending from Tyumen railway station.

Then the man pipes up, 'Would you mind asking ... Could you ask from us ... How is the Little One?'

Pavel hears a catch in the man's voice and is grateful that their small huddle is engulfed by shadows and darkness. Vasily makes no acknowledgement of the request and moves swiftly across the railway lines to the station master's office as if he has far greater issues to resolve.

Then the man's wife calls after Vasily, in a voice full of tears, 'God bless you!'

They pull out just before dawn. All the curtains are drawn and the lights extinguished. Ghost trains. No trumpeting steam whistle signalling their departure, just the tug and pull of the carriages being shunted towards their destiny. Soon the prisoners and some of their household staff are sleeping but there is something about Vasily's circumspection that keeps Pavel awake and alert in the sumptuous 1st Class carriage.

The endless clatter of the train charges onwards.

After a while the Commissar settles opposite Pavel and seems inclined to talk, so Pavel commences with, 'Some of the men say we should be in Yekaterinburg by tomorrow morning.' He keeps his voice low even though the prisoners are at the other end of the carriage. It is an open carriage crowded with settees and well-padded armchairs from the decadence of yesteryear. The richly textured wallpaper in crimson and gold is old and disintegrating, reminding the travellers there is no going back.

Vasily takes his time to reply, 'Perhaps ...' He lets the word sit between them, and just when Pavel thinks that is the end to their conversation, the Commissar adds, 'I've decided to travel south-east ...' None of Vasily's men have spoken about heading south-east — they have talked only about the route west: first to Yekaterinburg, a Bolshevik stronghold, then Perm and on and on until they reach Moscow. 'Omsk is our destination,' supplies the Commissar, guardedly.

Interesting, thinks Pavel.

'And we are connecting there to the Trans-Siberian line ... that will, as you realise, take us to Moscow faster, while avoiding Yekaterinburg.' The fiercely anti-monarchical Yekaterinburg in the Urals would not think twice about seizing the prisoners and doing with them what they will because they are far from the reach of the Moscow Central Government.

But Pavel is no fool. Yes, Omsk is a key stop for those travelling east to west, such as Moscow ... but Omsk also offers the train line heading north — to the Arctic Sea and beyond. Over this past week, he has found himself caught up in a strange drama. Is the Commissar truly working for the Bolsheviks? ... or the White Army? ... or the Germans? — or even himself? It's not inconceivable that the prisoner might have bribed Vasily to secure their liberation ... But if that is the case then why would they have left their four other children behind? It makes no sense. Try as he might, Pavel cannot figure out what is happening. But something is afoot.

Pavel looks past the Commissar and thinks grimly that while he missed the opportunity to escape with Olga in Tobolsk, he has formed another plan. He has decided he will return to Tobolsk, while all of Russia is watching Trotsky's sensational cross-examination of the man for treason, and grab Olga and run. But if Vasily is hatching an escape for the prisoner to go north to where the Allies are landing in support of the White Army — then what the hell does this mean for his darling girl ... and him?

Vasily's mind is far from the comfort of the 1st Class carriage. He knows he has done the right thing by informing Pavel that their destination is Omsk because he needs an ally in someone who understands the family. If his plan is to succeed. Vasily stares at nothing and thinks about the telegrams he has sent. One to the Romanov children back at Tobolsk, one to Ambassador Mirbach in the German Embassy, and the last to Vasily's contact in Omsk. He thinks to himself, they're not out of the woods yet, and nor will they be until they get to Omsk, after that ... well the chips could fall either way. His mind darts back and forth between the possible outcomes of this train ride. He has no intention of delivering the man into the hands of Trotsky in Moscow, and up until a few days ago, he had every intention of handing him over to Ambassador Mirbach, who would be meeting them at Kazan, along the Trans-Siberian route, and from there the prisoner would be bundled off to Germany. But then another plan took shape ... one that he has decided upon ... one that will change history in a way neither the German Ambassador nor the Kaiser nor Trotsky could have ever anticipated.

The train rushes on and on, and with each passing hour, Vasily allows himself, just a little, to believe his plan will come to fruition.

He thinks about his wife and her short red hair and the way it never settles — their three sons have the same problem. He knows they are safe in their hometown of Tomsk, surrounded by grandparents and aunts, and uncles. Their hometown ... now occupied by the White Army. Vasily thinks about his initial commitment to the Bolsheviks and how they helped him make sense of his life and offered him hope for a very particular future. And then came the intimidation and coercion from the local soviet to do its bidding, and its dirty work, because the local soviet knew he could command the loyalty of men. The local soviet's mistake had been to threaten his family if he failed to move the Romanovs out of reach of the oncoming White Army.

It was the Chairman of the Central Executive Committee, Yakov Mikhailovich Sverdlov, who initially sent through the paperwork commanding Vasily to deliver the prisoner to Trotsky in Moscow and the awaiting show trial. But the slippery Sverdlov then telephoned Vasily at Tobolsk, just before he went into his meeting with the prisoner, with an updated and highly confidential change of orders: *Take the prisoner to Mirbach, the German Ambassador, in Kazan.*

Well, Vasily has made a different decision. Now that his own family is safe from the Party's threats and under the protection of the White Army, his mind is made up.

Vasily feels the train slow down and realises the locomotives probably need more water and fuel. They must be in Kulomzino or thereabouts by now, less than 100 kilometres from Omsk. And Omsk is where he will action his plan. He will bundle the prisoners onto a northbound train. Destination: Murmansk. This is where the Allies have landed. Under the cover of the mayhem of the civil war and while the struggle between the Bolsheviks and the Germans over the peace settlement continues, the man and his wife and their children will go unseen into their destiny.

In the darkness of the night, as the train comes to a stop, he can smell summer in the Siberian plains. His men would appreciate an opportunity to get off the train and stretch their legs but he has not permitted this at any point since leaving Tyumen, nor will he until they are firmly in Omsk. It shouldn't be much longer before they are there, he thinks and stands up. It is then that he decides to step out of the carriage and is surprised to see Pavel is up and intent on doing the same. He watches the Captain as he gingerly stretches his left leg and winces.

Vasily swings the door wide and he closes his eyes to inhale the warm night breeze that travels out of the east with scents of pea-trees, elm, and home. He jumps down from the train and because he doesn't hear Pavel do the same, looks back. The Captain is standing stock still in the doorway of the carriage with a strange expression on his face. Slowly, Vasily turns back around to face the benighted Siberian landscape and sees what Pavel sees. The silhouette of Red Guards on horseback. Hundreds and hundreds of them.

The man, who was once Tsar of all the Russias, moves quietly behind Captain Pavel Konoplev because he has seen him unlock the safety catch of his revolver. The man watches Commissar Vasily standing before hundreds of mounted Red Guards.

One of them leans across his pommel and says they are *The West Siberian Soviet, acting on behalf of the Ural Soviet.*

Meanwhile, the man knows it is not just his fate in the balance but the Commissar's and Pavel's and every man in Vasily's entourage. The destiny of all is being determined right here, right now.

The man hears someone shout, and one of the words clearer than all others is *BETRAYAL!* and the man feels his skin crawl.

Then he hears Vasily's measured voice respond with something about, *Following orders from Moscow.*

Red Guard from the West Siberian Soviet yells again and everyone must hear him cry, *TRAITOR!*

A pause follows and then Vasily calmly insists he *Speak directly with my superior in Moscow.*

More loud accusation and anger.

Vasily coolly demands the train be allowed to *Continue to Omsk so that my contact, Chairman Sverdlov of the Central Executive Committee in Moscow, will confirm to the West Siberian Soviet that I speak the truth.*

The man sees Pavel grip his revolver more tightly but he is unsure whether he would use it on Commissar Vasily or the West Siberian Soviet or, even, on himself. He looks back to check his wife and daughter are not alarmed. In the shadows, he discerns his daughter is sleeping but his wife is standing by the settee, rigid with anticipation.

Someone from the West Siberian Soviet is charging the Commissar Vasily with *CONSPIRACY TO PERVERT THE COURSE OF JUSTICE!* And *DELIBERATELY REROUTING THE PRISONERS AWAY FROM YEKATERINBURG!* The man hears the West Siberian Soviet accuse Vasily and Chairman Sverdlov of the Central Executive Committee in Moscow of, *ANTI-BOLSHEVIK INTENT!*

The man listens as the West Siberian Soviet argue amongst themselves. Initially, he hadn't allowed himself to believe Vasily's plan, to hand them over to the German Ambassador, but now he has to admit it could well have been true. His wife had said, *Better that than a show trial in Moscow with Trotsky performing his monkey tricks.* He hadn't replied at the time. Whether the man is cross-examined by a Jew in the Red Square or hauled off to kowtow to the German Government, both courses of action would be shameful and he has no will to endure either.

Pavel steps back suddenly and Vasily pulls himself into the carriage. He glances at the revolver in the Captain's hand and then momentarily gathers himself before he speaks.

'They are unhooking one of the carriages closest to the locomotive and I will be escorted to Omsk. Alone.' Vasily's pace and tone are an imitation of its former voice. He looks warily at Pavel but addresses his next statements to the man, 'They have accused me of working for the Germans when in fact I have been working for my superior who is Chairman Sverdlov of the Central Executive Committee in Moscow.' He adds slowly, 'As you all well know —'

'Commissar Vasily,' interrupts Pavel quietly. 'What are your orders for me?'

The tall dark-haired Commissar is relieved and places a rough hand on Pavel's shoulder, 'Guard the family until I return from Omsk.' He looks at the man standing behind Pavel, 'The West Siberian Soviet has decided I must go alone to Omsk and face the accusations. They say that in Tyumen I sent a telegram to the Germans … Allegedly I had deliberately intended to reroute our train away from Yekaterinburg to reach the Germans already occupying Ukraine.' The Commissar can't stop himself adding, 'Which is ridiculous —

but many of these men have no idea ... they are filled with dire predictions and wonderous paranoia!'

The man hears Pavel chuckle in response, which is curious considering that over the last few months Kobylinsky, the Socialist Revolutionary Commissar who had been overseeing their house arrest, had mentioned to him that Captain Pavel had, like many of the guards, developed Bolshevik sympathies.

'I'm not worried,' the Commissar is addressing his words to both Pavel and the man. 'As I've mentioned, my superior is Sverdlov ...' Vasily lets the name settle into the shadows of the carriage. Everyone knows Sverdlov is the Chairman of the Central Executive Committee and thus Russia's first head of state — now that the man has abdicated. 'When the West Siberian Soviet hear Sverdlov restate his orders over the telephone then we shall proceed to Omsk — to pick up the Trans-Siberian heading directly to Moscow. Oh, Yes. Their attitude will shift when Sverdlov gets on the line.'

Pavel wonders whether Vasily is trying to convince his listeners or himself.

There's a shout from outside and the Commissar nods to Pavel, then turns and leaps down from the carriage. Now that Vasily's train is ready to depart for Omsk there is no time to waste. After a while, the locomotive chugs into life as it begins the journey south-east, with Vasily and some of the militant leaders of the West Siberian Soviet on board. Meanwhile, the rest of them wait in the stationary carriages surrounded by hundreds of Red Guards. Sentinels in the Siberian plain.

Time passes slowly. The man hardly sleeps and when it is morning, then midday, then afternoon, he has little to say to his family. He watches Pavel play a couple of games of draughts with Marie but both of them seem to go through the motions of the game without any banter or jocularity. It is a strange day. Outside they hear the comings and goings of horsemen and the movement of Vasily's men, occasionally knocking on their carriage door to deliver food or ask if there has been any news. A strange day.

The man realises that in the last six months this extraordinary course of inaction has been his usual practice. To wait. To hold back. To bide one's time. To stay behind. Up until their house arrest last year he had not known the tired little sleepy verb, *to wait*. All his life the rush of events and circumstances had swept him along in such a way that there was never a moment where he had to wait. Back then he longed for the pause, the hiatus, the rest. Back then when the Crown was thrust upon him at the early untimely death of his Papa, a difficult unlovable man whose hardened core could only be breached by the Empress Dowager, he felt it was all too soon and too much. He had still so much to learn. Indeed, it was only the arrival of Sunny, with her soft touch and endless capacity to soothe him, nurture him, take care of him, that he felt able to shoulder the burden of this gift from God — to be the Tsar of all the Russias and never wait.

The man looks through the tears in the threadbare curtains, that Captain Konoplev insists they keep drawn and sees the afternoon peel away. Summer wants to burst out in its full-bodied beauty and in a month wildflowers will dance across the Siberian plains. The man thinks that it is only now when he is forced to wait, that he can see the way summer never repeats itself in the exact same way. The purple primroses, yellow coltsfoot, pink lily of the valley, white anemone, blue irises, and fluff balls of pussy willow that litter the loamy grass fields are similar to what grew last summer — but not the same. The seasons are singular and unique.

Time is singular and unique. Once lived it is gone forever.

The man drops the curtain. They had left the windows covered all day, although they had already been discovered by a horde of Red Guards. But the curtains had stopped the gawking ignorant faces of these West Siberian men who seemed desperate for a glimpse of

Russia's greatest enemy. The man sighs. While Lenin and his mob have given Germany one-third of Russia's most arable land he, the disgraced and forsaken ex-Tsar, is regarded as the greatest enemy. The irony smarts and he thinks to himself that it is mere folly to have looked beyond the window to the promise of eternal summer.

The man glances across to his wife and daughter. They are kneeling in front of an icon, saying their prayers. He can't quite see which particular icon his wife has chosen but he suspects it is the *Stabat Mater*. The suffering mother. The eternal feminine grief. He knows he should join them but he remains seated. He listens to them recite the ancient prayers that, for centuries and centuries and centuries, followers believed were heard.

'*Those who put their trust in the Lord.*'

Prays his wife.

'*Are like Mount Sion, that cannot be shaken.*'

Responds his daughter.

The man hears his wife intone the psalter with a certain dread but in contrast, his daughter's response is full of hope and light.

'*Jerusalem! The mountains surround her.*'

Calls his wife.

'*As the Lord surrounds his people. Both now and forever.*'

Responds his daughter.

The man tries to remember when he had that kind of faith. That sense of optimism that the world will right itself.

'*For the sceptre of the wicked shall not rest.*'

Calls his wife.

'*Over the land of the just.*'

Responds his daughter.

Does he imagine it or does he hear his wife's trepidation as she calls out the words, composed so long ago by the great King David?

'*Oh Lord, my heart is not proud.*'

Calls his wife.

'*Nor haughty my eyes.*'

Responds his daughter.

He sees the Captain look across scornfully as they recite the psalm.

'*I have not gone after things too great.*'

Calls his wife.

'*Nor marvels beyond me.*'

Responds his daughter.

He listens to his wife's voice and remembers that there was a time when all of this would have offered him comfort, offered him direction, offered him determination. Nowadays, he stumbles about unable to find his way. He is a man who no longer knows himself.

'*Oh Israel ...*'

Calls his wife.

And the 16 year old's response rises above the head of her mother and the heavy silence of her father and the disapproving gaze of Captain Pavel.

'*Hope in the Lord. Both now and forever!*'

So be it, thinks the man to himself but his heart is empty.

Just as the man is wondering when the lamps might be lighted he hears the return of a locomotive and knows it is Vasily's train. Several of the dismounted West Siberian Soviet, who have been waiting patiently all day for the return of Commissar Vasily, assist his exit from the train and escort him across the short walk alongside the railway tracks and manhandle him into the carriage in which sits the prisoner who was once the Tsar. The tall sharp-featured Commissar is, by now, used to the shoving and pushing after spending a good deal of the day in Omsk where he was treated like a traitorous criminal. The faces of Pavel and the man and his wife and daughter look up at him expectantly. Vasily has already made up his mind that all of them would be best served by having the same information he has been given.

'We have a change of plans, I'm afraid.' No one moves and he wonders for a moment whether they need clarity, so he adds, 'My superior, Sverdlov, believes, in the end, it is better to comply with the West Siberian Soviet who are acting on behalf of the Ural Soviet. Therefore we are travelling to Yekaterinburg.'

'But why?' the wife's voice is filled with pain.

The Commissar looks away and steels himself by thinking about his wife and what would become of her and his sons should the White Army lose their foothold in his hometown. Sverdlov has retracted his orders, without explanation. To defy orders would mean death by firing squad and severe reprisals against his family.

'Yes ... Why?' The man asks, 'What are the reasons ... um ... behind this decision? Do we know?'

Vasily has heard the man speak but all of a sudden the weight of today's frustrating farce is too heavy and he can barely rally himself to offer any support at all for the prisoners.

'It is the decision,' says Pavel softly, fatalistically. 'There is nothing any of us can do about it ...' He is thinking about the beautiful Olga and her cheekbones like the endless plains of a Siberian summer and he is so filled with sorrow that he thinks he might weep right here as he stands in this godforsaken carriage. It is the prisoner, that man, who has brought down the vengeance of the Ural Soviet on all of them. For that is what it is, there can be no mistake.

The Ural Soviet, renowned for its uncompromising brute will and a capacity to never forget what they have endured for decades and decades to make Tsarist Russia rich in mining resources, will not let this opportunity for retribution pass by.

'But, I'm sorry — I still don't understand!' Everyone hears the woman but no one can look at her, not even her daughter who is quietly crying although she doesn't quite know why. The wife pleads, 'What does it matter whether we travel through Yekaterinburg to Moscow or through Omsk to Moscow — why does it matter?'

Her husband thinks it is not his place to answer. Besides, she must know that the Red Urals have nothing but animosity toward them and then it dawns on him that she is asking because she cannot come to terms with the fact that the rest of their innocent children will follow and be exposed to such hatred.

'Vengeance is a powerful engine,' says Pavel. His words seem to have frozen them into a tableau. He looks at the man who has brought such suffering upon his people and such utter destruction upon this country and now such mind-numbing misery upon his innocent children. Pavel looks at the man's wife who clutches an icon to her breast and in susurrations attempts to invoke her God. He looks at the young sister of his beloved who has covered her face with her hands. And then he looks at the Commissar who stands like a man who has lost the battle but has every intention of getting out alive.

Pavel asks Vasily bitterly, 'What is to happen?'

The Commissar has had time to think through Sverdlov's duplicity. *Take the prisoners to Moscow. Take the prisoners to Kazan. Take the prisoners to the Red Urals.* The journey back from Omsk, after the astonishing phone call to Moscow where Sverdlov agreed with the West Siberian Soviet that the prisoners should be rerouted to Yekaterinburg, allowed Vasily time to work out his plan.

'The Romanovs will be escorted by 300 Red Guards to Yekaterinburg. I have been asked to stay behind. In fact ...' A small smile appears on the lips of the Commissar, 'The West Siberian Soviet here has invited me to attend the Regional Soviet and explain, in full, why we diverted at Tyumen, heading away from Yekaterinburg for Omsk.'

'Look here,' says the man. 'Surely, they can see we need you to travel with us? The thing is, we need to be able to trust —'

'They've arrested you?' Pavel's interruption explodes in the carriage.

Vasily lets out a slow chuckle, 'Yes. I suppose I have been arrested.'

Pavel is incredulous. He is incensed. How has this gone so awry? One moment he is headed to a life with Olga, and then the next moment he is utterly bereft of hope.

'I can do nothing more for you or your family,' Vasily's tone is one of relief. I cannot change the course of history, the Commissar tells himself, not at this juncture. The wily Sverdlov has outfoxed them all. 'My orders were to move you out of Tobolsk because the White Army is advancing into that part of Siberia with great force.'

Pavel can't help but feel that it is as if the Commissar is rehearsing this for his impending cross-examination at the Regional Soviet.

Vasily adds, 'My orders were to reach Trotsky so that the people of Russia could have the prisoner answer to a court of law.'

Neither the Commissar nor the man mentions the German Ambassador.

The adults look from one to the other. The man thinks about the blessed lifeline Cousin Willy had thrown when their allies had abandoned them to the devil. His wife thinks about their young son back in Tobolsk who will not know kindness or care in this next hell of imprisonment. Her daughter thinks about her parents standing in the carriage unable to make any of this right. And Pavel thinks about the end of a love story and the willowy fresh body of desire that pressed and pressed and pressed itself against his skin. And finally, Vasily thinks about the way he has been outmanoeuvred. Sverdlov had strung the German Ambassador along, making him believe the prisoner would have been transferred to him in Kazan and smuggled out of Russia to Germany. At the same time, Sverdlov played Trotsky along convincing him that the prisoner was indeed being brought to the new capital, to face the trial of the century. But in the end, Sverdlov decided the West Siberian Soviet, acting on behalf of the militant Ural Soviet, was not worth a counter-move.

And as Vasily takes his leave, without emotion and doubt, he thinks about his next move. He knows that the toothless Regional Soviet will go through the motions of a hearing only to dismiss him because who in their right mind would cross Sverdlov? That slimy weaselly bastard who goes by the name of Isaac Sverdlov ... or Yankel Sverdlov or Andrei Sverdlov or Mikhalych Sverdlov or Max Sverdlov or Smirnov Sverdlov or Permyakov Sverdlov or Jacob Sverdlov. Chameleon. Liar. Traitor.

Vasily steps down into the night air and realises it has only been 24 hours since he last stepped down from this carriage — before he was confronted by the West Siberian Soviet and the accusations that *he* had been a traitor. Damn you all, he thinks as he is jostled into the hands of his captors, once again. Some of the Red Guards bundle him off, their job being to escort him back to Omsk where the Regional Soviet Committee has been instructed to assemble and judge whether or not Vasily is a traitor. His horsemen will follow him down there over the next day or so.

But the Commissar, who nearly got away with his plan to have his contact in Omsk move the prisoners north to freedom, has already decided what he will do, as soon as the shambolic trial by his peers is over. He smiles to himself in the dark of the night and believes summer will come sooner than they all believed. He is going to join the White Army, just as soon as he untangles himself from this mess, and then maybe he can help turn this great nation into the true revolutionary vision established in February last year!

West Siberia. May 1918.

Olga is happy because in the next hour they should be in Yeka-terinburg. As the warm column of airbrushes through their carriage window she looks away from Anastasia, gently teasing Baby about his floppy hair, and gazes out at the May summer. She even ignores

Tatiana's commentary that no sign of the other train is following behind them. Olga espies colours across the landscape which are so vivid it is as if she is inside a fairy-tale picture book.

The *chuggchuggchuggchuggchuggchug* of the steam engine, hauling them to Mother and Papa and Marie, fills Olga with excitement ... but more than anything it fills her with longing for Pavel, her darling Captain Konoplev. This is what keeps her wide awake throughout this long long journey to his ever-loving arms.

'Olga, please close that window. I don't want Baby to get a chill.'

Tatiana is so tiresome, thinks Olga, but she does shunt the window down and looks across benevolently towards her younger siblings.

'I really can't see Tutor Gilliard's train ...' Tatiana sounds genuinely concerned. 'Why would they be told to travel down to Tyumen with us — only to be waylaid there, as we continue to Yekaterinburg?'

The name of their destination races down Olga's spine and she looks across at Tatiana wondering whether her desire for Pavel, shows. But the second oldest Romanov daughter, who has quite taken on the role of the family boss, is still craning about as the train takes an endless curve, to catch a glimpse of the ever watched for but never seen the second train that seems to have remained in Tyumen.

After witnessing firsthand the months of humiliation in being under house arrest their tutor, Gilliard, the girls' maid, Shura, their mother's maid, Schneider, and the rest of their party, have seemingly been held back at Tyumen. Only Dr. Botkin and Kharitonov, the cook, and the 14 year old kitchen boy who sometimes plays with Baby, whose name always eludes Olga, have been allowed to continue with them, on this train.

'Maybe Gilliard's train has been delayed,' their younger brother offers, with his irresistible smile. 'Maybe he is getting to know Shura a little better ...' He ends his hypothesis with exaggerated kissing sounds. This, inevitably, sets Anastasia off into peals of laughter. Even Tatianna smiles. But Olga turns her face to the window because she feels the blush of blood rise up her neck and across her cheeks. How she longs for Pavel's hands on her breasts and hips, and his lips on her mouth and neck!

'Not long now!' Olga hears herself cry aloud and quickly adds, 'Papa and Mother and Marie will be getting ready for our arrival!' And the four of them look out the window expectantly, as the trees and grasslands and the occasional peasant farm-hold flick by.

Olga tugs at her blouse beneath the cotton travel jacket. It is not the white blouse with its handmade flax-lace collar that is causing her discomfort but the corset and belt of her pantaloons that scratch and dig into her skin. Throughout this journey, she has seen both her sisters pull and tug at their undergarments, just like she is doing now.

Olga thinks back to the arrival of Mother's letter a month ago, while the four siblings were still in Tobolsk.

April 17, 1918

My darlings,

We have arrived all safe and sound ... Praise be to God ... Papa is well, although, a little tired as it has been a long journey. How are you my dearest sweetest chickens? I hope you girls are looking after Baby and not letting him get away with too much mischief!

Here their mother had interrupted her written text and included one of her badly drawn, but somehow endearing, images of — they had to assume — Alexei tip-toeing past three girls, presumably his sisters, all in nightdresses and kneeling with eyes shut saying their prayers. Their brother had guffawed saying it was more likely Anastasia who would try to get out of evening prayers to which she had wholeheartedly agreed.

Now my Cherubs, I need you to dispose of the medicines as we agreed

... Get Shura to help you girls, and don't forget — dispose of the medicines ... All will be well My Loves if you do this, and before you know it, we will be together, once more!

Mother had sketched all seven of them standing in descending order, with Papa first and when she drew Baby she had him standing on a chair, which they all agreed was quite cute!

Did I mention that our new accommodation is a two-storey house? Apparently, it was once owned by a merchant but now we have the top floor! So it is very cosy xxx. When you arrive it will be summer — and there's lots of noise from the streets because Yekaterinburg is filled with bustle — all — day — long ...

And Mother had scratched a lopsided two-storey building with a palisade fence down one side. It looked as if it was on the corner of the street — which made Anastasia exclaim that she preferred it to the dreary old Governor's house in Tobolsk where nothing ever happened and no one ever came to visit.

Much love and say your prayers because the Lord hears the prayers of children above all else ... And remember, girls — dispose of the medicines as discussed and you all shall be well. My arms ache to hold you all — and especially my Baby! Until then — May the Blessed Mother of Our Sweet Lord Jesus Christ, hold you in her arms and keep you safe — as I know she will. That is always her promise to you, My Little Ones!

Kisses, My Darlings — so many kisses xxxx

The girls had worked diligently in *disposing of the medicines*, which of course was code for *jewels*. Mother had pulled the girls aside before she had left and explained that they were to sew the family's jewels into their corsets, petticoats, pantaloons — wherever they could — if they got word to *dispose of the medicines*. Mother had said if this was her message it meant that they had been searched, and so the girls were to smuggle in the jewels because it was the only means they had left to buy their freedom.

Olga listens to the train roaring toward their destination. She is sure of her decision. In this last month, she has had time to consider her decision and she knows there is no other way. She will run away with Pavel just as soon as he can arrange matters because she cannot go on like this, as if she is a child! She has the body and mind and desire of a woman and there is no reason on God's earth why she needs to rely on her parents or be obedient to their wishes. Besides, she knows they love her and will come around, eventually. The world is changing and she wants to embrace this new and modern time that no longer tolerates differences between people in terms of class or wealth.

Oh, and she has been keeping up her reading. Pavel will be surprised and proud that she has completed the *Communist Manifesto* and made notes! Indeed, she had quoted Marx to Gillard. Predictably, he had cautioned her against these new-fangled ideas when she said she refused to be a *grave-digger* in upholding the traditions of the past. Well of course she didn't mean *all* traditions but it was so utterly annoying having a tutor and a foreigner, of all things, lecture her about what he thought was appropriate and inappropriate when it came to expressing opinions. The All-Russian Communist Party had made women equal to men. Personally, she didn't like Lenin, but Gilliard was so irritating, asking her what sort of woman needed a man to make her feel equal. So she had responded by quoting Lenin: *Petty housework degrades and chains women to the kitchen and the nursery*. Obviously, she had no experience of either but she had to look to the future, as Pavel's wife.

Olga presses her forehead to the cool window of the train. She longs to be part of building this brave new Russia. As they head toward Yekaterinburg, she feels her back straighten and her head rises higher. She is her own woman and regardless of censorial constraints placed on her by Gilliard, or Mother, she is going full speed ahead into her future — one that contains Pavel Konoplev in their wondrous new world.

13

Kresty Prison

Petrograd. June 1918.

Viktor sits on the top bunk alongside a fellow inmate in Petrograd's Kresty Prison. He gazes out the window that is recessed in the wall and set behind double bars. The white nights of early June are somehow comforting as if the atrocities here in the prison can no longer go unwitnessed. And indeed this is the truth in Viktor's cell where he has been imprisoned for the past few weeks. Initially, he was placed here alone. Rudimentary solitary confinement. But now there are 13 other prisoners wedged into the space designed, back in 1860, for one person.

Last week the guards brought in two rickety bunks with no mattresses or bedding. So the inmates lay on or beneath these bunks or sit or lean against the walls of the cell for time to pass. There's a bucket in the corner that usually gets emptied once a day — the stench of faeces and urine no longer affects the men. It is strange what one can get used to, thinks Viktor.

The inmate alongside him, whose name Viktor knows but has no need of using, again tries to draw Viktor into his information gathering. Something has been whispered about this chap that he is a plant for the Chekist. A double agent. Even his scars, bruising, and wounds are suspect. Not fresh like Viktor's or the other inmates here in the cell.

'Do you ever wonder, Brother, if the prisoners who built this hell hole thought about putting in trap doors or false walls — you know — so the prisoners could have a chance to escape ... Maybe there could even be something here in this cell?'

Viktor watches one of the men on the opposite bunk look vaguely about the fortified walls and floor of this box in which they sleep, stand, shit and drink, using the single tap over a cracked basin.

'What do you think? It's worth a look, right?' When Viktor doesn't respond the inmate alongside him continues, 'Brother, you never said why you are in here ... What do you have that those goons want?'

Someone from below them answers, 'Shut the fuck up.' But it is said without force or menace as if the speaker is rousing momentarily from a thick sleep and can't quite figure out how this has all come to pass. No one wants to know anything about anyone else here in the cell, except for the inmate alongside Viktor, because knowing is dangerous. Hands can be broken, toes can be cut, hair can be scalped for less than a morsel of information hungered by the Chekists.

Viktor has no intention of saying anything. He knows that Moisei Uritsky will come good and soon the beatings by the leather coats will end and his Bolshevik convictions will be believed and he'll be offered immunity in the form of working undercover for the Head of the Cheka. Then once he is released he knows exactly what he will do.

The nacreous morning sunlight shines through the bars and there is no disputing that the white night sky is well and truly over and somehow today feels different to Viktor.

'I mean Brother, there's so many more of us ... We could overpower them — one guard per corridor. I saw it with my own eyes.

When the next feed is brought in we have to be ready! We could charge them and ...'

The June light seems to infuse the cell with warmth and calm despite the torn and tattered bodies of the men who are jammed up against each other in this godforsaken fox-hole.

Viktor was surprised he had been taken to the Kresty Prison, in the Vyborgskaya Storona, just a hop, skip, and a jump from Lidia's apartment. The notorious Trubetskoy Bastion Prison in St Peter and Paul Fortress had been closed by the Bolsheviks just months beforehand — so it is no surprise that Kresty overflows with human misery.

'Brother, I'm just wondering what the information might be that you have that they want because — you know — I think we are probably, you know, the same ... sort of people ... you and I ...' And once again someone hisses *Shut up!*

Viktor is elsewhere. His face bleached in the searing morning light that will, he knows from experience, soon move on and leave the cell fetid, overheated and steamy. Nine days of continual mid-morning rain, followed by a steamy summer heat glancing off the tranquil Neva flowing beside the prison will do that to an overcrowded cell.

Then one of the cellmates somewhere in the mess of bodies below Viktor begins.

'*There was once a man ...*'

The generic opening to any story.

'*A goodish man ...*'

Viktor listens as his co-inhabitants settle into the ancient rhythm of listener and storyteller. '*A man from Vladimir ...*'

There is a murmur of positive reception from some who recognise the Tolstoian story. '*Askyonof was a young successful merchant —*'

'Bloodsucking kulak —' adds the inmate alongside Viktor and those in his line of vision nod accordingly.

'Of course,' confirms the storyteller smoothly and Viktor looks down at him. A Socialist Revolutionary, he assumes, sitting on the floor, back against the bunk frame. It is rumoured that there are 800 Socialist Revolutionaries imprisoned in Kresty at this moment.

'Askyonof was on his way to a fair. His wife had tried to stop him on account of the strange dream she had had the night before ...'

Viktor feels the frisson of tension in his fellow inmates caused by any Russian tale referencing superstition. Meanwhile, the inmate alongside him leans over the top bunk where they sit and scours the cell for any poor bugger making the sign of the cross, a Russian instinct. He quickly lowers his eyes at Viktor's naked stare and slumps back into the gentle reverie of storytelling.

'She said, 'Last night, dear husband, you came to me in the dream, but when you took your cap off your lovely dark hair was thin and grey.' But Askyonof reassured his wife all will be well and began the long journey to the fair.'

Most days are filled with a recitation of a tale, like this one, or a poem or, even sometimes, a very hushed song that creeps out of someone's childhood and into their cell of waiting.

'... And after he completed his business at the fair Askyonof booked into a local inn. He then ate his evening meal and decided to retire to his room. A good inn ...'

Some of the men are shifting about and the storyteller responds by slowing down the tale, fleshing out the details, offering his take on Tolstoy's well-known story.

Viktor turns back to the window as the storytelling proceeds uninterrupted except for the occasional corrections offered up by the listeners. It is a story that most Russians would have heard as children. Its message, uncomplicated and true. And although it offers a balm of sorts it is clear it has become a tale that now belongs to another time, another place.

'... The inn had not only provided this sumptuous repast but when

Askyonof opened the door to his room he saw that the mattress was wide and thick and ...'

Viktor rarely lets himself think of Leonid and when the image of his beloved steals into his mind, Viktor offers up the mantra: *Leonid is safe. He is safe.* He watches the sunlight dull slightly and smells the onset of rain. Leonid always says no one can smell rain — *What you are smelling old man*, Leonid would say, *is the wet earth.*

I can smell rain, thinks Viktor, and then it thunders overhead and the storyteller pauses as the faces of the inmates turn to the flash of blue lightning somewhere up in the freedom of the skies. And then the white eye of the sky opens and rain crashes down. Viktor thinks about the rain's diluvian torrents washing over the outer red brick skin of the prison.

Kresty is made up of two enormous five-storey buildings, each constructed in a cruciform shape and linked by the St Alexander Nevsky Cathedral with its five onion domes. Kresty Prison was, of course, built when Russia believed in a God who would forgive and save the sinner. Regardless of the efforts by the Bolsheviks to enlighten the vast hordes that there is no God, thousands and thousands of men are forced to remain in a state of crucifixion, awaiting death or redemption, here at Kresty.

'... So when morning came Askyonof paid his bill at the inn and got into his cart to start back home on his long journey ...'

Viktor listens to the rain outside and he thinks about the men being stuffed into the prison cells here at Kresty. How will it all end? he wonders. When will it end? But he knows these questions cannot help him. His only hope is *Leonid is safe. He is safe.*

The rain slows and then stops altogether. Outside, the smell of Petrograd, or at least the Vyborgskaya, rises up ... washed and laundered.

'... On his way home, Askyonof was stopped by some officers and one of

them asked him if he might be permitted to search his cart. Askyonof was an honest man and someone who had nothing to hide ...'

Was it yesterday or the day before? Yesterday confirms a part of Viktor's brain that refuses to erase the memory of the bone-cracking blows that accompanied his most recent interrogation session by the leather coated goons. He has nothing to hide because he does not know where Kerensky is and he has said, again and again, that he has not seen Leonid — who is referred to by the Chekists as, *Your young faggot who will lead us to the traitor.* There are times, after weeks of beatings and threats, where Viktor actually believes that he has not seen Leonid since Finlyandsky Station. He plays the farewell, like a moving picture, repeatedly in his mind. The hug and the surreptitious kiss followed by the scream of the train whistle signalling Kerensky and Leonid's departure for Helsinki.

'... They bound him and threw him in the cart after discovering the blood-stained knife. It had been placed in a tin box and tucked deep inside Askyonof's bag ...'

Viktor watches the steamy humidity curl inside the cell window and presses itself against the dirty walls until it perspires like feverish skin. He thinks of Feiga and Lidia who must be well away by now, out of Petrograd and secure in Lidia's father's estate. He knows Leonid would have delivered them safely, just as he knows that Feiga would have survived her bout of cholera, and Grishka would have actioned the Battle Unit's plan to generate terror into the elite ranks of the Bolsheviks ... they have no idea what is about to hit them, thinks Viktor and allows himself the faintest smile.

'... Askyonof was afraid and stammered and said again and again that he had never seen the knife nor did he know how it had found its way into this strange tin box inside his luggage ...'

There had been a distinct shift in the interrogation room, yesterday. Less commitment to damage his hands and feet, which were bleeding and bruised. Less interest in Viktor's declaration that he has *no idea where the traitor Kerensky is!* and that *Moisei Uritsky will personally vouch for me!* Viktor knows the interrogation and punishment is nothing but a sham, a pretense, a fiction. He is being recruited by the Head of the Cheka. Viktor knows the beatings are a test. Perhaps it is Uritsky's way of assessing how committed Viktor can be and yet in the last few days, the intensity has lessened. Something is different, thinks Viktor if only I can figure out what ...

'*... And when Askyonof's young wife heard the terrible news that her dear young husband had been arrested for murder, she travelled the long journey to where he had been imprisoned for the term of his natural life — accused of a murder he had never committed and with a weapon he had never seen before ...*'

Kresty is renowned as the most advanced incarceration centre in Europe, with its electric lighting, central heating, and effective ventilation but this makes little difference to the daily routine of random inmates being hauled out of the cell and into the interrogation room where a couple of leather coated Chekists sweat it out to demonstrate their love of Russia by brutalising the prisoner until he is unrecognisable. Indeed, there is nothing secret about the secret police's sadistic pleasure in uncovering the truth — a truth that the pathetic inmates have no idea they harbour.

'*... And her eyes filled with tears when she realised her husband had been accused of the most heinous of crimes — the murder of a fellow Russian. Thus, Askyonof's own sweet wife turned her back on him ...*'

No one attempts to correct the storyteller and say that the murdered victim was a fellow merchant and, now that merchants are the enemy of the people, his death should result in celebration. No one interrupts the seductive consolation of being told a Tolstoian tale because each and every one of the men cramped in the cell is identifying with the unjust fate of Askyonof.

Viktor feels the dampness of the cell wall on the back of his head and lets the steamy morning fill up his nostrils and lungs until he can nearly believe that they are sitting about in one of Petrograd's saunas, alongside one of the more insalubrious taverns.

'... *Askyonof realised his lovely young wife believed the officers, the judge, and the guards. She turned her back on him and left — never to see him again because, in her eyes, he was the criminal they said he was ...*'

Viktor nurses his right hand, which is the worst. He is sure there are no more bones left to break. He tries not to think about the whispers over the past few weeks within this cell concerning the unchecked ruthlessness of other Chekists beyond the jurisdiction of Petrograd. It had made the goons at Kresty Prison seem like mere ingénues. So while his fellow inmates staggered into the cell or were dragged back with blood-soaked wounds or purple swelling joints or broken noses and eye sockets, and missing teeth, somehow it was better than rumours of the punishments inflicted by Chekists in other cities and villages across Russia: drowning, live burial, impaling, burning in a vat of oil, being skinned alive, drawing out the intestines of a living prisoner and crucifixion. Rarely the mercy of a bullet.

'... *twenty-five years passed but despite his innocence, Askyonof remained the ideal prisoner. He spoke well to his fellow inmates, worked hard, and did whatever was asked of him — never complaining, but all the while maintaining he was not guilty of this terrible crime ...*'

The walls in the cell are drying. Viktor knows that soon they will hear the clunk and shunt of other cell doors along the corridor being hauled open so that a basket of dry bread can be swung inside to the inmates. Somehow the gnaw of hunger hasn't galvanised a single rebellion against the oppressive goalers. But there is something else. Every man here believes he has been unjustly accused and arrested. Every man here believes that the truth will out and he will be released. Every man here believes in the Revolution, its hopes and dreams.

'*... twenty-five years had gone by and Askyonof had seen many a fresh batch of convicts arrived. Then one day a hardened brute called ...*'

The storyteller hesitates for a fraction and another prisoner in the cell immediately supplies the name, *Semyonitch*.

'*...* Yes, that's right, thank you.' And the storyteller goes on.

'*Semyonitch had been convicted of a number of terrible crimes. The weeks passed and this criminal got to hear of the innocent Askyonof because everyone knew that ...*'

The Bolsheviks are justifying the Cheka's powers. Lenin and others openly validate the imprisonment, torture, and elimination of Russians by the secret police. The new leaders of the government declare that all this is central to the class struggle. The enemies of this new revolutionised society must be exterminated to build a just and new world order. *Red Terror*. The men call it, whispering amongst themselves as if they are diagnosing a condition to which they are victims.

'*... And so it happened that one-night Semyonitch crept into Askyonof's cell where he was sleeping. But instead of bringing down further suffering and mishap upon the head of our innocent hero ...*'

Viktor realises that no one now bothers to correct the storyteller and remind him that Askyonof is a merchant and therefore nothing but a kulak, an enemy of the state.

'*... Semyonitch wakes Askyonof and tells him that it was he who murdered the innocent victim in the inn all those years ago and that he planted the evidence in Askyonof's luggage in an old tin box because he ...*'

So, thinks Viktor, out of the box that sprung such suffering and anguish comes, finally, hope. This tale, like our lives, is nothing more and nothing less than the tragedy of a Greek myth. Viktor's mouth forms a sour moue as he reflects on Tolstoy's message that applies to their own lives, here and now. Out of this cell in which we are boxed, with our lives precariously balanced on some bloody knife-edge, must emerge the hope of release. Either that or we await the last of the evils to leave Pandora's box.

Viktor hears the guards at the other end of the corridor.

'... *The grey thinning-haired Askyonof answered, 'Yes, I will give you my forgiveness'. He then asked Semyonitch to stand up and beg no more. Semyonitch went to the authorities and ...*'

Viktor is sure no one is listening any longer to the storyteller. They know the Tolstoian adage: *Forgive the unforgivable*. But more importantly to any Russian who loves his Tolstoy, which is every Russian, here is a tale worth telling — one where the innocent suffers without reason and without end. But there will be an end, Viktor thinks to himself, as he listens to the cell doors bang open one-by-one so that a basket of inedible bread can be thrown to the inmates, their stomachs growling audibly. Caged beasts bellowing for their feed.

'... *So Askyonof's order to be released came down from the authorities after Semyonitch made his confession — but it was too late. By the time the guards arrived at his cell to escort him out beyond the prison walls, they found, to their dismay, Askyonof had died peacefully ...*'

Viktor thinks about this tale and the title Tolstoy gave it: *God sees the truth but waits*. The cell door next to them slams back in place and he hears one of the guards grunt a reply to another before the key scrapes into the lock of their cell door. And it occurs to Viktor that despite his lack of faith he recognises this God from Tolstoy's story — a God who holds back, a God who bides his time, a God who abandons the innocent, with complete indifference.

When the steel door swings open, instead of a basket of food, a small leather coated man steps inside the doorway. Not a guard, a Chekist. This is new. This has not happened before and every inmate in Viktor's cell recoils as their universe shifts. The beady-eyed tightly-clad secret police officer takes in the moil of the prisoners, most of whom have turned their gaze away in case they win the random lottery. Then, eventually, his wide-open face alights on Viktor. 'You!' he commands. And Viktor thinks — *This is it!* Although he has told no one in the cell, Viktor knows Moisei Uritsky would not have been able to resist the message he passed on via his torturers: *Viktor will become an agent for the Cheka.*

Viktor slides awkwardly off the upper bunk and says to himself: *Leonid is safe. He is safe.* He can feel the adrenaline pump through his veins as he takes a few steps to reach the Chekist whose broad nose stretches even further across his face as he smiles at Viktor. Recognition. Viktor is now to be recruited.

His fellow cellmates say nothing, and those cramped on the floor, quickly pull back their legs to allow him passage and not to draw attention to themselves.

I must have my wits about me, Viktor thinks to himself as the small leather coat amicably turns his back on Viktor to step out of the cell — his bald head a good 20 or so centimetres below Viktor. The guards waiting outside the cell with the breadbasket watch on impassively.

Then the Chekist turns and surprisingly pops his fresh plump face back into the doorway of the cell, points, and says, 'And you.'

To Viktor's surprise, the inmate who had been sitting alongside him saunters out of the cell.

By the time they reach the end of the corridor, following the Chekist who despite his petite statue has the capacity of moving quite fast, Viktor realises they are not being taken to the usual shop of horrors. Its door is closed firmly on the plight of some other forgotten soul.

The short leather coat is met at the top of the staircase by two other goons and Viktor can sense nothing but disinterest and knows he must be utterly convincing when he is taken to the Head of the Cheka over at number 2 Gorokhovaya Ulitsa, 4th floor. Everyone in Petrograd knows the address of Moisei Uritsky. He moves gingerly down the staircase and at a slit window he greedily takes in a different view — a glimpse of the St Alexander Nevsky Cathedral. Not that he has any interest in religion of any kind but the sumptuous joy of seeing something other than the sky fills his heart and belly. The descent continues until they reach the bottom. They are a group of five. Three goons and two prisoners.

Viktor doesn't notice the wooden door at first but then sees it and realises with an intake of breath that they are on the ground floor and this will lead them out of the prison and into the yard and then to the main gates.

The small bald broad-nosed Chekist opens his eyes wide and looks directly at Viktor as if he is about to explain what happens next, 'Kerensky is in France.'

Viktor says nothing because he doesn't understand.

The perceptive little fellow in the leather jacket seems to have anticipated this so he continues, 'There was speculation that he was heading to Australia, of all places — where his wife's family reside — or even to the United States, but he has surfaced in France ...'

Viktor looks at the small man and realises this means he will be free to go because his claims that he didn't know the whereabouts of Kerensky are now utterly indisputable.

'The French countryside,' drawls one of the goons as if proving the ex-prime minister was always a decadent and cowardly traitor.

The inmate who had sat alongside Viktor, sniggers.

The goon in charge, who has so far only directed his comments at Viktor, looks quietly at the other prisoner and says with no emotion whatsoever, 'You are no longer of use to us.'

Viktor knows this confirms the cell's suspicion that this fellow inmate is nothing but a snitch, an informer, a rat.

'What do you mean? Brother? We have an understanding — I have a — I need to speak to Comrade um, hang on ... Comrade ... he is in the interrogation room on the 5th floor! I need — I —' The inmate has stopped jabbering because there is a distinct click from behind as one of the goons pulls back the hammer on his Nagant revolver.

Quiet.

Then Viktor smells the ammonic stench of urine and in his peripheral vision, he sees the inmate begin to shake.

'Take off your clothes,' instructs one of the goons from behind.

'Comrade? ... Please ...?' They all hear the plea but no one responds. Viktor has fixed his gaze on the wooden door and knows it will only be a matter of minutes before this filthy business is completed next to him and he, alone, will be escorted out of the Kresty, across the Neva via the Liteyny Bridge and downtown to Gorokhovaya Ulitsa.

'Take off your fucking clothes.' This comes from the goon standing behind as the barrel of the revolver presses perfectly into the back of the inmate's head.

Viktor notices the small Chekist in front of them turns away quite leisurely as the inmate, a rattle of bones and numb fingers attempts to strip himself of his worldly possessions — oversized gymnastyorka and trousers.

The bald, broad-nosed Chekist in charge slowly checks the time. The wristwatch seems far too large for his diminutive size and Viktor knows this is one of the many perquisites of his job, taking what won't be needed anymore by some prisoner.

The cellmate is now crying and blathering something about someone.

This wretch has done nothing but betray every one of us cramped up in that filthy cell, thinks Viktor to himself and he feels nothing but fatigue and he just wants this bastard to be finished off so that he can get out of this nightmare. He knows being recruited to be a Chekist may mean he will be required to prove his allegiance to the Head of the Cheka. And here in the small foyer before the wooden doorway, Viktor concedes he might have to arrest or even punish one or two suspects — but it is the big picture that he must keep firmly at the forefront of his mind. Viktor will be a double agent. On the other hand, he will seemingly report on disloyal Russians but, unbeknownst to Uritsky, he will infiltrate the Communist party as a Chekist. He will then strike terror in the hearts and minds of the Party with his targeted assassinations of the leaders.

He knows it is the proximity to the wooden door that has allowed him, for the first time since he has been taken prisoner in Kresty, to believe the Socialist Revolutionary's Battle Unit might succeed.

The small Chekist sighs when he looks back at the inmate who cowers beside Viktor — a forked thing that cups his genitals.

'Would you mind ...' he says distractedly to Viktor who realises immediately that this is the test of his loyalty — he is being asked to shoot the fellow prisoner. Where? Here? In front of the door — within earshot of the other prisoners stacked in pitiful suffering in the five flights above him? Once again the good-natured leather-coated Chekist seems to have anticipated Viktor's confusion and adds, 'Yes. Viktor. Would you mind stripping off ...' It is said with such cordial calm that Viktor reaches for what is left of his thin jacket but then stops as he tries to make sense of what is being asked of him. 'Quick as you can,' the broad nose stretches across the goon's face in a sincere smile.

Viktor's clothes are rags of their former selves and he realises that he cannot be taken to Uritsky looking like this. His jacket seems to slip off easily and one of the goons tugs slightly at his shirt, which does the trick, and as he is chucking off the trousers he is glad of the underdrawers he wears, regardless of their stains. But where are the fresh clothes that they must have brought for him to change into?

The small Chekist in front of him blinks a few times as if coming out of a daydream, smiles to no one, then turns about and moves swiftly to the wooden door. Inserting the key and drawing back the long tongue-and-groove bolt noiselessly. It is a good sound, thinks Viktor. The sound of freedom. The door opens wide! And then the stairwell and the foyer in which they stand is flooded in June sunshine and Viktor knows he has never seen anything as glorious as this before.

'Step out.'

Every one of them responds to the command and as a locked body they move into the liberation of a domed sky. There is cool grass beneath the prisoners' feet and even a fledgling oak tree alongside the four-metre high brick wall that surrounds them in the prison yard. Viktor inhales deeply and although he is convinced they will ask him to pull the trigger on the weasel beside him he puts it out of his mind just for this minute, just for this second. He tries to think about the endless sea of feldgrau rushing toward them at the Battle of Lodz, then Przemysl, then Warsaw when he was a lieutenant with the Russian 12th, and how easy it was to pull the trigger again and again and again. A matter of life or death.

But that was before the enemy was a fellow Russian.

The inmate begins to wail and one of the goons smashes his fist into the side of the bastard's ear. The prisoner staggers drunkenly, regains his foothold, and whimpers.

'This way,' instructs the leather coated Chekist and he leads them on a toe-path that seems to run between the sky-high brick wall and the swelling of the cathedral's chevet. Viktor permits himself to follow immediately after the Chekist and lets the inmate stagger behind. The less he sees of this poor bastard the better. Will he be asked to shoot the informer here on the grounds or just before the monolithic gates where a cemetery sits?

The noonday light of summer glances off the cathedral's stained glass windows and the prisms of colour cavort and whimsey across their pathway.

The Chekist ahead has stopped. He turns his round untroubled face to Viktor and those behind him. Again, like a strangely well-lit snapshot, the five of them seem to stand perfectly still.

And into Viktor's brain scurries a fugitive from his boyhood days at the temple.

The Lord is good to those whose hope is in him,

To the one who seeks him.

Viktor shakes his head slightly. Then the inmate next to him is roughly man-handled to his knees, face to the brick wall, back to his captors.

Again, another line — like a fleeing escapee — surfaces from Viktor's Jewish Tanakh.

For I know the plans I have for you, declares the Lord,

Plans for good and not for evil plans to offer you hope.

Viktor can smell the sweat and shit and urine and fear and humanity on the fellow before him, whose whole body shakes uncontrollably. He wants to step back behind the two goons who have the revolvers cocked and ready but he also knows this may be seen as a weakness, a loss of faith in the glorious promise of salvation offered to them by Russia's triumphant Communist party. So he waits and tries to steady his breathing because he knows he'll be asked in the next instant to shoot his inmate.

Nothing has changed, Viktor tells himself. Skin and bone. Friend and foe. Survival. Nothing has changed. Bones are breakable, joints are stretchable. Bodies bleed, cry out and then stop. Nothing changes. Before, during, and after the war, Russia knows only wretchedness, misery, and pain. Nothing changes, Viktor tells himself.

'Kneel,' instructs the small Chekist but Viktor is looking down on the inmate who is already kneeling, his naked dirty body offers no more resistance to his fate. That is when Viktor looks back at the agreeable round-faced Chekist who opens his eyes wide and nods to Viktor indicating he is speaking to him.

Out of a past that had been long forgotten races an ancient incantation that fills Viktor's brain.

The Lord roars from Zion

And utters his voice from Jerusalem

So that the heavens and earthquake:

I am your refuge your stronghold!

Viktor tries to think but he cannot.

He tries to make sense of this beauteous June day with the blonde light of summer warming his shoulders and face.

He tries to say the words to himself: *Leonid is safe. He is safe.*

But nothing comes.

Then he is thumped to his knees and his body is numb so he does not smell the loamy soil beneath him nor does he hear the chortle of oak leaves above — instead he sees the child within him standing at synagogue, head bowed, kippah in place, heart believing.

They shall run and not be weary.

They shall walk and not faint — those who wait for the Lord.

And in that fraction of a second, before he cannot, Viktor thinks about his beautiful beautiful Leonid.

14

Rabbit Stew

Forest beyond Luga, 140 km south of Petrograd. June 1918.

He is still. She has him in her crosshairs. She holds her breath as she begins to squeeze the trigger. Softly. Slowly. His nose twitches.

BANG!

Shoulder crunch.

Metallic whiff of gunpowder.

Lidia lowers the Mosin-Nagant rifle and breathes. The brown hare is no longer a flash of fur and muscle — it's now dinner. As she slings the rifle back across her shoulder and begins moving across the 80 or so metres to the dead animal she hears Feiga call out something to her from the thick birch forest behind.

'Hare!' yells Lidia over her shoulder as she strides across a small clearing to collect it. Lidia doesn't bother prodding it with her toe because she can see that half its head is a cave of blood and bone. She picks it up by the hind leg. The body is warm. She then turns and begins her walk back to the edge of the birch forest.

And that is when Feiga appears. Lidia swings the hare up as Judith might Holofernes's head and Feiga's delight is luminous.

'Hare and Mushroom stew!' Feiga exclaims.

'Look at you,' Lidia says as she reaches her friend. 'Six weeks ago you would barely eat a thing!'

The dash through the night with Feiga in the back seat of a requisitioned automobile, her hot and feverish head on Lidia's lap, Grishka upfront and Leonid next to him driving recklessly without lights through the warm dark streets of Petrograd and then out past Gatchina. This was how they eventually found their way to her father's estate. It all seems a lifetime ago. No one spoke on that journey. Leonid's rage over Viktor's sudden arrest by the Cheka, simmering from the front seat.

'The boys will enjoy the stew!' Feiga has dropped her stack of birch branches and is feeling the long body of the hare and thinking about its dark flavoursome meat.

'Hey — what happened to your shooting practice?' laughs Lidia after spotting what Feiga has collected. 'You were about to make a besom, weren't you? You want to bathe — again!'

Feiga collects her branches sheepishly and mumbles, 'It felt so good — the kitchen sauna last week ... I just thought it might be nice before the boys come home ... You know to wash ...' And nonchalantly Feiga whips her back this way and that with the bunch of birch branches and her elfin face lifts up in the noonday sun as she mimes the besom effect.

Again Lidia laughs. It has been good to see her friend recover so heartily while staying in the safety and seclusion of her father's estate. Even yesterday, after her father left for a few days fishing at his dacha down in Lake Oredezh, Lidia had felt no fear and thus no compunction for her and Feiga to go with him. Instead, they would wait for Grishka, Leonid, and Viktor, Lidia had assured her taciturn father. They will be fine, she had said repeatedly and kissed his hard weathered cheek.

Now that it is summer, and Feiga is improving every day, they take walks on the grounds of the estate and even beyond into the surrounding forests. At first, only Lidia would take one of the old Mosin-Nagant rifles to shoot small game but after a while, Feiga gave in to Lidia's insistence that she carries a rifle and learn to shoot.

'Well, let's start back to the homestead. Maybe you can have a quick bath before Leonid and Grishka return — hopefully they will have Viktor!'

From the thick yolk of the sun above, light pours through the slender white bodies of the birch. The two women move along a path, their chatter mingling with the click and twitter and snap and rustle of the birch world about them.

'... Viktor will probably need his rest ...'

'... Maybe we can bake pashka tomorrow night ...'

'... Well, I can chop the mushrooms and the ...'

'... Yes, I think there is a little birch tar left ...'

Lidia knows she should feel flummoxed by Feiga's lack of interest in developing her marksmanship, a skill every woman must have. Actually, Feiga is yet to shoot a squirrel or woodcock. In fact, some days Lidia has wondered whether she should take her revolver out, set up some target on a tree trunk, and get Feiga to practice. But Lidia's father had started Lidia and Pavel off with a rifle when they were young, and that is what honed both their aim and control, making them great marksmen as adults. Feiga should learn in the same way.

Lidia leaps easily across a small stream and turns back to see if Feiga needs help but her small friend waves away any assistance and holds tight the rifle that she has not fired. Then Feiga bounds awkwardly after her tall companion lands just on the boggy edge of the stream, and gracelessly slips backward, knees buckling, until she is sitting sideways in the slosh of water.

'Oh no!' cries Lidia but she can't shut down the laughter because Feiga looks like a child in a bathtub incongruously holding aloft a Mosin-Nagant rifle.

'Just catching some fish to cook up a pot of ukha,' Feiga giggles.

Lidia drops her hare and strides down to the bank. She reaches hold of the rifle butt that Feiga is extending and yanks her up and out of the wet. Feiga's cotton skirt and petticoat are soaked but it's not far to the estate, so she flaps and fans her clothing in the warm sunshine as they hurry back home.

'We'll be back soon,' Lidia says. 'You can change while I skin the hare —'

'No, I can do that, Lidia. Really it won't take me a minute to change and ... Let me make the stew ...'

Lidia knows Feiga wants to tell Viktor, when he arrives tonight, that she made it herself, especially for him. Everyone knows Feiga loves Viktor — everyone loves Viktor, it's true. In many ways, he is the glue that holds them all together.

Lidia espies the rough driveway to the estate's homestead. Unless you are looking, it would be nearly impossible to see.

Yes, Feiga adores Viktor, thinks Lidia to herself, even a little more than she adores me. Which is a relief. And it's not just that Grishka still resents sharing Lidia, it is because, as he says, Feiga is the weakest link. Lidia doesn't say anything to this comment but she knows what Grishka means. Unlike Viktor, Leonid, Grishka, and herself, Feiga offers no assistance in the radical destabilisation of the Bolsheviks and without a doubt, this is now their sole and collective purpose. The entire Socialist Revolutionary Party is charged to do the same. Everyone knows the Socialist Revolutionary Party has the majority and *that* Bolshevik, Lenin — she spits automatically — must be eliminated.

Lidia pauses while she waits for Feiga to catch up. She looks at the tiny frame of her friend bending and collecting twigs and small branches, even though the firewood is chopped and stacked to overflowing outside the kitchen door. Feiga wants so desperately to contribute, to be a part of their intimate circle.

'We'll need a rip-roaring fire for the stew,' asserts Feiga as she comes up alongside Lidia.

They move along companionably and then, up ahead, the chimney of the homestead emerges.

'No need to mention who shot the hare ... What do you think?' Feiga's large eyes look up in earnest.

'No need to mention who sat in the stream either ...' Lidia responds and then adds, 'But think of the laughs we'll get!'

Feiga switches her friend with her besom and pleads, 'Come on, Lidia be a ...'

Lidia has stopped still. Quickly she reaches out and pulls Feiga into the undergrowth behind her. Neither of the women speaks.

There is a motorcycle parked at the porch of the homestead.

Lidia reloads her rifle. Feiga fumbles for hers and tries desperately to remember, through the fug of panic, what Lidia has taught her to do with it.

Grishka and Leonid left the women a week ago in the same motor vehicle in which they had driven down. Where is the motor vehicle? Who has ridden here on a motorbike? Where are Leonid, Grishka, and Viktor? This strange unknown motorcycle means only one thing. Their cover is blown because there is no way three men, Grishka, Leonid, and Viktor, could have ridden it, all the way down here. Lidia is thinking fast and knows she will have to handle this herself. Feiga will only get in the way.

All of a sudden the front door cracks open and she can hear voices. Men. Lidia realises they are about to step outside so she half stands, half crouches behind the bush, and aims her rifle at the old splintered doorway. She blocks out the faintest humming coming from Feiga. Lidia balances her finger softly, determinedly, against the trigger and breathes in. The front door pushes open wide and a lanky dark tousled-haired man strides across the porch.

Lidia lowers the rifle and steps out of the undergrowth.

Grishka starts, then blinks, then raises his hand half in salute, half in the gesture of a wave. 'Lidia!'

'It's Grishka,' calls Lidia back to Feiga as she hurries towards him, forgetting the hare and her fragile friend.

By the time Feiga catches up to the porch, hare, and besom in one hand, her rifle strap in the other, soggy skirt rucking inelegantly between her legs, Lidia and Grishka are still in each other's arms.

'Hi, Grishka,' says Feiga shyly. 'Is Viktor inside?'

Grishka breaks away from Lidia quickly, 'Don't go inside ... Not yet.'

Both women look at each other and then Lidia turns slowly to the motorcycle and asks, 'Whose is this?'

Grishka says nothing and as if it might give her answers Lidia leans towards the motorcycle and reads the make: *Lier & Rossbaum*. She straightens up and looks at Grishka. She had felt something in his kiss just now and the way he had held her. A desperation. A despair.

So she asks, 'What is it?'

He doesn't answer her.

She insists, 'What's happened, Grishka?'

He starts with the Lier & Rossbaum: 'We liberated the motorcycle on the outskirts of Gatchina ... It was a pest really because the teeth on the sprockets are gone and ...' Grishka looks at Lidia and drinks in her fair-haired beauty and wishes it is just the two of them. Living here. Just them. No politics. No rebellion. No inciting civil disobedience. No recruiting zealot hopefuls. He gives up on the motorcycle and says, 'Leonid is inside. He's ... He's ...'

'Is he unwell?' It's Feiga because Lidia can't quite follow what Grishka is saying or rather, not saying.

Grishka is gazing at Lidia as if he has just seen her heterochromia eyes for the first time and he is trying to understand what this might mean. 'No ...' he answers vaguely and finally adds, 'Just tired. He should be resting. Hopefully ...'

'Let's go around to the kitchen,' Lidia says evenly because she knows she needs to take charge. 'Feiga do you have the hare? Good. Now let's just go in through the back and put on the samovar for tea. Let's go. Come on Feiga.' Lidia knows that Grishka will follow them but at first he stands fixed, looking out at the ever-moving sky with its scattering of cotton clouds effortlessly sliding westward.

The women enter the kitchen and Feiga lights the samovar quietly after placing the hare on the scrubbed wooden table. Lidia is taking down the tea glasses and prising the lid off the tin with this morning's leftover jam blinis. As Grishka enters Lidia nods towards a kitchen chair and he sits down. Lidia turns away from the dazed look on his face and fusses about the hare with a sharpened blade bidding Feiga sweeten the teapot before the tea is filled from the samovar. Feiga knows how to make tea but the stretch of quiet between the three of them is too disturbing so Lidia speaks softly as they all pretend Leonid is sleeping.

'... Yesterday Father left for the lake ... Hoping to fish and relax ... Promised to bring back salted fish for us ... So today we were target practising ... Well Feiga got distracted by the birch trees ... Shot this hare ... Obviously ... No she didn't fall in, just stumbled a little ... Would you mind? ... Now Feiga just slip off the skirt ... Dry it near the fire ... Tea's ready? ... Good ... Blinis? ... Eat one anyway ... Good ...'

The sunlight pushes past the hornbeam trees that grow close to the back of the homestead and reaches in through the milky kitchen window. Let us stay like this, forever, thinks Grishka. Even Feiga's mousey nibbles of the sweetened pancake is bearable. Lidia reaches across and holds his hand in hers, a gesture so tender he turns his face away. I cannot bear it, he thinks. But he knows he must.

In the sitting room beyond the kitchen, they hear the stirrings of Leonid, and then before long the curtain is drawn back and the fair-haired blue-eyed chiseled-jaw ex-aid-de-camp of Prime Minister Kerensky is standing there looking at them without recognition.

Feiga stares back.

Grishka drops his head into his hands.

Lidia gets up and pulls out another kitchen chair for her friend. 'Leonid ...' Her voice doesn't sound like her own so Lidia tries again, 'Leonid. Come and sit with us. You look ... You look tired ...' He doesn't look tired but it is the best she can do because his face is not his. He is not Leonid and yet he is.

Like a sleepwalker he moves to the chair she offers him and he sits. Lidia passes him a glass of tea. He remains still. Arms down beneath the table. Mouth slightly open. Eyes, vacant and fixed to a mid-point at the centre of the table. Lidia puts a plate of blinis in front of him and begins to cut up one of the gnarly apples that they picked a few days ago.

'We got to Petrograd ... Checked on your apartment ...' Grishka has pulled his hands away from his face and is now speaking in a monotone. 'We went to Viktor's place — well I did — Leonid went to Maria Spiridonova's apartment ...' Grishka stops and Lidia pushes his glass of tea closer to him and he picks it up and sips. 'Other people have moved into Viktor's apartment ... The landlady said she had been ordered ... to rent his place out ...' Grishka's voice is getting quieter and then he sits up and continues more determinedly. 'Petrograd has gone to shit. Lenin and his henchmen are pushing this food acquisition policy which is just leading to revolts all over the countryside and ...' For a moment Grishka loses his train of thought and then he gets back on board. 'There are pocket uprisings everywhere. The nationalisation of all large industries has not quelled the ire and discontent! Russians everywhere can see that these bastards — Lenin, Trotsky, Volodarsky —'

'Moisei Uritsky.' Everyone looks at Leonid, not because of the name he has just spoken but how he said it. In a voice that is sightless and broken-jawed.

'Yes, and Uritsky,' confirms Grishka. 'These bastards are *not* our leaders!'

Lidia is not convinced Grishka is ever going to arrive at the truth of what has happened. She can do nothing but sit and watch him and wait. Grishka's face is filled with misery and hatred.

He inhales deeply and pushes on. 'The Czech Legion and the Socialist Revolutionary leadership — funded by the White Army — are taking back control. They are going to put an end to this Bolshevik lunacy — They've gone mad — Lenin's gone mad! His fucking goons are now in their tens of thousands in Petrograd alone! Our city! This country we fought for — this revolution we fought so hard for and spilled blood over ...'

And then in a whisper, Feiga asks 'Goons?'

Lidia doesn't look at her but responds with *Cheka*, by way of explanation, but the moment she does Leonid starts to rock on his seat, eyes ghastly in his lifeless face. Just as Lidia opens her mouth to ask, again, *What has happened?*, Grishka continues but this time his voice aches with the most awful pain.

'Leonid, here, went to see Spiridonova. She wasn't in her apartment. But he found her. She is in hiding — she moves constantly but ... anyway. Leonid found her ...'

All three of them turn and look at Leonid.

'So much has happened ...' Grishka's voice fades and the four of them morph into a Russian genre painting entitled *Friends gathered at a kitchen table*. Grishka steps back to reality with, 'The city is filled with the news ... Kerensky has left Russia.'

Lidia can't help herself and her shocked intake of breath is audible.

'Yes. It's true,' continues Grishka. 'France. He has escaped to France. The newspapers are full of it ...'

The light through the kitchen window is turning pale pink and the fire has gone out. The wood of the table and chairs and bench and beams, darken. The room itself seems to be hunkering down.

'Grishka, my love ...' She cannot sit through this any longer, so Lidia pushes him on, 'What happened when Leonid found Maria Spiridonova?' The name of the leader of the Socialist Revolutionary Party, to which they are all affiliated, hangs in the afternoon quiet. Lidia has her eyes on Grishka. She will not look at Feiga or Leonid. She watches her lover put his hand across his eyes and for a moment she thinks he will say no more.

But then he sits up and says to her and her alone, 'Leonid spoke to Maria. She has received the news. Hundreds have been arrested. Thousands. Army officers. Socialist Revolutionaries. Jews. Strikers. Anyone. Because the Cheka can arrest anyone. Viktor ... You see ... He was among those who ... Well, Maria received intel that ... After his arrest ... Kresty ... And then ... It was confirmed, you see.' Grishka thought he could say it. Make sense of it. Contextualise it. Say it. But.

The kitchen has filled up with shapes without form. Dark shadows slink out of the walls and down from the ceiling and up from the floor. Only the window lets in a thin grey daub of colour that runs its paint over the profile of a glass and a blade and a plate.

And then Leonid says the words that were never meant to be his, 'Viktor was executed.'

Grishka covers his eyes and feels the sharp crack of the executioner's bullet as it hits the base of his friend's skull. Lidia sees the top of Viktor's head and hears the gentle slosh and drip of water as he washes her violation away, one evening in her apartment in Vyborgskaya. Feiga scrunches up her face and can hear nothing but the rabbi of her childhood temple intoning.

Place me like a seal over your heart ...

For love is as strong as death,

Its jealousy as unyielding as the grave.

It burns like blazing fire, like a mighty flame.

And although not one of them dares look, all of them hears Leonid whisper, 'My Viktor. My Viktor. My Viktor. Dead.'

It is Lidia who eventually gets up when the kitchen is filled with the white night or, more accurately, the shadowy half-world of day and night with its murky grey, illuminating everything and nothing. She moves to the side bench and fumbles about with the kerosene lamp until Grishka is beside her, taking the match and dipping the wick into the fount. The whoof of fuel catches fire and the soft light emerges with the smell of every evening. Grishka then moves to the stove and fills its belly with the wood that has been chopped and stacked by Lidia's father.

Meanwhile, Lidia, with no interest in food whatsoever, takes the hare and expertly makes an incision just above the knee on each back leg. She pushes her fingers inside the cut and frees the skin from the legs, the back, and the belly. Once or twice she reaches for a short knife to assist in the skinning because the hare has now been dead for a few hours. She is careful not to pierce the stomach or intestines because the contents can contaminate the meat.

Behind her Feiga and Leonid sit at the wooden table and beside her, to the left, Grishka busies with the stove. Snap of wood. Crackle of fire. A couple of exaggerated puffs from Grishka to get it moving.

Lidia holds the skin she has removed from the hindquarters of the hare and lowers its carcass to the kitchen floor until she can step on the hare's feet to hold it steady. Pulling the skin toward the head she gathers up more and more hide until it peels up and over the body. At one point she reaches out and grabs the small blade and nicks the skin here and there away from the meat and wiggles her fingers inside to loosen it free. And then, in a succulent pop, the skin pulls off over the front legs and neck.

Grishka has moved behind her to gather more glasses, shorter ones this time, and a bottle of homebrewed Vodka that is stashed in the same cupboard as the glasses.

The hare thumps back on the side bench as Lidia reaches for a larger chopping knife. *Thwack.* Head. *Thwack. Thwack.* Feet. She taps the tail off with another nick of the blade. The gralloched hare takes seconds and the windpipe is the last of the internal organs she removes, carefully cutting it to the end of the neck. Usually, the dressing of game is satisfying, but not tonight.

Grishka has prepared the pot with herbs and wild mushrooms and chopped onions. She places the body of the hare gently, tenderly into the pot and stands aside as Grishka pours in a liquid combination of stock and her father's brandy. Normally such a luxury is forfeited but today it just seems necessary.

'Viktor said ... *Targets are locked ... Do not stand down.*' Leonid's voice seems to come from a long way, away.

The kitchen is over warm, now that the woodstove is chugging along, cooking up a mushroom and rabbit stew that they may or may not eat. She knows she has been moving about the kitchen, desperate to do something, anything. Just as long as she can keep busy. Just as long as no one says anything to make the awful news, real. Lidia notices Feiga has her head on the table with her eyes closed. This doesn't mean she is asleep. Grishka has set a glass of vodka in front of Leonid.

To Lidia's surprise, Grishka responds to Leonid's statement with, 'Targets *are* locked. And I am far from standing down ...'

And despite the summery evening outside with its never-ending pale night sky, Lidia is chilled to the bone. There is something in Grishka's voice that makes her realise their fate is bound to this one catastrophic moment of Viktor's bewildering death. She looks between Leonid and Grishka.

'What targets?' She asks. Lidia knows this is a dangerous question and she also knows she does not want to hear the answer because this would mean there is no turning back.

Grishka doesn't answer her but says to the room, 'I will leave tomorrow. There are others I have to mobilise. Spiridonova said that those who have been already executed by the Cheka have been publicly named and shamed as enemies of the state.' He waits for the horror to sink in and although they all know that in Russia this inevitably leads to something even far more brutal, he says it anyway, 'They are now going after their family and friends and ... Lovers ... All those in contact with Viktor are now to be arrested by the Cheka.'

The rich aroma of roast hare fills the kitchen. The fire pops and sparks. Feiga lifts her tousled head and blinks about her as if trying to make sense of what she sees and smells.

'Now, Leonid,' Grishka is using a voice that one might use when speaking to a sick child. 'I need you to take care of Mouse and Lidia. Can you do that? Can I count on you to do that?'

They all look at Leonid who seems incapable of caring for anyone, including himself. His face is drained of colour, his eyes are blank and bleached.

Grishka looks at Lidia, 'I have no choice, my love. You know this ...' It is his eyes that fill with tears as he continues, 'We always knew this day would come and ... so it has ... tomorrow I will go back to Petrograd.'

Much later, after the stew has been pushed around on the plates or ignored, Grishka holds Lidia in her bed and tells her over and over again he will be safe. He must do what must be done. There will be no hope for true revolutionaries like themselves until this has been achieved. His whispered phrases skid about the darkened bedroom: *Trained and focused ... A web of cells ... Infiltrate then strike ... Terror ... Selective assassination ... Individual targets ... Linked to a much greater plan ... Return Russia to the February Revolutionaries ... Reclaim our hijacked Revolution ... Our nation's true future ...* Lidia says little. It is Grishka who talks and holds her and drinks in her smell and unburdens himself as he quietly, slowly, and carefully strokes her hair, her face, and her neck.

A few weeks back, when they were still in Petrograd, she had told Grishka what had happened to her. On her return to the Vyborgskaya. Crossing the frozen Neva in her brother's skates. After coming from her father's estate. The bridge. Two Red Guards. The warehouse. The rape. Her gun. Afterward, Grishka and Lidia had slept together and she had let him hold her but they didn't do anything more.

She knows Grishka will be gone by the morning and it will be her job to care for the broken Leonid and see whether he can ever return to the person he once was. Just like she had to nurse Feiga back from cholera. As for her own need to be healed — to be put back together, to be cleaned in a way that might wipe away the rape — she knows it will never happen.

At about three in the morning, Lidia rises from the bed and leaves Grishka in search of a glass of water. Not because she is thirsty but because it is not in her nature to wait for the inevitable.

Leonid is standing at the kitchen window and although he doesn't turn around he says softly, 'Cat-eyes ...'

She moves to his side and gazes out at the pale shaded light that keeps the midsummer night ever watchful. He feels cold against her shoulder and arm but she leans into him, nonetheless, and after a minute or two he moves his head just slightly to rest against hers.

'I can't sleep,' she says. The skin on her face feels tight and strained. She knows that later she will regret this lack of sleep but she just needs to get through Grishka's departure and then, maybe, she can rest. She feels the fatigue in her bones because she is tired of caring for the wounded when she just wants to curl up in bed and never have to speak or interact with another human being again.

'I am lost ... I have lost ...' Leonid doesn't continue but stands there with her watching the dirty white light of the sky outline the trees beyond the window.

'I know. You have lost too much ...' And it occurs to her that not only has he lost his darling Viktor but his faith in Kerensky. The man who should have led them out of the revolution and into their great 20th Century victory. Leonid, like herself and everyone else, believed Kerensky would return any moment and seize control from the Bolshevik madmen. But Kerensky has betrayed them.

Despite this Lidia tries to rally and says, 'But Leonid we must go on.' She feels him pull away from her which spurns her on even more, 'We are always losing people ... That is what it is to be human ...' She thinks about Grishka leaving in a few hours time and knows she must once again seal up her heart.

'No more. I can't do ... I don't want anymore ... I ...' Leonid is barely audible and then he asks, 'What possible reason is there for ... me ... to ... go on ...?'

She wonders the same but replies, 'We must go on living all our appointed days.'

2

Several days later, Leonid picks up the framed photograph off the mantlepiece. He can hear Feiga humming in the kitchen and he thinks Lidia is outside somewhere. He isn't sure. It is an old family portrait. He recognizes no one but has to assume the girl child in it is Lidia and the boy alongside her, Pavel Konoplev. Leonid thinks of his father. A wealthy, successful, and unloving man. He had been a mechanical engineer and Head of the Black Sea Shipyards. Leonid recalls that his father was regarded, by many, as a leader in the Russian Ukrainian community, despite being a Jew. A fact that those outside his family never ceased to point out. What Leonid remembers most because it has been years since he has seen his father, is that he was a hard man with a closed mouth and a quick temper.

Leonid leans against the mantlepiece and looks closer at the family portrait. To the right of the composition, the father is seated on a cane chair, the mother and the son stand alongside him, and propped up in a high chair is a fair-haired four year old girl in a voluminous white smock. Leonid smiles, slightly. The girl child looks cross-eyed because the old sepia photograph casts her different coloured eyes as shadow and light.

'Ah, you're admiring the good looks in my family.'

Leonid swings around and raises his eyes in mock surprise asking, 'So, this is you?' He points to the boy standing erect and uncertain next to his mother — the tips of his shoes shiny, his socks long, his knickerbockers pressed, his white shirt too large, and his dandy tie, enormous.

'Yes,' answers Lidia taking the photograph off him, her smile widening. 'You see I was a boy, once, a long time ago ...' Leonid smiles a little as she adds, 'Actually Pavel had head lice when this photograph was taken — according to family lore.' And she looks closer at the boy as if seeking some sort of evidence of this childhood affliction.

'What was your mother like?'

She is unready for this question. She looks with Leonid at her fresh-faced mother, who remains forever young, forever between Pavel and herself, propping them up with a warm sturdy hand on each of their backs. Dark serge dress, long necklace, brooch at the throat, and hanging earrings. A nice face. And her blonde hair pinned up in a fashionably fixed pompadour.

'She was ... I can't remember her very well. She was ... I don't know.'

Leonid thinks of his mother. A tall beauty who seemed to float through life ignoring her temperamental husband. She was a doctor and considered quite an intellect. But she had died before he had left the Crimea. After that, his father's plans for him could not be brooked: the Mikhailov Artillery School of the Imperial Russian Army.

'My father brought us up,' continues Lidia, pensively. 'We had nannies of course but he ... You know, underneath his gruff exterior ...' She sighs, 'Well, he is a darling.'

Leonid watches Lidia look fondly at the portrait. He doesn't share the same view of the ex-Colonel. Retired. Taciturn. Aloof. Leonid is glad Lidia's father has remained at his dacha. It is enough dealing with the kindness and the good intentions of Feiga and Lidia, let alone an ageing ex-military man who believes there is nothing but the charge of combat to right all wrongs.

'Did you see this photograph?' Lidia asks as she reaches for a smaller frame at the other end of the mantlepiece, alongside one of Feiga's endless jars of fresh wildflowers. She is glad Leonid is showing an interest in something other than the speculation of what is happening in Petrograd, or the battle lines between the White and the Red Army, or how Grishka is faring. It has been more than a week now and they have heard nothing.

'Yes,' he answers as he takes the only other framed photograph from her. Behind him, Feiga comes into the living room and he can hear the chatter of tea glasses and smell the sweet yeasty pastry of vatrushkas — Feiga's latest baking achievement.

The photograph had been taken ten years ago. Lidia stands behind her seated brother and father and she seems fuller in the face. Her long blonde hair is tied back but some of it has pulled away and frames her face. She looks directly into the camera, pale-skinned and paler-hair with her mismatched eyes wide open. Her brother, olive-skinned and dark-eyed, looks straight into the camera as well. He is her opposite and yet there is something about the square jaw, strong nose, and wide forehead that make them the same. The brother,

Pavel, is in Royal Infantry uniform. Legs crossed, boots polished and a thick mop of black hair protruding from his regimental cap, set as every Russian soldier, on a jaunty angle. Both he and his sister seem unhappy and it occurs to Leonid that maybe they have a special bond, thrown together with the death of their mother and their rather remote father.

'Tea is ready,' announces Feiga as she places the tray on the small table in front of the mantlepiece. Neither Lidia nor Leonid looks back as she scurries to the kitchen.

'Look at father,' says Lidia fondly. Leonid looks at the ex-Colonel with his epaulettes and medals and cross-belt and braiding. He is bald but sports a dark beard and moustache. Unlike his grown-up children, he looks off-camera and out beyond to the left. It is as if he is remembering something ... a long time ago ... perhaps another family photograph ... when she was there.

'Come on!' says Feiga proudly as she lumbers in with the samovar. Leonid springs into action and takes the silver urn from her and carries it across to the table. Waiting there is a teapot and tea glasses and a small plate of individually sized pastries filled with cottage cheese.

'You are spoiling me,' he says and he sees the joy fill up in Feiga. While the girls fuss with the boiling water and the pastries, Leonid takes one of the overstuffed armchairs next to the fireplace. In the middle of summer, there is no need for a fire and he notices for the first time that they have hung herbs to dry in the hearth. It has been more than a week since he found out ... No, he will not think of it ... Besides, now he has made his decision and there is no coming back from it. He accepts the tea glass and then a plate from Feiga who seems to get younger every day. She has flourished in this rambling homestead where learning to bake and collect flowers fills her days. Lidia complains to both of them that Feiga needs to develop her marksmanship and recognize the importance of being able to defend herself. But Leonid can see why Mouse is the way she is. He sips his sweet tea and listens to the girl's chat about the pie that Feiga is fixing for their supper tonight. He will travel to Petrograd soon. Tomorrow. This should be done swiftly. Expediently. He cannot wait here any longer. He is not invalid and there is nothing to restore. His heart is dead. It is nothing but a rusty sardine tin of yesteryear.

The girls smile at each other when they see him take another vatrushka.

Leonid knows he will have to deal with Feiga's tears and Lidia's pragmatic explanation of why they all must lie low until Grishka returns. But Grishka has been gone a week and although he is renowned for his resourcefulness, there has been no sign of him or message from him. He notices that Lidia does not mention this fact. Instead, every day she takes one of the rifles and shoots game for their meal or brings in wood for the stove or fetches buckets of water from the well or patiently instructs Feiga on how to cook with the provisions they have stored. But he knows that Grishka is always on her mind, how could he not be?

Leonid turns to Lidia who is still smiling from something Feiga has said.

'What is it?' she asks and then sadness moves across her face.

Leonid squares up to what must be said, 'I have to leave tomorrow.' He waits for this news to separate himself from them. The beginning of their farewell. 'There is something I must do —'

'No.' Lidia interrupts, quietly but determinedly.

Leonid wonders how this is going to play out because he *is* leaving. Tomorrow. No matter what. 'I have to do something and I will come back as soon —'

'No!' Again, she stops him. 'We need to be together. We have to stay together. Until ...' He waits to see if she can say it. 'Grishka comes home.' Of course, she can, thinks Leonid. 'And then we can assess what needs to be done.' She is made of sterner stuff than me, thinks Leonid. He feels tired. Fatigued by what life has thrown at him. He turned 22 in March and after the news of ... No ... He will not say it ... He feels weary with this drudgery called life.

'I will leave tomorrow. But I will come back,' announces Leonid and places his tea glass and the half-eaten pastry, in which he has lost interest, back on the table. He notices Feiga is now sitting deep into the settee with her head pressed back, eyes shut. They are used to how she tries to cope with the world. Lidia is leaning forward, as if in the hope that he will see her and realize his responsibility is as much to her as vengeance is to him. Because this is what it is.

Of course, a part of him wants to strike terror in the Bolsheviks by picking off their leaders, one by one. An assassin's field day. A sniper's festival. Especially now that Kerensky has abandoned them to these morons who know nothing of Russia because every single one of them had been abroad when the rest of the nation was fighting for their lives on the Front and then shaping a nation into a revolutionized constituent democracy.

But his motivation has nothing to do with the collective or with ideology. If he could say it out loud he would ... The real reason for his plan is nothing more and nothing less than for the sheer unadulterated pleasure of revenge.

3

It is still early and no one has slept well. Lidia can hear Leonid outside with the bicycle, grunting and shoving the chain back into place. Feiga is in the kitchen wrapping food for his journey up to Gatchina and then on to Petrograd. There is no talking him out of it but in many ways Lidia understands. He has lost everything so what does risk matter, now? She just hopes Leonid will find Grishka and bring him home, as he has promised he will.

She turns her attention back to the letter she is writing her brother. It is long overdue and Leonid assured her he will get it dispatched while some of his contacts are still operating out of Gatchina. So, she must have it ready before he leaves.

Dear Pavel,

Father has left for the lake and before long it will just be Feiga and me, here at the estate. The weather has been lovely and ...

Lidia breaks off and realizes this is not it at all.

We are well. Leonid has promised to get this letter off today — but we are better off here than in the city! When will things get back to normal?! I can't remember the days of normal ...

No. This is not why she is writing — she shakes her head and straightens her shoulders.

Pavel, the newspapers are all indicating that the prisoners are being escorted down to Moscow. Leonid said it is true that there is to be a show trial and Trotsky will be prosecuting the Tsar — who would have thought that in 12 months the revolution would have achieved so much ...

Again, she is frustrated by the way her pen seems to veer off course and fill Pavel's letter with noise as if avoiding what she so desires to ask but has so little hope will come to pass.

Brother, when you get to Moscow, please do everything you can to come here to us — surely, they can do without you for a day or two? It has been so long and so much has happened ...

Why is she being so vague? She needs Pavel to realize the horror of their lives, now that the Bolsheviks have seized total control. She needs Pavel to know that they are at the crossroads of history. She needs Pavel. She inhales deeply and writes.

There is something I need to tell you — Leonid's Viktor is dead. He was shot by the Cheka. They just rounded up Socialist-Revolutionaries and shot them. Hundreds of them. It has been so awful, so unbelievable, so ...

Again, she breaks off in her bid to find the right words, the truth.

Everything has changed here. Nothing makes sense. You must turn away from the Bolsheviks. When you see how it is here and how our very lives are at the mercy of these animals — you will not only be horrified but you will want to help us ...

She looks down at the word *us*. Such a little word. And then it hits her that there is not much left of *us*. Socialist Revolutionaries were arrested and executed in their hundreds. Viktor gone. Grishka MIA. Leonid is on the move. And she knows with growing certainty that she, like the men all around her, must take a stand. Her skin prickles.

We must bring about a Constituent Assembly and offer a true democracy for Russia! We have no time to lose. Spiridonova is calling for us to overthrow the Bolshevik leaders.

She needs Pavel. She needs him to come back here with family and friends. Besides, who knows where the truth lies? But anything is better than Bolshevik rule! They have so much to lose if they don't take back what is theirs. And time is running out.

So much has happened. Grishka has gone into Petrograd to meet up with the other Socialist-Revolutionaries and Spiridonova. Leonid is following him, this morning ... I need you home. We need to be together, now. On your way here from Moscow, please stop by father's dacha and persuade him to come back as well. We all need to be together. And there is no time to lose.

Lidia sighs. A part of her knows it is useless. Any journey across Russia is dangerous but if Pavel is headed to Moscow as part of the entourage escorting the prisoner, then he will most probably be safe. It is, after all, touted to be the trial of the century and the greatest display of Bolshevik supremacy. She knows her brother is wily enough to make his way up to the estate. After that, she will have to convince him to join forces with her and the others to turn this leviathan around.

Lidia hears Feiga carrying out the food parcel to Leonid. It will be time, soon, for his departure and even though she has been left to her letter-writing Lidia feels that the message she so desperately needs to get across requires even more clarification. But what else can be said? A dirty memory casts a shadow across the letter.

And there is something else I need to tell you, Brother...

She hears Leonid and Feiga talking outside and tries to concentrate on their voices because all this talk of the Bolsheviks and their filthy stranglehold on her country — has a face ... it has a smell and a body and a fist and a ...

Something happened on my return to the city last January ...

She tells herself that she has no intention of writing about her ordeal. Not to her brother, not to anyone. Grishka tried to make her talk about it but apart from the bare facts of the matter, she refused to speak more. And yet, it is as if her pen has a mind of its own as it dips its nib in and out of the inkwell and scribbles on. She knows that it is this information, and this information alone, that will bring her brother home. Sharply and factually the scrape of the pen's nib across the paper recounts what happened to her in that warehouse, alongside the frozen Neva.

Not much later, the two women watch Leonid cycle down the path away from the homestead, around the thick shrubbery, and then out of sight. They have said their goodbyes, kissing and hugging their sad handsome friend as he tied the food parcel to the back of his bike, checked his tires, buckled up his backpack, and said *I'll be back soon with Grishka*. Still, they watch his retreating back as though there might be a chance he will stop and turn around and cycle back to them. Long after they hear the last of the bike as it rattles off in the distance, both women, arm in arm, stand on the white sunlit patio. The long snaking track left by Leonid is the only tie they have to their men. Viktor dead. Grishka missing. Leonid gone. Pavel away.

'Do you ever wonder why ... why this is happening? To us?' asks Feiga.

Lidia doesn't look at Feiga but she feels her petite body snug under her arm, like an imprinted memory of a younger sister, ever sure of the older sibling's tolerance and protection.

'No,' Lidia responds. 'I don't think why ... I guess because it is happening to all of us — all over Russia.' Lidia knows she needs to focus on the shooting practice which now, more than ever, has to be their number one priority. Besides, she has no intention of sitting indoors, waiting to see how history will unravel.

'Not *everything* that is happening has happened to *all* of us ...' Feiga is speaking quietly but determinedly. 'I mean,' she continues, 'That is to say ...'

Lidia wonders what it is that her friend is struggling to tell her.

Feiga looks up into the painted blue sky above them and says, finally, 'You see — I know what happened to you.'

No response.

'In the warehouse.'

A chorus of birdcalls starts up across from where they stand.

'Back in January.'

The taller woman pulls away from the shorter.

'Viktor told me.' Feiga lies but she is desperate for Lidia to hear her and know that it is she, Feiga, who can love Lidia and protect her from the world outside. 'Lidia!' Feiga exclaims as her friend turns to go indoors and then before she can stop herself, she rushes on, 'It happened to me as well. Before. In the labour camp. I understand ... I ...'

Lidia turns back and says, 'I must get on. There is so much to do but first, we must go into the forest for rifle practice.' It is as if she has not heard Feiga. 'We must be ready for any eventuality.'

And then Lidia is gone and Feiga blinks back the warm tears that suddenly blur the morning. She thought if she raised it Lidia would see how it can only be Feiga who truly understands. She, alone, can help. Of course, on the surface, Lidia always seems to be the one bustling about after others but Feiga knows when they are alone or when Lidia has forgotten she is there in the forest with her gathering mushrooms or herbs or berries — that she is still wounded.

The cool off the living room works its balm and Lidia feels her heartbeat slow down. She took care of the bastard then and there. In the warehouse. Three bullets. There is no more to be said or done. But she knows that she is at a turning point. This waiting for Grishka, now Leonid, and the loss of Viktor confirms what in many ways her father always knew and prepared her for which is that in the end, women must also take up arms if the great battle is to be won. She knows that it is now up to her because no matter what men have promised, in the end, she must ensure her protection. Even now, at this critical point when the world is thrown into chaos, her father is probably fishing on the lake at his dacha, her brother is probably playing soldiers out in Siberia and her boyfriend is probably running amuck in Petrograd. She hears the door open and knows Feiga has come back inside.

'Let's have tea,' Lidia hears the forced cheer in her voice and Feiga responds by bustling about with the water and the samovar and the teapot.

Lidia pulls out the Nagant rifles that they used yesterday and lays them on the kitchen table.

Feiga begins cutting and slicing.

Lidia says, 'Nothing for me to eat — just tea,' as she takes the first rifle, clamps it in a vise, and removes the bolt.

Feiga fusses with the samovar and opens the kitchen door to let out the escaping steam.

Lidia runs one of the gun-rags up the bore a few times.

Feiga moves the tea glasses to the countertop furthest away from Lidia's tasks.

Lidia removes the magazine spring assembly and carries it carefully to the sink for close cleaning.

Feiga tips the boiling water from the samovar into the teapot.

Lidia turns back to the shoulder stock and begins rubbing it down.

Each woman is absorbed in her essential task.

Feiga carefully pours the hot tea into the glasses and places them at the far end of the wooden table.

Lidia reinserts the bolt and adds gun oil to the breach and world the bolt back and forwards. She then tucks the rags and small bottles of spirit and the jar of lubricant into the rifle satchel.

Feiga says softly, 'Tea's ready.'

Lidia responds, 'Rifle's ready.'

They both know that it will take Feiga far too long to check and clean the rifle she has been using. Indeed, frustrated by Feiga's inability to retain just about anything she has taught her, Lidia will, like always, take over and clean it for her. Besides, Feiga is so reluctant to shoot at anything, fixed or moving, that it is better to get all preliminary tasks out of the way so that they can get out in the forest and get on with what they must do.

Lidia sips her tea.

'I'll check my rifle in a minute,' says Feiga vaguely.

Lidia has no idea how long it will take Leonid to find Grishka or for her letter to find Pavel but what she does know is that she has only a finite amount of time to teach Feiga to use the rifle. And it's not being out here in the seclusion of her father's forested estate that worries her — two women alone. What worries her is that she is not sure how many Socialist-Revolutionaries are still operative and what it will take to stop the Bolsheviks.

Feiga smiles at her from across the table and the two women drink their tea. One of them thinks of the companionship of sitting together in the mid-morning warmth, alone, just the two of them. The other thinks about a plan that is hatching deep in the recesses of her heart because she knows she cannot wait forever for Grishka or Leonid or Pavel.

Lidia knows the targets. Grishka and Viktor made no bones about the fact that all Bolshevik leaders were now marked. And considering she is a better shot than any of the men she knows, apart from Pavel who is her equal, why not take out Hydra's most poisonous head, the one that leads all others?

Feiga asks, 'More tea, Lidia?'

Lidia replies, 'Let me just clean the other rifle for you.' As she stands up she adds, 'We must get out before the day has run away from us.'

And in the last of the indoor tasks for the morning, both women move about the kitchen. Feiga, resolute in her love and protection of Lidia. Lidia, resolute in her decision and commitment to do what no man has yet succeeded in doing. Unbidden, Lidia sees in her mind's eye the round mashed face of her rapist, snarling and gloating, and then, like a trompe l'œil, it shimmers and morphs into the visage of *that* Bolshevik, Comrade Vladimir Ilyich Lenin. She knows they are one and the same.

15

Obukhov Factory

Petrograd. June 1918.

SPIRIDONOVA ARRESTED!

A special report by Comrade Volodarsky. Commissar of Propaganda and Information & Editor of the Red Gazette.

Grishka looks at the newspaper hanging in the window of the closed recruitment office. His back is to the steelworkers pouring into the Obukhov Factory and his relaxed stance belies the rage coursing through his body.

The notorious terrorist and ardent man-hater, Maria Spiridonova, was arrested in Moscow yesterday, following her anti-Bolshevik, anti-Treaty of Brest-Litovsk speech, delivered in a vain attempt to destabilise the valiant Russian Communist Party.

The screech of the siren rips through the summery afternoon as the second shift for the day commences. The Obukhovsky has not missed a day's output in its manufacture of land and naval guns, torpedos, aircraft artillery, armoured plates for warships, rifle scopes and binoculars, since its inception in 1872. Now the workers are being instructed to produce tractors, railway carriages, and drive shafts for the hydroelectric power stations. This has generated much discontent because the workers are not being rewarded for the extended hours they are forced to work. Needless to say, those talking of strike have been threatened with Chekist gunfire.

On arrest, Spiridonova claimed responsibility for the assassination of the German Ambassador, Count Wilhelm von Mirbach. It was reported to this newspaper that just two weeks beforehand Spiridonova called on her Socialist Revolutionary Battle Unit to use terrorism to disrupt the following victorious achievements by the Russian Communist Party: Peace with Germany, Dismantling the bourgeois Constituent Assembly, and Requisitioning grain from rural areas to feed all!

Grishka bares his teeth at the blatant disregard of the rural peasants' hunger and poverty that has come about because of the introduction of War Communism by Vesenkha, the Bolshevik's economic committee. Its draconian strictures have had a flow-on effect on the workers here at the Obukhov Factory. And if that's not bad enough, Lenin's new government is replacing worker-led soviets with nationalised industries with the Chekist overseeing the strict discipline and punishment of workers. Moreover, rumblings of discontent can be heard everywhere about the government's control of foreign trade and the introduction of rationing. And everyone knows, thinks Grishka bitterly to himself, that the requisition of agricultural output from peasants is the Bolsheviks making sure the Red Army is stocked with food and weapons during this filthy civil war with the Whites.

While this newspaper and all those committed to the revolution acknowledge the contribution Spiridonova has made in the past, it is unlikely that comrades in this present climate will regard her as anything other than a retrograde deviant attempting to undo all the triumphant and fearless gains by Lenin and his heroic team of party leaders, as well as the rank-and-file.

Grishka glances over his shoulder at the mouth of the Obukhov Factory. Its monumental red brick entrance with its A-frame roof suggests the solidity and certainty of work for the Motherland. And yet the militant discontent rising within the ear-crushing factory is beginning to offer another story. The harsh Cheka reprisals have done nothing but intensify the workers' resolve to demand a Russia they fought so hard to achieve. Spiridonova has requested the Socialist Revolutionaries agitate unrest amongst the workers in these very sites, until the Bolsheviks, usurpers of the revolution, are overthrown.

Under the guise of a rabble-rouser and agent-provocateur, Grishka has been able to get closer to the sites where his targets might come into view. Bolshevik leaders are always coming out to the Obukhov Factory in an attempt to quell the dissenting masses who dare to challenge the Bolsheviks. Moreover, beyond the hotbed of Petrograd, the White Army in the south as well as the combined forces of the Czech Legion and the White Army in Siberia, are all threatening the Bolsheviks.

It's only a matter of time before we take back what is rightfully ours, thinks Grishka bitterly. A revolutionised Russia!

It was made known to this newspaper that when Spiridonova was interrogated, she decried the dominance of men in the leadership of the Communist government. She asserted that women often outnumbered the men who were exiled and imprisoned in Siberia in the labour camps for the decade leading up to the Revolution, suggesting that it was they who contributed largely to the outcome of 1917. Yet, comrades, throughout Russia we all know that it has been the ordinary people themselves who have brought about this cataclysmic change to our nation, one that has forged a glorious path ahead where every man and woman can enjoy liberty, peace, work, and food!

It's only been a few weeks since Grishka left Lidia. The only way he can stay and do what has to be done is the belief that Lidia will stay out of trouble. If anything happens to her he could never live with himself. It is enough that she is now burdened with the weak: Feiga and Leonid. But Lidia is good-hearted and Grishka knows she will never abandon them. He feels her absence most intensely when he is alone. Grishka tries not to think too much about her back at her father's estate, it is easier that way. Besides, he is doing this for her, for Viktor, for Spiridonova, for every Russian but, most especially, for all his fallen comrades at the Front who died for nothing. He spits and reads on.

Maria Spiridonova joined the terrorist Socialist Revolutionaries back in '06 and assassinated the pro-Tsarist land-owner Luzhenovsky. This became one of 200 individual acts of terror for which the Socialist-Revolutionaries took political responsibility! This is the same Spiridonova who was raped repeatedly by her Cossack captors before being handed over to the police. At the time, she was the tender age of 21 with a pleasing figure and face. She, along with five other infamous female political prisoners, known as the Shesterka, travelled to Siberia. Sources claim that throughout the years their anti-male pro-feminist vitriol is nothing but a cover-up for their degenerate sensibilities as inverts or Sapphists (women who have formed romantic friendships with other women!).

Grishka snorts derisively. A bit of salacious rubbish to push the so-called truth along. Every Russian believes that Spiridonova is a national hero, regardless of what the Bolsheviks say. Good luck with that, he thinks and turns momentarily to face the warm afternoon sun and scan the courtyard. Despite his blood pumping palpably through his veins he slouches against the office door frame in an affectation of nonchalance. He appears as a lone worker, tall and lanky with his dark head of curly hair tumbling out of his slouch cap. Worn-out overalls. Cigarette in mouth. Dirt-encrusted hands. Anyone passing might think he is awaiting supplies or that he is wanting to register for a job when the recruitment office reopens. After a moment he turns back to the newspaper in the window.

While this newspaper realises terrorism is a natural reaction to autocracy and was the weapon of choice before the patriotic October Revolution, it can no longer be tolerated! The Bolsheviks have revolutionised the na-

tion in that one man can no longer have absolute power over all of Russia.
Hence terrorism — in the actions of strikes, sabotage, and assassination —
can no longer exist in, this, our brave new Russia!

Grishka hears a vehicle pull up in the courtyard behind him. He watches through the reflection of the office window as a group of Bolshevik leaders scramble out. They cluster before the entrance of the factory with a proprietorial air. Shoulders back, clean suits, well-fed bodies — all in stark contrast to the bent and lean factory workers who entered the broil of their shift not long ago. Grishka hears a second car drive into the courtyard but casually continues reading the newspaper in the window, not wanting to draw attention to himself. He can only surmise that the rumours of the stop-work meeting today have been leaked to these Bolshevik leaders who want to strongarm their so-called comrades back into line.

He watches as a small, neatly dressed man in his early 30s, sharp-beaked nose and round-framed spectacles, jumps out of the second car. Grishka catches his breath. It's Volodarsky! The Commissar for Propaganda and Information.

Grishka tells himself to keep calm and he slows his breathing. His plans are now utterly altered. For the last few days, he has been here at Obukhovsky fomenting anti-Bolshevik sentiment and provoking striking. He has got to know many of the workers on their way to and from the two shifts offered over the 24-hour work-day.

But now. Now. Everything has changed, utterly.

The uncanny moment of reading the lies and propaganda written by Volodarsky and then seeing the traitor, here, on these very grounds just cannot be ignored. It is a sign. He reaches into his thin jacket and feels the grip of his revolver.

The Bolshevik leaders have entered the Obukhovsky and Grishka hears from the Factory floor the boos and hisses of a crowd who has come too far to give up now. And rising above the calls to *Shut Down the Cheka!, End the Death Penalty!* and *Permit Rival Newspapers and*

Parties to Exist! He hears Volodarsky's high sharp voice — a leader impervious to the voices of his fellow man. On and on Volodarsky talks over and above the thousand or so workers who have downed tools. Not because they believe the Commissar for Propaganda and Information will change their minds but to demonstrate their unbreakable faith in themselves and their power.

Grishka pulls away from the entrance of the Obukhov Factory and scopes the road that runs alongside the Neva. He decides the vehicles will turn left as they leave the grounds, to head back into the city.

He pauses.

Behind him are cries of anger: *The Obukhovsky belongs to us! The Worker's Committee to control its labour and output!* And then shouts *Free Spiridonova!* The catcalls and whistles and jeering and hooting and booing generate a violent aural brickbat that cannot be silenced. *Free Spiridonova! Free Spiridonova!* No one is as popular as this fragile, softly-spoken, bone-thin woman who is as unafraid now, as she was back in '06, to empty a round of ammunition into the face of the oppressor. And Grishka feels fiercely proud of his fellow Russians and knows that those Bolshevik leaders have no idea what they are up against.

He leaves the factory and starts making his way up the Obukhovsky Prospeckt. About 200 metres on is a thick green hedge that frames a small parkland running beside the road. Grishka heads toward this cover. He feels the strangest sensation ... as if he is walking on his breathing. His footfalls catch the beat of his heart that surely can be heard by busy passers-by. The colours of the street, the people, the vehicles, the Neva to his right seem to shimmer and dance. The very edges of this over-lit sun-bright mid-afternoon, tingle.

Grishka looks behind him as he comes to the hedging. No departing vehicles from the Factory's entrance. Yet. He lights a cigarette, coolly looks about him, and then pushes himself in through a break in the shrubbery. His redoubt is stellar. He is close to the Obukhovsky Prospeckt with only a thin coverage of foliage to camouflage him but it allows a perfect view of all oncoming vehicles.

He waits.

Grishka thinks about the steelworkers back at the Obukhovsky and he knows they are raising hell. There isn't a single Russian who will accept the Communist Government handing over large tracts of their nation to the Germans! Indeed, Trotsky has incurred outrage now that he has forbidden troops to fight against the Central Powers in Ukraine.

Grishka crushes his cigarette underfoot and un-pockets his revolver. Any time now, he tells himself. He checks the cylinder. Seven bullets.

He looks down the road to his right. An unblocked view to the entrance of the Factory. Grishka doesn't think about Volodarsky. He doesn't feel hatred toward this man, only great love of country and a desire to secure the future that he and Lidia and every single Russian deserves. The future that Viktor and his other fallen comrades fought so hard to secure.

The street and the hedging in which he stands offers up the occasional clop clop of the passing horse-drawn carts, the trill of birdcall as it scampers by and the distinct clangour of the steelworks as the factory starts up. But it is the silence that Grishka feels. A quietness that creeps in through his brain and heart and entrails. A stillness. A static invigilation.

And then he sees it. The nose of a vehicle. One of the two that entered the courtyard of the Obukhov State Plant.

Hidden in the shrubbery no one sees Grishka's semi-raised arm, the revolver in hand, and his finger gently resting against the trigger.

The first vehicle slides out onto the Obukhovsky Prospeckt. It changes gears and pulls laboriously left, catches its breath, then hauls its heavy load of four or five bodies up toward him.

Grishka feels nothing. The summery end of the day is forgotten. His hedged hideout, forgotten. The horse-drawn carts and the foot traffic, forgotten.

The first vehicle lumbers towards him over the very slight rise, that he hadn't at first noticed, from the Factory to his sentry post. Then the first vehicle passes him. Unknowingly. And is gone. Forgotten.

A minute or two passes.

Grishka imagines the first vehicle roaring toward the Smolny in the city, over-throttled and overloaded with the weight of the Bolshevik deputies, congratulating themselves on their success in heading off a strike at the Obukhovsky.

Then he sees the second vehicle pull left out of the Factory's grounds.

In.

Perfect.

Slow.

Motion.

Onto the street in which Volodarsky's destiny awaits.

Grishka inhales, slowly.

The vehicle takes its time. It creeps onwards, leisurely enjoying the view of the Neva to the right and putting behind it the stench of sweat, metal, and oil as well as the burning fuels of the Obukhovsky.

Grishka exhales and raises his right arm, the revolver secure, as his left-hand cradles the right.

The driver of the vehicle carries only one passenger. A small man who sits upright in the open backseat. From his vantage point, Grishka can see the dark hair plastered down on his small head, neat and tidy, like a schoolboy. Then Volodarsky's round spectacles glint once, then twice, like a semaphore message signalling danger. Grishka inhales and holds his breath as the vehicle chugs closer and closer and closer toward him and just as the vehicle drives up alongside him, Volodarsky's small narrow shoulders turn, as if something has caught his peripheral vision in the hedge ... a fancy, a folly.

Grishka squeezes the trigger.

BANG!

The small head flies back and back.

BANG!

The slender chest flowers into a red corsage.

Even before there are shouts from Obukhovsky Prospeckt, Grishka is moving back through the park to a road that will take him to the tram stop. His instinct is to run, to charge rapidly out of the park and as far away as possible but he forces himself to move at an even pace. He does not look back when he hears the commotion behind him or when he sees people running past him in the direction of the shouts. Grishka lights a cigarette puts his hands in his pockets and mooches on toward the tram stop. Eventually, he reaches it. He steadies his breathing as he leans casually up against the tram shelter, in an attempt to appear nondescript.

Grishka inhales deeply.

He hears the whine of the notorious Black Marias, now used by the Cheka, racing toward Obukhovsky Prospeckt. Others are waiting at the tram stop. A woman with a fussy baby, some students talking amongst themselves about what might have happened, and a few, like himself, knowing it is safer to show no interest. He looks down the tram line and sees it labouring toward them. Foot traffic crisscrosses the road on seeing the approach of the tram. Grishka hears its bell as it trolleys closer and sees the spit and spark of the electrical connection fizz overhead. Any moment now, he thinks to himself. And the other commuters begin to move forward in readiness to board the tram. Everyone wants to move on and get out of here as quickly as possible.

Then racing out of the side road speeds a Black Maria. It flies around the corner. Slams on its brakes. Right in front of the tram stop.

Those waiting for the tram move back as one and the woman with the baby is ashen-faced. For a fraction of a second Grishka thinks to run but decides against it when he sees how quickly the first Chekist alights. Leather-coated, indifferent face, revolver-ready.

'Identification!'

Grishka is closely corralled with the others and knows how this will play out. The 10,000 newly recruited Cheka are itching to be part of any search and destroy mission. It must have been radioed in by Volodarsky's driver and for the first time, Grishka wonders whether he should have taken the driver out as well. Could have bought me a little more time, he thinks to himself, as he, like the others at the tram stop pull out their ration books. One by one they are carefully examined. A charade of sorts considering the Cheka isn't picky when it comes to arresting and executing — whether or not the individual is guilty is irrelevant because what matters is the public demonstration of retaliating against civil disobedience.

Three goons are checking the ration cards. The two bigger ones are obviously illiterate but they are making a great show of examining the snapshot inside the ration book, where every woman and man looks like every other woman and man. But to his dismay, the smaller one, the one who stepped out first takes up Grishka's ration card.

'Grigory ... Ivanovich ... Semyonov,' reads the goon out loud.

It is at that precise moment that Grishka realizes he still has his used revolver in his pocket. At first, he curses silently but then calmly notes how the small Chekist, who has his ration book, has put his gun back inside his overlong leather coat. The other two are too busy in their dumbshow to have the wherewithal to take out their weapons.

'You're a long way from home. Comrade.'

It's a statement but Grishka knows he needs to explain why he is living in the Vyborgskaya Strona District but standing here dressed as a factory worker, so many kilometers south.

'Heard they're recruiting —'

'At the Obukhov State Plant?'

The goon is getting far too interested in him and some of the other patient commuters at the tram stop, now relieved the focus is not on them, have also turned their attention to Grishka.

'No. Over at the warehouses.' Grishka doesn't falter despite having no idea where these alleged warehouses would be, but the great meandering Neva carries goods up and down its watery body so warehouses are everywhere.

The goon looks back at the ration book and Grishka knows he has four bullets still in the cylinder of his revolver.

'So, you don't know anything about those shit-stirrers over at the Factory and the meeting there with our leaders?'

Grishka only has to reach into his pocket ... slowly ... so he takes his time to answer the question, 'What's that? Look, I don't know what you are talking about ... What Factory would that be?'

The two other goons have stopped looking at the ration cards and watch on. Greedily.

'You see the Obukhovsky is a ... hot cooking pot,' Grishka looks on as the Chekist is clearly pleased with his metaphor. 'And inside is a stew that is mixing and cooking and ...'

Grishka steps back, almost imperceptibly, and cocks his head to one side, indicating he is listening. And then he slides his right hand into his pocket. The eyes of the goon dart immediately to Grishka's pocket and Grishka makes the mistake of a lifetime — he freezes.

The goon reacts instantaneously. A revolver is pointed at Grishka's stomach.

The tram stop is blank-faced and still.

'What's in your pocket?'

Grishka smirks, 'Cigarettes.' Which is true, but not the whole truth.

'Check his pockets.' The other two ruffians push and shove Grishka, a promise of what they can offer in the near future, and pull out a squashed packet of Turkish cigarettes and then, of course, the gun.

'Ahh,' says the small Chekist in front of him. 'And why would you be carrying a weapon on your search for work ... at a warehouse?' The two larger goons are already pulling his arms up behind him.

'I carry a gun. What does it matter?' Grishka is being manhandled aggressively but he pushes back so that he can stand upright and tower over the Chekist in front of him.

'What does it matter?' says the Chekist eyes widening in feigned disbelief. 'What does it matter?'

Grishka stares back, defiantly, 'Last I heard it wasn't a crime to carry a gun.'

The Chekist smiles sweetly and responds, 'But it is a crime to assassinate one of our great leaders!' The Chekist can't remember *which* Bolshevik big-wig is lying dead out there on Obukhovsky Prospeckt, they all seem the same to him.

'Volodarsky,' offers one of the brutes manacling Grishka.

'That's right. Commissar Volodarsky. Assassinated.' There's an audible intake of breath from those innocent bystanders who have backed as far away from Grishka as possible.

'That's why it matters. *Comrade.*' The last word is dripping in sarcasm but the Chekist is looking past Grishka to those huddled in the tram stop — eyes downcast, baby whimpering — and he wonders momentarily if he should arrest them for harboring a fugitive.

'I am being falsely accused! Get the fuck off me!'

The Chekist ignores him because he doesn't matter. What matters is that he, the self-appointed captain of these two other half-wits, has outwitted another enemy of the state and he will be remembered for catching this despicable assassin! And this time he has proof — the gun ... not that proof is ever really expected from their superiors. Only commitment. And enthusiasm! Here is an arrogant, over-confident factory worker with no legitimate reason to be searching for employment outside of his district and carrying a gun close to the scene of the crime. Guilty! He nods to the two apes holding Grishka and they roughly haul him into the Black Maria.

2

The Chekist conducting the enhanced interrogation session has nothing against the prisoner, personally. He watches as Grigory Ivanovich Semyonov, known as Grishka to his friends, slumps on his knees, hands bound behind. His back, a mad and bloody roadmap of welts and gaping wounds. It's not personal. Davydov hands the long rubber hose back to Ligachev and returns to the steel table so that he can look at the prisoner should he raise his head.

'Once again I am asking you to save yourself and many others by telling me the names of your co-conspirators and the person who ordered the assassination of Volodarsky.' Davydov's tone is quiet and calm. He watches the prisoner drop his head to the cement floor, his breathing is laboured. Davydov knows that a man can be whipped to death — but not while he is in charge. On the other hand, his sadistic assistant will often suggest in his wheedling voice to use other methods: lower the prisoner into a vat of boiling water or saw through the bones in his legs or sodomize him with various objects and then slice up his abdomen. Slowly. Davydov spends most of his working days ignoring Ligachev, who is subhuman.

The prisoner has steadied his breathing but does not look up. He has been in the facility now for a few days and they will not be keeping him for much longer. Besides, they know it is Maria Spiridonova who is urging these otherwise good Russian men to sabotage the true pathway of the Revolution.

'I told you ...'

Davydov is somewhat surprised that the prisoner is making an effort to respond. Usually, they cry for their mothers or pray to a god who has never existed or beg to be finished or spared.

'I ... acted alone ...' The last words are barely audible.

In a way, Davydov believes him. After all, he is an eternal optimist and has faith that the majority of Russians believe that their nation is in the rightful hands of Comrade Lenin and Comrade Trotsky. Indeed, the government they have assembled is, without a doubt, the beginning of a new Russia, a new world! Soon, no child or woman or man will ever know hunger or suffering or injustice or ignorance ever again.

'So, Maria Spiridonova did not order the assassination of Commissar Volodarsky?' Davydov is not tired, he can go on all night but he would prefer to not be in the same room with Ligachev for too much longer. The assistant offers the occasional sadistic kick into the mash and splendor of the prisoner's back. Davydov has no intention of asking his superiors to replace Ligachev with someone more enlightened and dedicated to the real task, which is to re-educate his fellow Russians, because this may be misunderstood and reported to Moisei Uritsky. Davydov has an unblemished record as a warrior for the cause, and the Head of Petrograd's Cheka is never going to hear otherwise.

'No ...'

Davydov sighs.

Behind the prisoner stands Ligachev, who has taken it upon himself to uncoil the rubber hose and drape it teasingly, like some giant phallus, across the shoulder of the naked man kneeling between them. Ligachev sniggers.

'We have been told by some of your colleagues in the Socialist Revolutionary Battle Unit that Spiridonova called for those amongst you to generate terrorism by assassinating elite leaders of the Party.'

The reason it is not personal is that Davydov hates anything that is anti-Bolshevik. His motivations are ideological. Every other political alternative is a corruption of what they fought so fiercely for in the Revolution. Those who support the Tsar, those who wish for the war to continue, and those who sabotage the policy of War Communism, are all morally corrupt. And it is his job to pursue the morally corrupt religiously, ruthlessly, and relentlessly.

'We already know. So —'

The prisoner's murmurs interrupt Davydov.

The room waits.

'What did you say?'

And then they hear the prisoner sniff, inhale and repeat, 'She didn't ...'

It's irritating really, Davydov thinks to himself. He looks away from Ligachev coiling the rubber hose about the prisoner's neck. The noose is wrenched tighter and tighter, and then in an ecstasy of breathlessness ... released. The naked prisoner flops back onto the cement floor. Ligachev licks his lips like a nearsighted lizard.

'You see, Grishka, there's no glory — there's no selfless sacrifice here.' Davydov doesn't know whether the prisoner is listening but his doxology is so strong that he wants others to see the light and know the truth. 'We know you are a good man.' His voice, as always, is reasonable, measured, well-paced. 'We know that it wasn't your idea. We know you fought for your country and have even contributed to the glorious October Revolution — we know all this and yet ...'

Ligachev is moving to the side of the prisoner who is slumped forward on his knees with his head on the floor. Davydov knows what Ligachev wants to do next and there have been occasions when he has allowed him, but right now he can see that the prisoner's genitals are semi-protected in the cave of chest and thighs. Ligachev is, of course, deviant and unhinged, but what can you do?

'Unless you confirm the facts of those who have recanted, there will only be brutality and cruelty for *them* ... and *you*, Grishka.'

Davydov pauses because he wants to allow the prisoner to join the side of righteousness. The true faith. He wants him, of his own volition, to see how he has been manipulated and used.

'It's true, isn't it, that Spiridonova ordered you to act as an individual terrorist cell and assassinate one of the leaders of the Party.'

Personally, Davydov despises Spiridonova. He has nothing but contempt for this woman who believes herself to be some kind of living martyr. She has no real interest in the people of Russia. If she did, she would support the Party and not interfere with the natural course of the Revolution.

The prisoner pushes himself back onto his haunches. He is no longer young and handsome and strong. He is no longer fed or allowed to sleep. He defecates and urinates wherever he sits or stands during his re-education process. The prisoner does not see the Chekists. His eyes have been unable to open after his first beating. He does not smell their approach because his nose is broken but he knows Ligachev, who says little and enjoys much, is close by. Grishka can feel the intimacy of his breath on the side of his face.

'Those others who have obeyed Spiridonova's call to assassinate the leaders of the Party are now with us, and, unfortunately, suffering and will continue to suffer until *you*, the latest and most ...'

Davydov watches as Ligachev's boot slides gently, slowly, into the gap between the prisoner's naked knees. With a strength no one believes he still possesses, the prisoner hauls back from the hard boot and curls over himself, despite the roar of pain he feels when the wounds in his back re-open.

'Grishka. Listen to me.' Davydov can see the sheen of sweat on Ligachev's face and acknowledges that the sadist is employing great restraint that may or may not last for much longer. 'I can help you. I will help you. Your friends have all confessed and renounced their days as terrorists and want to rejoin the righteous path of freedom created by the Bolsheviks for all Russians!'

The prisoner is looking wildly to the side where he believes Ligachev stands. He knows that torture and abuse by the Cheka have been hitherto unimagined.

Davydov speaks more rapidly but with clear annunciation, 'If you also confess to being a terrorist, who was commanded by Maria Spiridonova, and renounce your faith in her heresy, then you and the others will not be executed.'

Ligachev is crouched next to the prisoner and is stroking his thigh with the tip of the rubber hose. The prisoner begins to whimper.

'It is utterly self-centered of you to refuse this offer to end the suffering of your fellow Russians. Their moans cannot go unheard. You must simply tell us what we already know.'

Davydov gathers up the few file notes he has on the prisoner and feels the weight of the world on his shoulders. Someone has to do this job for the moral certainty of Russia's future. And if not him, then who? When the Party calls, Davydov replies: *Here I am.*

'I have nothing against you, personally. The entire Party has nothing against you, personally. But as you are ...' He gazes momentarily at the twist of bloodied bone and ripped skin before him. 'As you are a terrorist and an assassin ...'

Ligachev slides the rubber hose lasciviously into the cave of the prisoner's thigh and chest.

'You are a danger to our nation.' Davydov feels moved by his declaration of love of country. And it is true — he will do whatever it takes to protect his vulnerable and nascent nation! 'The mighty achievement of Communist Russia is its radical social reform which will end poverty and provide education for all!' He wonders whether he has already said this and decides that it won't hurt if he repeats himself because the prisoner is, here and now, being re-educated.

Davydov turns his profile to the naked body now writhing spasmodically on the cement floor as Ligachev works the rubber hose with lubricious abandon in a part of the prisoner's body that Davydov cares not to consider. These matters undertaken by the likes of Ligachev should take place out of ear and eyeshot. Near the cemetery behind their building, for example. Not here in this place of interrogation. But the terrorists are multiplying. They are legion and only his — the screams of the prisoner interrupt Davydov's train of thought.

'Desist!' he commands.

Davydov hears the suck of the hose being withdrawn. He opens the file and scatters the few notes about, once more, on the desk. There is something here ... Something that caught his attention. What is it ...? Where ...?

'Yes. Here it is.' He shakes the paper, more as an audio cue because he is well aware that the prisoner is unable to see what it is that he has uncovered. Davydov is beginning to feel upbeat. 'Here it is!'

The prisoner shunts himself closer to the desk where Davydov stands, possibly in some delusional belief that he is clear of Ligachev. No one will ever be clear off Ligachev, thinks Davydov. The man is wantonly committed to the cause.

'Your girlfriend ...' The paper rustles a little as Davydov looks closer to confirm, 'Yes. Lidia Mikhailovna Konopleva was arrested on the Liteyny Bridge. 14 January. This year. She evaded capture and then she shot one of the guards.'

The accusation is stated neutrally enough and so both Davydov and Ligachev are surprised when the prisoner, for the first time in his entire incarceration, yells, 'SHE WAS RAPED BY YOUR FUCKING GUARDS!'

Davydov takes his time because the plan is forming as he speaks, 'Be that as it may, she is not judge, jury, and executioner. Your girlfriend needs to come forward and present her side of the story. The authorities will then ...' He stops because he thinks the prisoner is crying or maybe he is coughing and then he realizes he is laughing. 'Do you find this business of murdering a guard amusing?'

Ligachev is on the move again and grabs the rope around the prisoner's feet and drags him back into the middle of the room but as he does so the prisoner kicks out hard and luck is on his side because Ligachev is now doubled up gasping for breath and cradling his balls. Oh dear, thinks Davydov, this will not play out well for Grishka. But Davydov has had enough and knows what has to be done — Ligachev's foreplay is getting them nowhere.

'Get that cock-sucker away from me!' spits Grishka.

Davydov frowns at the scene before him, which, he has to admit, is both repugnant and fascinating.

'You see we must go down another path ...' Davydov allows himself a little license, 'This so-called cock-sucker, Comrade Ligachev, will now have to bring in your girlfriend, Lidia Konopleva, for questioning and he will ...' Davydov pauses deliberately, 'He will finish ... her ... off ...'

Ligachev has morphed into a gargoyle of stone mischief.

Davydov continues, 'I know you don't fear your death ...' His voice is mesmeric. 'But you should fear ... *her* assault ... and she will *long* for death ... believe me.' And Davydov looks down at the naked prisoner and knows it will be this, and this alone, that will break him.

3

A week has passed and Grishka doesn't look at the other inmates who are jammed into the train carriage that stinks of manure. The summer heat is alleviated by the rush of air that comes up through the floor and through the singular barred window to Grishka's right. Someone mumbles to anyone who's listening that they are bound for Moscow. Heads nod or look up expectantly, despite broken bones and seeping wounds. Amongst the 30 or so of them in the carriage, there seems a cautious optimism. Grishka hangs his head. He tries again to draw his knees up under him but the pain in his back and anus still screams in protest, so he leaves his legs out straight in front. The train rattles on and on and he tells himself there is nothing he can do. What is done is done. For the hundredth time, he says to himself *They knew already ... I was just confirming what every other poor bastard had already told them ...* But he is glad of the murky light in the train carriage. Here he is nothing, he is nobody. Faceless, nameless.

The person next to Grishka elbows him lightly and passes a ladle of water from a small wooden bucket that is going from man to man. When they were corralled into the carriage in Petrograd, like dumb beasts headed for slaughter, they were told by the Commissar they were no longer prisoners but detainees selected for re-education. Grishka slurps the water but the desert of his mouth returns immediately as he hands the ladle to the next guy.

In the end, it was Lidia. Grishka's shoulders slump. He loved her. He loves her. He will always love her. It was easy in the end. Grishka sighs so deeply he nearly expects to feel his rib cage burst.

He knows he is not alone. Every single detainee in every single miserable carriage hurling southeast sits in the waste of what he once was. Their shame is a stench that makes the manure seem sweet in comparison. These men, once political prisoners incarcerated at the pleasure of the Cheka, have surrendered their right to be themselves as they had once known themselves to be. They have given up who and what they were, and probably like him, have given it up to save a loved one.

Strange how, in the end, it never came down to ideology or courage or manhood or faith. Just love.

Grishka hears a fellow close by weeping. He scrambles about in his head trying to remember a memory, anything, something to take him away from the awful noise of the other detainee. A broken savage sobbing that catches in the throat and burns the back of Grishka's own eyes. He remembers a boat trip once when he was a boy after his father died. Grishka closes his eyes and blocks out the fellow crying and after a while, he hears the *chug chug chug* of the water steamer as it pulls them for days until they arrive at their grandparents' home. Warmth. Kisses. Food. Grishka asks his mother why his grandparents, and the uncles who live with them, speak so strangely. What country is this? He wonders to himself and forgets the emptiness that opens up in his chest because his father has just died. The fellow detainee has stopped crying.

And the collective relief is expressed in the chap by the window bobbing up to ascertain their whereabouts, calling over his shoulder to the shadowy numbed beasts behind him, 'Should be in Moscow soon ... Look — we are coming up to ... Klin! Not long now ...'

Then one bright spark from the other side of the carriage says, 'Hey Comrade — can you see Pyotr Ilyich Tchaikovsky?' A few chuckles and although Grishka, like every Russian, knows his composers, he had no idea where he had once lived.

'Yeah,' calls back the window-commentator good-humoredly. 'Oh, and I can hear him composing the 8th Overture now!' More laughter and then in the spirit of their liberation a few of the detainees spontaneously hum the masterpiece — known more commonly as the 1812 Overture.

But, Grishka is thinking about how quickly humans adapt to the situation in which they find themselves. One moment ardent Socialist Revolutionaries, like him, hand-picked to be part of the Battle Unit with its selected targets. Assassins. Freedom fighters. Liberation warriors. And the next moment they are bound for glory as recruits for the Bolsheviks just as soon as they survive the re-education program. Born again. Lightning rods. True believers.

The mood in the carriage lightens as they draw closer to Moscow but Grishka knows what the re-education program will teach them: The revolution offers each one of them a true place of belonging! Maria Spiridonova is the enemy of the state! Lenin is the great leader of the revolution! And so on ... The man who was crying before starts up once again but this time a few firm voices are telling him to *Pull yourself together, now!* and *Stop being the bad apple in the barrel!* and Shut up *you retrograde or we'll all be punished!*

A strong part of Grishka agrees. There is no turning back. He can either make the best of it or end it. And after seeing the wasted years he spent at the Front, with Russia achieving nothing but the loss of more men and land, he for one, is in complete support of Comrade Trotsky's bid for peace. And as Davydov pointed out to him, Grishka is a socialist and as such should have no hesitation in agreeing with the Bolsheviks' aggressive deliverance of land and bread to the people. Also, he does agree that the bourgeoisie and the aristocracy should be stripped of their land and resources for the workers, peasants, and soldiers of Russia to survive.

Besides, and this fact just about broke Grishka, Volodarsky is replaceable. Everyone is replaceable. Davydov had assured him that the Socialist Revolutionary's terrorist cell, established to assassinate high-profile Bolsheviks, will only strengthen Lenin's resolve to forcibly prevent dissent of any kind. Just a few months is all that is needed for the victorious Communist Party to establish order and all sanctions then will be lifted. Even this job, Davydov had added expansively, will become redundant.

All of a sudden there is a shift in the bodies of those in the cramped carriage. The train is slowing. The coupling rods pushing the huge steel wheels are slackening. The pistons driven back and forth by steam pressure are decelerating. And the coal and sweat-encrusted bodies shoveling fuel from the coal bunker to the coal box are ceasing ... leaning back on their shovels, taking off their neckerchiefs, and rubbing the gritty black coal dust from their eyes and mouths and noses.

The carriage then fills with the long screech of the steam-powered whistle because this is Moscow, the future of Russia, where there will be no negotiation.

Grishka watches from the window as they shunt into the railway station. He has to admit to himself that there is a grand sense of purpose here, in this brilliant summer afternoon. The new capital of all of Russia. The city with the red obdurate heart. The Kremlin. He knows that he has no choice other than to get on board this monumental machine of socialism that will not stop until the entire world of workers is liberated.

The brakes scream and gradually ... eventually ... like a fact that cannot be altered, the train comes to a halt. The carriage shudders.

Even the man who has been weeping has quietened. Most of them are on their feet when the huge doors are unbolted from the outside and the world of extravagant light and sun and color and sound pours into their fetid den. Each man stands taller and looks wide, wanting to see his destiny here, somewhere, anywhere.

A well-fed and well-washed corporal of the Red Guards is standing below them on the platform.

I did it for Lidia. Grishka says to himself, I had to, otherwise, she would have been arrested, assaulted, and shot. I had no other choice.

'On my orders get out of your shit hole and line up behind me.

No talking and no lagging!' He lifts his revolver in the air and says, pointing at one of the men closest to him leaning on the door jamb of the carriage, 'And if you do talk or piss about, I will shoot. NOW GET THE FUCK OFF!'

Leaping, shuffling, jostling, jumping, pushing, shoving.

They already knew about Spiridonova's orders, Grishka thinks. They knew we were recruited to assassinate and even who the targets were. I gave them nothing they didn't already know.

'On my orders, we will march to barracks. And if one of you apes can't march ...' Warming to his theatre, the corporal of the Red Guards points his revolver at a random in the middle of the line, and adds, 'I will shoot. FORWARD MARCH!'

Left. Right. Left. Right. Left. Right.

'I'LL MAKE RED GUARDS OUT OF YOU, ARSEHOLES, YET!'

She will understand, Grishka assures himself. How could she not when he had no other choice? I did it all for her. Everything was and is for Lidia. And as they march through Nikolayovsky Station beneath hundreds of pure bright red flags hanging from the wrought iron roof of the platform, Grishka holds his head high because he knows she will understand!

16

Heatwave

Petrograd. June 1918.

It's a heatwave.

The thick hot air seems to suck the oxygen out of his lungs as he cycles slowly along the Fontanka canal. Despite it still being morning, the day promises to be a stinker. Leonid passes an early morning shopper — a bent old woman with her shopping bags billowing empty about her. The sky above hangs low and the white disc of the sun fries his leather-coated body. Already he can feel the trickle of sweat down his back.

Leonid doesn't ride fast. He has time on his side and there is nothing to do other than to carry out his plan. Indeed, it feels as if his whole life has brought him to this day. He rides alongside the canal and he can almost convince himself that there is just him and the bike and the soupy heat.

Petrograd seems to sleep on, exhausted by the rebellion, the Chekist reprisals, and the ongoing civil war — as well as the promises and the innumerable lies. Truth shifts from day to day, hour to hour. In many ways, it makes sense to stay at home, stay indoors, swelter inside in the unrelenting thrum of 37 degrees.

Leonid's bike glides left into Gorokhovaya Ulitsa, leaving the tired grey-wash of the Fontanka behind.

To his surprise he sees a lone tobacconist propping up his hand-cart in hopeful readiness of the day's trade.

Leonid slows right down. And stops. He doesn't know why he is doing this — he doesn't bother with cigarettes usually — but this day, of all days, is not usual. And it is not that he is pretending to be someone he is not, it is that he has never been more himself than he is right now.

The tobacconist looks wary at first but there is something about the way Leonid is leaning back in the saddle of the bike, one foot on the pavement, the other poised on the pedal that makes the seller continue with his chores. He props up the signage, faded and obsolete, indicating he sells *Ogden's Guinea Gold* cigarettes from England, *Mal Kan No. 3* cigarettes from Turkey, and *Gauloises* from France. Of course, he doesn't actually have any of these but what he does supply is some roughly made cigarettes that he and his young sons put together in the evenings from the harsh cheap ex-military issue of Mahorka tobacco. He also has a large assortment of boots and shoes, none being a matching pair, cast about in the cart.

'Cigarette, Comrade?' the tobacconist eventually asks having made sure that Leonid offers no threat.

Leonid swings his leg over the bike and wheels it to the newly erected stall. He picks up one of the boots, no laces but the leather is fairly good.

'Do you need a boot, Comrade? I can dig around and see if there might be another the same — if you have been unfortunate to have lost two?' The tobacconist chuckles, he says the same thing every day to any prospective customer. And in the ease of this morning, with no immediate danger of protests or street fighting or Black Marias roaring up the street, he feels he has the time to banter.

'No,' Leonid puts back the boot and espies a child's shoe and something in him makes him recoil. 'Just a couple of cigarettes.'

Another bike whisks by and both the tobacconist and Leonid crane around to see who has spoiled this moment in Petrograd, where no one but themselves exists. A woman in her 30s, skirts hiked over the crossbar, cycles on. She doesn't look at either of them but peddles fast and as she leaves them behind a little face clinging to her back, a small boy or girl turns and smiles and Leonid raises his hand in salute. An acknowledgement that right here and now at this moment they have crossed paths. Then they are gone.

'Now. You wanted cigarettes, Comrade?' The tobacconist's face is, half wiry-grey beard and half blue-sky eyes, wide open in their question.

'Yes.'

Leonid is in no hurry and he would rather be in the company of this fellow, who has probably pushed the same cart since he was seven than in the company of his thoughts. The point is, Leonid says to himself as he accepts the two cigarettes, there is nothing left to think or say or consider. What's done is done. Leonid offers the tobacconist one of the two cigarettes, with an accompanying nod to indicate the gift.

'Why thank you, Comrade.' And the seller nimbly takes the offering and in a flash has the coruscation of a match burning at Leonid's face and then his own.

Leonid turns and faces the street, his bike now neatly leaning against a shopfront that has been closed, it would seem, for a couple of years. Something is soothing in this companionable act of smoking together and watching the street fill up with the morning sunlight, burning madly about their heads.

'I'd say it'll be a scorcher,' says the tobacconist.

Leonid nods in agreement and inhales the sticky thick smoke until it gives him a sharp kick in the heart and head. Nearly as good as a vodka shot, he muses.

'You work on down there with the other ... police?' The tobacconist asks his question easily enough but he has been eyeing Leonid's leather coat.

'No,' Leonid exhales slowly and realises that this feeling he has of total abandonment is both liberating and dangerous. 'Just borrowing the coat from one of those goons.'

At the use of the derogatory appellation his companion chuckles and then comments, 'Most days they are charging up and down this street.' As the tobacconist speaks he thrusts his cigarette to the left and then the right. 'Full of their self-importance ...'

'Dogs,' offers Leonid sociably.

'Yeah! They bring nothing but trouble.' The tobacconist looks sideways at Leonid, wondering whether he is risking too much.

In the week that he has been in Petrograd, Leonid had tried to make contact with the Socialist-Revolutionaries but so many of them had gone underground. Or had been executed. He had witnessed the discontent and defeat of ordinary people, everywhere. Leonid had gone to Lidia's apartment in the Vyborgskaya Strona and the old neighbour next door had said she rarely left the building because the Chekists were everywhere! She had gripped his arm with her surprisingly tight claw and whispered, *The Head of the Cheka lives close by! In the Vyborgskaya!* Her eyes were shiny all-seeing beads, her skin a cross-hatching of lines. *Moisei* ... she let the word out slowly ... *Uritsky.*

'Difficult times, Brother. Difficult times ...' says Leonid and drags deeply.

This encourages the tobacconist to chat on and pass the time of day, with this fair-haired ex-soldier. Most of the other vendors had packed up their carts and taken off, God knows where, but this just makes the pickings better for him. The truth is, no matter what the politics, there will always be a need for cigarettes and boots.

'Ahh Comrade, it has been worse than difficult. These last few weeks have been a bloody mess. Uprisings against the government in Moscow caused by the Socialist Revolutionaries, of course, and that's what's turning the Chekist into a pack of dogs!' After the tobacconist finishes his appraisal he looks directly across at Leonid to see his reaction to this opinion.

'Most probably,' responds Leonid as he flicks the butt of his cigarette into the road.

'It's true, Comrade! The newspapers say there have been 10,000 men recruited for the Cheka! No wonder we hear nothing but purges and executions. Those bastards are having a field day!' The tobacconist has warmed to his subject. He has seen enough in his lifetime to know that a cigarette is about the best a man can hope for — that and a drink. Because life is brutal and short.

Leonid closes his eyes to the heat. He tilts his head back and lets himself think about the only man he loved and the way he would exhale the smoke of a cigarette through his nostrils, with his arms crossed at his chest and his hand holding the cigarette close to his lovely mouth.

'No. I have no time for those Cheka wankers.' The tobacconist has come to the end of this cigarette and is unsure whether the customer will offer to purchase another two. 'But the government ...' The tobacconist continues in an attempt to draw out the other man who seems to be adrift in his closed-eye reverie. 'Now the government is making some good moves. The paper has said that priests, nationalists, Tsarists —' He spits, 'And landowners now have no voting rights! Only the workers and peasants ... and soldiers.' He actually cannot remember whether it includes soldiers because weren't they now the enemy of the people? Wanting war and all that rubbish. But he had added it because this fellow looks a bit like a soldier with his neat hair and something about the way he carries himself. Sharp. Watchful. Disciplined.

'Sounds right ...' Leonid responds vaguely. What does he care about the government and their heavy-handed policies? The only thing that matters is the intensity of love that he felt — that he feels, and will always feel — for his beloved. It's a cliché he realises, as he blinks back into the scorching sun, but love doesn't die ... it just changes into something hard and cold and absolute.

Leonid says, 'Did you see, Brother, in yesterday's papers that ...' He has nothing to lose, 'That Lenin has ordered the execution of entire villages if they refuse to send grain to the Kremlin.' He pauses for effect and adds, 'To feed the Red Army and the government workers and their families ...'

The tobacconist wants to like this young man but is starting to think he might be a little disturbed. He wishes now he had kept his mouth shut. 'No,' the vendor answers quietly. 'I haven't seen that news yet.'

The tobacconist is indeed proud of the fact that he can read, well at least pick out the headlines and have his sons read the most interesting bits of news. But the news, like everything else in this stinking city, is stale. 'But did you read that the American President is sending ...' The tobacconist can't remember the number so he guesses, 'Five thousand troops to support the White Army up north?' The tobacconist knows it has become a bit of a pissing contest but this is his cart and his turf. Besides, when he comes to think of it, he has never seen this guy around these parts. 'Where are you from?' the tobacconist asks.

Leonid smiles at the non sequitur and knows it is time to push off. But he has enjoyed the rightfulness of this man. Doing his thing as he has always done in probably this very same place for most of his life. Through Tsarist oppression, war with the Germans, blood-soaked revolution, and now the glorious present — where Russia has gone mad — the tobacconist has sold cigarettes and the occasional shoe. Will the tobacconist outlast them all? Leonid wonders as he pulls his bike off the shopfront. In the end, no matter the politics or the ideology or the weaponry ... in the end ... is this all we have? An individual reaching out to another. A connection — passing, fleeting, gone.

'Thank you, Brother, for the chat and the smoke.' And with that Leonid pushes the last of his roubles into the fellow's hand who immediately protests the generous tip as he stuffs it into his trouser pocket.

This is all there is, Leonid thinks, as he swings his leg over the crossbar. This is all we have in the end. He pushes off. You and me. And he cycles off down the street headed for his destination. His destiny. Number 2, Gorokhovaya Ulitsa. Everybody in Petrograd knows the address of the Head of the Cheka.

Five minutes later, Leonid dismounts and pulls his bike up alongside the side of this infamously non-descript building. There is a tingling sensation in his body. He puts his back to the street and pulls out Viktor's gun, which he took months ago when hiding in the cloak press at Lidia's apartment. That day. That fateful day when those bastards, on Moisei Uritsky's orders, arrested his beloved.

Leonid quickly checks and rechecks the chamber then slips it back inside the breast pocket of the leather coat. He takes out an officer's cap from another pocket and pulls it low over his forehead. It is usual to wear caps high and at an angle but he knows he is a target, because of his association with Kerensky. Leonid doesn't think of his father and the consequences for him after what he is about to do. He doesn't think of Lidia and Feiga and the retaliation that will follow. Nor does he even think about Grishka who, he has heard, has defected to the Red Guards in Moscow.

What he thinks about as he enters the building is how cool and right the foyer feels. A relief really. The glass doors close quietly behind and the dark shadowy interior enfolds him, womblike. It is just him, here. Breathing.

As his eyes adjust to the lightless foyer he notes the wide open staircase directly in front of him several metres away. He looks around and sees there are wooden polished bench seats against the walls and he chooses the one tucked next to the doorway. In this way, he has an unobstructed view of people coming in through the glass doors and using the staircase. He sits down and stretches his legs out in front of him and knows he needs to look as if he is waiting for an appointment in this building. Survival in Russia is a strange combination of not drawing attention to oneself and, at the same time, being ready to strike.

The doors yawn open and a hot puff of air pushes two leather coated goons in and up the staircase. Neither one of them looks about and their conversation continues uninterrupted about someone who has a ramshackle dacha but a very good-looking wife.

Leonid is in no rush. His intelligence gathering over the past few days allows him the certainty that his target will not be arriving until 9.30 am. He still has time on his side. Strange how a childhood in Mykolayiv, with its briny Black Sea stench and ear-smashing clamour of the Shipyards, is so far away from this moment, to which he has always been moving. Normally, he never thinks about the Mykolayiv Shipyards and yet here in this cool palatial entrance, it seems like a ghostly marker of someone else's life.

The doors push open and three Chekists frog-march a worker, probably no more than 17 or 18 years of age, up the staircase. One of the goons keeps up a paint-stripping tirade of obscenities that seems loosely aimed at the youth.

Leonid gently touches his breast pocket. The murky light is beginning to fade a little or perhaps his eyes have adjusted so much so that he feels everything around him is hyper-real. The bench seats, the banister of the staircase, the low hanging chandelier, even the tiling on the floor begins to reveal its patination. Curious how his success at the Mikhailovskaya Artillery Academy took him to Kerensky which took him to war, in a way that he would never have imagined. And it occurs to him that if there is one thing he has learned, it is that the enemy is never expecting the unexpected.

The doors push open and a well-suited individual walks briskly through the entrance and takes the staircase two steps at a time. The back of his boots wink and shine, a definitive indicator that he is high up in the echelons of this strange world that no longer seems familiar, relevant, or of any consequence to Leonid.

He knows his time has come. He stands and as he does so he stretches his arms long and twitches his fingers. He allows his beloved Viktor, the only one who saw him, knew him, loved him, to fill his mind for a moment. Leonid smiles quietly in the corner of the foyer because he has had all that he ever wanted.

Outside the sounds of vehicles and footsteps can be heard.

He is glad his time has come.

The doors push open and one, then two more civilians cautiously enter. Their heads crane about the building's foyer, ogling at nothing in particular until one of them sees Leonid and, mistaking him for a guard, whips off his worker's cap and offers an obsequious nod. After some hesitation, the civilians begin their way to the staircase. They ascend uncertainly, as if their ordinariness may cause affront. Before they reach the top of the first flight Leonid hears someone outside approaching the glass doors and somehow he just knows this is it.

He swiftly pulls out his gun and steps a little closer to the entrance.

The light seems to pulsate through the doors, then shimmer and pool in the foyer, as if forming an oasis in a desert of desperation.

This is my appointed day, Leonid thinks to himself.

Sun rays cavort across the internal metal door rails and he

watches the particles of dust glisten and glide in the beauty of the morning.

The doors push open and the target's pince-nez glints, his prominent aquiline nose is visible and then the dark voluminous head of hair appears. Somewhere at the back of Leonid's mind, he registers that Uritsky is smaller, more compact, and less hurried than he normally seems. There is no elan, no ruffled expanse of one of the most formidable leaders of the party. Just a quiet man en route, mid-step, mind elsewhere, entering the foyer of the building in which he works.

The revolver is cold and sure in Leonid's hand. He raises his arm. There is no one else. Just the intimacy of this moment.

The target is moving leisurely toward the staircase.

There is almost an inaudible click of a safety catch being released. Leonid's cold body floods with satisfaction.

Inexplicably, a part of Moisei Uritsky's brain begins to crackle and so he turns slowly, quietly, unperturbedly — as a somnambulist would — in the direction of the glass doors and sees the gleam of a metallic barrel, a trompe-l'oeil.

BANG!

Uritsky reels sideways but before he falls the echo chamber reverberates with another.

BANG!

And again *BANG!*

The foyer fills up with the acrid smell of absence.

Leonid is already moving to the glass doors when he hears upstairs shouting and stampeding — so he pushes through and the doors exhale behind him and he is out — wrenching his bicycle off the wall, running hard, bounding onto the saddle and, standing high on the pedals, pushing *down up down up*, feeling as if he is in a quagmire and there is no getting out of this street, this neighbourhood, this city — *down up down up* — because he's got to put distance between himself and the crumpled suit with the bloodied mashed head — *down up down up* — Petrograd roars up around Leonid's ears, which are still ringing with the shots he fired, and his bicycle belts on down the main streets and side streets and footpaths and shopfronts as he tries desperately to slow his mind and recognise his whereabouts. He tries to catch his breath. His heart is cracking.

Sirens vehicles faces
push down up down up
sirens shouting running
down up down up
horns pointing faces sirens shouting
breathe breathe breathe —

Leonid doesn't see the Black Maria leap out of the side street as he races by, its huge bulbous body like a giant cockroach. It accelerates behind him and then on impulse Leonid swerves left and instead of making it onto the rickety footbridge to cross the canal — he — is — air — borne —

Windmilling arms
Nothing to breathe
Slow-motion
Gulping air
Canal slurping
Viktor!

And then the sureness of bone, skin, and brain smashing into obdurate cobblestone. Leather coat, officer's cap, eyes frozen, twist of bicycle wheel.

The Chekists are already out of the Black Maria before the blood oozes sweetly from Leonid's ear. They have already cocked their revolvers before his skin drains of all colour. And despite the strange angle of the body, that no mutable life would imitate, one of the leather coated goons empties seven rounds of bullets into the lifeless face, throat, shoulder, and chest of the dead cyclist.

17

Yekaterinburg

Yekaterinburg, Urals. July 1918.

Apart from her arrival, Captain Pavel Konoplev has not caught another glimpse of Olga. So far, his job has been to oversee the transportation of resources from the township of Yekaterinburg to the *House of Special Purposes*. Pavel hates this term that most people use for Ipatiev's house, which now serves as the residence for the man and his family. Pavel thought that after the excitement had died down with the arrival of the first lot of prisoners, the ridiculous nomenclature for the house would be abandoned, but six weeks later when the second lot of prisoners arrived, Tatyana, Anastasia, Alexei, and his Olga, that had not been the case.

Unsurprisingly, the term *House of Special Purposes* is bandied about with more and more invested meaning. The term is foreboding if he is to put a word to it because it somehow implies that this is not just some midway point en route to Moscow. Any day now the man and his family will be escorted down to the capital for the trial of the century. It has surprised Pavel how long they have been holed up in Yekaterinburg but everything takes so much time, here in the Urals.

It is now summer and Pavel is billeting with the Dyatlov brothers. Born and bred Yekaterinburg Bolsheviks, who enjoy getting drunk and occasionally hunting in the forested hills that surround the town. It's not a bad setup. Evgeniy and Mikhail Petrovitch Dyatlov are happy to receive Pavel's board, being ardent believers in the world revolution and all things Bolshevik. This suits Pavel who wants to blend into the background of the daily life of the town, one teeming with Red Guards and committed supporters of Lenin. As is he, Pavel hurries to remind himself.

On arriving in Yekaterinburg, Pavel swiftly put distance between himself and the man, his wife, their daughter, and entourage. Indeed, fortune smiled and Pavel was jostled out of the arrival scene with locals hissing, anti-Tsar banners flapping and an impressive absence of clergy signalling that the light of Christ had been snuffed out — not that Pavel believes in that rubbish. Anymore. Yekaterinburg's protest was loud and clear. Centuries of slaving in the Urals will do that to you. And, with the locomotive still cooling and the prisoners being bustled out of their carriage, Pavel found himself pushed further and further to the outer reaches of the mob, catching only the briefest glances of the man and his wife staggering under the weight of their suitcases to the waiting carriages. Let them suffer the indignity — after centuries of what they have done to the rest of us. He had turned his back on the enemy of the people and pushed out into the township.

Pavel has every intention of surviving. It is just the unresolved matter of Olga that keeps him fixed in Yekaterinburg. Luckily there has been so much coming and going with the Civil War uprooting hordes of people, including soldiers like himself, that he has easily found sanctuary in the red hot breast of the eastern Urals.

After a short while, the elder Dyatlov brother, Evgeniy, managed to get Pavel a job as one of the regular guards at the *House of Special Purposes*. In part, this came about because Evgeniy had not only survived the Front but also the Battle at Tannenberg, like Pavel. So they drank each night to their shared good fortune. To the amusement of the Dyatlov brothers, the night before Pavel began his first shift up at the *House*, he shaved off his beard. He told them that he found the early Siberian summer too bothersome to have facial topiary. They had laughed companionably for some time, drunk on the homebrew vodka that every Siberian keeps in abundance. But of course, Pavel had no intention of being recognised by the man and his family, hence he had lost the beard and hacked away at his thick dark hair until he saw a thin unrecognisable face looking back at him from the small mirror. Not that the man and his family noticed anyone but themselves.

Today, in the delicate heat of a Ural summer, Pavel is overseeing the unpacking of bread and milk from one of the transport carts at the *House of Special Purposes*. His attention is caught by something beyond the unloading of goods. It is Commissar Yakov Mikhailovich Yurovsky standing quietly near the entrance of the house. He is a lean and intelligent-looking man with a wide forehead and a short black beard that falls from his nostrils and ends below his chin as if his mouth is lost in the undergrowth. While his nature is restrained and muted, his presence generates alarm.

Yurovsky and his 11 men are the only guards allowed inside the *House of Special Purposes*. The local Red Guards, of which Pavel is accepted as one, keep their distance and are assigned to guard only the perimeter of the *House*. This is marked by a rough-shod fence thrown up hastily so that the prisoners are confined to the house itself and not the garden nor the streets of Yekaterinburg. Indeed, the prisoners are only allowed access to the top floor. Yurovsky and his men take up the ground floor. Their militant vigilance is a far cry from the days of Tobolsk.

What Pavel has heard from the Dyatlov brothers and some of the other Red Guards is that the window frames upstairs have been nailed shut and he can see for himself when he looks up that the glass in the windows has been painted white. Not that he ever looks up because he has no intention of being caught showing an interest in the prisoners other than making sure the transport to and from the town runs without a hitch.

Pavel stops the Red Guard who is busy moving the provisions into the back kitchen in a trusty handcart because he sees a hastily scrawled note tucked into the basket of bread. He doesn't know that Yurovsky hears him bark an order at the Red Guard to unload the rest of the supplies in front of him to see if there are any other messages secreted away in the supplies for the prisoners. Unbeknownst to Pavel, Yurovsky had asked one of his men to find out the name of this gammy-legged guard, overseeing the coming and going of resources for the prisoners. When the name had been brought to him, Yurovsky tucked it away in a small compartment of his brain, as is his way.

'Are you sure that's the lot of them?' asks Pavel of his comrade, a poor washed-out fellow who has probably earnt a little on the side to bring these messages from a handful of local Loyalists to the man and his wife. The guard nods but his eyes slide out to the end of the cart where the milk crates glint in the sunshine.

'Lift those crates,' orders Pavel as he shifts his weight and moves to the end of the cart. The crates are hauled one by one off the cart bed and there beneath the last one is a letter wrapped in oiled cloth.

'Give that to me, and get these goods out of the sun and into the kitchen —'

'It must have been the boys packing the cart who let these messages slip in ... I had my back turned for just a minute and —'

'Yes, yes. Get on with it.'

And with that, the guard repacks the cart with the milk crates, abandons his handcart, and tugs at the horse's bit to move slowly down the side of the house and around the back where the cook and his kitchen hand are waiting.

It is then that Pavel bristles because he sees that Yurovsky has left the entrance of the house and is cutting a direct path toward him. The Dyatlov brothers have discussed Yurovsky at length. They were resentful when he first arrived because he stripped collective command from the local guards and appointed his men to keep control, night and day, of the prisoners. Yurovsky trusts no one, or so it is believed, and he has been sent by the Cheka. A Jew, Mikhail added and then hastily said, like our beloved Comrade Trotsky. A bobbing of heads from both Evgeniy and Pavel confirmed their agreement.

'Comrade Konoplev,' acknowledges Yurovsky.

Pavel is startled but keeps himself in check. It is not usual that the head of the operation here at the *House of Special Purposes* would speak to him, let alone know his name. Whether he had been sent by the Cheka or not, Pavel is wary.

'More letters have arrived, I see, from the Tsar-lovers in town?' Yurovsky's voice is crisp and sharp around the edges. He seems to avoid Pavel's eye and looks beyond to a point in the horizon that has not yet revealed itself to others.

'Yes,' Pavel wants to turn around and look over his shoulder to where Yurovsky's gaze is fixed but steels himself not to. 'I've handed the other letters to your men, for your consideration. Commissar. And here are a few more.'

Pavel passes across the paltry effort of today's epistolary hopefuls. They are always the same. Sad desperate letters from Loyalists telling the man and his family that they must be ready for their rescuers who are arriving at any hour. Or copied out Bible seductions: *In God, I trust and am not afraid. What can mere mortals do to me?* Pavel had snorted at that one — he had seen firsthand what mere mortals could do to one another, in the trenches of war and the streets of revolution. These pathetic messages had, Pavel suspected, been getting through to the prisoners up until the moment before he was put in charge.

'Rubbish,' says Yurovsky as he finishes reading the notes. 'But I suppose it is human nature to hope.'

Pavel stands still and looks directly at Yurovsky, but the man who may be a Chekist is once again preoccupied with something a long way off, in the distance.

This turns Pavel's thoughts to the rumours flying wild about the town: *The White army is closing in on Yekaterinburg! ... The old Empress Dowager in the Crimea is sending an envoy with a priceless ransom! ... The Kaiser is moving to snavel up his cousin! ... Trotsky is sending Muscovite Bolsheviks to haul the prisoner down to a public trial in the nation's new capital!* ... Nothing but rumours, thinks Pavel. He alone knows the truth. An escape plan. For Olga and himself, that is.

Then Pavel notices Yurovsky has shifted his gaze and is now looking directly at him. There is a distinct pause before he speaks and when he does Pavel notices Yurovsky is sizing him up, 'Later, some of my men will need someone to take them into the forest. Somewhere away from prying eyes. Somewhere only a local would know ...' Pavel doesn't flinch. 'You would know of a place like that, Comrade Konoplev?'

He cannot tell whether Yurovsky is testing him but he thinks on his feet and replies casually, 'Of course, Commissar.' And leaves it at that because what he has learned over the past few months is the less said the better. Besides, how hard can it be to find an isolated spot in the forest behind the town?

'Good — very good,' replies Yurovsky quietly and then walks away to the front entrance of the *House of Special Purposes*.

Pavel moves off towards the back kitchen. He is not worried about taking some of Yurovsky's goons to a secluded place in the forest. It might be an opportunity to form an alliance or two and be taken into their trust. He knows he may need this at some point soon.

As Pavel rounds the house he sees that the Red Guard, who has long since unloaded the cart, is now drinking tea and eating some left-overs with Kharitonov, the cook. Meanwhile, the young kitchen hand is ducking out the back door with a large pot of dirty dish-washing water which he throws across the yard. On seeing Pavel, the Red Guard puts his tea glass on the window sill and shambles back to the impatient horse and begins, without difficulty, in leading it away. Kharitonov looks a bit ashamed, being caught in the act of chewing the fat with a Bolshevik, and abruptly disappears into the kitchen.

That is when the boy stops. Instead of hurrying in after the cook, he looks across at Pavel and murmurs, 'She gave me something ...'

Pavel waits.

Despite the ever-vigilant inner guards, Yurovsky's 11 who enforce the imprisonment of the man and his family, Pavel has managed to surreptitiously befriend Leo Ivanovich Sednev, the kitchen hand. The boy is most impressed that Captain Konoplev asked him to take a note to the oldest girl. It was no problem at all because he is frequently asked up to play with Alexei, even though the invalid is a whole year younger than him. So much is happening in these last few months that he can hardly believe his luck. Once he was just an unseen worker for the great Kharitonov, back in the days when he first began in the kitchen at Tsarskoye Selo and his grandmother had cried with pride. Now he is a go-between for the love-struck Captain!

'Good. Give me her note,' says Pavel. He knows that the boy wants to please him but he also knows money is everything. 'Here, buy yourself something to eat or drink.' Pavel hands him a few coins and adds, 'When I was your age I was hungry all the time. I'm sure you are the same.'

The letter Leo passes to him is folded over and over into a tight cube as if to ward off the kitchen hand from prising it open. Which would have been ridiculous as Leo cannot read nor has any wish to learn because, as his grandmother had said, it is not his destiny. The Captain gives him a quick affectionate pat on the shoulder and walks off. Leo is so filled with elation, not just with the coins he is shoving down inside the side of his boot, but with how he has been singled out by the Captain. Leo smiles to himself. People usually don't see him but as his grandmother said, one day someone will and it will make all the difference.

Pavel returns to the sentry box and sits just inside the doorway, legs outstretched and crossed at the ankles. It is a quiet, lazy afternoon that slumbers about him. He knows he will be left undisturbed. Yurovsky's men rarely leave the house and when they do, they flaunt their superiority — that's why so many of the Red Guards say Yurovsky and his inner guards are Chekists because a Red Guard would never put himself above a fellow Bolshevik.

The letter paper crackles open and her handwriting races across the page in a breathlessness that fills him with joy.

Pavel, my love,

Yes! I will be sure to be ready at any moment! So many Loyalists have sent Papa and Mother similar messages — well not similar — but notes of hope and plans afoot! At first, I lost hope when I arrived here — especially when the guards living downstairs refused to treat us with respect — but I will not complain!

Pavel raises his head and listens. Nothing. A skylark, perhaps.

It is because of those other letters smuggled in that Papa and Mother have us all in readiness most days and nights. It's all rather thrilling, actually! Just to think when I turn 23 I will be your wife! Living somewhere far away from here ... I dream of it every day — do you?

Pavel smiles. Of course, he dreams about her night and day. Her soft chestnut blonde hair and perfect skin, her wide open cheek-bones, and her wrap-around eyes.

But I have so much to ask — I am bursting to know what and when and how — but in answer to your question I <u>DO</u> trust you and I <u>WILL</u> put myself in your hands... quite literally xx

Hurry Pavel — because I am yours —

Olenka xoxoxoxox

Yes, I burnt the letter you sent, just as you begged!

For a moment he taps the letter against his leg and looks up to the expansive sky that seems to promise the possibility of every-thing. Then he strikes a match, allows the flame to catch the corner of her note, and watches it burn until it is just the flotsam and jet-sam of ash, which he then rubs vigorously under his boot into the dirt floor. Something stirs in his heart. Doubt? Faithlessness? Then he realises it is fear that he feels.

Pavel stands and shakes his left leg until it comes good and he can place some weight on it. He leans up against the doorjamb of the sentry box and surveys the *House of Special Purposes* to his right, an ugly two-storey building with its hurriedly painted windows up-stairs, and Yurovsky's man standing at the entrance, ever alert. To Pavel's left are the street and the local housing that has recently been commandeered by the Red Guards for their temporary barracks. Like all Red Guards, Pavel is not permitted inside the *House* under any circumstances and must work the entrance gate or patrol the outside perimeter of the hastily-erected fence.

He takes a cigarette from his trouser pocket and cups his hand about the match he strikes. Pavel fears failure. He believes she would have burnt the letter he sent immediately because she is smart. Olga knows that should they be caught corresponding, let alone plan-ning an escape, they would be shot. It is not death that bothers him, thinks Pavel sagely, it is never having lived a life that is truly his be-fore he dies. Fighting in the war for Mother Russia was a God-given duty, especially because his father had been a Colonel, but so much had changed with the revolution and for the first time, Pavel believes he can live a life that is not bound by the traditions and ways of the past. That's why he has to succeed! Taking Olga for his own and beginning a life together proves that the old ways are dead and only those committed to revolutionising Russia into the 20th Century have a right to live a full life. This he knows to be true.

The crunch of gravel underfoot jerks Pavel's head to the right and there, only a few metres away, is one of Yurovsky's men.

'Konoplev?' Although it sounds like a question both know it is a command.

Pavel stubs out his half-smoked cigarette, puts it inside his pocket, and pushes off from the doorjamb. A performed insouciance. He follows the Chekist to the back of the house and fights down his terror that the kitchen boy has, for some reason, declared Pavel a traitor. But what awaits him is a cart with two more of Yurovsky's men, and a third shoving a member of the Romanov staff out of the kitchen doorway and onto the cart.

Then he hears quietly, 'Get in,' from the Chekist behind him.

Despite the balmy sunset, Pavel feels cold. He tries not to look across at the young male staff member who has been bundled onto the cart. Poor bastard Pavel thinks, as the horses pull away from the *House of Special Purposes* into the dusty street and then past the tired faces of wooden cottages, the markets abandoned to the dusk and a handful of Yekaterinburg residents watching on, with unchecked curiosity until they reach the fields that roll onwards to the forested surrounds.

Yurovsky's men loosen their shoulders and tongues and the corks of a couple of bottles of homebrew vodka. And not long after they have left all traces of the township behind, each man, including Pavel himself, is enjoying the conviviality of a drink and joke with fellow workers. Or at least this is how it may appear to some, but

Pavel is careful and while he can only guess, he suspects the Romanov staff member, across from him, is also ever vigilant. Then it hits him — it's Nagorny — the boy's dyad'ka or nanny. Pavel watches him now a little closer and sees the way the sailor, who has for some reason continued to stay with the family and care for the youngest Romanov, turns his head about as if taking constant note of his bearings. Back at Tsarskoye Selo, Pavel was vaguely aware of two sailors appointed to care for the Tsarevitch but the other, understandably, disappeared just days after the family had been placed under house arrest.

'Captain,' says one of the Chekist laconically. 'You know why you're here, right?'

Pavel looks at the small compact man cramped up beside him in the cart and tries to stay calm because he is not sure who or what to trust.

'Yeah,' Pavel lights the tail end of the cigarette he has in his pocket. 'Comrade Yurovsky wants a local to help you stooges navigate your way into the forest.'

The Chekist chuckles but after a pause adds, 'Yes. You will take us to a quiet secluded place.'

Pavel notices the dyad'ka, Nagorny, is shifting about in the cart as if in readiness to make good his exit. He is clean-shaven with thinning hair and even a thinner moustache. He wears the uniform of the Imperial Yacht Standardt but in the waning light, Pavel sees him as an animal, wary of his unfamiliar surroundings.

'Up ahead — follow the track to the right. Stay on it.' Pavel is surprised by the strength and conviction of his voice. Of course, he has been here with the Dyatlov brothers, occasionally, to hunt and trap hare or grouse but he would have no idea how to find his way through the maze of the forest with tracks crisscrossing this way and that. If he can't find a secluded place in the forest, he will claim that it's the growing darkness that is tripping him up. One thing is for sure, he is certain he has no interest in partaking in whatever is to happen in this uneasy journey with a cartload of Chekists and the young boy's dyad'ka.

The summer twilight is brushed with moonlight so that the boughs of large trees and the trunks and even some of the foliage can be seen quite easily. The men have stopped joking and drinking and he can hear someone in the cart murmuring and he realises he must call out at some point for them to stop, as a local might.

'Here's good!' Pavel says out loud to the evening, which is somewhere between dusk and night, a strange liminal space of stillness.

The driver calls out softly, *Whoa*, and the horses come to a stop.

Pavel stays seated in the cart but the other Chekists are jumping down, all but one who seems welded to the dyad'ka. And then Pavel realises it is the dyad'ka who has been murmuring to himself. A susurration to someone or something beyond those here tonight. Although he doesn't know why, Pavel recalls some gossip he has heard about Nagorny, the dyad'ka. He demanded the Chekists show respect to the Tsarevitch and his sisters. One night Evgeniy had painstakingly explained to Pavel, drunk as he was at the time, that the cook reported that Nagorny was demanding some of the Chekist clean their drawings off the privy wall ... lewd acts of copulation, engorged cocks and redolent breasts with the occasional foul word or phrase.

'Nurse,' hisses the Chekist clamped up beside Nagorny. 'Move it!', and with a shove, the young man, who has cared and carried the invalid son of the Romanovs for several years, is pushed off the cart.

Pavel doesn't move. The dark isn't closing in quickly enough for him but he hears Nagorny continue with his murmurings as if he is elsewhere as if he is far away from this thick unknowing, this blankness of forest.

'*... Blessed Saint Joseph,*
Obtain for me all spiritual blessings

Through thy foster Son,

Jesus Christ Our Lord —'

'Over here,' Nagorny's supplications are interrupted by one of the Chekists the dyad'ka is pushed across the small clearing by the side of the forester's track to an alcove of tall trees. The indifference to his fate catches at the back of Pavel's throat as he hears the captive continue to pray.

'*... So that I may offer him*

My thanksgiving and homage ...'

Pavel hears the dull thump of something hard against a body and then sees, or thinks he sees, Nagorny slump.

'*... Saint Joseph,*

Whose protection is so great,

So strong ...'

He knows they will want to beat Nagorny hard not just because of the prayer but because he seems utterly elsewhere.

'*... I dare not approach*

While the Christ child is in your arms,

But press him in my name and kiss His fine head ...'

At first, Pavel doesn't believe what he has heard but then he hears another bullet being pulled back into the chamber. He stops breathing.

'*... And ask him to return the kiss when I draw my dying breath —'*

BANG!

BANG!

After the gunshots, there is nothing but the tossing of heads by the horses, and one of them nickers. Then Pavel hears the click and snap of the trees and the undergrowth, followed by a quiet instruction from someone and a dead weight being dragged off into the densely wooded area behind them. Pavel allows himself to breathe but does so, quietly, slowly, and without moving. This is the only way he will survive. He realises that his back is covered in sweat and he is cold to the bone.

The Chekists are returning and pulling themselves up into the cart. 'Well done, Comrade,' says the one slumping in beside Pavel. 'Now, can you get us out of here?' The other men chuckle but the horses have already responded to the driver's *Hup Hup* and are heading back the way they came, nosing their way home to supper. And then across the shared darkness, one of the Chekists says absent-mindedly, 'The nanny, the dyad'ka, told me earlier that he was from Kiev ...' The cart pulls on and someone else pipes up softly, 'So am I ...' And, although he says nothing out loud, Pavel thinks, *So am I.*

I cannot get involved, he says to himself. I have witnessed worse during the war. But this is not war, another part of him pleads. Well, it's a type of war! he throws back at himself. I just have to get through the next few weeks — or days, even. He shuts out of his mind what has just happened but he knows now that he must seize the moment. There can be no more waiting. He must send her a message tonight!

The bottle is being passed around once again and before long there are a few tales and jokes shuffled about between the men in the cart. A little duller, a little more tired but efforts are being made nonetheless.

'Comrade, can you get us more of this homebrew stuff?' It's the compact Chekist up beside him who is making the request.

'I can get you guys something better than this,' responds Pavel as he thinks about Evgeniy's supply.

Another Chekist on the other side of him drapes his arm lazily across Pavel's shoulders and begins crooning.

I beg you farmers
Don't sleep at night ...

Some of the other men in the cart heckle him to stop, but their protests are made good-humouredly, and the compact guy on Pavel's other side joins in. Meanwhile, the cart trundles on, passing into the wide-open fields.

I wouldn't ride a colt
To be fed at night ...

Pavel can see the wink of lights in the farmhouse up ahead and he knows he is going to make it. He and Olga will escape and head north then eventually west. No one will care, it is the man they want. The stupid stupid man is the one responsible for what has happened tonight. He should have cut such simple-minded devotion, free.

I passed a crossroad
And crossed myself ...

The folk song goes on but it is only two of the Chekists singing and Pavel can tell they are Latvian Russians. He takes a swig from the bottle passed to him and thinks, I, too, have passed a crossroad and there is no coming back. He listens to horses' hooves *clop clop clop clop* into the township and after a while a line from the novena, the dyad'ka was praying, slips unbidden into Pavel's mind ... *Blessed Saint Joseph, patron of departing souls, pray for me ...*

By the time they arrive back at the *House of Special Purposes*, it is close to midnight. Pavel feels nothing but determination. People all his life have talked lyrically about Mother Russia but he knows his country to be a killing field. Nothing more, nothing less. He tries not to think about Nagorny, the dyad'ka, who might have been the same age as himself. He doesn't think about the Dyatlov brothers, their good-natured trust and hospitality. And he certainly doesn't care to think about what will happen to the rest of the prisoners once Yurovsky finds out Olga has escaped. The fate of the man and the rest of his family is not his concern.

When he jumps off the back of the cart Pavel mooches around to the kitchen entrance. He finds that it is unlocked and so he lets himself in and waits in the dark for his eyes to grow accustomed to the shadowy shapes of baskets and pots on some of the benches and then someone sits up suddenly on the stretcher in the corner.

'Who are you?'

Pavel is momentarily caught off guard when he recognises the cook's educated voice and curses himself for glibly anticipating that only the kitchen hand would be sleeping in the kitchen. He answers quietly, 'Captain Konoplev. I'm after ... Leo ...'

The darkness bats about the heads of the two men, one standing and the other still sitting on his stretcher.

'Leo?' The cook seems bewildered and wonders whether he is still asleep, 'What do you want with my kitchen hand?'

Buoyed by his determination to move swiftly with his plans, Pavel offers, 'The boy has information for me.'

The cook says nothing. Of course, he knows the Captain to be one of the more dependable Red Guards, someone who has been with the family since last year but the cook is wary in this time of shifting allegiances. Who knows what information he has been gathering from Leo? But on the other hand, if there is one thing he is sure of it is that help is on its way for the family and perhaps the Captain is involved in their breakout. Still, he must be cautious.

The cook offers a timely yawn and then adds calmly, 'Get out of my kitchen. The boy is not here —Yurovsky ...' The name is almost spat. 'Gave orders earlier tonight, for him to go.'

Pavel doesn't believe it and growls, 'Light the lamp and show me! You are a lying —'

'Search the place if you don't believe me! How they expect me to cook for a family of seven as well as Dr. Botkin, and then turn around and feed the maid and the footman — I do not know! Never in my career have I had to peel potatoes and wash dishes!'

Pavel has no interest in Kharitonov's confected outrage but what he does start to see quite clearly in the dark, is that he is running out of time. He tells himself he is not shaken by the sudden dismissal of the young kitchen hand because if he was found to have been the go-between for Pavel and Olga, all three of them would be dead by now. Besides, if Yurovsky suspected Pavel of plotting to escape with Olga, he would not have sent him on a trusted errand to find a place for … he ignores the rest of that thought.

'I must get a message to someone in the household,' Pavel knows these words he has spoken are dangerous but he is running out of options.

'Wait a minute …' Now the cook is wide awake, 'You were on the cart with Nagorny this evening … Where did they take him? The family is beside themselves! Why, the Tsarevitch is desperate for his dyad'ka and would not even take a mouthful of his mushroom soup this evening!'

Pavel sighs, these loyal household staff members have no idea about the world beyond their own small lives. Kharitonov could not even discern that the so-called inner guards, living on the ground floor of the *House of Special Purposes*, are in fact Chekists, while the outer guards are a mix of local Bolshevik Red Guards.

'Look, I have no idea where the dyad'ka was sent … I helped Yurovsky's men …' He is convinced Kharitonov doesn't get his meaning. 'To find a quiet place to give him a beating and then they left him to find his way out of Siberia. They don't take to household staff challenging their every move.'

Pavel cannot tell whether the cook believes his story but instead of rambling on with his small world concerns, Kharitonov now wants to come across as compliant, even helpful.

'It depends which household member you are trying to get a message to …' The cook pauses. 'If it is the Tsar, Trupp is your man but if it is the Tsarina you are going to have to go through her maid, Demidova — but I'm afraid both of them are unlikely to help…' Pavel can hear the cook warm to this topic as he prattles on, '… You see both the footman and the maid are sticklers for rules. You know, the gatekeepers to the most powerful, and all that, so they think they are the powerful ones ...'

You mean the most powerless, thinks Pavel to himself.

He says to Kharitonov, 'My job is to guard the outer rim of the house and protect those of you inside from the unwanted attention of hostile outsiders.' He lets that sink in and then adds, 'And should there be a movement afoot, those of you inside and in particular the family ...' He projects every word with the coded unsaid, 'Would be best served by being informed and ... ready...' The last word stays in the darkness between them, like a yeasted bread set to rise, slowly, quietly, assuredly.

Initially, Kharitonov's career appeared nothing less than stellar after he was selected to replace the nervous French Head Cook who had abandoned his post at the start of the war and darted back to Paris. God knows Kharitonov's wife and seven children thought he had ascended to heaven. Even when Kharitonov was rudely packed off from the Winter Palace to Tsarskoye Selo, when the Tsar and his family were initially under house arrest, the cook's own family had meekly followed — believing that this time would pass and the man appointed by God, for whom Kharitonov was honoured to cook, would one day be restored to his divine destiny. The cook admits he had some convincing to do to move his entire family all the way out to Tobolsk but they finally accepted the truth that the Tsar, his family, and his entourage, of which Kharitonov was at its centre, was being moved for the reasons of safety. Coming to Yekaterinburg was different. Kharitonov was bundled along, under cover of night, and barely got a message to his wife other than, *I will send for you and the children on arrival at Moscow.* And as soon as Kharitonov gets out of this purgatorial waiting room of Yekaterinburg, with its lack of supplies and hard labour, he will once again bring his family to him so that they can be there when the Tsar is rightfully restored to his throne.

This is why Kharitonov leans forward and says conspiratorially to Pavel, 'So you see, I am your best bet ... I can get a message to the Tsarina personally. Once every three days she meets with me in her rooms to discuss the menus.' The cook is proud of this engagement with the Tsarina. Indeed, at the top of the daily menus, he draws the Russian Imperial Coat of Arms. The list of dishes these days is simply because of the limited resources, but they are also ingenious! A truth he never tires to reiterate to those who'll listen.

'Hmmm,' the Captain replies. 'I see ... but I would prefer the message go to one of the daughters ... The eldest daughter ... It would be less suspicious ...' The cook seems to be considering this and, as he does so, Pavel tries not to think about the fragility of his plan. One that is utterly contingent on circumstances playing out in a very specific way.

'Actually,' begins the cook, 'I have promised to show the older girls how to make pierogis tomorrow ... I taught them how to bake bread the other day and they were delighted ...' For some reason a stab of longing for his children hits Kharitonov and he wonders whether those who have already abandoned the Tsar, the once-loyal household staff, are much better off.

'Yes. That is a plan,' Pavel agrees. 'But the message must be given to Olga because she is the one Leo, the kitchen boy, has kept informed. To anyone else the message might cause concern and inadvertently find its way into the wrong hands ... Of course, if that were to happen the consequences would be dire for the family and ... for you.' Pavel knows Kharitonov is literate, what Head Cook of a Royal family is not? But even so, Pavel knows he must seize this one opportunity that is being presented.

So, there under the stump of a candle and on the hard notepaper and pencil, the cook shoves across to him, Pavel scribbles a note to Olga. As he bends over his task he is fully aware it will be read by Kharitonov.

Tomorrow night a parcel will be delivered. Come to the kitchen by 2 am and Kharitonov will ensure your safety. You must come alone and say nothing to your family.

A friend.

As he folds the paper Pavel says, 'Tell her the note is from me. She knows that I have been behind the messages that Leo has taken her. This is the only way she will trust what is written here.'

Kharitonov takes the folded note and says quietly as he watches Pavel through the flickering candlelight, 'How will I get the parcel that she is supposed to receive?'

'There is nothing for you to worry about.' Pavel is already moving to the door that will take him out to the back of the house, 'I will bring the parcel. Tomorrow night. 2 am.' And then he is gone.

Kharitonov stands alone in the dark and, for the first time in a long time, he feels hopeful that they all shall be saved!

2

Pavel is awake. He is vaguely aware of Evgeniy making chicory bean coffee, at least he assumes it is Evgeniy. The younger Dyatlov brother is usually nursing a hangover at this hour of the morning or complaining loudly that his brother has given him an early shift. Evgeniy's task is to write up the weekly roster for the outer guards, which is more often than not, discarded as the men swap and reschedule their allocated shifts. Pavel hears Evgeniy clear his throat, pour the steaming coffee, pull open the cottage door and shuffle outside.

He hauls himself off the mat and pushes it under Evgeniy's trundle bed, which is neatly made up, reflective of the man's orderliness and belief that all will come to pass as it should. Pavel pads about in the trousers and socks he wore to bed last night, shunting on the homespun jacket that he has picked up somewhere. The other brother sleeps on, a faint snore buzzing unrhythmically about his nose and an arm stretched wide overhead as if he has been flung off a church spire, his mouth open in the shock of the fall.

He opens the front door to a riot of colour.

The sky is a bright blue canopy stretched endlessly overhead, while as far as the eye can see, the verdant grass is a rich and creamy green. In the mid-ground, the world's viridescent floor is separated from its azure ceiling by strips of browns and greys and blacks and piebald tree trunks that catch the buttery sunlight on their silky skin. A race of scarlet poppies opens up in the field across from the Dyatlov cottage and Pavel admires it all and understands why Siberia, and in particular the Red Urals, generates such passions in its people.

When he glances down at Evgeniy he sees that the older brother is staring at the rise of the dirt road where the township settles, and, in the far distance, the edge of the palisades that cordon the *House of Special Purposes*. Pavel sits on an old log and leans his back against the cottage wall, alongside Evgeniy. After a while, Evgeniy hands Pavel the used coffee glass as well as the coffee jug. Pavel pours himself a glass. Its thick grainy surface hides the sugary content below. Evgeniy always makes the coffee too sweet. But this morning of all mornings, everything is exactly as it should be, thinks Pavel as he gazes over the world in which he finds himself moved by nature's beauty, by nature's boundless bounty.

'You missed the meeting last night.' Evgeniy has a solid way of speaking that makes those to whom he is speaking feel a sense of assurance that nothing will be wasted and whatever transpires is necessary to the everyday running of their lives.

'The Commissar asked me to take his goons out into the forest,' Pavel explains, enjoying the coffee that is warm enough to throw back. 'Took them out to a clearing ... Maybe 15 kilometres off into the forest. I think it was where we went last week for squirrels but I can't be sure.'

Evgeniy grunts some sort of assent and Pavel notes how he doesn't pursue the topic any further with questions like why was he asked to do this or why did Yurovsky choose him or what the Chekists did there. Perhaps this is what makes Evgeniy so dependable and why so many of the Red Guards at Yekaterinburg look to the eldest Dyatlov brother for guidance in circumspection ... and survival.

'Anyway, what happened at the meeting?' asks Pavel with no interest in the answer.

Both men look over the field across from the dirt road and watch the heads of the poppies dip and bow delicately. A dance of infinite grace.

'A unanimous decision by the Ural Soviet. Quiet unprecedented, actually ...'

They hear Mikhail yawn from inside the cottage. Soon the three of them will probably fry some bread and light the samovar for tea. Pavel already knows he needs to be up at the sentry box at the *House* by midday. He feels a little lightheaded with the day ahead as it brims with all its possibilities. In some strange way, in the absence of their physical contact, Olga has become more real, and their dreams for the future, more tangible. Although he yearned for her arrival in Yekaterinburg, a town swarming with Red Guards and tainted by Chekists, Pavel only caught a glimpse of her pale frantic face as they were bustled past his sentry box. She looked windswept and full of expectation like one of Neptune's nautical angels flying across the tumultuous seas to landfall. Pavel knows he will force the hand of fate to make good their escape. Tonight. In less than 24 hours they will be on the run. Putting as much of this Siberian wilderness between themselves and the rest of Yekaterinburg. But he is not worried. He sets down the finished glass of coffee and stretches out his legs and reaches high above his head, and stays like this for a few minutes.

Then the cottage door opens to release the shambles of the younger Dyatlov brother, desperately in search of whatever dregs of coffee he can smell. While he watches Mikhail stumble to another log and reach for the remains of the coffee in the jug, eschewing the used glass and drinking the lukewarm remains from the jug itself, Pavel goes over the plan, once again, in his head.

This morning he will sort a horse and cart from the stalls, beyond the *House of Special Purposes*. If asked by one of the outside guards, he will say that he has been ordered to do this. Later, much later, he will hand Olga the parcel of clothing in the kitchen and tell her to change in the privy. Khaki trousers, tunic-shirt, over belt, boots, and cap. Army issue. Found under Evgeniy's bed, neatly folded. When she has donned the disguise, hair tucked up high in the cap, they will move swiftly to the waiting horse and cart and head out of town, via the forest road and then north, keeping off the main roads and away from the endless flow of refugees, deserters, and White or Red Army fanatics.

Against the backdrop of this plan, he hears the brothers talk about the meeting last night.

If Pavel had not been called away at the last minute by Yurovsky to do his bidding — he reminds himself there is no good thinking about what happened out there in the forest — he would have attended the soviet meeting. They were usually long tired affairs where the more vociferous seized the opportunity to speak at length about all the injustices done to him or his ... greedy landlords, locals who have dachas, world revolution, the beauty of Pushkin (*One of the aristocracy!* yells someone, *A grandson of a black slave!* retorts another), a poor harvest, rising fuel prices, peace at an affordable price (*One that doesn't include the Caucasus!*), compulsory education (*Well, at least some assistance for those who can't read or write ...*), the elimination of the dowry and so on. To be honest, he is glad he missed last night's tedious soviet meeting.

Then on this hot summer morning, Pavel hears a buzzing of words hitting the windowpane of his mind and he realises the Dyatlov brothers are intensely conversing.

'All of them, right?'

'Yes. All of them.'

'... I guess it is the only way ...'

'That's right. The only way.'

'The children as well?'

'Yes. The boy. The girls.'

'And the household staff?'

'... Yes. That was the decision by the Soviet ... The staff as well ...'

Pavel shakes himself out of his sun-drenched reverie and asks, 'What? What are you talking about?'

There is a pause as the two brothers look across at their boarder, who asks little but pays his rent on time.

'Last night's meeting ...' says Evgeniy but Pavel looks confused so he adds, 'Soviet Ural meeting. Unanimous decision ...' If Evgeniy is irritated with having to repeat what he said only a few minutes ago, he doesn't show it. 'We are all in favour. There can be no survivors.' Evgeniy looks away because he has nothing more to add and quite frankly he needs to cut up the rest of the black bread and get some fat into the pan. His mouth waters as he levers himself up off the seat of the log.

'No survivors ... of what?' Pavel asks faintly behind him.

But it is Mikhail who answers because he doesn't need his brother to be distracted from making breakfast. Evgeniy has got to start frying the bread if Mikhail is going to be able to face another mind-numbing day, guarding a fence's perimeter, while he waits for nightfall and the liquid warmth of homebrewed vodka to work its balm on his pointless existence. 'The execution.' Mikhail's answer is blunt as he wonders whether Evgeniy might be persuaded to make another jug of coffee.

'Who is being executed?'

There is something about Pavel's tone that makes Evgeniy turn back, then pause in the doorway.

For God's Sake, fry the goddamn bread, thinks Mikhail. Deep down he knows that his brother only ever makes one jug of coffee and if you aren't a machine like him and can't get up in time to enjoy a hot glass, then that is your misfortune.

'The Ural Soviet has unanimously voted,' says Evgeniy matter-of-factly. 'On the proposal to execute the entire Romanov family. Here in Yekaterinburg. This order includes the servants and others who have served the man and his family instead of offering their allegiance and ...' For a moment the sure-footed Evgeniy seems lost for words but he quickly recovers by adding, 'And their loyalty to the Party and Russia.'

Pavel stumbles to his feet and stamps his left foot because his leg is corked. He is buying time. He can hear what is being said but he cannot understand. 'Look. There must be some mistake. I mean ...'

'There is no mistake.' Evgeniy is looking strangely at Pavel as if he is seeing him for the first time and cannot quite place him. 'The Soviet has decided. Yekaterinburg will be the place of their execution —'

'No!' interrupts Pavel desperately and stumbles a step or two toward Evgeniy but then stops himself. Hold it together! He warns himself. 'I thought ... I thought ... The Chekists with me yesterday ...' Yes, Pavel thinks to himself, put it on them. 'They were saying that the man is to be taken down to Moscow to stand trial. You know. For the crimes, he has committed against ... us all. I thought that was the plan ...'

'No.' Evgeniy seems tired, now. He wants to end this bewildering conversation he is having with Pavel who, up until this point, has been far better company than his ne'er-do-well vodka-soaked brother.

Evgeniy steps through to the inside of the cottage — a few comfy chairs that belonged to their parents, a small table cluttered with some provisions and cooking pans, and two small trundle beds that were once his parents and, after they died, now are his and Mikhail's. Two bachelors who will, eventually, die here.

Evgeniy fossicks around until he finds the gnarly old loaf of black bread and begins to slice three generous slabs, all the while thinking that last night's outcome is the best they could have hoped for.

Everyone hates the way the town has been turned upside down by the arrival of the prisoners. Yekaterinburg is a strategic location and they have enough on their hands having to stave off the White Army, which seems to be getting closer and closer each day. There is no way the Red Urals is going back to being a beast of burden for the rich, with the yoke of oppression laid across its shoulders. Those days are over and his town will not fall to the Loyalists. Evgeniy, like so many of his comrades, is concerned that in accommodating the prisoners they are making Yekaterinburg a sitting duck, a target, a bullseye. Besides, theirs is not to bow and scrape to the will of the All-Russian Central Executive Committee in Moscow. Those young upstarts. Jews. Were they all Jews running the showdown in Moscow? Whatever they were, they were going to learn soon enough that the Ural Soviet is the only reason the red blood of Russia flows. Without them, there would be no energy, no fuel, no machinery, no might. Without the Red Urals, there would be no Russia. Well, these young fellows who are running around in Moscow are going to learn soon enough that up here they call their shots. Sure, last night at the meeting that hardnosed closed-mouth Yurovsky, a son of a watchmaker from Tomsk, said he would carry the decision to Comrade Lenin for approval. The meeting had murmured its assent with little interest. They had made their decision and there was nothing those in Moscow could do about it. Yes, that's how it is, thinks Evgeniy to himself and surveys with satisfaction the interior of the cottage. He, like all workers, no longer pays rent to the landlord — some bourgeoisie who did not even live in Yekaterinburg but used to send his notary up from Tomsk four times a year to collect all the rents from all the properties that he claimed as his.

'Not anymore,' says Evgeniy quietly to himself and scoops a lump of fat into the pan.

Outside, Pavel stumbles away from the cottage, across the dirt road, and into the field of poppies. He tells himself over and over again that it makes no difference, none whatsoever. He has a plan, he whispers to himself, nothing will happen before tonight. He has a plan and it is for tonight. And if something is to knock this plan off its tracks ... He will drag over some of Mikhail's homebrew to the Chekists he took out to the forest last night and ... She's only a girl! He cries out in his head.

He chokes back a whimper.

What would they want with the children, for God's sake? Why kill them!? It makes no sense. Besides, everyone knows that the White Army is descending on the town. In a matter of days — hours maybe — it could be all over for Yekaterinburg with its fanaticism and uncompromising socialist vision.

But this is not his concern he tells himself roughly. The only thing that matters is seeing through his plan.

Tonight.

The package of army-issued clothing.

The horse and cart.

The ride north.

Man and wife.

Then lost in the streets of Petrograd, anonymous in the crowds of that stinking city. Eventually, they'll head down to his father's estate where only he and his sister and their father knew the old goat path that offered ingress and egress.

18

House of Special Purposes

Yekaterinburg, Urals. July 1918.

At the end of the day, the man stands by the window, upstairs in the *House of Special Purposes*. He looks through the right-hand corner of the windowpane that has not been completely whitewashed. The window panes upstairs have been hurriedly painted over. Crudely the brushstrokes criss-cross both the glass and the wooden frames and even, in certain sections, the walls themselves. After being cooped up here for weeks in the stifling summer heat, one comes to see most details including the places in which the paint has failed to completely cover the window. It's just a sliver of the world outside, a shard, really, nothing more — but for the man, who has little else, it is enough. So he stands and looks through the chinks in the painted glass to catch the interminable twilight. It makes him feel that he, once again, surveys all of the Russias.

The man snorts inaudibly at his foolishness.

He blocks out the murmuring behind him and stares down into the dusty street that edges the house in which they are imprisoned. There is no other way to think about their situation, any longer. Imprisonment. He knows his wife thinks the same without ever saying the word to him. He sees it in her hair which is quite grey now. The fuss and bother of baths and hair oils and body lotions and powder and hairstyling have all been packed away. The man realises he hasn't heard these sorts of ministrations since the days back at Tobolsk.

The man watches a small brown bird pop and pirouette on the fence. The fence that fortifies the house in which they crowd their lives of no purpose. Five rooms upstairs are the sum of their world. That's the thing about nature, he thinks to himself as he watches the bird, it has no need of us and goes along its way completely indifferent to our fate. There is something in the newly sawn wood fence palings that makes the bird pinch its head this way and that, occasionally thrusting its beak in the hope of an insect. Leisurely distracted, gloriously free.

And then it is gone.

The man's back is to the small room that serves as their sitting room, their dining room, their reading room, their study, their sewing room, and their games room. Dr. Botkin plays draughts with Alexei and the two younger girls are caught in the murmurings of his wife, who is probably reading from the *Bible* or *The Lives of the Saints*. It is usually one or the other. The older two are down in the kitchen with Kharitonov. Recently the cook has been giving them lessons. A source of great amusement. Last week they learned to bake bread and tonight, for their late supper, the girls are being taught to cook pierogi — the man smiles at the thought of these sweet and savory dumplings.

Occasionally, the *tap-tap* of the game of draughts is followed by his wife suspending her reading to answer a question posed by their youngest daughter. There must be a game of cards going on downstairs with the Commissar's men because every so often laughter meanders up the staircase and along the hallway to their open sitting room. Back in Tobolsk, and of course in Tsarskoye Selo, the man would have wandered down to where the guards were congregating and chat to this one or that about where they were from and whether or not they saw action at the Front. Those days seem so long ago, he thinks, as he espies some of the cottages, along the street, light their lamps.

The dusky summer sky is filled with the pearlescence of white and pink. The soft pale colours promise an endless summer and it is this very nursery palette that quietens the man's soul and calms his mind.

Behind him, his wife is saying something about mystics.

Wonderous ascetics ... Daughters of God ... Walled into the sides of churches.

She is interrupted with a question, of course, from Anastasia, which is followed by his wife's insistent response.

Saints! ... Penitence and the renunciation of this life ... Anchorites ...

The man watches the outside world through the gap in the paint.

The guard leaves the sentry box, limps a few steps away from his post, and looks up at the traces of colour sponging the horizon's twilight.

There is something familiar about him, thinks the man, as he observes the guard's leisurely movements and just for a moment the man knows he would give anything to exchange places with him. Not of course to wear the traitorous uniform of the Bolsheviks but to be liberated from this life — the one he never chose nor wanted. Or at least that is what he tells himself now.

The man watches as the guard puts the cigarette to his mouth and inhales.

Behind him, he hears a tumble of glee from his son, as, once again, he claims victory over his opponent in draughts. The kindness of these devoted few, he thinks to himself, who have left their wives and children to look after mine. Without turning around he knows that Dr. Botkin is now reaching for one of the slim books he carries about in his pocket: Akhmatova's *Evening* or Pasternak's *My Sister — Life* or once he saw Mandelstam's *Stone*. He finds it strange that a well-educated man like Dr. Botkin has a penchant for such formless poetry.

The man notices that the guard's cigarette glows like a tiny firefly against the nightfall.

The man hears the solemnity of his wife's voice behind him as she continues talking to the younger girls.

Vow of place ... Permanent enclosure ... When they entered their cell ... The priest read them the funeral rites —

But they weren't dead!

Even without turning around, he knows it is Anastasia making the indignant protest.

Patiently his wife continues, *They were dead to this world ...*

Her voice belies grief that could drown them all if they let it. The man notices that the guard below has turned around and seems intent on the side passage of the house that runs down to the kitchen. Meanwhile, his youngest daughter is arguing against her mother's unshakable benediction of the holiest of holy. Anastasia seems the only one who thinks she can somehow determine the world around her. The others have become more and more subdued, as the days stretch out to the great expanse of the Siberian wilderness. Perhaps, he thinks grimly, there is far too much vast unknowing.

The man thinks about the trial up ahead. All of Moscow will turn out to see him — the man who was once the Tsar — be interrogated by this peculiar Jewish revolutionary, Trotsky. Over and over again he is told by his wife that there will be thousands of Loyalist supporters attending the trial. There will even be Russians who thought they were progressive only to realise, when confronted with the alternative, that they must demand the reinstatement of the Tsar. The man shows no doubt because it is too difficult to explain why he has no belief in the goodness of the Russian people. As for Trotsky, or even those guarding them in Yekaterinburg, the man feels numb.

Their anchor-hold is a spiritual place ... His wife continues serenely. *They receive the eucharist through the hagioscope —*

What?! Anastasia again.

A hagioscope, a squint ...

The man marvels at the extraordinary patience of his wife as she continues.

And on the other side of their cell a small barred window through which ...

The man watches the guard limping slowly away from his sentry post down toward the side of the house, heading to the kitchen. This is unusual because the outer guards always stay on the outside of the house while the inner guards are the only ones permitted to watch over the man and his family in this claustrophobic eternal waiting room.

They did not answer to the authority of anyone other than God ... They prayed ... They never lost hope —

But couldn't they even go outside for a walk, Anastasia's interruption sets the other siblings giggling. *Or just, you know, have a dog?*

He thinks he hears his wife sigh, but maybe not.

They were chosen by God ... They knew what it was to suffer ... To be reborn in Christ ...

The man realises the guard is disappearing from view as he looks through his squint, his hagioscope. He realises it is late and soon the big girls will bring up their latest attempts at cooking. The family will eat and talk quietly, then Olga will insist, like she did last week, on taking the empty plater back downstairs to Cook.

A strange half-life they all live, he thinks to himself.

And out of nowhere, he realises that he does love his children and wife, he just cannot *feel* that love. The man peers upwards and wonders if there might already be stars in the cloudless summer night sky. What he can feel, when he allows himself — on the rare occasion he is alone in a room or marooned in memory — is the outstretched longing for country. For the sweep and reach of Russia's endless landscape, which includes the swelling ocean and the domed sky. This is what he yearns for. Not people, not politics, not victories, not rituals — just this — a land that goes on forever and ever. His land. His Russia. His beloved.

His wife's voice seems to have faded in the semi-lit room behind him ...

And in her cell, she contemplated ... Her visions ... Her surrender...

For a moment the man wonders whether his wife is speaking about herself.

She wrote about these things and the great insight Christ offered ... because she had withdrawn from the world ...

He knows he should be happy that winter is over and that he is here with his children, wife, and their doctor. An ordinary family waiting for supper with lamps lit and night descending. He can no longer see the guard but he hears his wife's voice go on.

And she wrote: All shall be well, and all shall be well, and all manner of things shall be well.

The man's skin prickles.

2

Hours later, Commissar Yurovsky steps out of the *House of Special Purposes* when the thunder cracks. He lights his cigarette and watches the summer storm roil and romp up ahead and he thinks to himself, any time now, any time. Right on cue the dense towering blue-black vertical cloud roars and Yurovsky inhales and watches its belly split to unleash the deluge.

Nothing beats a Ural summer storm, he thinks. But deep in his heart, he knows that nothing is greater than what has been asked of him and in so doing he not only secures the future for his sons in Tomsk but the sons of every Russian!

The portico beneath which he shelters shakes and cowers. Thunder crashes around him and the relentless hammering of rain unfurls its violence on Yekaterinburg. A long way off is the persistence of white light and even the illusion of indigo as if this will pass and the summer sky will, eventually, resume its watchful eye.

The Commissar crosses his arms against his chest and lets his nostrils fill with the downdraft of the storm, a musky petrichor of earth and geosmin. Like a thirsting animal, he cannot resist the atmospheric charge, and his heart races. The diluvian cascade of rain up ahead momentarily falters as the inky clouds thicken and skid about restlessly. The entire sky is an ocean and Yurovsky stands on the seabed. Infinitesimal. Indistinguishable. Invisible.

He knows he cannot take much more time away from the men and the prisoners upstairs. The letter has been signed off by Chairman Sverdlov in Moscow and the Ural Soviet decision has made it perfectly clear that they will brook no postponement. In a matter of hours, Yurovsky must steady his men and follow through with the order. There is no turning back. How can there be? The White Army flanks Yekaterinburg to the south and is less than 12 hours away. They have traitorously skulked into the region under the cover of this stormy summer night.

What must be done, will be done.

But still, the Commissar, who is in charge of the *House of Special Purposes,* stands outside under the portico with the bluster and promise of the moving storm above.

3

Meanwhile, upstairs Olga is inconsolable.

The man turns away from the drama of the storm that he has been watching through the chink in the window paint and says to his daughter, 'Please do as Mother has asked, Olenka. You are upsetting everyone with your ...' He stops himself from saying *gloom* because he knows she has every right to be filled with despair. She is young and beautiful and at the very threshold of being the woman, she is meant to be. *I can do nothing with her* ... His wife had said as she slipped out of the sitting room they have been allocated upstairs in the *House of Special Purposes*. The man looks about him. The rest of the children are next door playing cards and succumbing to bouts of laughter or protests. Dr. Botkin's voice can be heard occasionally shushing the children's exuberance.

'I know it has been trying, sweetheart, but this time we are sure.' He looks down fondly at the soft chestnut blonde head that his 22 year old daughter cradles in her hands. The man knows this is the moment where he might put his hands upon her shoulder to comfort and reassure her that things are not as bleak as she seems to think. But he hesitates.

And then the moment is gone.

Her pale face looks up into his and with the weariness of age that is not yet her burden she says, 'I must be allowed down to the kitchen. I just must. I cannot ... I cannot stand it here a moment longer.'

The man sighs, 'I really don't see how it matters. We are about to leave and in the next place ...' He puts the destination of Moscow, where his so-called trial awaits, out of his mind. 'When we settle into our next place, you can resume your cooking lessons with Cook Kharitonov ...' He can't quite see why she has become so fixated with going back down to the kitchen. He smiles vaguely but she turns her head away from him and says something in response.

'I didn't catch that, dearest ...'

The man has always found being one on one with this particular daughter rather challenging. On the one hand, she has a whip fire mind and he enjoys her banter when she is not expressing her more radicalised views, but on the other hand, he is uncomfortable with the intensity of her emotion that lies just below her skin. Out of all his children, Olga is the one he cannot fathom.

'I said,' she pauses and looks up into the face of the man who cannot help her in this life that has careened off course. 'I said — I don't want to leave here. I am sick of ... of being on the run.' She leans back into her chair and crosses her arms, 'I want a real-life ...' And then she knows she is about to say the unsayable, 'I want to be ...' She inhales and forces herself over the precipice, 'A wife.'

The man is taken aback. He looks down at his daughter who now sits petulantly in the late evening shadows, seemingly unperturbed by the impact she has had on her mother and siblings, all of whom chose to be in the sunny company of each other, in the other room. Unlike Olga, his other children are delighted to be in their travel clothes because this time they have been instructed to prepare to leave — not from a clandestine note smuggled into their parcels from outside — but from Commissar Yurovsky himself! The man knows he must chide Olga and busy her along to prepare for the journey they are about to make but he is reluctant to do so because, strangely, her resistance, is his resistance. Even though he hates it here, and hates it he does with its white-washed windows and endless restrictions, he would prefer in many ways to live out his days here in this limbo than be dragged down to Moscow and publicly stand before his people, as a traitor might, and answer to the most despicable of all Russians, the one who gave away so much of his nation to Germany. Trotsky.

The man grimaces at the Semitic appellation.

He sits down across from his daughter and, with the heaviness of the oncoming journey upon him, he says, 'All will be arranged for your marriage in due season.' The quietness of his voice surprises him and it is in that instance that he realises his firstborn, his darling Olenka, will soon no longer be his. He looks across at her fierce and passionate glare and thinks to himself, I have not loved her enough. I have not loved any of them enough.

But Olga is having none of it, 'This is a different time now Papa — can't you see that? It's — times are different now! People ... can choose their husband or wife. It's not like the old days. Not anymore!'

There is a certainty in her voice and the man wonders whether the whole world has left him behind. He hears the subdued shouts of his family in the room next door and it feels like he will never join them — he will never find his way out of this room and back to them. He wants to reach out to his daughter and draw her into the story that should be theirs but he has lost faith in that a long time ago.

'Look. The thing is ...' He makes a start and as he does he tells himself she just needs reassurance because she is still, in many ways, a child. 'We all have to be ready to leave tonight. There is no other way forward. This is the last of the journeys ...' He doesn't quite know if this is helping either of them. 'We are going to Moscow and, well, as Mother says, people will be there to support us —'

'But Papa, I don't want to leave —'

'No, no! You must listen to me. In Moscow, everything will be different. We have friends there, do you see? And you children — and I know you are a young woman, now — you will all have an opportunity to see your lives unfold ...' He feels himself losing momentum partly because even though he says the words they feel hollow and meaningless. 'To unfold in the way they are meant to ...'

Olga has turned her face away from him. She has changed so much in the last year and how could he blame her? He would have liked to have known her better but it is too late. How can a father who was once Tsar of all the Russias truly face his daughter, his children, his wife, his country — after he has been stripped of all pride.

When Yurovsky strode into their sitting room earlier this

evening and said that they were to be ready in their travel clothes because tonight, after supper, they will be on the move, the man felt both relief and dread. *The time has come*, Yurovsky had said. At that moment he saw his wife drop her head and make the sign of the cross. This was the blessing, the miracle she had been praying for. Again and again Sunny had reassured him that in Moscow their fate would change. Their friends and the world would see that they had been treated abysmally and God's succour would be theirs. Her unwavering faith, her utter belief in him and their destiny have carried them all.

Again he hears the shouts of glee from next door and cannot help but smile.

'It may seem like the world is in flux, my dear, and that everything is different to how it once was ... for Mother and myself ... but the thing is — Russia is always Russia. No one, not even these ...' He decides to avoid an argument with his daughter and so leaves out the pejorative descriptors, 'Bolsheviks, can change the way this ancient and powerful nation of ours has always done things ...' He feels as if he is speaking to himself, in a room alone because his daughter is lost to him, her head slightly turned away as if she is listening for the approach of her beau ideal. 'So, hurry now, and change into your travel clothes, as your Mother has asked.'

The man stands and waits for his daughter to do the same.

She remains seated. Impassive. Unmoving.

'When you have done this, my dear, come and join your sisters and brother with the rest of us in the other room ...' He knows she has a will of steel but he also knows she has no choice. None of them do.

Then Olga stands up and turns to the door but the man impulsively reaches for her wrist and holds it. Her skin is silky soft and warm. His heart floods with a tenderness he has long forgotten. His darling. His firstborn. His daughter — and then she slips from his hand and walks out the room, closing the door behind her.

Just outside, Olga stands quietly. Her heart is so filled with choking anger and tearing despair that she thinks she will die. She hears the guards downstairs speaking in muted tones and wonders if she could risk it and try and make her way downstairs. Her cheeks burn with the humiliation. How dare those men shout at her to return upstairs when she tried to take the supper tray back to Cook.

The electricity of the storm makes her hair dance about her face.

The sheer frustration of it all! And her plans, once again, are thwarted. It cannot be endured! Pavel will go without her or think she has changed her mind or ... find another girl. She must get downstairs and into the kitchen so that she can send Cook to get Pavel. It must be tonight because in a few hours or less they will be travelling to Moscow — and who knows when she and Pavel will see each other again!?

Olga has her hand on the banister when she hears footsteps approaching the staircase below. She pulls back into the shadows. Waits. The person begins to ascend and as she catches a glimpse of Yurovsky's thick dark head of hair she turns swiftly and flees to the bedroom she shares with her sisters. With the door closed behind her, she listens as the Commissar passes by and moves to where her family is gathered. Again she waits. There is something in the slowness of the footsteps that makes her hold her breath.

4

Commissar Yurovsky hesitates a moment at the door. The storm is abating and his men are restless. Their orders are clear. Meanwhile, foreign forces are spewing into Murmansk — American Marines and British soldiers. He grips the doorknob. Indeed, 45,000 Czechs are heading toward Siberia not to mention the White Army descending upon them. He pushes the door open and walks into the expectant faces of the prisoners. All except the woman, who half lays, half sits on the settee closest to the window. The children seem to be playing some sort of game of charades.

The man stands and opens his mouth to speak but Yurovsky is in charge and so with a single gesture, a wave of the hand, the Commissar dismisses Russia's autocratic power that was established some 300 years ago.

'I see you are ready.' Yurovsky's voice is filled with quiet authority. 'The Czechs and the White Army are close to Yekaterinburg and therefore the Regional Soviet has decided that in the next hour you will be leaving.'

Two of the younger girls look at each other and smile, even the invalid boy — thin and pale — leans over happily and pats the spaniel on the head.

'Thank you Commissar Yurovsky,' says the man. 'Is our destination still to be Moscow or ...'

Yurovsky lets the man's question hang heavily in the room. He is not curious about the man or his family. He understands why they want to know where they are headed but he cannot help them. Instead, he responds, 'I have sent for Father Storozhov —'

'But will there be enough time?' interrupts the wife. 'Father must hear our confessions before we take the Eucharist and then our staff would also like a blessing —'

'The priest will have only a few minutes with you,' responds Yurovsky because he has no patience for such idiocy. 'Until then, pack nothing but be ready to move out at my command.'

The Commissar looks around at the children and the parents and their Doctor, 'I would prefer that all of you are together in the one room. I will instruct the other members of your staff to join you here in this room.'

The man looks at his wife to see what her reaction is to this impropriety. How are they expected to remain comfortable with the cook and the parlourmaid and the footman cramped up in the same room while they wait for the priest? But his wife has her hands clutched in prayer and her eyes closed to the ignominy of it all and so he lets it go; besides, the taciturn Commissar has already left the room.

The man picks up a novel that one of the older girls has been reading. English! *The Scarlett Pimpernel*. A delightful distraction, he thinks and makes his way to an armchair in the corner of the room. And although life goes on around him, Dr. Botkin playing charades with the younger children and his second eldest embordering a sampler next to her mother, the man feels disquiet. Frayed. Unsure. He knows it is the aftermath of the storm and tells himself that soon they will be outside and on the move and even though he wishes to slow down his inevitable and humiliating future, indeed to avoid altogether the ridiculous laughable show trial that he must endure, another part of him yearns to be free from this godforsaken prison.

His son is chortling at something Anastasia has just said. The man thinks of his children and the comfort they have been to their mother. He tells himself that in the next chapter of their life, wherever that takes them, he will try harder to connect, to feel what a father should feel with his children. To truly be inside the heady mix of their wants and dreams and aspirations. For a moment the man imagines himself outside the Mariinsky Theatre production of *The Nutcracker*, listening to Tchaikovsky's magic and the enraptured applause of the audience. But try as he might, he cannot find his way inside. Is it all too late? he asks himself wistfully as he cradles the novel he does not read.

Not too much longer, but after Kharitonov, Demidova, and Trupp have already moved obsequiously into the now crowded sitting room, and Tatiana has been sent to hurry Olga along, there is a quiet tap on the door.

Father Storozhov has come without a deacon and stands for a moment at the entrance of the room. He is careful not to bow to the Emperor and Empress because he is relatively young and has every intention of growing old in Yekaterinburg. He steps into the room and despite the large gathering and Yurovsky's stern countenance close behind him, a hush comes down on the group.

The priest makes his way to the small table below the windows. He notes that the Empress' most beloved icon, Our Lady of the Sign, the Znamenskaya, has already been placed there.

He does not know why he was so rudely dragged from his home and meal a little while ago. And he does not know why this couldn't wait till morning. But he wants no trouble from these Red Guards and so he grabbed his prayer book and followed them out into the summer night, washed clean by the storm.

The priest turns his back on those in the room and decides to begin with the call and response of the *Anima Christi*. He hears the rustle of people kneeling behind him. He intones.

'*Soul of Christ …*'

They reply.

'*Sanctify me.*'

He calls.

'*Body of Christ …*'

They reply.

'*Save me.*'

And on it goes.

'*Blood of Christ …*'

'*Inebriate me.*'

'*Water from the side of Christ …*'

'*Wash me.*'

'*Within Thy wounds …*'

'*Hide me.*'

The responses are faint, but there. He has only been permitted to offer the service to the Royal family once before, but he recalls back then that their prayers were more robust and assured. Now, he has the strangest feeling that there are only one or two people in the room behind him.

'*Suffer me not to be separated from Thee…*'

He pauses as he holds the icon high above his head and wonders whether he should have sung the brief service. He then realises what is coming up and quickly rushes through the rest of the prayer.

'*From the malignant enemy, defend me.*

In the hour of my death, call me.

And bid me come to Thee.

Forever and ever.'

He lowers the icon and hears them murmur, *Amen.*

When Father Storozhov entered the *House of Special Purposes* he was met by the Commissar who said tersely and unequivocally he was not to hear confession or give the Eucharist. The priest had no intention of causing problems and had nodded immediately and made his way up the stairs with the Commissar following. Perhaps the Tsarevitch is sick, once again, and that is why he has been brought in — not that he noticed the young boy when he entered the room — he was more intent on being seen as complying with the command of those now in charge. He turns about and faces the room. His eyes are closed in supplication and his arms are held wide in cruciform. Father Storozhov continues the recitation.

'*With the Saints give rest,*

Oh Christ, to the souls of Thy servants,

Where there is neither sickness, nor sorrow, nor sighing, but life-lasting.'

As he prays out loud he thinks about his own need for support in this sea of troubles where illiterate peasants are being encouraged by the Reds to turn on the clergy and even in some terrifying instances, take their properties!

'*Thou, only, art immortal, who hast created and fashioned man.*

For out of the earth were we mortals made,
And unto the earth shall we return again.'
Father Storozhov opens his eyes and notices there is only one other person in the room not kneeling. The Commissar. He stands unmoving at the back of the room, near the door. There is grit in that man's eye, thinks the priest, and hopes he can take his leave just as soon as the service is over.

'*For earth, thou art, and unto the earth shall thou return.*
All we mortals wend our way, making of our funeral dirge, and thus we sing ...'
There is no response from those kneeling in front of him so he is compelled to prompt them.

'*Alleluia ...'*
They respond like dry grass whispering in the wind:
'*Alleluia, Alleluia, Alleluia.'*
When it is over and the priest has allowed the prisoners to kiss his pectoral cross, Yurovsky leads him from the room. The Commissar can now see that there was no need for him to oversee the service, which, ran for approximately 15 minutes, because the priest cannot get out of the place fast enough. Yurovsky sends Father Storozhov on his way to the front door. He should have directed him out the back, through the kitchen, but the Commissar wants to drink in the stony-wash of the summer evening as he stands beneath the portico, once more. He watches as the young over-fed clergyman scurries down to the gate and one of the outer guards, the one with the limp opens it wide and lets him pass.

Religion is a disease that sickens the mind and body of Russia, mulls Yurovsky, as he stands in the clear night sky that still seems wet and unsettled after the summer storm. The sooner all priests are done away with, the better, he thinks irritably. The visit has calmed the prisoners before starting on their journey tonight and that is a good outcome.

The smell of grass and something else fills the night sky and then he sees the small glow-worm in the sentry box at the gate and knows the guard is smoking.

It is time, he tells himself, but before he turns to go back inside the house, he looks up once again and wonders at his great fortune. To be born into this astonishing country at a time where the nation itself is being reborn. His sons, and in the future, his grandchildren, and great-grandchildren, will be in awe of the impossible that they are now achieving. A new Russia. A modern power that will change the destiny of every man, woman, and child worker in this world.

Yurovsky knows it is time.

When he re-enters the house he nods to his men to follow him into one of the rooms they have been using for meetings. When all 13 are gathered, and the pocket doors are slid shut, he looks them over.

'Tonight we will do what we have been ordered to do.' The men before him mirror back to him the surety he feels. Their destiny is to secure the safety of the Revolution. 'I want all the weapons collected from the outer guards. This must be done immediately. Their weapons will be returned in the morning.'

One of his men clears his throat and the Commissar nods his head to indicate he may speak.

'Just to report Commissar Yurovsky that I, and a few of the boys, have sorted a place about 25 kilometres west of here. Locals call it the *Four Brothers*. An abandoned mine shaft.'

'Very good. And you have the equipment?'

'Yes, Commissar. Gasoline. Sulphuric acid. All ready to go.'

'The carts need to be brought around immediately afterward,' instructs Yurovsky. 'And any queries or problems between now and when we move the prisoners — must be brought directly to me. Is that understood?'

His men nod their assent.

As they move out Yurovsky feels their energy rise and knows the worst is behind them. The perpetual waiting is no good for morale. But now it is time and he watches as his comrades move purposefully into the balmy summer evening to do their duty.

He picks up one of the oil lamps and takes himself off down the small rickety staircase, just before the kitchen, that leads to a door in the basement. He gives it a slight shove and opens into the loamy smell of what was once an old cellar that has long been robbed of its Georgian wine and French Brandy. He stands in the compact room and knows he is part of the great good that is restoring Russia to justice.

When he returns upstairs a few of the men are coming back into the house with the cache of weapons they have collected from the local Red Guards, who have been protecting the outer rim of the fence. He hears his men boast of how easily and willingly these locals surrendered their weapons.

And then one of his men sidles up and begins, 'Excuse me, Commissar ... The guard out in the sentry box ... Well, he asked whether he might be permitted to assist in ... Moving the prisoners ...'

Yurovsky allows some of the other men to chortle at this quietly. His men should be held firmly but never in a stranglehold.

He thinks for a moment and then asks, 'You mean the guard who found a place to dispose of the Tsarevich's nanny? The one with the limp?'

No one comments on the fact that the Commissar usually refers to the prisoners as *prisoners* and never with their former titles.

'Um ... Yes. I think that's right, Commissar.'

Yurovsky believes in rewarding ambition and tonight he feels a magnanimity in this opportunity they have been given. 'Tell him to stand by. Keep his weapon, for now. But we will need him to ensure the carts and horses are ready ... We might need some assistance in moving the prisoners out of the house ... So, yes. Tell him to stand by.'

'Right you are, Commissar.'

All is ready. Yurovsky feels quietly pleased with how everything has so expediently been sorted. After his men have checked their weapons he orders them into position. He then walks calmly up the staircase to the sitting room in which all the prisoners are waiting.

In less than 30 minutes the prisoners would have left the *House of Special Purposes*, forever.

As the Commissar enters the room the man stands.

'We are ready now to move you and your family and staff.' Yurovsky speaks quietly but everyone in the room has heard and is scrambling to their feet, collecting summer shawls and other essentials.

All except Olga, whose tall statuesque figure remains unmoving.

'Certainly.' The man then adds, 'We may need a few minutes.'

But rather than give them this, the Commissar stands at the wide-open doorway revealing some of his men close behind.

The man wants his wife or even one of his other daughters to speak to Olga who seems to be determined to make a scene. But the river of children and wife and doctor and footman and cook and parlourmaid flow about her, unseeingly.

The man moves across to her, 'Come on, Olenka.' His voice is upbeat and a lie. 'Do you have your ...' He looks about where she has been sitting, but unlike her sisters and mother, she has no shawl or hat or gloves or small beaded purse. He takes her elbow because her eyes are far away as if she has lost something that she will never find again.

Trupp, the footman, is kneeling before the son adjusting the military cap. The man smiles and pulls out a similar cap from his coat pocket, tugs it on and winks at his young boy — who beams, bravely, back.

'Right,' says the man. 'Are we all ready?'

He sees his wife nod to her parlourmaid, Demidova, who bends down and retrieves from under the settee two small pillows. He has seen the care with which their family jewels have been sewn inside the pillows by his wife and her maid.

'Quite ready, Your Majesty,' responds Dr. Botkin as he takes the small hand of Anastasia and then that of Maria. The doctor has never stopped referring to the man in this way and, despite the orders of every jailer they have endured, he refuses to change his ways. The man smiles at the doctor and knows that it was the right decision to ask him and the cook to remain with them, even though this meant both men left behind their wives and children.

The man draws strength from the faces of those still with him. 'I will carry my son —'

'Sir, allow me,' insists Trupp.

'Thank you, but I will carry my son.' And the man picks up his beloved, his heir. Light as a sack of feathers. Pale as death. His son's head lolls against his chest and the man stands perfectly still, forcing back the roar of tears pricking his nose and eyes.

And it is then that his eldest daughter steps across to him and lays her soft tender hand on his arm. The entire room simply watches.

Olga looks into her father's eyes and says, 'Yes Papa, let's go.' And she and he lead the way from the sitting room and the man knows that this great sacrifice she has just made, to journey on with him to the next stage of their desperate lives, is love.

Down the stairs, they move. Dr. Botkin, Anastasia, and Maria are behind Olga and the man, who carries his son, then comes the man's wife with Tatyana and the parlourmaid, followed by the Cook and the Footman.

There is dignity in their procession.

No one speaks until one of Yurovsky's men, waiting at the bottom of the stairs, indicates that they are to move toward the back of the house.

'I thought we were to be collected ...' begins the man vaguely.

'Down the next staircase, if you would, Citizen Romanov — yes, toward the kitchen.'

The man doesn't know of another staircase at the back of the house and so he hesitates but Cook Kharitonov speaks up from the rear-guard and indicates that just before the kitchen swing door is the smaller staircase down to the cellar. The man looks back at the Commissar and when he thinks there is nothing more forthcoming he hears Yurovsky speak.

'White Army gunfire close by. We need to protect you until the transport arrives.'

The man hesitates for a second time at the top of the staircase, the one that will lead to the cellar. He feels his daughter's hand on his arm tighten. Then he steps on down and as he does so he hears her say, softly, cautiously.

'Papa ...?'

There are a couple of guards down in the cellar but other than that it is empty. The wooden racks that once held the potable collection are bare. The man carries his son into the cool. The eldest daughter, the doctor with the two youngest girls, the second eldest daughter linked to her mother, then the parlourmaid, the footman, and, finally, the cook follow him. Refugees without country.

'Commissar,' the man says calmly. 'May we have a few chairs brought in? For my wife ...' Such a personal term, *wife*. He would never have said such a word out loud to someone like — Yurovsky — in his former life. 'And one for my son ...' He feels his boy grip his collar as if indicating he has no intention of leaving his father.

The Commissar looks steadily at the man. He refuses to look at the eldest daughter because there is something in her eyes that unsettles him.

'Two chairs,' says Yurovsky tightly to one of his men.

It takes no time for the guard to carry down two of the dining room chairs and they are placed in the centre of the room, as a photographer might in his studio. Then the Commissar and his guards have left them alone in the basement.

The woman who was once the Tsarina sits down gingerly, her sciatica playing havoc in the small of her back. The parlourmaid fusses one of the pillows behind her mistress and steps immediately behind her hugging the second pillow as if waiting for instruction.

'We may need another round of charades,' the man says in an upbeat tone but his wife makes the smallest discernible shake of the head and so he settles beside her, and, as he does so, his son slinks cat-like across to his mother's lap. An unusual decision for the boy. She buries her nose into his tender sticky neck. The rest of the children seem to form a tight knot about their parents. Excited to be gone. Hopeful of where they might end up. Glad to see the end of this last place. Yearning for their adult lives to commence.

'*The Angel of the Lord declared unto Mary ...*'

His wife's voice seems bold and defying.

'*And she conceived of the Holy Spirit.*'

Respond his daughters immediately and then they are off and racing.

'*Hail Mary, full of grace*
The Lord is with thee;
Blessed art thou among women
And blessed is the fruit of thy womb, Jesus ...'

A strange choice, the man thinks but knows his wife and the womenfolk find the Marion devotion deeply comforting.

'*Behold the Handmaid of the Lord ...*'

His wife pauses and the man hears his beautiful Olenka's crystal voice respond.

'*Be it done unto me according to Thy word.*'

The others follow up.

'Hail Mary, full of grace
The Lord is with thee;
Blessed art thou among women
And blessed is the fruit of thy womb, Jesus ...'

The man wonders whether the Commissar and his men are listening on the other side of the door or whether they have gone back upstairs to ascertain when the transport will arrive so that they can commence their long dark way to Moscow.

'And the Word was made Flesh ...'

His wife doesn't need to wait because the Doctor and the Cook and even Trupp join in the response.

'And dwelt among us.'

The rest pray.

'Hail Mary, full of grace
The Lord is with thee;
Blessed art thou among women
And blessed is the fruit of thy womb, Jesus ...'

The man hears the voice of his son and leans over and kisses his cheek.

'Blessed art thou among women and blessed is the fruit of thy womb, Jesus ...'

And then he knows. The man knows that this is all there is. Just this moment. The closeness of bodies. The need for each other. The being together at this very point in time. This is all they have — this is all there is ... He still feels the grip of his eldest daughter's hand on his shoulder and knows, this is love.

At this moment he hears the boots descending the staircase.

His wife's faith fills up the room.

'Pray for us Oh Mother of God!'

And the entire basement, including the man, responds.

'That we may be made worthy of the promises of Christ.'

The words that had forsaken him for so long — are now his. Inexplicably. Inscrutably.

'Hail Mary, full of grace

The Lord is with thee;

Blessed art thou among women

And blessed is the fruit of thy womb, Jesus ...'

Even when the Commissar strides into the basement, the guards close on his heels, the man's wife continues. Inexorably. Unrelentingly. Her voice alone.

'Pour forth we beseech Thee, Oh Lord,

Thy grace into our hearts —'

'CITIZEN ROMANOV!' interrupts the Commissar loudly. He ignores the noise from the wife because she is of no importance.

The man takes over from his wife and responds.

'That we to whom the incarnation of Christ, Thy Son —'

'YOUR RELATIVES!' shouts the Commissar. 'TRIED TO SAVE YOU!'

The man feels the warmth and strength of his eldest daughter's hand on his shoulder. The man's wife calls out.

'Was made known by the message of an angel —'

'BUT THEY HAVE FAILED!' interjects Yurovsky.

The man recites assuredly, unhurriedly.

'May, by His Passion and Cross,

Be brought to the glory of His Resurrection —'

'SO YOU WILL BE —' Goddamnit, thinks Yurovsky, will he not shut up! 'EXECUTED!'

No one speaks.

The man tries to stand.

His legs are water.

The man thinks, *My God, My God why hast thou forsaken me?*

The guards step forward. They are legion.

The guards think, *Show no mercy to the enemy!*

The man opens his mouth.

Thirteen black revolvers.

The man cries out from the cavernous darkness of himself ... *THE LORD IS MY LIGHT AND MY SALVATION!*

'AIM!' Thunders Yurovsky.

And the 22 year old girl knows her lover is not coming to save her.

Someone somewhere bays *NO! NO! NO! NO! NO! NO! NO! NO! NO! NO —*

'FIRE!'

The horses neigh and thrust their manes hard into the summer night sky. Pavel grabs the bridles and pulls their heads low and Evgeniy manages to steady the cart as both men look toward the *House of Special Purposes.*

'What the fuck was that?' spits Pavel.

'Gunfire,' Evgeniy replies.

And then Pavel is running toward the house, tripping in the dark, unable to find purchase on the ground beneath him and, as in a nightmare, the distance, from the gate to the kitchen, seems to stretch further and further away from his reach. He is stumbling and gulping air. Pavel pulls open the kitchen door roughly and there stands one of the inner guards. Eyes blank in the lamplight.

'Hey — what's going on? Is everything alright?' Pavel has no idea what he is saying and he knows he needs to start thinking and he must start thinking now!

The Chekist recognises the sentry guard with the limp and says, 'All good, Brother. I'd say you can bring those carts around now.'

For some reason, this fills Pavel with relief. 'Yeah — sure — will do ...' And then he hears Evgeniy pull up one of the carts alongside the kitchen door with a quiet *Whoa* to his horses.

From somewhere inside, there is a yell, then boots running and

BANG! BANG! Pavel's eyes stretch wide but the Chekist is blocking the doorway to the kitchen and to whatever filthy business is happening within. Pavel strains his ears to hear ... A few voices. Men. Followed by what sounds like a chair scraping on stone. Then more yelling, a cry like a field mouse caught in the talons of an owl. The thick smash of something.

Once.

Twice.

A third time.

Just as Pavel is about to step into the Chekist, throw him to the ground, grind his brains into the kitchen flagstone and run to find her, he feels a hard steel hand on his shoulder.

'Go get the other cart, Brother.' It's Evgeniy. 'I'll take it from here.'

Pavel does not move because he cannot. He must get to her and do whatever he has to to get the hell out of this place. He should have done this months ago! But now there is no turning back. And just as he takes his destiny into his own hands he sees someone move into the kitchen and approach the doorway where the other Chekist is standing. Pavel recognises Yurovsky immediately.

'Sir ...' Pavel is not sure what to say next and so waits there in the threshold of the night, with Evgeniy's calloused hand on his shoulder and the Chekist with his rifle pointing laconically at Pavel's chest.

'Yes. Good. You've brought the carts.' Yurovsky is pleased the summer evening is starless and devoid of its usual white light on account of the storm earlier. 'One of you stay with the horses and you ...' He points to Pavel as a gesture of goodwill and trust, enabling him the opportunity to join his men, 'Come with me. We need help bringing the prisoners out.' The Commissar doesn't wait and the Chekist, barring the door, steps aside insouciantly but Evgeniy's hand remains for a fraction longer on Pavel's shoulder who shrugs it off and makes his way into the shadows of the kitchen following Yurovsky.

Pavel steps out of the kitchen and into the wide hallway. He pauses behind the Commissar. He realises they are to descend a small flight of stairs. Which must be where the family is waiting. Pavel wonders why the two guards carrying the sack up from below are making such a meal of it. One drops a corner. Giggles. Picks it up. Trudges on up. Pavel tells himself that he must keep his eyes downcast in case Olga reacts to his sudden appearance. The goons continue up the stairs in front of him. They stop. Nearly overbalance. Someone swears.

'Come on, lads,' growls the Commissar but there is no bite in his words.

At last, they arrive at the top of the stairs and that's when Pavel sees the hand.

He hears Yurovsky say, as if from a long distance away, 'As quick as you can.'

And then Pavel is stumbling down the staircase to what appears to be a gloomy basement with a number of the other guards hauling up weighted laundry and all around is the smell of gunpowder and shit and blood and ... One of the guards shakes out a cigarette and lights up — it's an excuse for the others to do the same. Someone offers Pavel a smoke and he takes it automatically. He bends his head to the flame and inhales sharply. The wall at the back of the basement is a mess of pockmarks. A couple of the guards are grunting behind him as they lift the dead weight of something from the floor, they haul it through the doorway and begin their ascent up the staircase. Someone next to him swears and drops to his knees. In the scrum of rags that he cannot, and will not, look closely at Pavel sees a string of pearls, a diamond collar, a gold buckle, and blood-red rubies.

'Look,' says one. 'Look — the maid had them in her clothes ...' He listens as the men scramble to their knees, 'Here! They're in her pillow!'

Pavel moves away from the treasure trove and allows himself to glance down sideways, here and there, for her chestnut blonde hair. At the back of his head, he hears the hurried crunch of boots descending the staircase and then the Commissar's voice, far away, commending the men on the find and assigning one to gather what he can of the jewellery and for the rest of them to bring up the prisoners and load them on to the cart.

Pavel drops his cigarette.

He sees her hair. He goes to her because she is his. Her wrist is flung close to her face and her lovely wrap-around eyes are closed. He doesn't look at the thick black wound on her white blouse. She is lovely in sleep. He drops to his knees beside her. He hears the other guards grunting under their burdens or calling out for assistance to help drag the next body up the stairs and out onto the cart. They are all getting on with the business of following orders.

Pavel scoops his right arm tenderly beneath her neck and her darling head shifts to his chest. He shuffles his weight so that his feet are firmly beneath him then burrows his left arm beneath her dark skirted knees. He closes his eyes and feels the warmth of her young body against his chest and arms. Then he heaves her up so that he is standing with his beloved.

A long way off he is aware of the quietness of the room. The men are subdued. Secretive. Vigilant. Everyone is more or less hurrying now as if this moment needs to be removed from their memories and the *House of Special Purposes* and the town and the very country itself.

Perhaps Pavel is the last to come up.

He takes his time.

Cradling her tenderly so as not to bump her head on the doorway in the basement, he turns about at the bottom of the staircase and ascends slowly, quietly. His fingers on his right-hand press against the side of her face and he says gently to her ... *Nearly there now my love ... A few more steps ... Hold on to me, sweetheart.*

There is no one to see him or hear him. He is simply one of the outer guards recruited to bring up the prisoners out of the *House of Special Purposes* so that history and Russia can move on. He is no one. Pavel arrives at the top of the staircase and follows the last of the other guards through the kitchen and out into the summer night. He doesn't see the Commissar or his men or even Evgeniy — who gets off the cart and moves towards Pavel, guiding him with the weight of the dead girl, to the other cart that has been brought around.

In the melee of this underworld horror, no one notices, except Evgeniy, the way Pavel refuses to throw the body onto the stack of bloodied limbs and hair and clothing in the tray of the cart. Instead, Pavel lays the girl on the front seat, ducks under the two hitched horses, and scrambles up beside her. He then takes her head and carefully rests it on his lap. When Evgeniy climbs into the seat of his cart and shakes the reigns of his horses, he sees that Pavel is leaning over, whispering something to the dead girl. And then they are clopping out into the summer evening.

It must be well past midnight, thinks Evgeniy. He doesn't look behind him because he can hear Pavel's horse has automatically followed. Behind the two carts is a bunch of Chekists already singing softly and drinking. He is glad the business is over but Evgeniy knows that he has misread his boarder, Pavel, who seems to have lost his mind over the business.

They pass out of the township. The Commissar is not with them on the prisoners' last journey but he spoke directly to Evgeniy when Pavel went down to the basement about where they are to take the prisoners. Of course, Evgeniy knows the four pines that stand lonely 20 kilometres out of town near the abandoned mine shaft. *Yes,* he had said to the Commissar, *I know the place called the Four Brothers.* Evgeniy looks back once and sees the outline of Pavel leaning close to the ear of the dead girl, stroking her hair. He turns back around, apprehension gripping in his heart. It is enough having to worry about his drunken brother let alone a boarder who has lost his marbles!

The guards in their carts are now way behind and they are singing with more gusto.

On and on they travel, a plan forming in Evgeniy's mind. He will not be brought down by someone he barely knows. These are dangerous times, he thinks to himself as he pulls left and clicks encouragement to his horses as they move onto a rubble path that leads to the forest. You can only trust those you have known all your life. But he thinks of his brother stinking of homebrew and vomit, and missing shifts. You can only trust yourself, he decides grimly.

There are no stars but the night is now beginning to whiten with summer light, more dirty grey than white, and it is this that allows Evgeniy to lead the entourage to the *Four Brothers*.

Four lonely pines that stand sentry to the head of a makeshift mine. He pulls over in the clearing and hauls on the side brake. By the time Evgeniy has jumped down, Pavel has also pulled his horses to a stop but instead of dismounting he is — there is no other way of describing this, thinks Evgeniy — crooning to the dead girl who lays across the front bench of his cart.

When Yurovsky's men arrive, Evgeniy joins them as they drag the dead from the cart, and either in pairs or alone they haul the bodies over to the mine shaft. Although he doesn't keep count Evgeniy suspects there are about a dozen bodies. Once or twice he notices a guard quickly frisk a corpse, as if in search of some random trophy, before it is swung over the abyss and into the mine shaft.

Everyone seems to ignore Pavel who is now talking in a subdued tone to the dead girl he caresses. Evgeniy feels the flutter of nerves and wonders if any of the Commissar's men know Pavel is boarding at his house. There is no way he is going down with that guy. When one of the men says something about collecting the gasoline and sulphuric acid from their cart, Evgeniy joins him. He needs to be seen as loyal to Yurovsky and having nothing to do with Pavel.

As Evgeniy hauls out the barrel of gasoline he hears a bit of a scuffle — then Pavel is yelling something and it is on! The men charge across to the other cart and haul the dead girl off and Pavel roars like a wounded beast and the night sky watches on as the guards rough handle him and the dead girl to the mouth of the mine shaft. Evgeniy knows that, like himself, the guards have been ordered to dispose of the bodies, discreetly. They cannot afford an unreliable witness. Certainly not a madman who cannot stop the deep wild outpouring of ... grief. The noise Pavel makes is unbearable. The men hit him again and again with the butts of their rifles. They kick him, they spit and hiss but he continues to sprawl on the ground before the abandoned mine shaft howling. Howling ...Howling ... *Olenka! ... Olenka! ... Olenka! ...*

Then the crack of a bullet ends the unbearable. Everything is pitch-perfect in its quiet.

One of the guards returns to where Evgeniy is standing and begins to help drag out the rest of the tins from the back tray of the cart. Evgeniy doesn't hear the two last bodies being thrown down the mine shaft. He does not hear the barrels of sulphuric acid being unscrewed and the *gulp gulp gulp* of it being poured after the body of Pavel and the girl and her sisters and the young lad and his mother and the cook and their doctor and the maid and the footman and, somewhere in amongst it all, the man who was once Tsar of all the Russias. And Evgeniy does not hear the hiss of bones being eaten by the acid. He has moved back with two others to tug and pull the gasoline barrels off the cart.

Soon it will be over, Evgeniy tells himself. He breathes through his mouth as he helps carry the barrels back across to the mineshaft. It'll be morning soon, he says to himself. And he realises he will have to go through Pavel's small belongings when he gets back to the cottage and burn whatever can't be of use. There should be no trace of his connection with the poor soft-headed bastard.

Then one of the men produces a hip flask from his long leather coat and passes it to Evgeniy. And when he takes a swig, he knows he will be fine. Yurovsky's men need him to get them back to Yekaterinburg.

19

Red Flag Flying

Moscow. July 1918.

Comrades! The kulaks must be crushed without pity ... You must make an example of these people. Publicly hang kulaks because they are rich bastards and known bloodsuckers. Publish their names. Seize all their grain. Do all this so that the people see it, understand it, and tremble. Lenin.

Lidia lowers the newspaper and looks past Feiga to the countryside racing past their carriage window. Soon they will be in Moscow. She knows Feiga's eyes are causing her trouble because she has had them closed since this morning after they climbed on board the train at Petrograd. Lidia glances back at Lenin's call to the nation — to round up and hang those peasants withholding grain from the Bolsheviks. So this is what the so-called leader of the revolution thinks will bring about an enlightened society. It makes her blood boil!

In the last few days, she and Feiga made their way from her father's estate to Petrograd. She was determined to find Grishka. What she found was news from one of Maria Spiridonova's Shesterka, who told her that Grishka had been arrested for the assassination of Volodarsky, the Head of Propaganda. Lidia went numb. She was then told that instead of being shot, he had chosen to become re-educated. Grishka wants to be a Red Guard. A Bolshevik. A traitor. He was last seen with a group of other shameless turncoats, all under heavy protection, boarding a train for Moscow.

Lidia watches the dachas and the run-down garden lots whizz past the window. The relentless rattle and pull of the train across the 650 kilometres is both soothing and frustrating. All she wants is to get to Moscow and find Grishka. She knows him to his core and she knows nothing would have made him betray their cause. Nothing.

'How much longer?' murmurs Feiga, eyes soldered shut.

'Not much longer.' Lidia calculates, 'Probably another three to four hours. Past halfway.'

Neither of them has spoken about Leonid. The assassination of the Head of the Cheka in Petrograd had been the hot topic for weeks but by the time Lidia and Feiga had arrived in the city, it was old news. Leonid was dead. Shot on the street for the assassination of Moisei Uritsky who was, of course, responsible for the death of Viktor. Leonid's Viktor. And Lidia tells herself for the hundredth time, as she grinds her teeth, that she will not cry. She folds the newspaper on her lap. She must find Grishka. As quickly as she possibly can.

Up ahead she hears the girl pulling the tea cart down the centre aisle. How strange that in these times, where nothing seems real or familiar, a task as simple as selling tea could prick her eyes with tears.

'No tea for me ...' she hears Feiga say.

Leonid comes unbidden to her mind and although she tries to shake off his memory, he holds on tenaciously to her heart. *Wonder boy.* She smiles sadly at Viktor's affection. The loss of Leonid is as painful as the loss of Viktor.

A few minutes later, Lidia is nursing a cup of strong tea and feeling the comfort of this drink.

Perhaps it is best this way, she thinks to herself. Leonid was bereft without Viktor. It's just that ... She sips the hot brew ... Leonid always seemed vulnerable — how could he have lived on without Viktor? Again she blinks away the tears and fights back the physical tug of wanting Grishka's arms about her. She knows she made the right decision. She will find Grishka and together they will assassinate the very man who has usurped their Revolution and their future. Her veins pump with rage. Lidia leans across Feiga and holds the glass of tea close.

'Just a sip ...' She waits and then watches as Feiga, eyes shut, leans forward and takes a morsel from the steaming glass. 'Better?' Lidia asks.

The train rickety-rackets over a wooden bridge and across the farmland.

'Better,' answers Feiga.

Lidia looks out the window at the small indistinct farm holdings. She starts to think about those peasant farmers, kulaks, unlucky enough to have their own farm. She shakes her head imperceptibly. The enemies of the state are growing by the month, the week, the day, the hour. She lets her eyes wander over the undulating farmlands, patchworked in barley and wheat as if looking for the unfortunate kulak who has been lynched by his jealous neighbour.

'Grishka's in Moscow ...' Feiga's statement is almost inaudible, a soft susurration, and Lidia smiles across at her petite friend who is blind to the world about her but seems to see everything.

'Yes ...' responds Lidia. 'I will find Grishka in Moscow. And we will sort it all out ...'

Firstly, they will sort out this inexplicable decision of his to join the enemy. Because there is no way he would ever betray the Socialist-Revolutionary's terrorist cell that has been ordered to destroy the usurpers, the Bolsheviks. Secondly, she will see through a plan that, up until now, had been merely an aspiration while she waited on her father's estate. Then it became an ambition, while she was in

Petrograd after she discovered what had happened to Grishka and Leonid. Now it has become an obsession. Lidia is determined to answer Spiridonova's call to *all* committed Socialist Revolutionaries to destroy the leadership of the Bolsheviks. Terror via assassination. The Head of Propaganda has been eliminated. Grishka is nothing less than a national hero, she says fiercely to herself. The Head of the Cheka has been eliminated. Leonid gave his life to save Russia, nothing more and nothing less! She purses her lips determinedly. She will join Grishka and together they will, like Hercules and Iolaus, eliminate Hydra.

The train is chugging slowly now, pulling back on the remaining fuel. As its long whistle blasts across the countryside, she watches long-tail ducks rise out of a waterway and into the afternoon scrap of colour across the sky.

Eventually, the locomotive comes to a halt at an isolated station.

Lidia looks through the window and notices how the bodies of rail workers move about purposefully on the platform, while others refill the locomotive's tender with wood. My brother will be in Moscow soon, she thinks. All the newspapers have reported that the prisoners have left Yekaterinburg and so the Kremlin awaits the show trial. Lidia puts it out of her mind that she has not heard back from Pavel for quite some time. She feels the train shunt forward and wonders whether her brother received her last letter she sent via Leonid. If he didn't receive the letter, he wouldn't know about Viktor. Nor would he have any idea about Leonid ... No — she will not cry. She will not think of it — the waste — the carnage. Lidia bites down on her bottom lip to stop the memory of Viktor's beautiful dark face and Leonid's, cornflower blue eyes. How she loved them both ...

As the train pulls out and leaves behind the nondescript refuelling siding Lidia can't help but feel Russia is getting away from them all. She glances across at Feiga who has one hand propped against her eyes and forehead. The momentum of the train builds and just as she is about to ask if she can do anything for her friend, Feiga drops her hand and although she keeps her eyes shut, her face seems to relax. Almost as if she is sleeping.

All that hunting practice at the estate amounted to nothing, thinks Lidia but without resentment. There is nothing more she could have done to persuade Feiga to show more interest in her training. Lidia, of course, loves shooting out there in the forest and the Browning pistol she pocketed from her father's eclectic gun collection fills her with confidence and determination as they head to Moscow.

Lidia looks over the afternoon fields. They are changing colour now that it is edging toward the end of summer. Paddocks race by in autumnal reds and oranges. Neither she nor Feiga asked why Leonid did what he did. The world knew why. The Head of the Cheka was responsible for the execution of thousands of Russians — but most importantly, Viktor. That is why Leonid assassinated him. There was no other reason that existed. Lidia sighs and wonders why she hadn't seen it coming, why she hadn't tried to stop Leonid from leaving her father's estate. Now she knows that when he left for Petrograd he had no intention of looking for Grishka. Leonid had only one goal.

Enough. Perhaps she says the word out loud, she is not sure, but Feiga's small hand reaches across the seat and finds hers. *Enough.* Lidia exhales the command to herself and feels the weight of grief, as heavy as an entire country, press down on her thin body.

'Won't be long, now, Lidia,' comes the faint voice of Feiga. 'Soon we will be in Moscow.'

2

Let us raise our banner boldly,
Even though a storm of hostile elements is howling!

Even though sinister forces oppress us today!
Even though everybody's tomorrow is uncertain!

The song of the freedom fighters fills Moscow's Kursky Railway Station and, as the two women clamber down from their train, every living thing seems to be celebrating this new Russia — even the starlings are freewheeling in the early evening sky. There are crowds everywhere and trains are screeching in or whistling out of the station and amongst the mayhem, a sea of people is parting for the Red Guards who fly and sweep their blood-red flags through the throng.

Oh, this is the banner of the whole mankind,
The sacred call, the song of resurrection!
It's the triumph of labour and justice,
It's the dawn of the brotherhood of all peoples!

Feiga clings tightly to Lidia, who stands tall, one hand clutching their old leather suitcase, with a folded umbrella strapped across its side, and her other hand clenching the pistol within her skirt pocket. Around them swirls the banner-wielding fanatics and dewy-eyed believers.

Forward, Russia!
To the bloody fight,
Sacred and righteous!
March, march, Russia!

There are women, men, grandparents, children, workers, ex-soldiers, shopkeepers, peasants, people in Western dress, people in traditional Russian attire, worldly Muscovites, and wide-eyed newcomers from the east and south and north. All are cheering or marching or singing the *Varshavianka* led by about 50 prominent Red Guards.

And that's when Lidia sees him.

Today when the working people are starving,
To indulge in luxury is a crime!

And shame to those among us, who in our young age,
Are afraid to mount the scaffold!

At first, she is unsure. It is someone who looks like him, she tells herself breathlessly. But she cannot tear her eyes away and although he is looking in the direction of where she stands, he doesn't seem to see her. Lidia can't look away. He strides on, with the other guards, tall and proud and utterly inscrutable. Eyes glazed. Face empty.

Oh, we will never forget the deaths of those,
Who gave their lives for the cause!
Because our victorious chant will make
Their names honoured by millions of people!

She needs to breathe. She hasn't even put her bag down or moved off the station — is it really him? And as she tries to talk herself down off the precipice, she realises that the crowd, which is swirling around her, has not only been singing but calling out one name over and over and over again. Their chant. Their hope. Their saviour.

LENIN! LENIN! LENIN!

Slowly Lidia looks to the space that has been funnelled behind the windmilling red flag-bearers and sees a small balding man appear. Shaking hands. Calling out to this one and that. Raising his fist in victory. Singing vociferously. Her hand tightens on the pistol.

Forward, Russia!
To the bloody fight,
Sacred and righteous!
March, march, Russia!

Then something makes her look back to where she had been scrutinising the Red Guard, the one she thought she knew. And in an instant she catches the same Red Guard, tall and rangy, bewilderingly familiar, look away from her. *Grishka!* And then he is gone. Lost in the bodies of singers, chanters, well-wishers, believers, supporters, workers, soldiers, women, men, children, and Lenin. All of Russia it would seem.

Hurrah! Let's tear down the crown of the tzars,
While people are wearing the crown of thorns!
Let's drown the rotten thrones in blood,
Thrones already stained purple with the people's blood!

'What is happening?' she hears Feiga ask beneath the heave and excitement of the unstoppable crowd.

And an older woman jostling past leans in and says, 'Comrade Lenin is to talk at the Mikhel'son Factory!'

Ha! Frightful vengeance to today's tormentors,
That sucks the life out of millions of people!
Ha! Vengeance to the tzars and plutocrats,
And we'll harvest the crops of the future!

The crowd is pushing and pulling in the same direction and without resisting, arm in arm, Lidia and Feiga bob along with the human river. They become part of the flotsam and jetsam supporting the government, the Russian Communists, and hailing its leader as the new Caesar, the new Tsar, the new God.

Forward, Russia!
To the bloody fight.
Sacred and righteous!
March, march, Russia!

Wedged into the crowd the women have no choice but to leave the railway station and move north with the crusaders. Up ahead trams have stopped to collect the crowd and take them on to their destiny because the fanfare of flag-carrying Red Guards, as well as Lenin himself, is enough to stop traffic.

Unable to disentangle themselves from the zealots the women find themselves inside one of the trams that have become a cacophony of song and chatter, all devotees of Lenin and his government's promise to give them a new Russia. The two women are part of the human cargo being hauled across the city to the great leader's destination. Surely all of this is just an antidote for the Civil War crisis, thinks Lidia bitterly to herself. Not to mention the invocation of War Communism that is threatening another famine, greater hardship, and more deaths.

The tram plashes through sheets of silver puddles on the city's roads and then scoots across the bridge over the Moskva River. Lidia cannot see past those closest to her and although she squirms about in an attempt to discover if one of the Red Guards at the front of the tram is actually him, she cannot be certain. But she knows it *was* him back at the station. She knows it *was* him.

'Where do we get off?' Feiga's question prompts Lidia into action.

From the moment they alighted their carriage till now, there has been no time to think — especially as all her thoughts are of Grishka. But now she knows she must figure out a plan.

'Soon, just up ahead,' says Lidia, simply because she needs to stop the rattling momentum of time. She needs to get off this unrelenting tram ride forward and figure out what exactly happens next. By the light of the early autumn evening, Lidia can see markets and commuters up ahead. The tram slows down to pick up some more supporters who have seen the display of red flags flying from the tram windows — they too want to be part of whatever it is that is more exciting than their own tired lives of simply trying to exist. Lidia seizes the opportunity — grabs Feiga and pushes past passengers attempting to board — and exits through the tram's back door. The two women watch the tram pull off and they are left in the electric lights of a bustling evening with sellers calling their wares and people scrounging for supper.

'Come on,' says Lidia. 'We will find somewhere to eat ...' because the last time either of them ate was the night before, in Petrograd. It is then that Lidia notices four or five men, collarless shirts, trousers with braces, pushed back caps, and thick moustaches, coming out of a doorway filled with the aromas of supper. The women wait until the men have passed then Lidia reopens the door and follows a small set of steps leading up to the hiss of frying onions, someone shouting instructions, and the clink of glasses. The dining space is lit up with workers smoking and talking and eating and drinking. Lidia moves towards a small bench table pushed up against the window that overlooks the street from where they have come.

'Nice place, Lidia,' comments Feiga good-heartedly.

Indeed, the life of the café brings momentary cheer to both the women as they settle into their seats, with their suitcase, the umbrella still firmly strapped to its side, between them on the floor. Lidia watches Feiga squint out the window where, below, pedestrians come and go in the dusky night.

A woman, old enough to be their grandmother, carries a large bowl of potato peel gruel to their table and plonks it down, deftly. It's hot and steamy. Then out of her apron, she pulls two spoons and a smallish piece of black bread.

'Drink?'

Feiga shakes her head but Lidia is already responding.

'Yes. What do you have?' But instead of answering Lidia's question, the Babushka gazes long and hard at her mismatched coloured eyes. Then, after some consideration, she turns her hefty hips and moves back to the kitchen.

Lidia smiles across at Feiga and nods to encourage her to begin. Their heads lean over the thin liquid companionably, their spoons dip and rise, dip and rise, over the shared bowl. Before long a large, watered-down beer is placed beside Lidia's elbow.

'Use the bread,' says Lidia, and her friend tears it up into small birdlike pieces and scatters it across the gruel. It is warm and comforting.

Lidia knows she must find Grishka and tonight might be her only chance, so she says, 'Mouse, I need to leave you at the address we have been given.' The Shesterka has organised for them to stay at an address close by. 'We'll go there directly after this and ...' Lidia hasn't been to Moscow for years but her sense of direction is good and she knows that the safe house is close enough to the Mikhel'son Factory.

Feiga puts down her spoon, looks across at Lidia, and asks softly, 'Why? I want to stay with you.'

'It's too dangerous.' Lidia doesn't say anything more. Grishka is clever and resourceful. For all she knows he is probably planning the assassination of the top-end target at this very moment while masquerading as a re-educated Red Guard. A ruse to get up close to the leaders. Grishka is lulling the enemy into a false sense of security and when he has done that — he will strike!

'But why, Lidia?' The pain in Feiga's voice has to be ignored.

Lidia needs to be alone when she approaches Grishka. And it needs to be tonight, under the cover of the madding crowd.

'Look, Mouse.' Lidia deliberately uses Viktor's pet name for her, 'I just need to go on to this factory and see for myself what is happening. We can't go together — with our luggage — I need to be ...' She knows it is cruel but says it anyway, 'Unencumbered.' Feiga closes her eyes. 'Just tonight, Mousey, and then tomorrow we will meet up with some of those contacts we were given and sort out a plan —'

'But we know the plan!'

Lidia looks around quickly after Feiga's unexpected outburst, but everyone is busy eating and talking, and drinking. 'Let's go,' says Lidia pushing back her chair and standing up.

The babushka immediately appears at her elbow, snatches up the few coins Lidia offers, and makes no bones about staring at the tall blonde with her ill-fated eyes. Feiga stirs, picks up the suitcase and umbrella, and follows her friend. Out on the road, it has become even busier. The pitter-patter of rain eases, and bodies move hurriedly home or back to night shift, and the smells of cooking curls around the shopfronts.

Before long Lidia points out, 'There's Dubininskaya Ulitsa.' She is determined to see through her decision. Lidia knows they are in the Zamoskvorechye District but hadn't realised that the street where they are to stay would be so easy to find. Feiga looks down the busy road with its traditional wooden houses. 'Do you remember the number?' Lidia asks quietly.

There is a long pause but eventually, Feiga answers, 'Yes.'

Lidia waits and then after a few minutes, she says assertively, 'Go on. They are expecting us at the address and I will only be an hour two behind you.'

Eventually, reluctantly, Feiga pushes off down the road. Her diminutive size and half-hearted steps, with the small suitcase and umbrella strapped to its side, make her appear like a child-runaway.

Lidia doesn't wait a moment longer. She must get to the factory and make contact with Grishka. The evening continues to be busy but there are strands of the revolutionary song being sung up ahead and as she turns across a small footbridge she feels the droplets of an evening shower begin. She espies the belching smoke of a factory and knows she is close. It must be the Mikhel'son Factory with its never-ending human effort to generate electrical machinery. Lidia's heart is aflutter. Tonight she will face Grishka and figure out what they must do, together, to stop the pretenders. Lidia moves through the main gates of the factory, across the docking area with its long shadows, and doesn't have to look further because there in front of her is a huge crowd of people, including many many workers from the Mikhel'son.

Behind her, unseen, scurrying along with the suitcase banging her legs, follows Feiga.

The tall blonde woman moves about the periphery of those gathered to hear Lenin as his fist pumps his promises and assertions and declamations in the air. There is so much noise and cheering and movement in the mass of swirling bodies that she is neither noticed nor observed. Lidia keeps her eyes on the banners flown by the Red Guards and like an arrow, to her target she hones in, checks out the flag-bearer and when it is not Grishka, moves on. There are Red Guards in the centre of the crowd whipping up the people into cheers and calls of *LENIN! LENIN! LENIN!*

And just as she is halfway into the centre of the mob she feels his stillness. She looks across to her left and there, about three metres away, stands Grishka. Tall. Lanky. Dark curly hair, now cropped short. Holding an unfurled red banner and looking straight ahead. But she knows he has seen her. He raises his chin asserting the direction of his gaze, which is at Lenin and no one else, and she steps across to stand as close to him as possible.

On the far edges of the crowd is Feiga. She has seen Lidia insert herself into the centre of the crowd but decides it is best to wait here, where she can open the umbrella should the rain get any heavier.

Grishka is rigid. There's another Red Guard to his right, who seems older and more senior. Lidia decides she will stick to his left side as best she can, until an opportunity arises where she or he might be able to speak to each other, without drawing attention to themselves. She notices Grishka lean toward the Guard next to him, listen and then nod his head. He is being held on a tight leash. And then Grishka begins to unravel his banner but as he does so he manages to block off the Guard to his right and in that second he looks directly at Lidia and mouths the imperative *LEAVE!*. His face is thunderous.

She looks immediately at the speaker, the Head of the Communist Party, and then back at Grishka but he is nonchalantly preparing his banner and nodding to whatever it is that the Guard beside him has just said. Lidia's heart is racing. What just happened? Why did he look at her like that? Why does he want her gone? Who the hell has he become?

And then Grishka rises the treacherous red flag high into the dripping evening and begins to wheel it about. Effortlessly. Lidia, like a few of the others, needs to step back a little to avoid being hit by the flag and that is when she realises Lenin has finished his speech. The crowd is cheering and some of the other Guards have begun to sing their song of revolution. The crowd starts to disperse. The speech is over. The call to continue supporting the government's policies must come to an end, for tonight.

Grishka is then on the move, following the other guard and wheeling his flag, cutting a path to his right. Lidia follows because she cannot do otherwise. People are moving out the other way, re-tracing their footsteps back from where they have come. They are thinking about the walk home and the need for supper. It is getting darker and wetter as she follows Grishka and his fellow guard and then she notices a Black Maria idling in the side street.

Feiga sees Lidia moving out to the right, away from the crowd that is picking up their pace as they head homeward before the bad weather closes in. Feiga lifts the suitcase and pulls out the umbrella but doesn't open it because she must hurry after Lidia.

The spontaneous rally surrounding Lenin seems to have ended as quickly as it began. The small bald man, wedged between a posse of Red Guards, makes his way to the parked car awaiting him. A few stragglers are hanging about, a few dozen die-hards wanting a word or two with their leader. Lenin looks tired but the Red Guards know he will stop and shake hands or offer a clipped answer to a question or even wave in recognition to one or two of his supporters.

And it is there in front of the Black Maria, that Lidia finds herself. Not once has Grishka looked about to see if she has left. Not once. There Grishka stands with a bunch of other Red Guards, they form a semi-circle about the back of the vehicle. Lidia feels as if her heart has been ripped out. What has it all been for? Viktor? Leonid? Why has Grishka turned his back on us? What has happened to our cause? To the terrorist cell for which he and Viktor risked their lives? And with her veins ice-cold, she asks herself, *Why did I even come here?*

There are people behind her and others who crowd closer to the vehicle to snatch a chance to meet the man who will lead their beloved Russia into a world-class revolutionised modern nation. And then she knows why she is here.

The tall Red Guard standing nonchalantly with his peers at the back of the vehicle sees, without looking, the tall blonde woman standing in front of the Black Maria. He has also noticed the small woman lurking in the shadows behind the blonde. Mousey brown hair, a suitcase against her legs, and holding a closed umbrella. Around him, he hears his colleagues complain about the rain and the ever-increasing hours of duty, and the burden of early morning reveille.

'Look lively, Comrades,' says one of the guards next to him as Lenin, at last, steps across to the Black Maria. Soon the leader will be driven back to his apartment within the Kremlin while the rest of them will either jump on the back of their trucks or take the long way home to their barracks, via the local public transport. Already some of the guards are quietly breaking ranks and moving back to the trucks to secure their ride.

But Grishka doesn't move.

He watches the blonde reach inside her skirt pocket.

Slowly.

Carefully.

The blonde has called out something to Lenin. The small mousey woman has also started moving in closer to the vehicle. Lenin is momentarily distracted and turns his face toward the tall blonde woman. He opens his mouth to speak and Grishka glimpses the small Browning pistol.

BANG!

Grishka sees the suitcase drop.

BANG!

BANG!

Grishka watches an umbrella open.

Then someone is yelling, '*LENIN'S DOWN! LENIN'S DOWN!*' and Grishka is surging forward and already he can see the leader writhing on the ground, clutching his neck and coughing up globs of blood so terrible that that closest move back in horror. Disbelief momentarily stuns the bystanders.

Then the driver is charging around to the side of the car bellowing 'GRAB THE CULPRIT! GET THE BASTARD!'

People are running and yelling and someone is screaming and the dark broiling sky above opens up and rain hammers and hammers and hammers down.

Grishka knows he has to get to her before any of the other Red Guards do — he leaps over the two guards attempting to staunch the blood coming from Lenin's neck and dives into the crazed melee running this way and that in front of the Black Maria. He's temporarily blinded by the rain and all around him, guards are firing warning shots in the air which is just making the helter-skelter worse. Workers' caps bob this way and that, scarves fly thither, faces terrified they'll be wrongfully arrested, arms reaching forward, bodies shoving, legs pounding, feet scrabbling and an umbrella cartwheels overhead.

Then he sees her.

She is picking something off the ground.

Grishka stops in front of Feiga.

Her small nest of hair is flat and spiky from the rain. She looks up slowly at him as she cradles the Browning pistol in her hand.

'IT WAS HER! IT WAS HER!' A young worker is yelling his face off pointing at Feiga. The panicked crowd freezes as if catching the scent of the prey. 'ANARCHIST! BOURGEOISE! KULAK! LOYAL —'

Grishka smashes the young worker effortlessly across the face and he crumples to the ground. But others are pushing back in to see the thing, the monster, the terrorist who has done the unthinkable. Grishka is trying to press Feiga into the crowd but she seems heavy-footed and stumbles just out of his reach, her vise-grip pressing the Browning to her breast.

'Mouse! Get the fuck out of —'

Then a Mosin-Nagant is cocked and standing next to Grishka is his senior Red Guard. Lizard eyes, body unflinching, revolver poised.

'Comrade,' he says forcefully to Grishka. 'Take her weapon!'

Grishka knows the moment for her to run has passed. And as he reaches for the pistol to which she clings he is calculating what it would take to convince his fellow guard that she simply picked up the dropped murder weapon.

'You are arrested for the assassination of Comrade Lenin!'

This is all happening too fast and where the hell is Lidia? Is she safe?

'Guard, bind her wrists! Now!'

Feiga doesn't struggle as Grishka ties her hands together behind, loosely, quickly, all the time figuring out his next move.

The people seem to have returned to the scene of the crime. They are desperate for a glimpse of the bleeding Lenin or at least the terrorist who did this. Before long, the damp jittery crowd begins murmuring *She's a girl! She's just a girl!* and Grishka also hears the less cautious, *Is she mad? What the hell is wrong with her?*

'Comrade ...' says Grishka as he is made to haul Feiga through the gathering crowd toward the trucks. 'Comrade, I saw this girl pick up the weapon off the ground ... I did not see her fire the gun ...' He wonders whether he is moving too fast but he is running out of time. The older reptilian guard has his pistol in the snug of Feiga's small back and says nothing. Grishka holds one of Feiga's arms, lightly, willing her to make a run for it. 'I think it was one of the workers, Comrade.' Asserts Grishka carefully, 'I don't know who pulled the trigger but this girl just bent down and found —'

'The Party will need the assassin brought in! The nation needs to know that the strongarm of the Party will not tolerate these old Narodnik methods!' The lizard is on a roll and seems to be speaking, not just to Grishka, but to anyone around them who is willing to listen. 'Assassination may have been the preferred weapon of the last century — and God knows we needed to kill off the bloated aristocracy — but this is a new Russia!'

He gestures to Grishka to haul Feiga up into the truck.

'Yes but the real gunman is still out —'

'Listen, Comrade,' the senior Guard leans in quietly, eyes lidless and full of menace. 'This is our job done ...' Grishka doesn't need to look down at the Mosin-Nagant pistol because he knows it is pointing at him.

Feiga is featherlight to lift into the back of the truck but before Grishka can follow, the senior guard has swung himself up beside her and is banging the sides of the vehicle to indicate the need to leave. Now!

He turns back arrogantly to Grishka standing in the wet muck of the night and says, 'I'll take it from here, Comrade.'

And the truck moves off into the arteries of streets that will somehow pump Feiga out into her destiny.

In the back of the truck, her face is a small white moon of calm looking — without seeing — the receding image of the tall Red Guard who used to call her *Mouse*. Inside the truck, she is roughly pulled down onto the bench beside the senior guard. There are other guards with them but they keep their distance as if she is some strange angelic witch who might give them the evil eye or, worse, bless them unawares. Even the senior guard is quiet. He is unsettled by this business of doubt that Grishka has raised. What good does it do? One guard questioning the validity of another guard's decision. It's no good. Let it be someone else's problem when they get to Lubyanka.

Then the girl begins to hum. The men in the back of the truck draw closer to one another and the hair on the backs of their necks, rise when they hear her faint incantation.

'Do not be afraid or discouraged,

For the Lord God will not fail you or forsake you.'

One or two of them in the dark of the truck make the sign of the cross but the senior guard growls at her, 'Shut the fuck up ...' The swearing is more for the benefit of his comrades, and to model to them who is in charge. What he is thinking, as the truck seems to be taking forever to get to the Cheka headquarters, is why the fuck is it taking so long to get her out of the streets and into the hands of the secret police.

'How long will You forget me, Oh Lord?

How long will You hide Your face from me?'

The senior guard presses the muzzle of his pistol into her ribs.

'Out of the depths, I cry to You, Oh Lord.

Hear my voice!

Let Your ears be attentive unto my supplications!'

The girl's voice is an undertone, nothing more, a murmuration, a susurration, a purr.'

'My soul waits for the Lord,

More than those who watch for the morning —'

'SHUT THE FUCK UP!' He's about to slam home the instruction when the truck pulls up, at last, and turns off the engine. There is a palpable relief amongst the men as they scramble over each other to jump off.

'GET HER OUT!' the senior guard commands and they respond gingerly because she has not stopped, nor will she, as she is manhandled off the truck and hauled up to the yellow bricked façade of the massive Neo-Baroque building.

'Do not fear nor be afraid,

For the Lord, your God

is the One who goes with you!'

They push her in through the main entrance, above which hangs a mighty clock face. The men half pull, half carry this frail girl-woman across the parquet floors.

'For the Lord is my light and my salvation.

Whom shall I fear?'

A posse of leather coated Chekists who, unfortunately, have had a slow night, spring to their feet when they realise there has been an arrest. They immediately block the path of the Red Guards.

'We'll take it from here, Comrades,' says one.

The leather coats look condescendingly at the Red Guards. One of the Chekist wears the official chest badge, a red cluster of oak leaves with a sickle and hammer in the middle. The rest of them sport the cap cockade with its red five-pointed star and the hammer and sickle in yellow.

The Red Guards are glad to be done with her but it is their reptilian senior guard, gliding in behind them, who responds, 'She is our prisoner. Arrested for ...' The entire entrance area waits with interest, 'The assassination of Comrade Lenin!'

The announcement doesn't have the expected effect because one of the Chekists replies laconically, '*Attempted* assassination. He has survived.' The other Chekists nod and shuffle respectfully.

'The Lord is the strength of my life,

Of whom shall I be afraid?'

It is well past midnight and it has been a long day so the senior Red Guard spits, 'She's all yours.' Besides, the witch-girl is freaking his men.

3

The Commissar for Internal Affairs and Head of the All-Russian Cheka, Felix Edmundovich Dzerzhinsky, bides his time. He realises with surprise that morning has arrived as he looks out over the square from the window of his 7th-floor office in the Lubyanka. What he sees is a dirty egg-shell sky that indicates nothing other than the quickening of autumn. He thinks wistfully of his Polish Russian homeland and how it holds on more tenaciously to summer than the cold-hearted Moscow. Dzerzhinsky can hear the approach of footsteps and knows they are bringing the prisoner to him, as per his instructions.

'Enter,' he says to the knock at the door but doesn't bother to turn around.

He had been informed immediately when they had arrested the person who had attempted to kill Lenin. He knows that throughout the night, despite the rigorous efforts of his men, the assassin has refused to admit she was working on behalf of the British. It makes no difference. Dzerzhinsky's mind is made up. This is the catalyst he has been looking for to introduce the disciplined plan the nation needs. The sharp sweet stink of urine and shit is there, somewhere, behind him.

'So you have refused to cooperate with the Russian Government?' His voice is quiet but everyone in the room hears him.

From his window, Dzerzhinsky can see some of his officers moving across the Lubyanka square purposefully. He has been pleased with the sheer numbers of dedicated Russians who have lobbied to join the Cheka. A growing industry. He hears one of the Chekists behind him hiss at the prisoner, *Stand up!* Still, his reluctance to turn around continues. He had told Lenin he would only take on the Directorship if he had full powers, no supervision, and no one to whom he need answer. Of course, he is right to demand this level of independence if he is to ensure the success of the Revolution.

'Yes, Commissar, that is correct. The prisoner has refused to co-operate!' Dzerzhinsky ignores the Chekist who has taken it upon himself to answer for the prisoner but he recognises that it is this level of enthusiasm that will ensure the security of internal affairs.

'Our aim here is to fight against the enemies of the Government,' says Dzerzhinsky calmy as he continues to look out the window. He is their iron leader who never sleeps and never uses expressions of any kind — because rest and revealing one's inner thoughts are a weakness. It is his purview to utter clear and precise statements that outline the work he, and his fellow Chekists, do.

'We judge quickly. In most cases, only a day passes between the apprehension of the criminal and his ... her sentence.'

The three Chekist who have led the prisoner into the Dzerzhinsky's office stand to attention as he turns to face the prisoner they hold. They watch as he gazes disinterestedly at the mess of blood and bone as well as her torn and tattered dress. Unblinking. Assured. Assuring.

The prisoner does not look at the Commissar for Internal Affairs and Head of the All-Russian Cheka. One eye is completely closed and her eye socket is damaged beyond repair. The other eye seems to gaze unseeingly.

Perhaps this is what prompts Dzerzhinsky to add, 'You and your scruffy rag-bag group of malcontents do not incite terror into those of us protecting the principles of the Revolution! It is the Cheka and the Cheka alone who will ensure that the likes of you will know the full and terrifying reach of the Russian Revolution!'

The Chekists are filling up on this truth. In many ways, it alleviates the memory of the disturbing night that they had to endure with her, as they tried to make her renounce her co-conspirators.

The whole time she kept whispering to the God who would not forsake her, yet clearly, he had.

'The fact of the matter is that when confronted with evidence, criminals like yourself, in almost every case, confess. And you confessed.' Dzerzhinsky looks away from the prisoner's broken face because it is not relevant. 'And what argument can have greater weight than ...' Dzerzhinsky's voice fills up the room in hard cold determination, 'A criminal's confession.'

The prisoner's confession was brought to him almost immediately after she had been taken into the custody of his men. Dzerzhinsky moves from the window to his desk and picks it up. And this is what these people's lives amount to, he thinks sourly. A few lines of misguided assertions. And whether it is the silence of the prisoner in front of him or perhaps even her unseeing eye he decides to read her pathetic statement out loud.

'Today I shot Lenin. I did it on my own. I will not say from whom I obtained my revolver. I will give no details. I had resolved to kill Lenin long ago. I consider him a traitor to the Revolution.'

Dzerzhinsky pauses here for the room to register the enormity of the prisoner's foolishness, nothing but a child's deadly protest.

'I was exiled to Akatoi for participating in an assassination attempt against a Tsarist official in Kiev. I spent 11 years in hard labour. After the Revolution, I was freed.'

Again Dzerzhinsky waits so that those gathered with him will note the generosity of the Revolutionary leaders in releasing those, including himself, who had been imprisoned by the Tsar for daring to dream of a better Russia.

'I favoured the Constituent Assembly and am still for it.'

It is over. He tosses the sheet of paper back onto his desk to show its insignificance, its uselessness. A mere scrap paper. The prisoner's life has amounted to nothing. He can spare no more time on the matter.

'You have been investigated and now you will be executed for the high crime of treason!'

The prisoner makes no plea.

'Take her to the Alexander Gardens.'

The prisoner does not collapse or cry out.

'IMMEDIATE EXECUTION!' Dzerzhinsky roars.

The prisoner's face peers up at him as if she is trying to see who he is and whether this might help her make sense of what is happening.

The Commissar for Internal Affairs and Head of the All-Russian Cheka turns his back on her and says briskly, 'Take her away!'

Through the window, he can see that there will be no blue sky today, just a thin grey shine with the occasional suggestion of sun. He has studied the techniques of espionage and counter-espionage and knows that his first and foremost task is to ensure that the nation does not succumb to the forces of counter-revolution. He listens to the sounds of the men and the prisoner retreating down the corridor and wonders what really happened last night. It is the third time this year that someone has taken a pot-shot at Lenin. He received a call informing him that Lenin refused to go to the hospital and walked himself from his car to his apartment in the Kremlin. He lives.

Dzerzhinsky snorts derisively. He has what he needs. Now, no one will stand in his way. The Party will have to endorse his Decree.

He watches the prisoner being bullied and bustled across the square to an awaiting Black Maria by a growing number of Chekists. How could she have pulled the trigger? He wonders idly. Poor eyesight ... No training in marksmanship ... Encumbered with a suitcase and an umbrella ... No ideology. It does not matter. He watches her being tossed into the back of the awaiting vehicle. A dirty bundle of laundry. It is of no consequence.

Dzerzhinsky turns back to his desk, sits down, and pulls the typewriter close to him. He waits. The wording begins to come to him and he commences the *tap tap tap* of the draft of the Decree.

Meanwhile, it takes no time at all for the Black Maria to drive across to the Alexander Gardens, just outside the Kremlin. The leather coated goons pile out and the passers-by scatter. It is best to neither see nor hear the work of the secret police. A small woman is hauled out unceremoniously and dragged through the gates of the gardens and along to the western red walls of the Kremlin. She stumbles along between her brute handlers, not because she is reluctant but because she cannot see. Someone behind her tries to steady her by grabbing the tuff of her hair but he cannot find purchase.

She has the body of a child and the face of a vandalised city.

'This is good enough,' one grunts and pushes her to her knees, her face to the giant red belly of the Kremlin wall. The truth is the men are torn. On the one hand, they want to be commended as the officers who took the treasonous bitch and executed her, but on the other hand, her quiet calm is unnerving. The woman is still.

The scent of fading crocuses in the Alexander Gardens takes her to the synagogue of her childhood in Kiev. The morning sky above the Kremlin walls is soggy and grey and sad but the rabbi has still to finish the Kaddish and she is waiting with her obdurate faith and patience. Next to her is a ruined grotto, part of the Alexander Garden's folly, and alongside this are her siblings and her father who bows his head and cradles his face in his hands.

She doesn't feel the muzzle of the pistol at the base of her neck.

The Kaddish goes on and on and it fills her with the cadence of something more than the sum of herself. She knows that Lidia and Viktor and Leonid and Grishka are behind her on the synagogue's bench seats and in that instance, she understands the absolute certainty of her life.

A dark starling takes flight at the crack of the bullet and spearheads into the sky above. It is immediately joined by a larger group and, to the wonder of the morning, they commence their swarming behaviour. The flock aggregates and swirls this way and that above and beyond the mighty Kremlin. There is no central coordination to their murmuration. They plummet and soar and turn and dive for the sheer pleasure of being alive. And in their exuberance is separation, alignment, and cohesion. The display of the starlings' flight would be breathtaking in its complex interactivity and instinctive unpredictability — but no one is looking up. The morning foot traffic scurries head down so as not to attract the ire of the Chekists, who seem reluctant to scrap up the mess in front of them.

All of this is commonplace and unremarkable.

Back on the 7th-floor office in the Lubyanka, the Commissar for Internal Affairs and Head of the All-Russian Cheka, Felix Dzerzhinsky, is finishing off the Decree that will be published in the *Krasnaya Gazeta,* tomorrow. He does not think about the prisoner anymore. Feiga Kaplan ... Fanya Kaplan ... Dora Kaplan ... Whatever her real name is — it does not matter. His complete focus is on the Decree which he has just about finished typing. He pauses. The ending is vital because there can be no question — just pure realisation — that they are now in a new age, a new Russia. This is the Decree, he thinks to himself as his beautiful hands hover over the keyboard, that will secure the future for the Party, for the people, and for Russia!

We will turn our hearts into steel, which we will temper in the fire of suffering and the blood of freedom fighters. We will make our hearts cruel, hard, and immovable so that no mercy will enter them. We will not quiver at the sight of a sea of enemy blood. We will let loose the floodgates of that sea. Without mercy and without sparing, we will kill our enemies in scores of hundreds. Let them be thousands — let them drown themselves in their blood. For the blood of Lenin and Uritsky and Volodarsky, let there be floods of bourgeoisie blood — more blood, as much as possible!

And let this be known to the enemies of the people as the Red Terror.

20

Brave New World

Petrograd. October 1918.

Lidia takes the tram down Ligovsky Prospekt after leaving her apartment in the Vyborgskaya Strona. The truth is she is glad to be back in Petrograd. In her apartment. Back at the school. Teaching is all-consuming now that everyone is trying to take advantage of compulsory education. Boys, as well as girls, come in droves. Better that and the promise of a school meal, which hasn't yet eventuated, than letting them roam the streets like a generation lost. Lidia fills her hours with either reading and preparing or instructing and encouraging. Helping these children build their future is the only reason she keeps going.

The tram swings into Nevsky and she looks out at the pedestrians, some with umbrellas others with scarves or caps, but all bowing into the wet westerly wind. An October morning, bleak, autumnal, and filled with quiet triumphalism.

Lidia doesn't think about Viktor or Leonid or Feiga or the way her letters to her brother have gone unanswered. She was a different person back then. She, and a small band of idealists, were trying to change the course of history. Ridiculous. Dangerous. A madness had crept into her soul.

Lidia looks out the tram window and sees the dirty slap of the Fontanka Canal. The tram skittles on.

She knows when that madness took hold ... In that abandoned warehouse ... Last January ... After she had skated across the Neva ...

The tram is quite full now, and women, old beyond their years, jostle to sit on the wooden bench seats and ease their bones before they face another mindless day of searching for food to fill the empty baskets they nurse on their laps.

Lidia only has till noon and then she must be back at school. She has been given a furlough to attend a morning session at *The Conference for the Masses,* at the Winter Palace. *Palace of the Arts,* she corrects herself immediately. Using the right language is paramount to survival. When she had asked the Commissar at the Central School if she could attend the conference there was no hesitation. The Commissar, who last year had been fighting at the Front, had no intention of being reported at the local soviet for obstructing such a request.

As the Nevsky Prospekt gets closer to the Neva it narrows and meanders through the edifices built centuries ago. A squabble of tenant buildings and shop fronts and administration offices and tired workshops. She realises that it is showering more determinedly now. Lidia touches her unfurled umbrella that she carries in her leather satchel. The tram is stopping and so she gets up, flings the satchel across her chest, pulls her black chequered scarf down lower on her forehead, pushes through the swaying bodies who couldn't get a seat, and steps out of the stationary tram.

The air is briny and billows about her as she shunts open her umbrella.

Lidia moves quickly through the cobblestone alleys and then under the double archway on the Bol'shaya Morskaya Ulitsa, until she is there, in the square. The enormous dark red façade of the Winter Palace, the *Palace of the Arts,* no longer exists. Lidia is fleetingly disorientated as she stands to the side of the archway. In place of the palace's façade is canvas — thousands and thousands of metres of canvas painted with strangely exuberant Cubist and Futurist images. Flattened, two-dimensional, multi-perspective, funny, horrifying, and far too new to be real pictures. A jigsaw of discombobulating colours and shapes and dimensions. An imagining made by a giant's child.

How strange, she thinks, to stand in front of one of the most formidable and familiar buildings in the city and see it for the first time. Its enormous edifice that once had the power to reduce and dominate its people, has been transformed into a vast outdoor art gallery — so that every worker, peasant, soldier, and passer-by might see and feel modern times. A new Russia. All of us, born anew.

Breath-taking thinks Lidia.

She looks up above the palace that once housed the Tsars, their families, and their eternal entourage, and sees the fresh new national flag, frenzied and thwacking. She wonders if this is part of the art installation or whether the new Russian flag will always fly above the palace. Gone is the two-headed eagle with its tricolour and in its place, a red banner soars with *RSFSR* in the top left-hand corner in gold Cyrillic lettering.

'Russian Socialist Federative Soviet Republic,' she murmurs the marble of words to herself.

She looks slowly to her right. The Staff Building is also swathed in the artist's canvas. It is a colossal bandage seeping up the colours from a child's paintbox. The infant images are bordered in black. They pop and shout.

Even the central red granite column, which Lidia is certain no longer bears the Tsarist appellation of the Alexander Column, soars up into the wet boggy sky of this morning, plastered head to toe with sculptures of twisted steel and balls and smoothed wood with wiry teeth.

A small laugh erupts from the back of her throat. Perhaps it isn't just me who is going mad, she muses.

Even though her time is limited Lidia finds herself standing longer in the palace square. A part of her feels she should have expected this — the conference is, after all, being organised by the poet Mayakovsky and even though she doesn't buy into his enthusiasm for all things Bolshevik she, like so many of her contemporaries, finds his faith seductive. He and his confrères preach that every Russian can contribute to the art and culture of their new nation.

She looks at the dazzling fresh skin that surrounds the palace square and despite her ambivalence, she feels a delight, an innocence, a hopefulness in this reborn body that is their true country. Lidia's eyes glass with tears and although she shakes them away, she knows it is the inordinate waste, the loss, of those who are gone, which hurts the most. Their lives were given for what?

She begins walking across the square, her umbrella buffeting a little in the wind.

The talk she has registered to attend should be commencing shortly. She grins at the memory of these words on the pamphlet.

Sanctuary or Factory? Comrade Mayakovsky will be discussing whether the Palace of the Arts, the former Winter Palace and home of the Tsar, should be converted into a macaroni factory! As Mayakovsky argues: We do not need a museum of art where people worship dead art — we need a macaroni factory, a living factory of the human spirit!

Lidia passes close to the column and sees a Red Guard look across at her with interest. He is one of many randomly patrolling the square in the lead-up to the nation's celebration: the 1ˢᵗ Anniversary of the October Revolution. The February Revolution is now to be referred to as the *Bourgeoisie Revolution*. Language is everything, thinks Lidia, and her mouth forms a moue.

She picks up her pace, not only because she thinks the Red

Guard is moving across to intercept her, but because she wants to look at the art inside. The *Free Exhibition*. No vetting, no competition — anyone can hang their art. The ordinary worker's painting will now be displayed alongside that of Repin or Bryullov — extraordinary. The newspapers have declared it a success with more than 2,000 paintings submitted ... but then again the newspapers declare all national celebrations a success.

'Lidia.'

She stops.

'Lidia.'

She lowers her umbrella until its ferrule taps the cobblestones. The Red Guard stands a metre or so away from her. People heading into the palace for the conference see nothing unremarkable about a guard stopping a tall woman to either check her papers or question her purpose.

'It's me ...'

She knows it is him. She knew the moment he said her name but she cannot move, she cannot speak.

'Here, put up your umbrella ... You will get wet ...'

Lidia lets the rain shuttle down lightly on her scarfed head and shoulders and face. He moves carefully and lifts the umbrella for her and holds it aloft. Her hand has dropped from its crook handle.

'I saw you and ...' He starts again, 'I was redeployed to the barracks in Petrograd ... Just last week ...'

She wants to run but her legs can barely hold her up. She gazes at the height of the lanky guard in front of her. His dark wavy hair visible beneath his cap, the breast badge, a red star with a yellow hammer and sickle, sewn onto his jacket. She even looks at his black polished boots — anywhere but his face, his eyes.

'Lidia. Please? Do you have a moment?'

'No.' Her answer comes too fast and is almost inaudible but he hears her.

'I need to talk to you — if not now, when? I must see you. I must
—'

'No.' This time it is more determined, more forceful.

The rain is easing but he doesn't lower the umbrella from above
her head. It is as if he has cast her in his spell from which she cannot
remove herself. With a superhuman effort, she steps out from beneath the umbrella's shelter as if to walk on, go through the gates of
the palace, mount the steps, and enter the foyer. He is bewildered.
He never imagined it would be like this. He has always loved her
and protected her — even in his darkest hour. It is her, Lidia, who is
always at the forefront of his mind.

She turns back to him, the conference and the free art exhibition
utterly forgotten. 'You were there.' The ferocity of her voice hits him,
'You were there — I saw you!' For so long she has locked the horror
of what happened that night into the dungeon of her mind.

'Yes, of course, I was there — I warned you to leave when I saw
you. I —'

'You and the others grabbed her!' Lidia's mismatched eyes flare
with such anger that he can barely follow her logic. 'You arrested
her and threw her to those blood-sucking goons!' The filthy, bloody,
sticky dungeon is open and all its bone-hard hatred and rage dis-
gorges, 'They shot her! You know that don't you? They shot her for
attempting to kill Lenin — but tell me ...' Her scarf has slipped
back in the frenzy of her fiery denouncement of him and her white-
blonde hair slips upward in an electric miasma. 'Tell me — how the
hell could she have shot him? Huh? In the dark and rain and with
her eyesight — or lack of — and her reluctance to have ever learned
to shoot? How the fucking hell could they have laid that at her feet?!'

Her throat constricts with the effort not to scream.

The morning moves on around them. Red Guards mooch about
the square, conference-goers hurry to get out of the cold and into
the warmth of the palace, and tired sellers pushcarts filled with

books liberated from aristocratic homes. And then she just feels exhausted. She wants to turn around and get back on the tram and go home — not home — not to the place fingerprinted with his memories, and hers, and Viktor's and Leonid's and Feiga's. But away from here. Away from him. Again, Lidia turns to walk off but he is reaching for her even before he decides to do so.

'Stop. Please ...' His voice is bereft of hope. 'It's wrong ... It's all wrong — that's not what happened ...' He knows it is probably useless. 'You don't know. It wasn't like that — I — you need to know it wasn't like that ...'

Lidia does stop. And for the first time, she looks into his face and a voice within her tells her not to believe, not to feel, not to let him in with his treacherous new faith. But what she sees is Grishka. Just Grishka. Not a Red Guard. Not a Bolshevik. Just a man she loves — had loved. Just a man.

'I tried to protect her — I thought that's what I was doing. She picked up your ...' He corrects himself, 'The gun. She picked it up and I nearly got to her in time. I was right there! I said — *Run! Go!* But she wouldn't. She just stood there. And then it was too late ...' But it was more than that, 'I pleaded for her to be released but they didn't care. Can't you see?' He lowers his voice. He, for one, knows how dangerous it is to say such things. 'They would have executed anyone for it — they needed a scapegoat to commence the Red Terror...' His voice has lost the urgency because it is all too late.

Grishka holds onto the umbrella even though the rain has stopped.

Some workmen pass close by and look with curiosity at the Red Guard with the tall blonde woman. The workmen are part of the huge consortium ordered to prepare the square for the upcoming festivities in celebration of the revolution. There is certainly anticipation of food and drink and frivolity, all of which have been promised in the newspapers. The workmen are also buoyed by the suggestion of liaisons formed, like this one they are passing!

It is then that Grishka sees her expression soften and hears her say, faintly, 'I haven't heard from Pavel ...'

He is surprised by her non sequitur but responds instinctively and steps a little closer to her to ask, 'Where do you think he is?' His voice is warm with emotion and Lidia looks away because she cannot allow herself to feel the flood rising within.

'I'm not sure ...' She thinks about the declaration printed in the papers last month that the Tsar had been executed by the Ural Soviet but the rest of the royal family had been transferred from Yekaterinburg to a place of greater safety.

'The family was moved. Did you hear?' Grishka is speaking quietly to her, his head bowed to hers, the umbrella above them. 'The Tsar was executed. Of course, you know that — but the reports say the family was moved. You know, because the Whites were about to enter Yekaterinburg ...'

Lidia's mismatched eyes are full of the desperate need to believe as she watches every word Grishka speaks. She has been yearning to ask about her brother's fate for weeks but has trusted no one. Until now.

'He'll be fine, Lidia. He is probably with the family or on his way back here ...'

Grishka concentrates on Lidia's lips and neck and shoulder and arm and hand. He pushes back the rumours he has heard in the barracks that the rest of the family was shot along with the Tsar. Who knows what's fiction or fact? He reaches out slowly and picks up her cold thin hand. She does not snatch it away. He understands why they were all shot — a live banner is something Russia's enemies can rally around. He moves a little closer. Besides, he thinks grimly, the Party needs to show that there is no turning back.

'And look at you!' She pulls her hand away from him but she just can't rally the venom she should. Instead, she feels like he is the only survivor left from the shipwreck of her life and if she does not cling to him, she will surely drown. 'Look at you.' She tries again, 'A Red Guard ...' And because somehow this is the saddest truth of all she begins to cry, right there, in the palace square, with her white hair flying about her.

Grishka steps into her grief and takes her in his arm and although she says *Don't* it is lost in his shoulder and her knowledge that she will never come to the surface again without him holding her.

'Don't cry, my love. Don't cry.'

And the Red Guard and the tall blonde woman stand together, like a Cubist or Futurist installation, suggesting the shock of the new.

'After I was arrested ...' He speaks into her hair, unable to stop himself because he wants so dreadfully to unburden himself. 'I was forced into a re-education program. You see ...' He knows it is his weakness for her that makes him tell her the truth because without her knowing, there can be no way forward. 'They knew about you — what happened to you ...' He is holding her gently but he can feel her body tighten. 'The other prick had reported on you and what had happened to his buddy. On the bridge in January and then ... in the warehouse ...' Grishka presses her white-blonde hair, wildly churning about them, into her neck. He inhales and says simply, 'If I didn't comply they were going to take you — and ...' He cannot finish the truth but there is no need to because every Russian knows the ending.

After a while, Lidia stops crying.

She drinks in the scent of Grishka. It is his smell, his body, his voice. And a part of her no longer feels forgotten, forsaken, abandoned. He is her Russia. Viktor, Leonid, Feiga ... even, perhaps, her brother ... are all gone. But Grishka is here. And she is in his arms.

For the first time, in a long time, Lidia feels she is home.

Perhaps this is all there will be, she thinks. Now that everything they believed in is gone. Maybe this is all they will ever have. She and Grishka. Their own country.

Historical Note

While *Abandoned by God* is a work of historical fiction it is based on the research of real events and real people.

Those assassinated:

- Volodarsky (born Moisey Markovich Goldstein) was the Head of Propaganda and assassinated on 20 June 1918 by Grigory (Grishka) Ivanovich Semyonov
- The Romanovs (former Tsar Nicholas II, his wife Alexandra Feodorovna, and their five children: Olga, Tatiana, Maria, Anastasia, and Alexei) were assassinated on 17 July 1918 by Yakov Mikhailovich Yurovsky and his Chekists
- Moisey Solomonovich Uritsky was the Head of the Cheka in Petrograd and was assassinated on 30 August 1918 by Leonid Joakimovich Kannegisser
- Lenin (born Vladimir Ilyich Ulyanov) survived an assassination attempt on 31 August 1918. Feiga Kaplan (born Feiga Haimovna Roytblat) was convicted for this crime but it is more likely, according to historical sources, to have been Lidia Konopleva

Other historical people in *Abandoned by God* include:

- Viktor Pereltsveig, Leonid Joakimovich Kannegisser's

real-life lover, was executed in July 1918 at the orders of the Head of the Cheka

- Andrei Derevenko was the Tsarevitch's bodyguard who abandoned his duty in the early stages of house arrest
- Klementy Nagorny was the Tsarevitch's bodyguard and was executed by the Chekists on the orders of Yakov Mikhailovich Yurovsky
- Ivan Mikhailovich *Kharitonov* was the Head *Cook* at the court of the Royal Family and was executed along with the Romanovs
- Leo Sevnev was his kitchen hand who escaped execution
- Aloise Yegorovich Trupp was the Head Footman for the Tsar and was executed along with the Romanovs
- Yevgeny Sergeyevich Botkin was the court physician and he was executed along with the Romanovs
- Anna Stepanovna Demidova was a lady-in-waiting in the service of the Tsarina and was executed along with the Romanovs
- Pierre Gilliard was the Swiss tutor to the Romanov children and escaped execution
- Alexandra (Shura) Tegleva, who had been a nurse to Grand Duchess Anastasia Nikolaevna of Russia, married Gilliard and escaped execution
- Alexander Fyodorovich Kerensky was the Minister of Justice, then the Minister of War, and then Prime Minister of the Russian Provisional Government
- Sir Robert Hamilton Bruce Lockhart was a British diplomat, journalist, author, secret agent, and footballer
- Vasily Vasilyevich Yakovlev was a Bolshevik revolutionary and transferred the Romanovs to Yekaterinburg
- Yakov Mikhailovich Sverdlov was the Chairman of the

All Russian Central Executive Committee from 1917 to 1919

- Yakov Mikhailovich Yurovsky was a Chekist and chief executioner of the Romanovs
- Maria Alexandrovna Spiridonova was a Narodnik-inspired Russian revolutionary who then lead the Left Socialist-Revolutionaries. Spiridonova was sent to Siberia in the company of five other prominent female SR terrorists. The group was sometimes called the Shesterka (Six)
- Yekaterina Konstantinovna Breshko-Breshkovskaya was a Narodnik, one of the founders of the Socialist Revolutionary Party, Russia's first female political prisoner (40 years in exile for opposition to Tsarism) and fondly known as the grandmother of the Russian Revolution
- Maria Leontievna Bochkareva was a Russian soldier who fought in World War 1 and formed the Women's Battalion of Death. She was the first Russian woman to command a military unit
- Trotsky (born Lev Davidovich Bronstein) was a Ukrainian Russian Marxist revolutionary, political theorist, and politician
- Felix Edmundovich Dzerzhinsky was the Commissar for Internal Affairs and Head of the All-Russian Cheka

Acknowledgements

This book owes its existence to the encouragement of my husband, Roger Murray, and my daughter, Madelaine Rose Guy-Moore. I am indebted to First Rider Publishing and to the talented designer, Zoe Castorina.

When I was 18 I came across something written by Anna Akhmatova and I copied it out and stuck it on my kitchen wall in my tiny rented apartment in Sydney. I read it many many times: *During the frightening years of the Yezhov terror, I spent seventeen months waiting in prison queues in Leningrad. One day, a woman was standing behind me, her lips blue with cold, who, of course, had never in her life heard my name. Jolted out of the torpor characteristic of all of us, she said into my ear (everyone whispered there) - 'Could one ever describe this?' And I answered - 'I can.'*

This haunted me and although I knew nothing then of Akhmatova or the Yezhov terror or what had led up to this point in Russia's 20th Century — I was utterly obsessed with all things Russian. I then studied Russian history; read its poets, novelists, and playwrights; visited Russia's galleries, museums, churches, and monasteries; and travelled to Russian cities and remote villages in a variety of transport.

Finally, it is with much love that I dedicate this book to my husband who has offered me an epic tale of love that could never be packed away or forgotten.